I0716080

DEAD & LOVELY

J. M. MILLER

Realm Stones

Clear

an overview of events

Haze

CLOUD
thoughts and memories

NEEDLED
amplifier

SMOKE
fears and desires

Opaque

WHITE
dead connections

EYE
animal control

BLOOD
human control

BLACK
endless

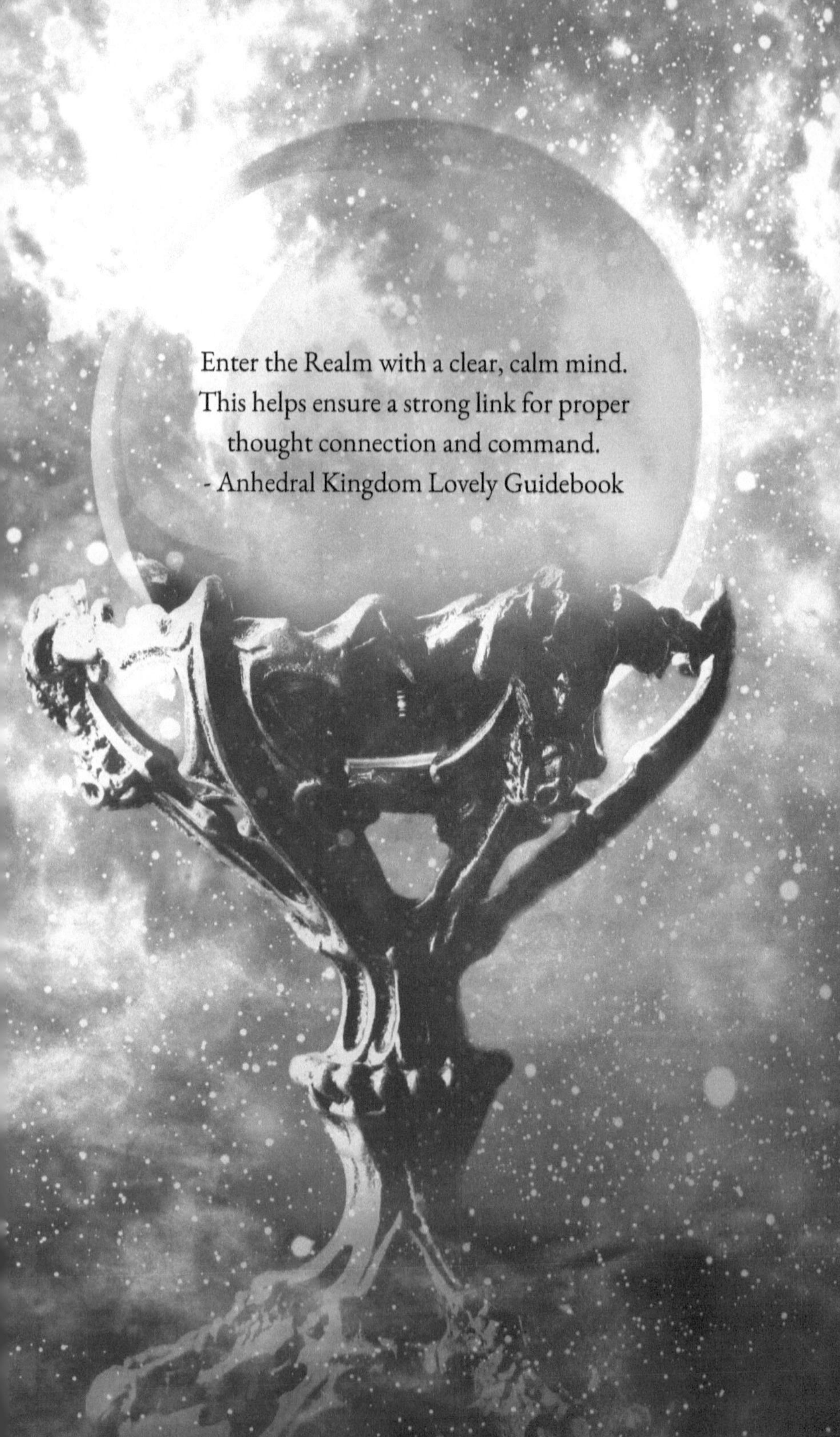

Enter the Realm with a clear, calm mind.
This helps ensure a strong link for proper
thought connection and command.
- Anhedral Kingdom Lovely Guidebook

Despite the crowd gathered inside the town hall, the only sounds to be heard as I approached the dais were the chancellor's breathy sobs, subtle creaks from his wooden chair, and the muted drips of his urine puddling below.

Two polished spheres sat atop the table in front of him. I knew the stones well, had touched them too often to count over the last twelve years. They were the second and third most valuable things in Shadowstone, monetarily and judicially. The first was me, since I alone could connect with both.

The Clear stone rested on a black iron base that twisted like a gnarled oak branch. A dried streak of red already blemished its pristine surface. At the table's center, the Cloud stone was no less impressive in elegance. Though its wiry copper base appeared thin and fragile, the milky white swirls inside the sphere held enough strength to captivate anyone, not just the Lovely who truly understood its power.

"P-Please," the chancellor choked out, his body trembling harder as I took my final step to the table.

A wave of whispers rippled through the hall, quietly condemning his tears.

"Proceed, Lovely," Count Ashboard's stern voice beckoned from his seat against the opposite wall.

I didn't have to look to know all three of his town advisers were at his side. Most everyone was in attendance for the trial of the count's own chancellor, but none wanted to see justice served more than him.

Following a steady breath, I gave a swift nod to the guard commander and took my seat in front of the Cloud stone. Lorenz stepped forward, as stoic and dutiful as always, and grabbed the chancellor's hand.

The chancellor's fear instantly surged, the restrained trembles and stuttered prayers turning into a bout of unhinged screams and wild thrashes in a single moment. He used whatever remained of his strength, but the effort was futile, the belts at his waist, feet, and wrists holding firmly to the creaky but solid chair.

Well adjusted to these situations, Lorenz seized a harsher hold of the man's hand as he drew the edge of a dagger across a new fingertip. Blood sprouted from the cut in an instant.

I closed my eyes for a moment, calming my own mind amidst the chaos, preparing to enter the Realm.

When I opened them again, the chancellor's bloodshot eyes were locked on me, lids nearly swollen closed from excessive strain and tears. Sweat lined his flushed face and frothy saliva gathered at the corners of his cracked lips. Terror had many faces. His was befitting given his knowledge in crime and punishment.

He knew all too well this was his end.

No risks were taken with the security and effectiveness of the stones. So Lorenz held a clean white cloth aloft before swiping it beneath the tip of the chancellor's finger, then smeared a streak across the surface of the Cloud stone.

The hall went utterly silent again.

With a deep inhale, I lifted my palms, feeling the Realm reach out, beckoning me even before I made contact with the sphere's cool surface.

The instant I connected, a jolt of energy burst forward, diving into my mind, supplying the familiar quick stream of blurred thoughts and visions. I was not a spectator of the chancellor's life, watching his history replay as any Clear stone allowed. Instead, I was a temporary visitor inside his mind with a limited view from within, hearing the whisper of his thoughts, seeing flashes of the world between blinks of his eyes, tasting the acidity in his mouth, and even feeling the heavy beats of his heart and the steady breaths in his lungs.

"Tell me what you see, Lovely." Count Ashboard's voice entered my mind, directing me.

Since mere days had passed from the crime, I didn't have to travel long. Beyond a tangle of memories from the chancellor's failed escape from town, the countess appeared in a mental haze.

Braided blond hair hangs past a corset I long to one day unfasten completely. Books line the wall on shelves from floor to ceiling at her back. Her thin lips hold a sad smile for a moment before they turn downward completely.

"I can't." Her melodic voice is a feast for my soul, but the words are a blade through my chest.

"You said ... You said you only wanted me." Other, more pathetic utterances threaten to spill from my lips, but I swallow them down to feed my anger.

"*You know I can't leave him.*" It's dismissive, as if I were asking her to do something unheard of, not what we've discussed in our many stolen hours together.

"*It's not that you can't. It's that you won't.*" The harsh truth has my body trembling. She lied. She never meant a single word.

Resentment builds. I will not share her anymore. I refuse.

My hands move without thought, seizing her braid and yanking her back onto the settee. Her startled yelp is the last unbridled sound she makes before I cover her mouth with one hand and take hold of her neck with the other. As my grip tightens, her eyes widen, finally realizing I've had enough of her games. I am respected in this town, even more than her useless husband. I will not settle for second.

I am no one's servant to command or toy to discard.

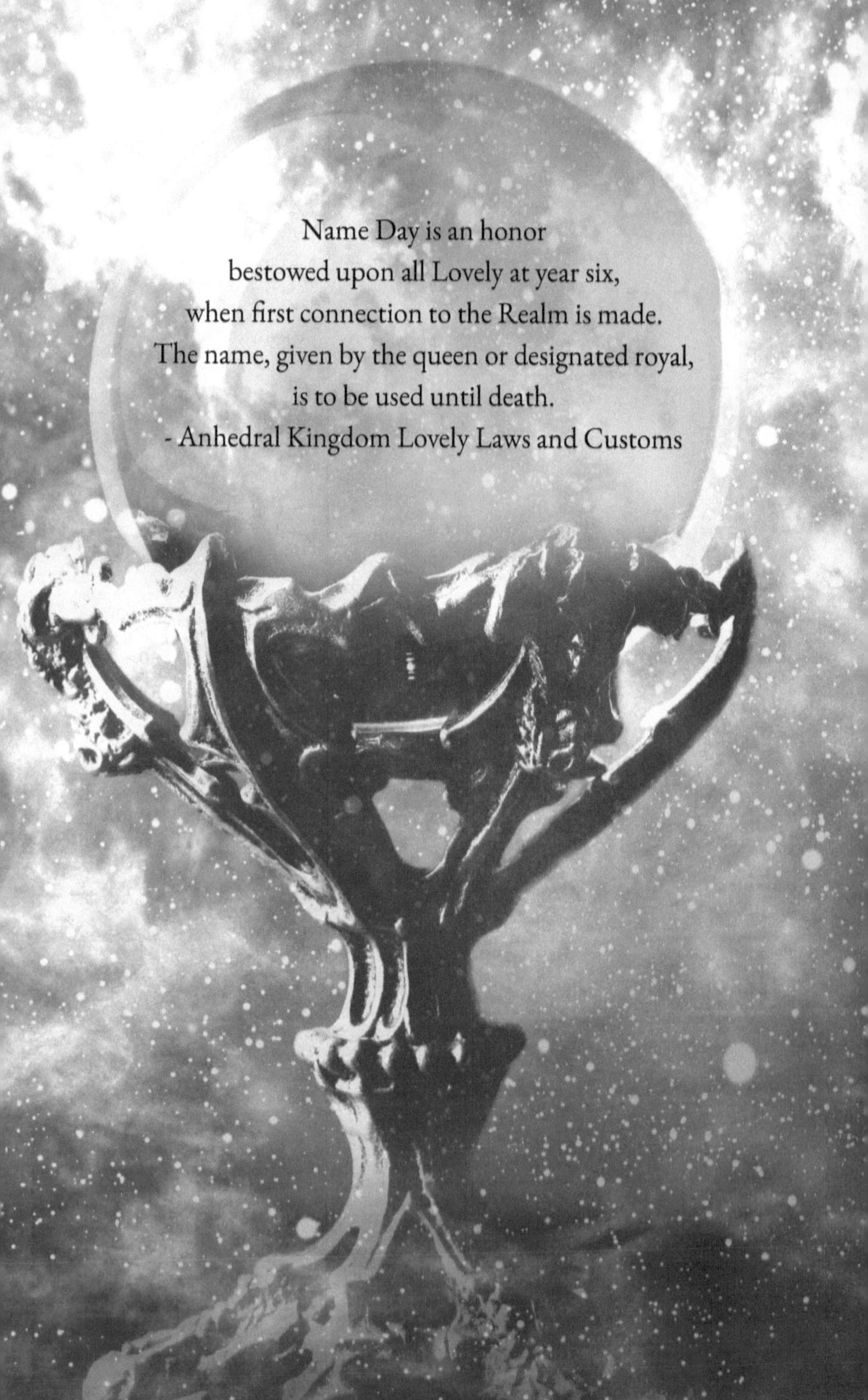

Name Day is an honor
bestowed upon all Lovely at year six,
when first connection to the Realm is made.
The name, given by the queen or designated royal,
is to be used until death.
- Anhedral Kingdom Lovely Laws and Customs

~ 2 ~

I didn't stay for the execution. I never stayed. The manner of punishment held no significance. Sometimes the guilty had a choice, but it was all the same to me. I held no bloodlust for justice like others did, that deep-routed need to watch someone pay for their crimes, with as little as confined isolation or as much as their final breath. Maybe it was because I'd already seen enough evil, vengeance, and death to last a lifetime. Never mind that I'd never seen an actual death firsthand, with my own eyes. Being a Lovely, I'd seen it all through the stones, through the Realm.

At age six, I'd learned about sex. Not from any farm or house animals, as children often do, but from the butcher's wife. She'd shown me adultery too.

At age eight, I'd witnessed real greed after a son poisoned his father to take over the family farm.

At eleven, I smelled the saltiness in a rush of panicked sweat before taking a husband's unfettered hit.

At thirteen, I tasted the tang of envy and the bitter thirst for revenge.

At fifteen, I felt true pain and terror through the pierce of an arrow.

And there was so much more in between and after, all of it growing stronger and more visceral as the years passed.

So there was no need to add to my undesirable memories with a real view of the chancellor's body swaying from the stout sycamore behind the town hall.

His thoughts had been grim enough to haunt me for weeks to come, easily the worst I'd ever seen. He'd known as soon as I'd arrived he couldn't hide his truth. No matter how horrid or pristine the skeletons or reputations may be, I would speak it. We all did. Because it didn't matter our stone class or how gifted we were. The Lovely never lied when connected to the Realm.

Everyone in Shadowstone had known the chancellor. All had liked him. He was a go-between for many, helping to mediate trivial town problems without having to involve Count Ashboard. But his soul was a vile one, darkened by guilty actions, plotted intentions, and devious thoughts so wretched that when I'd released hold of the Cloud stone, returning from the Realm, bile burned my throat and tears wet my cheeks.

An hour later, my eyes were focused on the fruit plate I'd prepared myself as the house's front door opened. I'd left immediately after the trial, unaccompanied, knowing in doing so I'd receive more chores and maybe a week's worth of extra town vanity readings like always. I hardly cared.

"Olean?" Cordelia's voice entered the room before she appeared in my periphery, the cheery tone surprising. While Cordelia's natural demeanor favored calmness, I expected a firm, irritated tone at my disobedience. As the Guardian appointed to our town's Nursery—also called the Lovely boarding house by locals—she tended to be more critical with me than with Begonia, Clem, or the youngest of the house, Girl. Cordelia's sternness toward me wasn't only because I'd been the eldest for several years, or that I often defied the mundane rules. It likely had to do with my stone ability, which was above her own. Though I had yet to ever read her, she couldn't completely hide her envy of my strength, and possibly her fear of it too.

As she stopped inside the kitchen's wide archway, the skirting of her favorite golden lace dress whirled out around her feet. If nothing else, the dress was the biggest indication of the day's importance. It, along with a few others she owned, was usually reserved for our rare formal occasions, like the quarterly dinners at the count's manor. But I hadn't understood why she'd risk tainting it, despite how grand today's trial had been.

My eyes remained on the plate, specifically a squashed raspberry, reassuring myself it looked nothing like a mess of bloody flesh I'd seen inside the chancellor's mind.

"Oleander." The word was whispered inside a burst of impatient air.

I finally looked at her, taking in her widened eyes, the pinch in her full lips, and the slight pink tinge on her honey brown cheeks. She was nervous and flustered.

Someone was visiting our Nursery.

She tilted her head, peering from across the room. Voluptuous was how some locals described her, in whispers and read thoughts. Her family had likely come from the northeast hills of Bloodweld, noted for curvy bodies of average height and broad, square faces. Her stature made everyone assume her soft and mild tempered, but she was mentally tough and not one to back down from arguments … or defiance. We were alike in that way and others. Though my face was narrower and my frame a bit taller, I was rumored to have been born in the northeast as well, with hips and a bust just as curvy and skin a similar dusky shade, unlike the paler people in our northwestern town of Shadowstone.

"You were supposed to wait by the carriage or ask for a guard escort. How many times do I—"

A clatter of footsteps came from the hall, cutting off Cordelia's words before three bodies overtook her in the doorway.

"It's my Name Day!" Girl shouted as she barreled past Clem and Begonia, stopping directly at my feet. Her eyes were as wide as Cordelia's, but I deciphered the emotion in hers much more clearly. It was equal parts excitement and fear. Her thin, flat-gray dress did nothing to conceal her nervous tremors as she waited for my reaction to her announcement, her face tilted upward and her lips pressed tight.

It meant the queen was the one visiting the Nursery, yet she hadn't been at the town hall for the trial.

Two notable days existed for the Lovely. The first was birth, when the one with whom we shared a womb also made an entrance into the world, only to forever join the dead. Our souls' connection never fully severed, though, leaving a tether between the living and the dead, creating our connection to the Realm.

The second day occurred during our sixth year, when we were deemed old enough for first contact with a stone to experience that tether. It was the first test of our sight, to confirm what we could offer the kingdom. That day was also known as our Name Day, each moniker given by the queen herself, overseer of all the Lovely.

If a Lovely's gift exceeded average ability, a third notable day sometimes happened around maturity. They were called upon to serve at the castle in the Realm division of the kingdom's army known as The Queen's Garden. Most never saw that day. They stayed in their towns, managed as their Guardian saw fit—to continue service in justice, to work for tax and profit, or released to live on their own, which usually happened if they were found to be weak, or worse, became addicted to the stones and madness slowly claimed them.

A tremor spread over my own body, knowing I had every right to be as nervous and excited as Girl.

There was a chance my third day had come.

But I wouldn't let my emotion show. Instead, I dipped my chin for a better view into Girl's eyes. "Just remember your studies ... and don't lie."

"Don't lie?!" she shouted up at my face, making me flinch back and hold in an actual chuckle. With her, I always had difficulty not succumbing to true feelings, not giving in to an actual connection. She was too innocent, too pure, and it made me ache to have that naivety again. "But I-I thought we couldn't when we touch them? Everyone's always said we can't!"

At the table, Clem rolled his eyes, loosened his ruffled purple necktie, and slumped back into a chair with a dramatic groan. I'd said the same to him on his Name Day five years before, wanting to break through his unease. I cast a glare his way to be sure his mood didn't sour Girl's. He'd been surly for the trial after learning he wouldn't be included. It was supposed to have been his turn with the Clear stone. But because of the trial's importance and possibly the level of violence, Cordelia had connected instead, to confirm the overall scene of the chancellor's crime before I was called to go deeper with the Cloud stone.

"Don't listen to her, Girl." Begonia huffed as she strode to the sink to pump a glass of water. Her plain black dress was identical to mine, handed down from all the other Lovely before us. The only differences were her slightly smaller size and the color of the satin ties at our waists—hers blood orange, mine pale pink. The tiny amount of orange only seemed to highlight the freckles she loathed. She claimed she didn't like the way they looked spattered all over her pale skin, but she really hated them because I had them as well, grouped over my nose and cheeks, blending smoothly with my darker skin.

Begonia didn't bother looking at us as she added, "Olean wants you to fail so she'll stay atop her shiny glass pedestal. Do well and shatter it for us, won't you?"

I gritted my teeth to stop a growl. She'd hated me since her Name Day, three years following my own, angry that her ability hadn't come close to matching mine. In the later months, I gave up on being friendly with her or anyone else who belittled me due to fear or jealousy. I would gladly stand tall as anyone's enemy if it meant not losing myself. Being a Lovely already came with a heavy threat of losing ourselves, our own thoughts and feelings drowned regularly by all the others we took in. We didn't need another way to lose more.

Sinking down onto my knees in front of Girl, I replied sincerely, "I was only teasing. There is no lying. You won't even need to think about what to say. Your mind and mouth will simply take over as soon as you touch the stone. And Begonia's mistaken. I'm excited for you to do well today, especially when you get your name, which will undoubtedly be more beautiful than hers."

A piggish grunt sounded from near the sink as Girl smiled wide, the idea of her name washing all other concerns away, including Begonia. Her golden beige skin shimmered under the light from the kitchen window as I traced the curve of her ear. Like the rest of us, her head and body were hairless. Our eye color was practically the same too—cloudy white irises with a shadowy gray outline. If there was anyone alive who didn't know about the Lovely, they might guess us all related despite our varied features and skin hues.

Begonia finally finished processing my attack on her biggest insecurity, and she gave a low grumble. "You wretched—"

"Enough," Cordelia cut off the impending argument and outstretched a hand. "Come, Girl. I hear the coach outside and you need to be ready." As soon as Girl took her hand, she turned to leave but not before calling over a shoulder, "No more fighting or you'll all pay with outdoor chores. Clematis, refasten the tie and sit with Begonia in the parlor. Olean, put your house shoes on and remove the flour smudges from your skirting. Quickly."

"Baker's wench," Begonia whispered before following the others out of the kitchen.

After leaving the trial, I'd taken advantage of the empty town and visited the premier baker's eldest son Jonah, who worked while his parents attended the trial. It hadn't been the first time. Like me, he enjoyed exploring the desires I'd only seen through the stones—the secret, delicious things people did behind closed doors. I longed to experience it all myself. Cordelia was aware of those indiscretions. She saw everything during my monthly personal readings, which were mandatory for all working Lovely within the Nursery to ensure we weren't compromised by others, accessing stones illegally, or becoming addicted. She let me have my stolen time with Jonah because she knew it was only curiosity. Or I'd assumed as much since she'd only ever spoken of it once, and that was to ensure our meetings remained secret considering that type of involvement with a Lovely could be negative for his future. We were revered for our gifts but still held at arm's length from most people due to our differences. The sneers and smiles we received were always in near equal measure.

But it didn't bother me so much. My life goal was not love, nor to be trapped in Shadowstone to become what Begonia's insult predicted—something hidden regardless of my stature or worth as a Lovely. Because we were never to marry and were also incapable of having children.

And I'd seen the way Begonia looked at Jonah in passing. The hateful words were a cover for her own desires, and that was yet another reason for her to hate me.

I was still wiping smudges from the hem of my dress when the front door opened and Cordelia's very loud and honey-sweet voice made a formal greeting. In a frenzy, I dashed silently to the parlor. Entering the room after the queen would be a terrible mistake, only slightly better than greeting her incorrectly. And as I had never been to Castle Anhedral—let alone anywhere outside the borders of Shadowstone—and hadn't seen her since Clem's Name Day, I would hate to risk any chance at being called to join the Queen's Garden on account of such a trivial error.

At least, I'd imagined being late would be one of the worst mistakes, until I turned into the parlor's rear doorway, tripped over something, and smacked straight into someone.

I had only a moment to release a startled yelp before colliding with a tall man and the box he had been carrying. He made no sound, only stumbled backward a few steps from my impact before we both fell. I landed on my knees over his legs, watching in horror as the polished wooden box clattered to the floor, its lid bouncing off, releasing the contents. Stone spheres launched across the planks in a chaotic race.

We both scrambled to chase after them at the same time, our limbs tangling. His body was hard and warm, muscles firm as they flexed and released, rushing to retrieve the stones. The sensation of him against me instantly reminded me of how Jonah's body felt, though Jonah wasn't nearly as large or solid and hadn't ignited me like some of the visions I'd encountered through the stones. Certain town women all but incinerated from the touch of their lovers. My body flashed nearly as hot, and the realization made me go still on my hands and knees. Embarrassment. That was the cause. Nothing more.

Clem, Girl, and Begonia all remained seated behind the tea table across the room. Clem snickered quietly from his end on the stretched settee, his lips rolled inward to contain anything louder. Begonia's button nose pointed to the ceiling in a practiced look of indifference. Her resentfulness shined through her downcast stare as always, though. And Girl ... well, she was bouncing lightly on her bottom in between them, twisting her little hands, her wondrous stare fixed on something behind me.

Unable to contain my curiosity, I swept my face toward the fireplace and was met with the sloppiest kiss I'd ever had, which was some feat considering the first time I'd kissed Jonah, his intention might have been to swallow my entire face. Even though he'd been physically incapable, there was a possibility the culprit of this kiss could. A long, slobbery tongue licked me from chin to forehead twice in quick succession.

As soon as the enormous, blueish-gray head came into focus, I released a startled gasp. The dog settled back onto its haunches with a twinkle in its eyes as it began to pant excited breaths, its tongue lolling out of its open mouth.

Before I could even categorize the level of disorder following my parlor entrance, someone chuckled, even and deep. "Now that's a grand entrance."

My eyes shifted around again as Begonia, Clem, and Girl got to their feet, curtsied or bowed, and all at once said, "Your Highness."

Climbing to my feet, I kept my eyes pinned to the floor and silently chastised the crooked pink ribbon at my waist, the tiny smudge of baker's flour still visible along my dress hem, and maybe most of all, the sticky mess of slobber coating my face. For a moment, I'd thought no one else had seen since the queen had yet to enter. But to my dismay, we hadn't been alone. The prince was a surprise. He'd never visited Shadowstone Nursery before.

"Your Highness." I curtsied low, then silently begged the Realm to reach out and swallow me whole.

Lovely are the conduit to the Realm,
serving a single, destined purpose
to protect the kingdom
from within and without.
- Anhedral Kingdom Lovely Guidebook

"I apologize for Argo's behavior." Prince Ren's smooth voice held a hint of amusement. "He's not normally so forward. Honestly, I've never seen him act so bold with anyone. But I suspect the ungentlemanly act was to show you he holds no hard feelings for tripping over him."

A strangled squeal came from Girl. "Argo is his name? Is he your dog?"

Begonia released a soft hiss, a reminder for Girl not to speak in a formal setting until addressed.

When I finally lifted my face and eyes, the prince smiled broadly, handed me a fold of silk fabric, then turned to face the others with a flourish of his hand. "Please, sit and relax. My mother's admiring the grounds and gardens, as she usually does, so she will be delayed. And yes, the dog's name is Argo, but he is not mine. He is Croft's. Our attendant."

Being the oldest of our group, I followed customs and remained standing at his side while hastily wiping the drool from my face with the handkerchief he'd offered. I honestly wanted to die in that moment. I'd never been so embarrassed. The mortification was even worse than when I'd fallen into a pile of horse excrement before a reading at the town hall when I was thirteen—something

Begonia had brought up at least twice a year since, lest anyone happened to forget.

While his focus was on the others, I took the opportunity to eye him fully. Though not nearly as brawny as the Nursery guards, he stood as tall as most, possibly two or so inches taller than my own five-foot-ten stature. His attire was for travel, with plain black pants and a trim, single-breasted surcoat, the very top showing a crisp gray shirt beneath. The tips of his shined boots held water speckles from the melting ground snow along our entry path outside. Despite the simplicity of his clothing, he was neat and clean, which most in our farming town had trouble with maintaining daily, especially when the melting snow soddened the ground and mud covered most surfaces. Cordelia had spoken of the gowns and suits worn at court from her time at the castle, but I still could only imagine, never having seen anything so resplendent in real life or the Realm. The occupants of Shadowstone were more mundane, tenders of the hearty crops and rugged animal farms—the primary assets of our kingdom's outlying mountainous town. Any distant acquaintances I'd witnessed through the stones were much of the same.

At a dinner earlier in the year, Count Ashboard had briefly regaled us with details of the prince's traditional twenty-second-year celebration, though his story leaned more heavily on the castle's available food and drink rather than decorations, gowns, or even the people. Seeing the prince for myself, I couldn't deny the reason for the town's rumors of his handsomeness. He was something to behold. His flaxen skin held a glow in the muted sunlight of the parlor. Having seen the queen a few times in my life, I knew he likely favored his father in most features. Dark brown hair cropped close on the sides of his head and along his narrow, angular jaw. His lips were fuller than most men, fluffed like pillows. His body was fit, though not as large with muscle as guards or even the attendant I'd so gracefully run into. I didn't know much about royal life, but he had maintained himself well in preparation to rule.

Prince Ren continued, "Croft is different in that he is deaf and doesn't speak. Argo is always with him to alert him when needed."

"An attendant who can't hear? Isn't that a bit useless?" Now it was Clem speaking out of turn, his words soft, tentative.

I knew him well enough to understand his question wasn't meant to be cruel, only inquisitive. He was too accustomed to our usual bluntness as Lovely and needed to learn how to phrase things more considerately when in polite conversation. Though I also didn't miss how he left out the part about speaking. He thought that wouldn't have been as big of a loss as most attendants didn't need to speak at all, just listen and follow orders.

I grimaced at him from the prince's side. Finally, he corrected himself with a quiet, "Sorry if that was rude."

To my surprise, it was Girl who spoke up next. "They look useful to me. Argo and Croft look very smart."

Prince Ren chuckled and cast an amused glance over his shoulder toward Croft. "You are right, little one. They are smart, work well together, and are very helpful to us. Those qualities and others make them very useful and most important to us."

Girl giggled and looked behind me with a tiny, shy smile. "And being handsome?"

Realm, save her. Was she flirting at age six?

Begonia closed her eyes and shook her head at Girl's declaration while Clem huffed out a breath. Both hadn't paid any mind to Croft or Argo, but they'd hung on the prince's every word since he began speaking. Begonia's eyes especially, her eyelids fluttering as if she'd had something stuck inside both. I itched to mention it but wouldn't dare tear her down in front of a royal.

As the prince chuckled yet again, seemingly delighted by Girl's cuteness, I couldn't help but glance over my shoulder. What I found was exactly as Girl had said—a very smart and handsome duo. Argo sat still and observant, his large head nearly on level at Croft's waist. And Croft ... Well, he looked like much more than an attendant. His sleeved uniform shirt in the kingdom's signature black color fit perfectly against the breadth of his shoulders, chest, and arms, the seams in silver accentuating his muscular size. He was a good deal taller than me, too, which was less like any local resident and more akin to our town guards. Thick, wavy brown hair was gathered and fastened neatly at the back of his head. His face was broad too and somewhat familiar, with a wide, square jaw covered in trimmed hair, a straight, slightly upturned nose, and a slim upper lip, which had lifted the tiniest bit at one corner while his eyes focused on Girl. The hue of his skin was a rich, coppery tan, not too different than my own, likely having family from the easternmost lands of Anhedral or even one of the kingdoms beyond.

With the box of stones clasped firmly once again inside his gloved hands, Croft's gaze shifted to me as if he'd felt me assessing him. With light amber eyes, his stare was beyond intriguing.

In a panic, I jerked to face the others.

"You, little one, are clever and sweet," the prince spoke to Girl. "I should hope that means you'll do well today. Are you excited to touch your first stone?"

"Yes," Girl answered, smile faltering and wondrous eyes blinking rapidly as worry replaced her excitement.

Prince Ren gave a reassuring nod. I focused on his short length of top hair, curious as to how many attendants they had for grooming and things. I had never been envious of ordinary hair. As a Lovely, I found our baldness to be beautiful and defining. But I longed to explore the use of something other than the simple color-identifying head ribbon we were permitted, and I quite liked the idea of wearing more elaborate clothes too.

That was one reason I'd been awaiting my invitation to serve the kingdom's prestigious Garden, knowing the tales of extravagant parties with unending choices for food and drink. Even Cordelia had briefly spoken of what might happen if I were to go. Though she tended to be vague about her own time there, she made sure to express how difficult and demanding the duties could be. She had struggled with her limitations, had been grouped with others for more basic tasks. I assumed that was why she'd been selected as Guardian of this Nursery years ago, taking the responsibility of raising Lovely instead of continuing with a position at the castle.

"Stay where you are. Stay where you are. Let me look at you all," Queen Reina Vidis of Anhedral said, abruptly gliding into the room, a scent of strawberry following as she lifted a weighty traveling cloak from her shoulders. Cordelia, who was on her heels, took hold of the black garment and hooked it on the stand by the foyer. The queen stopped in the center of the parlor, her lips parted in a practiced toothy smile, eyes roaming the room to take in all the occupants. Her travel dress was more intricate than some of Cordelia's best but still considered plain as it had very few layers and draped close to her body. Her sleek black hair was styled in layers of braids along the top, then flowed freely down the bottom, stopping somewhere in the middle of her dainty back. More subtle lines creased the porcelain skin of her heart-shaped face and exposed neck than at her last visit. I believed her to be nearing fifty years, like Cordelia, though appearing younger due to the smaller features from her southeastern heritage of the Jewel Isles. I had no doubt wealth and access to finer quality goods aided as well.

"Now, now," the queen tutted as her wide-set eyes continued to shift around. "I'm so glad you've gotten acquainted with Ren while I assessed the grounds. He already knows much about the Lovely but has more to learn before he takes his place as king. But enough of all that. You, my dears, have become so beautiful and handsome. Growing like weeds, though blossoming like your namesakes. Lovely in all ways. I'm sure your minds and abilities have blossomed as well. Begonia. Clematis. And look at you, Girl." Her graceful hand reached over the tea table and gently palmed Girl's cheek. "I have a feeling any of the names I have in mind will suit you perfectly."

Girl beamed at the attention, sitting as still as her excited body allowed.

"So ..." The queen glanced at Cordelia. Though it was fast, I couldn't help but notice the warmth that had been in her eyes flashed rather cold before she looked away. "Those other chairs ... so we can begin."

Cordelia jumped into motion, her head bowing as a flush rose in her cheeks. She was flustered in a way I had never seen. Or was I only noticing now that I was older? The queen's presence had always made her jittery. Then again, the more I thought about it, I never recalled the queen addressing her directly anytime she'd visited.

With a smile gracing her lips once more, the queen spoke to the prince. "Ren, take the opposite end to see clearly." Cordelia situated the first chair for the prince as the queen glanced my way. "Oleander. Truly pretty, you are. Take the seat across from the others here, darling. We regretfully missed today's trial where I hear you did splendidly. I am rather excited to see more from you. But first with Girl. Croft, if you will ..."

Cordelia had hauled the final wing-back chair to the queen just as she finished speaking. I took a seat at the same time and watched from the corner of my eye as Argo's head shifted into Croft's side. It might have been the way to alert him, though Croft was already in motion, already watching and aware. Could he read body cues? Understand words as they formed on a person's lips? The only person I'd known of with a physical and mental impairment had been one of the alpaca farmer's sons. He also didn't speak and would react to people in a disassociated way, but he could hear and had learned basic skills to help his family. When he'd turned fourteen, I'd read his thoughts at his parents' request. His mind was a vivid landscape, beautiful and chaotic, memories and thoughts categorized meticulously in his own method. He understood many things, only lacked the usual ways of showing comprehension and expression.

It seemed Croft understood and even reacted quite typically, though stolid like most attendants.

Croft set the box onto the serving table at my side and opened it facing the queen, revealing the stones I'd seen in a blur minutes before. Four stones. Not three, like all the previous visits.

Clear. Cloud. Smoke. And ... White.

Solid, opaque white!

The queen smiled broadly. "Shall we begin?"

For any persons on trial
and any mandated readings for those
under employ of the Crown (guards,
attendants, soldiers, etc.), no direct contact
will be made with a stone.
When blood is required, a cloth will be used.
This applies to all Lovely as well.
- Anhedral Kingdom Lovely Laws and Customs

~ 4 ~

As Croft removed the last stone from the case, grasping it firmly within his leather gloves and placing it onto its plain wooden stand at the center of the table, there was a gasp from the settee. All eyes shifted, looking to find the source.

Begonia looked sheepish, her audible response a shock to even herself. I couldn't blame her. I'd nearly done the same. Such a valuable and powerful stone had never been inside our Nursery as far as I knew. We only housed two. The queen always brought her own for Name Days, and the most powerful had only been Smoke. Until now.

Not dwelling on the reaction, the queen shifted forward in her seat as Croft backed away from the table. Because of the chair positions, he and Argo were once again standing close behind my side. I could hear Argo's breathing. Being a constant reminder of their close proximity, the rhythmic sound should have made me nervous, but it actually had the opposite effect. My heartbeat slowed, the airy cadence an unexpected assurance, calming me as the queen spoke again.

"First things first." Her gaze swept to Girl. "In addition to your normal academic studies, have you learned about our kingdom's history and the stones, to include their rules, and each class and use?"

"Yes, Your Majesty." Girl nodded emphatically from her position between Begonia and Clem.

I smiled as her little eyes flitted to me for support.

Before Girl could glance at the fireplace behind me—where Cordelia had positioned herself—the queen continued, "Good. Tell me about our history."

"The early travelers discovered the stones as they formed Anhedral Kingdom. Lovely were born soon after, but it would be years and years and years before anyone found the bond between us and the stones, and the link to the Realm."

Our true history was glossed over in the teachings and very rarely brought up in company at all, especially on Name Days. The deeper, darker truth found in older books recounted that the Lovely born then were intentionally slaughtered, generations of ordinary people believing we were either gifts who needed to be sacrificed to the early settlers' Sky Gods, or physical abominations who needed to be eradicated. And after the Realm link was finally found, it would still be years before our sights were believed and utilized for justice, defense, and then entertainment.

"And the years following?" the queen asked, her words rushed as always, as if she disliked the required inquisition herself or simply found the kingdom history boring.

"The mines were pl-plun-dered." Girl took a deep breath after struggling with the word. "Then in the Realm year one hundred thirty-two, the Raids happened. Stones were sold to other kingdoms or destroyed in revolt against the Crown."

"Yes, truly unfortunate times. And now?"

"Mining is regu-lated, though no new stones have been found in over a hundred years. Most left are owned by the Crown and other noble families."

The queen spared a quick glance at the prince, who sat diligently with a practiced, placid smile, silently observing the exchange.

After a nod, the prince cleared his throat and asked, "What are the rules for using the stones and entering the Realm?"

Girl blinked a few times, the shuffle and collection of thoughts evident in the wrinkle of her tiny forehead. "Stones are polished and blood is smeared to ensure the Realm link is pure and the connection is clear. Unless a crime is committed, no one under the age of fourteen may be read and no one older may be read against their will. Under the kingdom's indentureship, no Lovely, active or inactive, willingly or not, may connect with the Realm without consent from the Crown. All information from the Realm is also property of the Crown."

"Excellent. Very eloquent in your knowledge, Girl. You've practiced well," Prince Ren praised.

"Olean helps me," Girl replied without hesitation, only to frown a bit when she realized she'd let the secret slip.

It wasn't exactly against Nursery rules for us older Lovely to help the younger, but our influence could be viewed negatively since we were not the Guardians and also no longer pure of Realm connection and the corruption of other people's crimes ... and in my case, also their direct thoughts.

"Does she?" The queen hummed thoughtfully, eyes darting to me, then over my shoulder briefly. I didn't miss the pinch in her lips or the glare aimed at Cordelia. She continued immediately. "Let's move on. Name the classes, what stones are in each, and their uses."

Girl's hands twisted the tiniest amount on her lap until she caught herself and stilled them. Then she began reciting more of the information that was taught to us even before we could speak.

"Clear are the most common in use and in number. Some even have tints of color. They are the most basic link to the Realm, where levels of the past and the present can be seen. Haze class stones are less common and stronger yet. They are Cloud, Smoke, and Needled. Cloud stones have pretty white swirls. With them, we can view memories and present thoughts more powerfully from inside the person's mind. Smoke stones have gray and black swirls and can show us a person's deepest fears and desires, an asset for crime and punishment. Needled have lots of sharp, dark lines inside. They are used for distance and group readings, am-amplifying other stones when used closely together."

"Good, good. And the last class?" the queen asked with an encouraging nod.

"Opaque." Her eyes cast a look downward at the solid white sphere set on a plain wooden base. "They are the most rare and strongest. There are four: Eye, Blood, White, and Black. Eye stones are dark blue with a shiny streak of light that moves along the stone's surface. It connects us with animals, to read and control their minds. Blood stones are mossy green speckled with red. No one alive now has ever seen one. Our history says they can control human thoughts and actions. White is solid in color. They allow a direct connection with the dead inside the Realm, let us see, hear, and sometimes speak with them."

The last bit lingered heavy in the air, all of us Lovely thinking the same thing since we saw the stone set onto the table. Why was it here? Now?

"Black stones." Girl's words were barely audible in the roaring silence, so she repeated and continued on more firmly, "Black stones. They are a solid color like White. All remaining are owned by the Crown. They are the most powerful connection to the Realm, said to hold abilities above all else. Very few Lovely have been strong enough to connect with them. None who have connected have survived."

Those who did connect were trapped, their minds and souls captive inside the Realm before their deaths. There were stories of some who had endured for some time, though. The one most known was during the reign of the notorious Queen Rose, also called the Evil Queen, who had been the very first to bestow us with the collective moniker Lovely, gift us our names, and offer the kingdom's lawful protection in exchange for servitude.

Queen Reina clapped three times, jolting the rest of us from our musings. She straightened with a smile, oblivious to our unease or simply accustomed to disrupting silence. "We've been on quite a journey so far, visiting several of our towns for Name Days. The reason I brought the White stone along this trip is because we've had recent losses and are heavily replenishing our Garden. Since there are to be many joining, of all stone classes, we wanted a better idea of the abilities before the arrival at the castle. We will still hold a proper testing for all accepted, as per our usual induction custom, as well as hold our induction ball."

Cordelia had mentioned the induction ball when I was younger. Mostly, though, she discussed the events for dignitaries where Lovely were entertainment for vanity readings. They were the stories Begonia fawned over, begging for snippets from Cordelia at the times she slipped into nostalgia and let us peek into her younger life. It wasn't often. She was notoriously closed-lipped about her time at the castle. Noticing more about her and the queen's interactions, I wondered if they had once been acquaintances or had known each other to some degree. Given the look from the queen, I'd almost guess them rivals.

The queen eyed each of us, letting her last statement settle before glancing around the parlor, taking in the meticulously cleaned drapery and dustless tabletops, likely assessing more than the surface-level appearances. The Crown funded the Garden Nurseries. If anything was to her displeasure, she would have it changed regardless of Cordelia's or Count Ashboard's opinions. She'd ordered the drapery replaced on my Name Day, the garden excavated and replanted on Begonia's, and all the furnishings refinished on Clem's. We were left cleaning the house for weeks after the last time, our chore time tripling to get rid of the dust and varnishes.

So even though we lived in the house, nothing was truly ours. And I wanted that, something for myself. Aside from my stolen time with Jonah, my personal time and belongings were minimal. Perhaps at the castle, things might be different. Maybe there would be something more I could call my own one day, something I could earn from merit and ability. A gown or a pair of fine heels, like Cordelia's prized possessions kept from her time at the castle. Maybe joining the Garden would be better than imagined, maybe even better than Begonia dreamed, knowing she'd never have the chance to experience it. Well, that last bit stood as truth until the queen had shared the latest news. Were they really taking all stone classes from the towns?

And what had she meant about recent losses? Had something happened at the castle?

I peered over my shoulder again, eyeing Cordelia for any hints of knowledge. But her face remained blank, no twitches or rapid blinks, no hints at all to show she knew anything. Before turning back, my eyes decided to stick on Croft and Argo, still standing handsomely and obediently. Croft's eyes shifted to mine yet again, catching my fleeting perusal. They narrowed the slightest amount. Following a heavy pause, I managed to tear my gaze away, only then to catch the prince's eyes as well. There was no chancing a heavy pause there. Staring boldly at him might burn harsher—and in more ways—than the sun. Lovely were valued but nowhere equal to royalty. I knew my station well enough despite living so far from the castle.

But it had raised my curiosity. Had he been watching me for some reason already? Or perhaps merely looking around as his mother was?

"So," the queen said, abandoning her perusal of the parlor, lifting the edge of her dress, and shifting her legs into another position. She did the same with her lengthy black hair, moving it over a shoulder. "Shall we begin with Girl's readings?"

Girl's eyes widened, and her tiny body shook again, this time with nervousness. I gave her a reassuring smile and a small nod, hoping to encourage her.

"Sit forward, darling," Queen Reina continued. "We usually have a volunteer from town here to test for Name Days. Since we weren't quite prepared, we'll be doing something different."

Everyone's eyes moved to Croft, an automatic assumption as reading for the royals was exclusive and usually done with limited viewers. They each had their own assigned to them, handpicked and of higher skill level. It was *the* goal for most of us Lovely. A true honor.

So naturally, especially on a Name Day, they wouldn't be the volunteers for the reading. Since there was no one left aside from the Lovely ourselves, our eyes moved to the attendant.

"Oh, not Croft." The edges of the queen's lips tipped upward as she eyed him for a moment. "Croft is unreadable. It is his particularly unique trait and quite the gift to the Crown. Many have tried, and all have failed. His mind is his own. Of course he's still visible to others through the Realm ... but I digress. Cordelia. Please take Olean's place across from Girl so we can begin."

I barely stopped my sharp intake of air. Fortunately, the chair's rough movement along the floor in my hasty move to stand covered my shock. This was highly unconventional. I'd never seen Cordelia read by anyone in town. Her required readings were twice a year and performed by someone sent from the castle. It was the standard for Guardians, to be sure all was running well and our progress was strong. But those of us living here were never privy to them or their outcomes. She always went to the count's manor, and she was always unaccompanied.

So this ...

As I backed away from the chair, Cordelia passed me stoically. She had no reason to protest, I assumed, though even if she had, she would never voice it. She was given an order, so she must follow.

She sat gracefully while I took another step backward, bumping my hand into something cold and moist. Just as I realized what I could have touched, a wet tongue gave my hand a lick. My eyes glanced downward to Argo's appraising stare. Silently, I sneaked a pat to Argo's head before wiping the side of my hand on my dress. I'd never been drawn to the local animals. Most canines were farm aids, herders and protectors. None had been quite so friendly with us Lovely. Smart of them, really, obviously sensing our connection to death and the Realm and knowing it wasn't normal, or perhaps understanding it better than anyone else. Argo, though, seemed unbothered altogether.

I glanced up at Croft, whose eyes flickered forward as if he'd noticed and watched our exchange.

His mind was unreadable. I wanted to think on that more, about how it would feel attempting to enter his thoughts with the Cloud stone, or how his deafness might be a factor as to why no one could. But all of my attention was shifted to Cordelia and what was about to happen.

The queen remained in her stark straight position as she viewed the table. "Being as how we always start with the most powerful stone for the Name Day test, we will begin with White. However, given the nature of this stone, we won't need blood. The connection holds a wider scope, showing a broad range of the immediate area and everyone within. We can ask the Lovely from there who and what to focus upon. So, Girl, please reach out with both hands and place your palms upon the stone."

Slowly, and without a shake, Girl reached forward, fingers stretching wide as if she intended to fully encompass the surface of the glossy sphere. There was no chance of that. Its size matched the others on the table, all much larger than Girl's little hands. No one seemed to breathe as her palms came into contact.

And then, after two silent moments without any movement, Girl blinked and frowned.

"That's quite all right, Girl. It is a strong one, after all. We're moving to the next then, yes?"

Smoke. I'd connected with it on my Name Day and hadn't touched it again since because the queen hadn't given one to our town. Even though we'd had our share of crime, there was essentially no need to delve into a person's mind specifically for their deepest fears or desires. There was a reason it was considered a specialty examination as it could seek out manifestations in addition to actual memories if needed. It was mainly used for kingdom interrogations, or at least that was explained after I had outed our town guard Lorenz for his deathly fear of spiders and his desire to become guard commander.

While all the other Lovely still looked shocked by what was about to happen, the prince looked practically bored. His eyes roamed the room a few times, and his feet tapped some too. He'd obviously seen enough readings to not care, even though this reading wasn't a standard Name Day practice. If he was here to learn, he seemed less and less enthused.

"Croft, your knife," the queen said.

Croft had to read lips or had already anticipated the proceedings because he stepped forward with the dagger from his side and quickly sliced the point across the tip of Cordelia's finger. He extended a clean cloth to collect the blood, but the queen motioned for him to just hand it to Cordelia, which was unusual. I guessed her reasoning, though not voiced, was because Cordelia wouldn't connect with the more powerful stones even if she accidentally touched them.

Croft placed it inside Cordelia's other hand and moved to Argo's side with two quick backward strides.

Cordelia's shoulder had stiffened slightly with the slice of the blade. Then she collected the blood with the cloth and leaned forward, reaching for the closest stone. Clear.

"No, Lovely." Queen Reina tutted with a dismissive little wave, then pointed to the table's center. "In descending order of power, if you please."

Cordelia's arm remained suspended over the stones in a long moment before sweeping to the Smoke stone. The dark swirl within looked menacing in its beauty, more so because of Cordelia's obvious apprehension. She was afraid. Of what? Us knowing her fears and desires?

After she swiped the blood across the surface, Girl leaned in and repeated her previous action without hesitation. Her features had turned determined, longing for the first experience, to know her station as a Lovely now that she hadn't connected with the more powerful Opaque stone.

Once again, a lengthy moment had us all holding our breaths.

And once again, there was nothing.

"And now Cloud," the queen said with a faint purse in her lips. There was resigned disappointment there. She'd been hopeful but knew better than most how infrequent the higher connections happened.

From the back, Cordelia's posture hadn't eased in the slightest. She pinched her fingertip, gathering another drop of blood for the cloth, then smeared it over the Cloud stone.

Girl pressed her palms to the surface faster, eager. That time, there was no wait. No bated breaths or heavy, expectant pauses. Her body instantly tensed, and her eyes widened. The atmosphere noticeably shifted within the parlor, the Realm welcoming her.

With an appeased sigh, the queen sat straighter. "Good, Girl. Now tell me what thoughts Cordelia had been reluctant to share with us."

When a Lovely first connects
to the Realm and is awarded their name,
they pledge their servitude to the kingdom
and Crown with the Lovely Vow.
- Anhedral Kingdom Lovely Guidebook

"*I will not let them, Pearla. They can't. They can't. They can't.*" Tears flooded over Girl's cheeks as she spoke, her chanting soft and panicked.

Her connection had been instant. She'd jumped inside the memory and immediately begun to cry. Her descriptions were swift—her view of the dimly lit room, its damp, musty air, and the pain radiating from head to toe, most especially her stomach. Then she had grunted and groaned before speaking as Cordelia.

I hadn't been sure what to expect of Cordelia's memories. As far as I knew, she hadn't endured any horrible events in Shadowstone aside from our usual trials and occasional taunts from unfriendly townspeople. So it had to have been some kind of trauma before our time. But I never in my life would have imagined the words that came next.

"*'They can't take my baby.'*"

Baby?!

There was no controlling my gasp that time. And I was not alone. Begonia's hands had catapulted upward to cover her mouth before she instantly corrected her error, while Clem sputtered out a soft whimper I hadn't heard from him since the night of his first official trial reading. A guilty mother had beaten her boy so badly, he couldn't walk for a week, which gave her a sentence of the same punishment and a stripping of the child's custody. Clem had sobbed all night in his room. I'd tried to console him before he'd locked himself away. He woke the next morning and never mentioned it again. He hadn't wept since.

Despite not understanding how this could even be true myself, I wanted to comfort them both. Perhaps it was because I inherently knew it had to be true and needed comfort too, to be assured that what we thought about our ability to have children wasn't a lie. Had we misheard what Girl was reading from the Realm? Somehow misunderstood?

"*They know,*" Girl uttered. Her eyes remained open and unfocused, her hold on the stone firm, though her little body trembled in her seat. "*Please do as I asked you before ... should I not survive. Oh, Realm, the baby's coming. They will not let me keep what was never meant to happen.*'" Girl screamed in pain, sweat beading along her brow now. "*Quiet. You must be quiet now,' Pearla shushes me.*"

Cordelia trembled in her own chair, choking back a sob. "Please, no. Don't have her continue. She's too small. It's too painful."

The Cloud stone was entirely more visceral than the Clear. No one in the room would understand that as well as me. But despite our differences, we all knew that the connection and potency only increased as we aged. So while Girl would experience some amount of pain, she would not experience the full level endured during childbirth. The shock of the firsthand experience would be the main cause of her distress.

"She's doing well," the queen replied, seeming untroubled by the reading's information. Though she was queen and likely trained to maintain composure in all scenarios.

Girl's sobbing ceased, and she went utterly still. *"Pearla holds the baby up, tears slipping down her own plumped cheeks. The smile she shares with me is as real and true as ever. 'It's a boy, Cordelia. A white-eyed, Lovely boy.' I reach forward, begging her, 'Let me hold him.' He's beautiful, my baby boy. But he makes no noise in her hands, no movements, and Pearla's smile falters. Before I can take hold, the cellar door bursts open and a rush of guards enter. 'No! No! No!' My voice is weak, my head fuzzy. 'He's gone. Look for yourselves. You don't need to take him,' Pearla begs them for me as the room darkens. Then there's nothing."*

Girl's breaths evened out, awaiting her next instructions, suspended in the Realm's link with Cordelia's mind.

Queen Reina gave a small sniff and gently cleared her throat. Her poised body gave no other indication that the reading had affected her, but I suspected that might have been a small crack in her composure. "That'll be all, Lovely. You may remove your hands."

No one else dared speak. Cordelia was frozen in place. Standing off to the side behind her chair, I couldn't even tell if she breathed. Tears welled inside my own eyes, feeling not only the pain and sorrow Girl had experienced for the first time but also wondering what I'd never known about Cordelia's pain.

She had birthed a child.

Girl's eyes fluttered open and stared directly across the table as her hands dropped to her lap. She blinked, and her lips quivered slightly. Her hands moved to lift again as her body shifted forward, the intent plain. She wanted to hug the woman who raised her, someone as close to a mother we all had. Our Guardian. But her movements were interrupted.

"Quite a good job, Girl. Come around here," the queen said, standing and moving to the center of the room while signaling to Croft. Girl scooted around Begonia to follow, and everyone else stood too.

Croft and Argo were also quick to move. I took a step forward to give them space, to which Croft glanced sideways at me in acknowledgment between his strides. As much as I wanted to admit his presence as an attendant was nothing more than normal, there was this feeling in the base of my stomach that had me assessing my usual thoughts of stature. Our guards in Shadowstone never bothered me. I never looked down upon them even if they were ranked as servants below the Lovely. Croft, though ... With his simple glances, he had me feeling less than. His gaze wasn't exactly contemptuous or cruel, but it was sharp and hard, maybe judgmental, as if he had a general dislike for the Lovely or had been wronged by someone before and it followed him everywhere. His large body also didn't help with blending into a normal attendant role. It was difficult to ignore even if he made hardly a sound as he walked, a stark contrast to most guards.

The queen continued on, "While I would have you test your link with a Clear stone as well, I think you've endured quite enough for your first connection. There will be plenty of practice for you soon enough, and a test with an Eye stone as well. Since you connected with one Haze class stone, there's still a chance you can connect with a different Opaque class. Right now, though, I believe I owe you a proper name, one that compliments your proven level of skill and your obvious display of strength and determination to push through a rather challenging first reading without breaking stone contact. And so ...”

Croft and Argo were at her side. Croft extended an arm to display pairs of head and dress ribbons. The colors of moss green, pale honey, and red wine stood against his rich black sleeve.

The queen's elegant fingers moved to his arm and selected the moss green set. After sliding them off, she held them at her chest. “Now, Lovely, please recite your vow.”

Girl's eyes were wide as she took in the color the queen had chosen. With a soft inhale, she recited, “On kingdom and Realm, I Lovely, pledge to the Crown my servitude. I vow to this duty, for now and always, to connect with all stones that allow me and reveal the truth as it is shown, for the justice of crime or interest of others, as Crown law permits.”

She bent into a much practiced curtsy, not a wobble to be seen in her small frame.

“Rise now, young Lovely.” The queen waited for her to stand erect before extending the ribbons. “With your connection to the Realm by way of the Cloud stone, you have proven yourself worthy of your vow. From now until your final breath, you will be known to all as Ivy.”

Ivy took hold of the ribbons presented and curtsied again. “Thank you, Your Majesty.”

Clapping sounded behind us, startling me. Prince Ren's eyes were on them, those puffed lips in a soft smile as he applauded. He'd been so still during the entire reading, I'd almost forgotten he was in the room. While Ivy turned and smiled tentatively, Clem and Begonia looked as conflicted as me. The prince's uncustomary applause mixed with our concern and questions about Cordelia had us unsettled.

"Well …" Queen Reina clapped once, interrupting the prince's solitary celebration. "Ivy, please return to your seat. Olean, please retake yours as well. We will test your White stone connection before we leave."

The parlor fell silent of words again while everyone returned to their places. As I sat, I caught Prince Ren's eyes on me. He was far from bored now, his gaze seeming to blaze as he took his own seat at the end of the table. There was no mistaking his focus.

"As I stated before," the queen said as she nestled back into her chair, "we don't need blood for the White stone. As such, should you connect, we will discuss what you see and decide any topics during the reading. Do you understand, Olean? Are you quite ready?"

"Yes, Your Majesty, I am." The reply sounded lifeless to my own ears. My excitement after learning they had come today, hoping that it would finally be my chance to leave Shadowstone behind and go become something more for the Crown … Well, it had soured my gut like a tainted apple.

But I knew it was still what I wanted, what I'd longed for since the moment I'd learned it would be possible. Despite what Cordelia's reading revealed and the depth of sorrow for her pain, this test was essential for my goals, my dream to be part of something grander.

With a deep inhale, I straightened my back and glanced quickly over at Clem, Ivy, and Begonia. They all watched on with uncertainty, nervousness once again creeping in since we all knew the rush that came before connecting with a stone for the first time.

Then, as I released the breath, I stretched my hands forward and felt the Realm pull me in before my skin even touched the cool, brilliant white surface.

With a great whooshing, my mind levitated from my body, spinning up and out, twisting through consciousness, until everything abruptly stopped, my vision refocusing. I was not inside anyone's mind, nor was I watching a crime as it occurred. The parlor stretched out around me, blurred by a thin veil of haze. Everyone, including myself—my body—remained as they had been before, perfectly identifiable, though features not quite distinct. The sight was far different than any other stone connection to the Realm. No other time had I felt I was inside of a specific place—the Realm being more symbolic rather than the actual alternate plane that we learned it to be.

This was proof that it was real.

Specks of light streaked in wide, wavy ribbons through the air, suspended yet churning, creating a magical, glimmering atmosphere, like a starry night trapped inside a dull gray day. Some streaks dissolved into nearly nothing but wispy trails, originating from each body. No, not everyone.

Only the Lovely.

They were our tethers, I realized. Our connection to the Realm. They had to be.

And floating throughout it all were head-sized orbs of those loosely gathered specks, most hovering directly beside each person. The entities tied to us. Our dead.

A dull cry escaped my body below, echoing the emotion I felt and my immediate reaction. I wanted to weep, seeing the actuality of the Realm's existence for the first time. The noise below sounded deep and resonant, spanning out just like the ribbons, adding a feeling of hollowness to the space. As I watched closer, the movements of everyone were also extended, all motion and noise playing slower than normal.

My thoughts shifted while I stared at Ivy's eyes, watching them close in a long blink. I was conscious of my own actions for the first time while connected to a stone. It wasn't usual. Far from it. Could the reason be the Opaque stone class or the White stone itself? That made me wonder more, about the strength of the connection. I didn't know how long I would be in the space, how long I could hold the stone. I still hadn't heard the queen, only some body adjustments and my own faint cry. Nothing had been spoken aloud or inside my mind.

Was it my only time to see, to explore for myself?

Desperation had my view jumping around, frantically searching for the wisp attached to my own body and any clusters connected. Would it be my sister? Brother? It was something I'd never known. Most of us had no recorded history, being brought to the Nursery with little to no information about our births, our parents, or siblings. The questions had plagued me for years until I'd finally given up on ever having a response. All hope of the truth about family had been lost.

As soon as I spotted the light source connected to my body, I tracked its line upward, realizing for the first time the absence of the ceiling and the rest of the house. The only perceptible area was the parlor. All else faded into nothingness, gradually darkening into the deep, endless sky.

The cluster at the end of my tether hovered behind my chair. Cordelia was close to the fireplace, her own tether spanning out above, while a few orbs moved in a lazy orbit around her. The one nearest her stomach made my breath hitch. Was it …? Its internal and surrounding light was dense, with ribbons weaving out in all directions, one as thin as the wispy tethers, stretching outward toward the opposite side of the fireplace, not far from Argo and Croft.

I refocused on mine and willed myself toward it, stopping just before contact. I longed for it to have all the answers I ever wanted but needed to expect what I'd gotten all this time: Nothing. I reached outward and a transparent version of my hand appeared in my view, like an empty, outlined reflection of my true body. Twisting my wrist, my fingers splayed open, the sight transfixing me for a moment before I turned them toward the orb.

"Don't touch anything," a low, lilting voice said, the words a normal speed yet replaying a second time quieter. As soon as I hesitated, the echoed voice came again, and it sounded relieved. "Do exactly what I say, or they'll know something's wrong and make your death an accident."

Lovely cannot occupy the same Realm space.
Even if a single stone is used,
their experience will always be separate.
- Anhedral Kingdom Lovely Guidebook

~ 6 ~

I nearly choked on a gasp, having no idea if what I heard was real or if I somehow slipped into a dream. The intake of breath from my physical body was delayed and muted, like a hiccup of distress, loud enough to be noticed by everyone but not concerning.

"Listen," the low voice came again. "The queen is starting to speak. You must do as she requests. Answer how I tell you to as if you were speaking, and your body will respond for you. If you think strongly to yourself, only I will hear your answers. Do you understand?"

Confusion happened a fair amount while using the Cloud stone, when I was inside someone else's mind, but it was because of their own scattered thoughts during their crimes. There was no thinking on my part, not one conscious decision I needed to make. This was entirely different, and I wasn't sure what to do or who exactly was speaking.

The voice—a female's voice despite its depth—prompted. "Do you understand?"

"Yes." While that thought was spoken aloud inside the Realm, my body didn't utter a sound.

"Good," she replied. "The queen is finishing her question. She asked what you see and hear. Be specific of everything, to include the speed of sound and sight, but do not tell her about my voice. She's witnessed enough readings to know how the Realm manifests with a White stone."

Queen Reina was indeed finishing her question, the last word dragging to a stop before her tongue peeked out to moisten her lips in a slow sweep. The others remained fairly still around the table, while Cordelia, Argo, and Croft stood silently at the wall behind me, at either end of the fireplace.

I thought of my reply, making no sound, then rethought it all as if I were speaking and watching my mouth begin to move. The words that followed were heavy and sluggish, but most everyone's bodies straightened with rapt attention in response.

"Good. We'll have time to speak while your answers are relayed," the voice commented.

Before she could say another word, I asked, "Who are you? And why do you want me to lie to the queen? We aren't supposed ... We usually have no choice."

"It's more an omission than a lie. And yes, some of the most gifted Lovely are unable to lie even when having use of their own thoughts with the Opaque stones. We have access to more with them, and that allows us more freedom."

"Us? You're a Lovely? You're alive?" I'd wondered if I had already been speaking to the dead.

"I am."

"What's your name? How are you speaking here, with me? Can you see us?"

"I can't see, only sense and hear who is there. And I'm using both White and Needled stones in order to expand my range. Hoping to find … you." She paused a moment, as if there were more she wanted to say. "But we shouldn't waste the time we have. There's no way of knowing how long our connection will last or when the queen will finish."

There was so much more I wanted to ask her, so much more I needed to know. But she was right, so I'd listen to her first.

"The queen is now asking you to count the orbs you see."

Queen Reina had finished her next question. I felt it odd that I could understand, that my mind focused on both conversations without much effort. After a brief look around, I spoke the answer and refocused on the voice.

"Good. Now … Recently, Lovely have died at the castle, plus others are missing. Some believe they are either also dead, are break-vows for leaving their duties, or are murderers, since they disappeared after the others were killed. One who died was the prince's appointed reader. It's why they've traveled to all the Nurseries, to bring more to the castle and replenish lost numbers, and for the prince to see the newcomers individually before he makes a replacement choice."

My head spun. Had I been so clueless in regard to the kingdom and castle? We so rarely spoke about anything outside Shadowstone in less than an educational manner that I felt completely in the dark, naïve and ashamed. I'd been concerned with ball costumes and stepping my way into a Garden placement, hoping to be valued and respected on a level unobtainable in a small town. I hadn't even thought what that life might fully entail. I'd paid little to no mind to Cordelia's comments regarding her challenging time there, writing it off as simply her own struggles due to limited abilities. How foolish.

When I didn't reply, the voice continued, "I understand what you may be feeling. You have no reason to trust what I'm telling you. But please use the same concern when you get to the castle. Don't trust anyone except maybe those you already know if they are there too."

"The queen wants to know the orb names closest to her," I said.

"They are the echoes of our dead, not fully functional beings. They answer questions with information about their lives, but do not hold conversation in present time. She already knows who usually surrounds her but wants proof of your ability. Get closer as she said to do. Speak to them as you are to me. They will tell you their names, or some might show you images to relay."

I did exactly that, moving to the queen's chair and asking the gathered specks of light. Their forms shifted with their answers, pulsing in various degrees. There was no difference in tone from the six orbs as they all spoke their names, names I recited back to the queen without thought of their connection to her. I would have cared mere minutes before, but at that moment ...

"Why are you telling me all of this? Is there something you want me to do besides be cautious?" I asked the voice, backing away from the table and studying the ribboned air, searching for more. I located my tether again, and the orb attached floated up closer to where the ceiling should have been. The need to move to it, to ask its name, was strong. I also wanted to touch all those around Cordelia, Clem, Ivy, and even Begonia. It would be a gift to them, something to offer that they might never experience themselves.

I closed in on Cordelia, watching the orb at her stomach and the ribbons spanning outward. One in particular caught my eye again, the thin wisp spanning the wall before dissolving into nothing just past the fireplace.

"You're strong. Able to communicate with me here. You're also innocent of any crimes or biases at the castle. That means you are trustworthy. And with your Opaque stone ability, you will be placed in a higher Lovely position immediately. You will have access to more information and hopefully decide that the truth is worth uncovering."

"And if I don't?"

"Then I fear others will die. Maybe even you if you step in a wrong direction."

"Is that a threat?"

"No. It can't be a threat when you've already given your life to the Crown."

That made me pause. She was right, of course. My life wasn't exactly my own. But what Lovely's was?

"Listen. Before the queen can finish her next question. I know something that could help you learn more, beyond your own eyes and ears. Go to the attendant."

"Croft?"

"Yes. He is coveted by the royals and it's not only because he can't speak if anyone were to capture him."

"His mind is blocked," I replied absently, recalling what the queen had mentioned. No one had been able to read him, so she wouldn't use him as a Name Day volunteer. But how did the voice know? How did she know everything? Was she a member of the Garden or did she live somewhere else in the kingdom?

"What if I told you that you could connect with him?"

"With Croft? How? Why?"

"How? Through this space in the Realm. Why? Because he has access to information and is possibly the most trusted in the castle because of his uniqueness. Others might not care what's being done or said in his presence. Some are careful not to speak when he's looking at their lips, knowing that he can understand most things. Others don't care if he sees or understands at all."

"You think he's seen something, and that I'll read his memory in here without a Cloud stone?"

"No. I don't believe you'll see memories. I think you might see or hear something when it happens through his mind."

"I don't understand. How can that be true?"

"I can't sense anything around him. I'm too far. Are there orbs? Light?"

Focusing despite my confusion, I moved to Croft and Argo, taking in their unwavering steadfastness. Except, as I dropped closer, Argo's head tipped slightly, his big nostrils flared with a sniff, and his eyes locked on me. Or rather, my echo form. Could he see me? Smell me? His mouth opened slowly, and his trapped tongue escaped, falling out with a long pant.

Croft's chin dipped, eyeing Argo over his shoulder. He'd picked up on the dog's movements remarkably fast, which was only more evident with how slow the world was moving around me.

Pulling back some, I focused on Croft. "No. No orbs. Several light ribbons are really close to his body and head, though. It's almost making him glow."

"You need to touch whatever is near his head. The idea is to link yourself to him there."

"Will this hurt him? Or me? Are you certain this can even be done?" I was doubtful. How could I trust her to know for sure? I didn't know her or her intent. "What if he's affected and he responds physically? If he moves at all, everyone will notice."

"I can't answer what I don't know. This will be the only chance you get. That is the only sure thing. I've heard of similar connections. It's why I'm here ... looking for you."

I reached out, hesitating once again. "I don't know. I ..."

"Sielle is my name," the voice whispered, its echo so faint the words were only a scatter of air. "That's all I can tell you for now. We may not get a chance to speak after this. Your White stone interaction will be limited and likely monitored. But I will try to find you again. We need answers that could help save others' lives."

Conflict twisted my gut so harshly I had to force a breath. Mind. Heart. The clash of the two was stronger than I'd ever felt firsthand before. This was my choice. My decision. But it was unfolding much like being in someone else's mind, frantic and confused. Was I about to cross a line or walk away from the biggest truth I'd ever learned? Should I listen to her, trust her? On one hand, it might risk everything, risk my future at the castle, possibly even my life. And on the other ... My existence was about truth and justice, about seeking out the wrong to help protect others.

I didn't know if I could ignore that.

"When I do ... When I arrive at the castle ... They could read me, my memories of this. They could see. You said someone might kill me if they know something's different." Cordelia was a Clear stone reader, had an outside limited view for our required checks. She'd never been inside my head.

Others at the castle could.

"The White stone has a level of protection over the others because of the dead. If they use a Cloud stone on you, these memories will be too loud for anyone else looking in. They will hear and see everything with your physical body, the memories from the queen's questions. Some might view your thoughts of this place, what your projection of them are. But it's nearly impossible for anyone to see or hear what happens with your thoughts that occur outside your own body in this Realm space."

"But you can talk to me now, in here. How?"

"Because I'm inside with you from a distance."

"So if someone were to touch a White stone at the same time, they would be in here with me too?" All our lessons had said otherwise. Even if we touched the same stone, any of the stones, we wouldn't be together.

A lengthy pause followed. "No. The Realm would project differently to them. It would be the same space, but separate."

"How is it possible then? Why wouldn't they be the same as you?"

"My connection is failing," Sielle said, her voice even lower. "The queen has finished her question. We're almost out of time."

I stared at Croft, at my hand still raised so close to the trimmed hair along his jaw. My eyes flitted around the room again, hoping for some clarity on what to do. The queen's eyes were wide, lips pinched with impatience from my lack of response. She began to repeat my name in hopes of an answer. Clem, Ivy, and Begonia all continued to stare at me, their waning focus reigniting at my silence, knowing something was amiss. Prince Ren's blue eyes blazed with something equal to the desire I'd seen in numerous gazes through the stones, his body perched on the edge of his chair, leaning as far forward as he could while seated. Cordelia's pale eyes still brimmed with tears, her gaze straight ahead and vacant. She hadn't sobbed a single time, but the pain from Ivy's reading lingered enough to see.

And Croft ... Well, the intakes of his breaths were as steady as Argo's at his side. Both seemed to have little interest in my lack of response to the queen, though I supposed they stood through enough functions and readings to hardly care.

"This connection ... will I still be able to answer the queen and finish this reading?"

I waited a moment for Sielle's reply, watching as the queen's lips stopped and pressed into a thin line.

"Sielle?"

She didn't respond. Time was truly up.

I could answer the queen and continue on as if nothing happened. Perhaps I'd dreamed the entire thing, or my mind couldn't handle the connection with the White stone. Part of me wanted to believe that was true, that maybe my mind had had enough. And that reasoning had nearly won as I thought about the queen's question and prepared to answer, until ...

Croft's amber eyes narrowed in my body's direction, his eyebrows dipping lower on their prominent ridge. In another blink, they were aiming at me, and his face tilted toward my splayed palm at his cheek.

I knew I would regret either choice I made, but that simple movement gave me hope that I wasn't about to make the biggest mistake of my life.

My fingertip skimmed along his cheek, cutting through the thin stream of ribbon there before I reached out and snagged the brightest, thickest one at the crown of his head.

The jolt was instant, my thoughts seizing as the specks of light between him and my physical body crossed and intermixed, the exchange crossing through my hollow form. Croft's head swayed almost imperceptibly, though he made no other movement. A rush of warmth hit me hard, seizing my thoughts, making me shudder. My body below began to mimic my actions, a slow, torturous ripple running from head to toe, shaking the chair beneath me. Everyone else reacted, their mouths opening, the beginnings of surprised or fearful noises and panicked words booming through the space in delayed chaos.

I wasn't strong enough to hold the stone. My body revolted despite my mind grabbing more firmly, clinging with every bit of energy I had while the light wrapped around me stronger, tighter, digging in so hard my breath sputtered and my vision darkened.

Gasping and convulsing, my body dropped onto the floor and my hands slipped away from the stone, disconnecting me from the Realm.

The next moments came at me in rapid succession, one moment awake to the noise and loud voices, the next in darkness. Then all at once, I was being lifted to an upright position on the floor, someone supporting my back while the queen stood a few paces in front of me.

"Agh. Mm hhhdd." Jumbled sounds reverberated in my mind. Scrambled. Like words, only off balance. But my mind attempted to decipher, shuffling the sounds and tones. They somehow sorted themselves, and I understood the words. *"My head."*

"It may have been too much to handle, especially after such an important trial reading." Queen Reina's voice came into focus as she stared at me curiously. The frustration that had been set on her small features moments before had smoothed into understanding and maybe pity.

"Are you all right?" Prince Ren called my attention to his crouched position at my side. His voice was sharp and clear, not mumbled as the other had been. He was not holding me upright from behind my shoulders, but he did have a comforting hand upon my upper arm—a gentle touch to match the gentleness in his blue eyes. Being so close to him, I couldn't help but notice the rounder shape of his eyes and how he had a mild bump in his otherwise straight, slightly upturned nose.

"Yeah—Yes, Your Highness. I'm not sure what happened," I admitted, recalling everything but thoroughly perplexed just the same.

"Croft, I've got her," the prince said, glancing behind me, and I felt the other hands release their hold as the prince's grip tightened in support.

"Of course you do." Another voice seemed to answer, the depth resonant, the same muffled tones having to sort correctly inside my head. But the sounds hadn't come from my ears ...

"You did wonderfully, despite that lapse, Oleander." The queen busied her dainty fingers along the stitching at her waist while keeping her gaze on me. "Cordelia, she's to regain her strength here. A couple of our coaches and guards will stay behind and leave with her in a few days. They are also to bring whatever trinkets and possessions are hers as well as those of the others. No additional garments aside from what's needed for travel. They will all be clothed differently at the castle. As for now, Begonia, Clematis, and Ivy will come with us. Off now with you three. Pack only your travel clothing."

"Great." That confusing voice came again, the tone rich and oddly soothing. It was inside my head. It was—

"We're going with you?" Ivy squealed in delight, the high pitch burning through my achy head like a blazing fireplace poker. Luckily, the tapping of her bouncing tiny feet on the floor wasn't as harsh and actually made me smile a little in amusement. She simply couldn't contain her excitement. There was even a titter of excited sounds coming from Begonia and Clem.

The news was a surprise to us all.

"Your Majesty?" Cordelia's calm voice pitched with overwrought and nervous emotion.

I couldn't help but glance up, seeing even more distress in her usually placid features. She appeared so frail in that moment. She was losing all of us.

This time, the queen did look at her, a small flicker of empathy given in the tiny roll of her lips and soft sigh of breath. "It's not a reflection of you so much as what is needed for the kingdom at this time. They will be cared for well, and you will continue to manage this town's justice readings with the count as usual. Help guide him through this trying time following the loss of the countess. I'm certain you will be brought another infant to care for soon enough. There are a couple due to be born this year, and a few others we have yet to confirm."

"Right, let's get you up," Prince Ren whispered. Both of his hands grabbed hold of my arm, guiding me to my feet despite my unsteadiness.

As much as I wanted to keep my eyes on Cordelia, I had to be certain I wasn't having some kind of mental breakdown after contact with the White stone. There were times when a Lovely was overcome and rendered useless by contact. Most often, it was addiction by continued use that plagued us, but some had also been stripped of all logic and sense with a single touch of an Opaque stone. Entering the Realm was always a risk. I wondered if I'd made a horrible mistake by taking direction from whatever had communicated with me inside.

As I stood, Croft's gaze caught with mine, following me to my final upright position. Then I got the confirmation I needed that it wasn't a mental breakdown, that the jumbled words weren't my own in some form of confusion. The link had worked.

"He'll choose her."

The smallest recorded stone
to grant access into the Realm was
a Cloud stone 14 mm in diameter.
Connection time was less than three minutes.
- Anhedral Kingdom Lovely Guidebook

~ 7 ~

Despite the silence inside the house, the next few days of waiting passed in a daze. I didn't really eat. I barely slept. There were moments I'd thought I'd dreamed it all, but then I'd listen to the empty house, or hear the quiet sobbing from Cordelia's room and realize that I hadn't lost my mind.

All my attempts to speak to Cordelia had been denied. She'd locked herself in her room the first day, inconsolable despite my small offerings of comfort with plates of food or whispered words at her door. The following days, she left the house, likely realizing that finding peace inside so soon wouldn't happen without the usual ambient noise from the others. Her mourning ran deeper than the obvious.

I scoured all of our textbooks, searching for answers to several questions and never finding them. There were no voices to be heard inside my mind except my own thoughts puzzling endlessly over my time within the White stone Realm and those short minutes following.

It wasn't until the second day of book searching that I realized the name Sielle was unlike any usual Lovely name given by the queen. I'd even searched the small flower and gardening directory we had inside the Nursery. It was a book we often pored over as we

69

wondered what name the queen might give to the next awaiting their Name Day. But the reference book was not extensive enough to be sure in my assumption. When I reached the castle, I would have to do more research.

Then there was the voice I had heard after. Croft. While the denial still badgered me, there was no other logical explanation for what had happened except that I had actually connected with him. I'd done what Sielle had said, and then I'd heard him. The words weren't exactly clear, more jumbled than intelligible, but I understood them, my mind shifting and sorting to piece things together. And since I'd heard nothing more after everyone had left, my only assumption was that the connection was limited in reach. The words were limited, too, which likely meant I had only heard what he would have voiced if possible, not all of his thoughts. That felt similar to my interaction with Sielle—only those strongest thoughts were heard.

I took it upon myself to pack everyone's belongings along with my own on the morning the coach was due to arrive. We didn't have much in our individual rooms, as they only fit a slim bed, a bare pine dresser with three drawers, and a matching desk and chair, with just enough space to walk between each. Our things were simple treasures gifted from Cordelia, the townspeople who had regular vanity readings, or from trial families wanting to express their thanks.

Girl—Ivy had the least, with only her beloved stuffed pink alpaca named Petal, pencil drawings, and a handful of tiny wood-carved dolls. Clem had a fair amount of art supplies—paints, paper, charcoal—and a few favorite paintings. And while Begonia mostly hid her items away, I knew she had things from town that made her feel both as ordinary as the townspeople and extraordinary as a Lovely. There was an unending war within her, wanting to be something she wasn't, both normal and exceptionally stone gifted. All her items were already contained in a travel chest, so I hadn't planned to open it at all. But when I moved her bedding around for fear I'd miss something, a stuffed pink alpaca sat beneath her pillow. With worn, scruffy fur and black button eyes, it was identical to Ivy's, which had first been mine. Begonia had thrown hers away years before, when she'd no longer wanted anything similar to me. She had obviously retrieved it before the garbage had been taken away.

I tossed it inside her chest and tried not to scoff at the shiny copper hair clip or the torn piece of silver fabric she'd likely saved from an old gown of Cordelia's. Sure, I had imagined what it was like to have hair, and even longed to wear more fanciful clothing when arriving at the castle, but I didn't wish to be someone else, something else. I supposed one of her wishes had come true. She was moving to the castle, despite not being above a Clear stone class. Maybe she'd find her happiness there. As for me, my own happiness was uncertain now that everything had changed.

While I sat in stillness on the parlor's settee, trying to clear my mind of all the questions I'd continue to obsess over during the weeks of journey, the front door opened.

Cordelia's face was gaunt and smudged with garden soot. It was early for planting, but I doubted that had been her focus. Her yellow house dress was streaked with it as well. I watched her kick the shoes from her feet as she entered but didn't bother speaking to her, expecting there wouldn't be a reply like the previous days.

To my surprise, she approached and sat directly on the pristine chair across from me, not seeming to notice or care that the dirt she harbored would take well over an hour to scrub from the upholstery. She studied her messy fingers resting in her lap. After a deep breath, she lifted her eyes to mine.

"I'm sorry. I'm truly sorry, Olean. For my behavior these last days. For my lack of direction about your upcoming trip. I was simply ..."

"I understand," I answered.

"No, no, I don't think you can fully. And I am not saying that to lessen your experiences or your intellect. I only mean that you have never been a mother, or rather ... placed in a motherly role, only to have the children you've raised and cared for ripped from you in such a short time with hardly any notice at all."

"No, I don't suppose so," I agreed, grasping what she meant.

"I haven't seen anyone again, you see," she said, eyes dropping to her fingernails again. "I was Guardian to four others before you. The youngest was eight when I'd arrived. Tansy. She was the only one left when you arrived as my first infant five years later. I'm not sure if you recall her. You weren't even to your Name Day when she was asked to the castle."

"She had golden skin and smelled like oats." It was all I remembered.

"Yes." A breath of a laugh escaped her lips. "She had dry skin her whole life. Oats helped. We'd get extra from the baker so she could bathe with them. Though you helped add to that with your messy eating habits when she fed you as a baby." She took another breath, letting her eyes lift around the room, pausing on certain places and items before moving on, as if she were drawing up memories tied to each. "She has never returned. Neither have the others. Though two were only Clear class, they also chose to leave, and I granted their requests. The castle and larger towns have more opportunities, more draw. I knew it would happen. Service at the castle doesn't often come with travel anyway. But the other day ... I hadn't expected such a fast goodbye for the younger ones. It's no excuse for not helping to guide you. I'm sorry for letting you down."

I blinked, feeling my eyes sting. We weren't usually emotional with each other. We'd been closer when I was young, but after I'd started reading the Cloud stone, I believe she had a difficult time relating to me or possibly struggled with helping me navigate a more powerful Realm stone, since she'd never experienced it herself. I wondered if she'd struggled the same with the two other higher stone classes she'd raised as well.

"Listen, Olean." Her body shifted forward in the chair, her pale eyes staring at me intently. "You'll be treated decently there because of your abilities, so I know you will do well with your duties. And because of your status, especially now that you've connected with an Opaque stone, you will fare better than the others. In fact, even though I shouldn't ask this of you ... Will you do your best to look after them? I'm unsure what will happen with Ivy. They didn't take in many young while I was there, but they had Guardians for such occasions. And with her higher class, they might even keep her separate. But I feel I've done wrong by Begonia and Clem the most. I hadn't expected them to leave yet, so I didn't bother muddling their thoughts with the burdens of castle life and the reality of work most Lovely endure there. I need you to hear it so you'll know."

She sniffed, visibly holding back emotion. And I held my breath and kept completely still, not daring to interrupt the information she'd never offered before. "My time there wasn't as great as I'd hoped. The Clear class are more plentiful and the bottom tier of the Garden, entering the Realm at long intervals, overseeing the entire kingdom to maintain its safety. They are housed together in combined sleep quarters and also work in mass reading areas under supervision and direction. While it may sound like menial tasks, it is exhausting. Mentally and physically. Long hours spent inside the Realm take a toll. They will not be prepared ...

"As for me, I fell in love with someone who sparked life into my rather bleak soul, and ... As far as most anyone knows, Lovely are not fertile. We both are aware from townspeople's readings that females can tell such things easily enough, though we have always been different. I was unaware of the subtle differences until farther along. Luckily, I had a certain level of guidance and protection until ... Well, you heard when. After that, I was moved here, to the farthest town. As I could still be useful, I apprenticed, then ultimately relieved the previous Shadowstone Guardian of her position and made this Nursery my home. My grief eased immediately with the four young who were already in residence. Helping to comfort and teach them became my purpose, a fate better than I ever could have imagined at my lowest.

"I needed you to know this, to realize that not everyone there will be friendly, whether royalty or not, whether they act it or not. You may struggle too, under the weight of the tasks you will endure and by the pressure of those who either covet the role you end up placed in or because they solely want to see you fail. The station or reason is of no consequence. Like the people here, some love us, some tolerate us, and others despise our existence. Don't trust so easily. Especially other Lovely. I was wronged by someone I considered a friend years ago. I have no doubt that your experience will be far different than my own and the others, but be aware. And also, take care of your heart, all right? Love is not an easy thing. For us, this is most certainly true. I let your time with Jonah go on because I knew your goals were far bigger than staying here. I also knew it might be your only experience, since Lovely relationships are highly regulated at the castle if permitted at all. You needed to have something for yourself, if for only a little while."

I nodded, caught up in everything she told me and everything she hadn't. There would be things I may never know, but I understood why she'd hold onto those most personal and private memories. "I'm not sure what to say. Thank you for explaining more. I am also very sorry for what you endured. It couldn't have been easy."

"No, it wasn't. And that's what I fear for you and the others." Her soft smile held only sadness. "It's not all celebration balls and beautiful flowers. There's much more happening there. It can be easy to forget what's really important, whether you're being revered at the top or being dragged along at the bottom."

What's really important. And what was that in this life? My only concern before had been to make the most of my abilities, to reach for the highest position I could within the kingdom. To serve as my vow declared.

The doubt niggling inside wasn't Cordelia's fault. That had started three days before when I'd first learned not everything inside or outside the Realm was as I'd thought it to be. Could I tell her? Disclose what I'd seen and heard? Admit that I'd been able to withhold information from the queen, from them all? I wanted to. I had never wanted to confide in someone more, even if she'd have no advice to offer.

Cordelia lifted from her chair in a rush, glancing toward the foyer and the door beyond. Then I heard the coach wheels outside too. It was my time to leave.

She dug quickly into the wrapped bodice of her housedress. "I shouldn't do this. I ... It might be a risk, but you can decide if you want to take it or not. I just want you to be as prepared as possible." She pulled something free and extended her open palm, revealing a dirt-covered cloth, a silver chain and oval pendant tucked within. The letters A and V stacked on top of each other, nearly indistinguishable with the swirling background. As soon as she flipped the pendant over, my breath caught. The backside was partially exposed, revealing a sliver of Clear stone. "The encasement muffles its detection. It's the smallest a Clear stone can be to access the Realm with a very limited range."

I reached out, touching only the silver edging. A flurry of questions fought for position in my mind. The most important, though, was one that related to the pendant as well as the truths I wanted to disclose to her. "If I'm read?"

"An infraction with this size stone shouldn't cause you trouble, not at your standing. The punishment won't be severe. You are strong, enough to prevent addiction if you use it wisely. But know there might be others who conceal things the same way."

A knock boomed from the front door, and Cordelia shoved the pendant into my hand, shaking her head. "Hide it beneath your undergarments to be safe. Don't be concerned if it's found and taken. It's something I should have been rid of long ago."

Another knock came, more insistent, rattling the door's hinges.

I was too stunned to reply, but I did as she said, hastily burying the pendant beneath my bodice, taking care the stone didn't touch my skin.

She offered a tight smile, her eyes welling up once again, then moved into the foyer to answer the door.

Black stones were last to be discovered.
Since contact proved fatal to Lovely,
the power was coveted.
Because of this, Anhedral Castle was built
on top of the largest quantity found.
- Anhedral Kingdom Lovely Guidebook

~ 8 ~

Ever since I'd gotten my name, the tears I shed fell for others more often than myself. The reason might have been tied to the stones and the Realm. I'd seen and felt so much from many townspeople that my own burdens felt trivial, reshaping my emotional perception and empathetic response. There hadn't been anything substantial for me to cry over. My bouts with Begonia were minor, common sisterly rivalry. My lack of blood relatives had always felt more like the dull hollowness within an empty space rather than the true agony of a mournful loss, as I'd never known any true family. And my daily plain and placid life in Shadowstone had every livable necessity met without much strife, aside from the burden of mental and emotional pains of others, of course.

So I'd been a little surprised to discover the stream of tears spilling over my cheeks as Shadowstone disappeared into the steep, sloping landscape behind the covered coach on the first day of travel. I wouldn't have thought I'd miss home when I left. Even though their excitement had been plain to see, perhaps Begonia, Clem, and Ivy felt a little of the same after they'd departed—being old enough and fully aware of this separation, while we'd been too young to recall the first.

Queen Reina and Prince Ren had traveled with six coaches, at least twenty armed guards, and everything else they'd needed for their journey across the kingdom. They'd left two coaches and five guards behind for my accompaniment. The guards traveled in one coach, while the other held me alone and most of the supplies. I assumed the reason was for safety, though most hadn't spoken to me at all during our extended travel. Before we'd left, they'd mentioned the trip taking as little as two and a half weeks when the northern ferry across the Silver Sea was in use. The winter had been too harsh this year, though, creating irreparable damage to the access passes to the western port. Without it, we would have arrived at the castle closer to three weeks. But that time had extended even further. A late season snowfall had hit the main mountain pass a day before we'd reached it, making the terrain leaving Shadowstone treacherous and doubling the first days of travel. The royal coaches ahead had slipped through at the perfect time.

I hadn't complained. The coach was comfortable enough, with an interior fit for the royals. There were many pristine tufted blankets for bedding and elegant pillows stuffed to the seams with down. Heavy velvet curtains covered the windows, blocking the outside coldness. And while there were barrels of dried travel meats and grain for us to eat over the days, there were also plenty of fresh fruits and breads from Shadowstone's greenhouses and bakeries. The only possible complaint to have was loneliness, though talking with the horses during stretching breaks had helped.

The landscape changed through the days, from the thawing, snowy mountain base, to dense, wild forestry, to the steep mining cliffs and ravines of the nearly abandoned towns I'd read about in our history books. The lands had been pillaged for the precious stones that linked us to the Realm. Remnants remained, material relics gathered into piles near large caverns dug inside the passing cliff walls or dumped within deep trenches, some things partially covered, reclaimed by plant life, while others had disintegrated under the creeping devastation of the ever-changing weather.

Our journey was continuous, but there were a few cherished stops at outposts and tiny towns along the main road for longer rests and personal cleaning. I'd struggled with sleep one particular night when some people made their distaste of the Lovely known, spitting and calling foul language to the coach as we rode through their town. Usually, two of the guards were on watch of my coach during the sedentary nights. That night, we kept moving, and on the next, four had been posted instead. Then there'd been another small outpost where I'd glimpsed a Lovely on the side of the road. With tattered clothing and dry, ashen skin, he had a sign at his feet offering readings in exchange for food. His sunken, pale eyes tracked the coach as we passed, locking with mine peeking out from the window curtain. There was no change to the empty look upon his face.

The final day of travel, as the forest thinned then gave way to the sprawling farmlands surrounding the city, Anhedral Castle appeared. I'd never seen something so grand. The elaborate tales from Count Ashboard and a few vanity readings of his visitors had given some expectations, but their words and Clear stone visions hadn't been worthy of its magnitude. Buildings, markets, and houses spanned farther than my eyes could see. The tremendous castle perched high and wide at the center of it all, and I could imagine viewing the land's expanse from one of the many windows set into the gray stone exterior or the several towers reaching toward the cloud-speckled sky.

After navigating through the city's cramped cobbled streets, we arrived at the castle midday. I was grateful the din had abated as we reached the gatehouse. My ears hadn't been prepared for the amount of noise that came from such a large, condensed area. People, carriages, animals—my senses were overloaded and exhausted, so much so that I found myself yawning as the coach stopped outside the outer wall, and again as it pulled through the narrow entrance and into the main courtyard.

A few attendants hurried to the coach, helping me to exit and retrieving all the chests and belongings. As they exchanged information with the guards, I turned in a circle, taking in the wide space and the bordered center garden and walkways throughout. People milled around it all, groundskeepers working on the landscaping, other attendants carrying baskets of goods from the few carriages near the far side of the courtyard to what I'd assumed would be the nearest entrances to the storage pantries and kitchens.

"Lovely Oleander," a female said at my side.

I spun, taking in her short stature and the plentiful brunette hair wrapped into a neat chignon at the base of her head. She wore dark pants with a white undershirt and a gray vest, like some of the other attendants in the courtyard. "Yes. Hello."

Her chin dipped in greeting. "This way to your quarters, please."

I followed when she didn't offer her name. It wasn't exactly rude, I supposed, but I'd been accustomed to usual courtesies at Shadowstone, introductions at a bare minimum no matter the status. Her stride was swift, passing turn after turn, hall after hall. I attempted to take in all the gorgeous adornments, but there were far too many and we were moving far too fast. Silver sconces, lush, vivid paintings of scenery and people wrapped in fine metallic frames, tapestries and banners and more all blurred together with each step. Physical activity hadn't been necessary for us at Shadowstone, aside from menial household chores, so I was nearly out of breath by the time we passed through an immense vaulted great hall with thrones at one end before coming to a grand staircase and starting to climb.

"Is this where … all the … Lovely live?" It was a struggle to speak through my gasping breaths.

The attendant spared a brief glance over a shoulder as we continued down the hallway. "No."

No? That was it? I waited several seconds for more of an answer, taking in deep lungfuls of air to calm my racing heart.

"Only a select few live here in the northwest wing," a cordial voice answered, making the attendant stop in her tracks and causing me to ram into her backside.

She gasped and lunged sideways a bit before bowing low. "Your Highness."

It took me a little longer to recover from the hit, straightening up before turning into a curtsy toward the voice. "Your Highness."

Prince Ren stood at the mouth of another hallway—possibly one leading south, though all of them were decorated too similarly to distinguish yet. He took a step forward, his hand lifting in a motion for me to stand. His smile was humored. "On your way, Imogen. I'll show her."

Imogen bowed once again, handed the prince something with a leather strap, then scurried past him down the other hall.

"I'm glad you arrived safely, Olean. We were a little concerned after we received updates of the late storm. We were fortunate to have already gone through the pass."

"Thank you. Yes, it was quite the journey," I replied, as he moved to my side, eyeing the entirety of me before nodding forward in the direction to walk. I glanced around him, noting no one else save a single guard posted at the very end of the hall.

"Was it tolerable?" he asked, his strides slower than Imogen's had been, no doubt noticing my exhaustion after hearing my wheezing as we'd approached, the sound likely echoing off the walls.

"Most. The journey was delightful despite the extra time," I answered, keeping my eyes forward so as not to run into anyone else in his presence. Imogen had been the second after Croft, and given his humored expression, he had obviously remembered yet had the decency not to comment. I could feel his eyes on me, though. And in my periphery, I noted his crisp white shirt, pressed black pants, and shined pointed shoes. The look was more relaxed than his travel clothes had been in Shadowstone. His length of top hair was even mussed a bit, edges sticking outward over the close-cropped sides.

He chuckled lightly. "You would be astounded when the weather is pleasant then. It's far more bearable when the paths are clear and dry."

"Do not get her hopes up, brother," a soft, airy female voice said as we neared another side hallway. The body came into view a moment later, seeming to be swallowed whole by a luxurious gray gown with metallic embellishments that sparkled with the swaying, ruffled fabric. "If she's as good as you say, she might never leave the castle."

Princess Naomi.

I curtsied in greeting but didn't hold it with a higher royal already present. "Your Highness."

"Aw, come now, little sister. Don't frighten her into thinking she'll be captive here," Prince Ren replied. "But yes, she is quite talented. You will see soon enough."

"Oleander, it is a pleasure to meet you," the princess addressed me with a soft smile. Her small features were remarkably identical to the queen's, a copy in most ways, unlike the prince. At twenty-one, she was younger than the prince by a year yet looked even younger than me. Her black hair hung freely, lengthy strands grouped together over a bare porcelain shoulder. She was a tiny thing, but I had no doubt that was no reflection on her personality or presence. I'd learned not to judge a person based on appearance well enough. "I had just heard of your arrival and had to see you for myself. You left quite the impression on my mother and Ren, and you're in contention to be one of the highest class of Lovely. Quite remarkable. That could mean a really high position"—she glanced at Prince Ren—"depending on how you test against the others at induction, of course, and how you fare with other stones. Ah, there you are, Hem."

She glanced to her side as a male Lovely entered from the same hallway and gave a small bow to both prince and princess. He appeared to be somewhere over thirty, with shallow lines carved into the olive-toned skin at the corner of his eyes. While he stood taller than the princess, he was at eye level with me and greater in body size with a healthy stomach that hid only marginally beneath his loose clothing. A beautiful mix of blue and green spirals twisted in a small arc over the lower portion of his forehead, forming a decorative set of eyebrows where—like all Lovely—there was no hair. I'd heard about the custom of painting them from Cordelia and through Count Ashboard's tales, knowing that while our bald heads were almost respected, the lack of eyebrows and eyelashes were unnerving to some in the main city. We'd never been asked to paint ours in Shadowstone.

"Oleander, this is Hemlock," Prince Ren introduced. "He's Naomi's appointed Lovely. And when he manages to break away from her incessant needs, he's also the head of the Haze stone class and primary for the trial council, overseeing most high court trials held at the castle."

"Nice to meet you," I said with a smile, watching as he assessed me fleetingly.

"You as well. Looking forward to speaking more," he replied in a throaty voice, inclining his bald head, then looking at the princess. "Shall we?"

"Oh yes," she replied, gathering the bunch of dress at her front, preparing to walk. "We are to check in on the other new arrivals before meeting with Father regarding the latest readings about the deaths. Ren, see you at dinner. Make sure she's apprised of recent safety procedures if you haven't already. Olean, looking forward to seeing you again. Hem is right down the hall from you, so I'm sure it will be often."

"Thank you." My reply was short, not wanting to keep them as they had already started to walk. Imogen, who had reappeared behind them at some point, bobbed her head to the prince as she rushed off to follow.

After watching them leave, Prince Ren pointed forward. "You're just over here."

He led me to the final door of the main hallway, which had a surprising distance still before reaching the corner where a guard was posted. His hand revealed a key Imogen had given him. He used it inside the lock and pushed the door wide.

"There are several Lovely who live in the northwest wing, a few on this floor. All of you are Opaque class."

I had already started looking around the massive room. Rooms, actually. We were standing inside a gathering or lounging area much like the Nursery parlor, and there were four other doors inside, leading to what I could imagine to be sleeping and bathing rooms within. Why would I need so much space? I turned to ask if there was a mistake.

The prince's lips were rolled inward, and his gaze shifted around the room too, only his perusal seemed uncomfortable. "If your status changes and you're appointed to a high position, and things settle down ... you can decide on a different set of rooms if you wish."

Had I looked disappointed? "No, this is ... lovely actually. I just thought ... I'm not used to having so much space."

"Ah, yes," he replied, a smile tugging the corner of his lips. "Well, it is deserved as you're an Opaque class. But there's another reason too." He stepped farther inside, moving to the fireplace at the far wall, then peering through the drawn curtain and through the exposed window. When he turned back, he said, "It's about what Naomi mentioned. After the recent incidents, we're taking extra precautions with Lovely. I know my mother didn't elaborate when we visited Shadowstone. There have been some deaths and also some disappearances. The trial council are working to find out who's to blame, but it's been difficult. All the readings have shown nothing, so we believe the Lovely who disappeared are to blame." He waved a hand into the air. "There's no reason for you to be concerned, and I won't get into all the details, but we are being cautious. We've posted extra soldiers and guards inside the castle as well as attendants. You will have an attendant to keep you safe. They will tend to your needs and help you settle in."

That sounded … stifling. While it was concerning, especially the possibility of being targeted when I was in an unfamiliar place with no one to truly trust, I already felt as though I couldn't breathe for the same reasons. I'd hoped to relax in my own space, be myself if only by myself, not have to worry about acting properly or faking a smile. Then there was my concern with what had happened during the White stone reading, and whether it was something that had been in my head after all. It had been over a month, and I hadn't heard any voices. Though, I also hadn't touched a single stone since and hadn't been near Croft.

And now, on top of everything, I'd have someone watching me closely.

The prince cleared his throat, and my wandering eyes snapped back to his. "Forgive me. I'm sure you must need some rest after such a long journey. Know that I understand this is a big change for you. We will ensure your safety here. You are valuable to us, Oleander."

I smiled weakly. "Thank you, Your Highness."

He looked so sincere, his blue eyes studying me as he gave a quick nod. "Of course. Rest, please. Clothing and necessities are already inside the main room and bathing room. And if you require anything else, just ask Croft. He's been notified of his assignment change and will be here soon."

With that, he turned and left. As soon as the door closed behind him, I let out a long breath and allowed my shoulders to slump forward. It took a moment for his last words to sink in.

Ask Croft. My attendant.

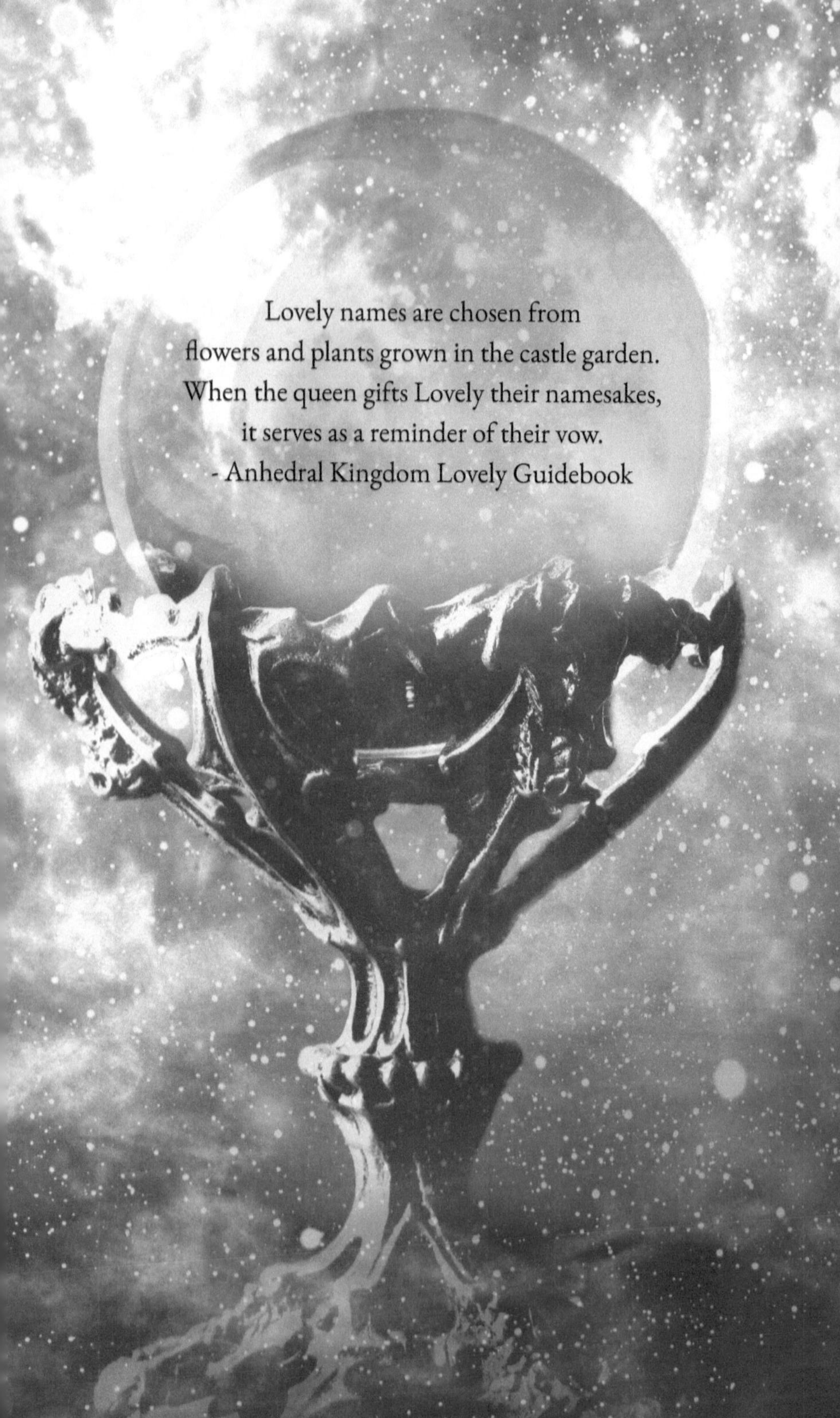

Lovely names are chosen from
flowers and plants grown in the castle garden.
When the queen gifts Lovely their namesakes,
it serves as a reminder of their vow.
- Anhedral Kingdom Lovely Guidebook

~ 9 ~

"Olean! You're here!" A high-pitched squeal sliced through my sleep like a sword, jolting my eyes wide just as something landed hard and fast on top of my still body.

Two big white eyes invaded my vision at the same time little arms squeezed me fiercely.

"I'm so happy you're finally here! I was worried you may never come, even though everyone told me you would. We've been here several days already. And I stayed in another room, but not now. Now I'll be here with you!"

"Easy, easy. Calm indoor voice, remember?" I said groggily, focusing in on Ivy's gap-toothed smile and loud, shrieking voice. She looked more adorable than ever with missing teeth.

"Oh, yes." She corrected herself in a much more tolerable volume as she dismounted my body, sliding onto the bed I'd found immediately after the prince left.

"You lost some teeth?"

"I did! Two on the bottom. They fell out along the journey. Croft and Clem showed me how to wiggle them out. But the new ones are starting up already."

I rubbed at my eyes to clear the sleep away. I'd only wanted to test the stuffed mattress, but I'd underestimated its comfort and instead fell into the deepest sleep as soon as my body sank inside.

"Isn't it like sleeping on a cloud?" Ivy asked, noticing my admiration of the bedding. "They have the best beds here. Blankets too. And tarts! Wait until you see the gardens too. Everything is so grand and pretty."

She was speaking so fast, I struggled to keep up. There were times she was excitable in Shadowstone, but nothing near as enthusiastic as this moment.

"Ivy, please, slow down." I chuckled and wiped at my eyes again. "I've only just woken. I need a moment."

"Oh, sorry." She sat upright beside me as I swung my legs over the edge to do the same.

"It's all right. I can see that you're already enjoying your time here."

"Yes, but more so now that you've come. I was staying with Guardian Calla. She just brought me here to the rooms and told me to stay and not wake you." She pressed her lips together with a soft giggle, realizing she'd just given her disobedience away. "She's nice and gave me extra tarts from the kitchen, but now I get to stay with you. The king and queen said I'm better here after my newest test."

"Stay with me? Newest test?" Oh no. My stomach flipped at the thought of what she'd already been made to do since arriving. "They tested you again?"

"Oh yes! They wanted to see if I could connect with an Opaque. They tested Clem and Begonia too to make sure they wouldn't connect with other stones. They didn't, though."

"Aren't the tests to be held at the induction ceremony?"

"Only for you and the others who are older. They told me I still have to wait and take school lessons before I can do more things. But they want you to help me since I know you and you already helped me with my studies before."

"I'm not sure I will be a good teacher for studies," I answered absently. Taking on responsibility of her and performing my own duties might be too challenging, despite not yet knowing what my position might be.

"No, I'm to have someone else teach regular studies, but I get to stay with you and have you help me with the stones since I'm Opaque now too!"

"Did you try the White stone again?"

"No, they had me try an Eye stone this time. It was so funny! They brought a bunny rabbit. He was so cute, with fluffy spotted fur and big black eyes. I cried because they poked him, but it didn't really hurt him. They only needed a tiny bit of his blood. And then ..." She began to bounce excitedly on her bottom, and I noticed only then the intricate green lace dress she was wearing, so different than the flat fabric I still wore from Shadowstone. "Then I connected to the stone, and it was amazing. It was more fun than the Clear stone I did after and far better than the Cloud stone on Name Day. It was like I *was* the bunny! I couldn't stop sniffing the air and looking around. And my ears were really itchy but could also hear so many things."

"That's really incredible. I wish I could have seen you do so well," I replied, grinning wide for the first true time since I'd arrived. Her energy was contagious, and I was happy her experience had been positive and not traumatic. I could only hope it would stay that way for quite some time, to prevent her innocence from being crushed.

"You will. They said it's almost certain you will connect with the Eye stone too. And if you don't, well, that will be all right. You already connect with so many others." She patted my hand in consolation, causing me to break out in laughter. "What?" she asked, beginning to giggle herself.

I shook my head and held back more laughter. "Nothing. I know it will be all right, Ivy."

A muffled bark made me jump.

"Argo!" Ivy yelled, getting to her feet just as the gray dog walked through the wide-open door of my new room as if he'd entered this room several times before.

"Argo."

And there it was. That jumbled voice that somehow made sense. Croft.

The dog's name sounded like an admonishment.

Ivy got down on her knees, greeting the dog by shoving her face right in front of his. "Hi boy! You're a good boy."

"Ivy," I said, getting to my feet too and pressing a finger to my temple unwittingly as if to push away the voice I'd heard. "You shouldn't get in his face. Give him space."

The dog's rear end shook, his long tail wagging excitedly even as Ivy stopped to look at me. Mouth agape, he took the break in Ivy's attention to move around her, stopping at my feet and sitting like a very good boy indeed.

"Hi, Argo." I bent to pat his head and give his floppy ears a small rub. "It's nice to see you again."

"Hi, Croft," Ivy said, bringing my attention up.

He stood just inside the door, gaze already on me until his eyes shifted to Ivy. He gave her a soft smile and lifted his hand in greeting. His amber eyes flitted down to Argo at my feet, his smile falling immediately. And had his lips dipped into a scowl?

I lifted my hand, thinking I'd done something wrong. "Hi. Uh, hi," I repeated when his eyes lifted again, settling on my mouth. "Sorry if I, if we shouldn't ..."

His head shook the slightest amount. *"Nothing's wrong."*

"We're allowed. Prince Ren and Croft both said I could, unless they were busy at their work. Right?" Ivy asked him, her words slower as she reached back with one hand to pet Argo again, keeping her face toward Croft.

He nodded once in reply, and she went on. "You have to remember to look at Croft when you speak to him. He can read most of the words from our lips and fills in the rest. Isn't that neat? But it's not easy if you speak too fast. Prince Ren told me to slow down when we were traveling. He said I talked more than the morning birds and the kitchen cooks combined." She giggled shyly, her round cheeks lifting high with her toothy grin.

"It seems you've found even more to talk about after leaving Shadowstone." I chuckled and gave her a warm smile. She had certainly become more lively, and I was grateful no one had trampled the joy she was experiencing. The positive interactions with Croft and Argo also fueled her excitement.

Croft's attire matched Imogen's, with a white undershirt and a slate gray buckled vest. And though it wasn't as formal as what he'd worn at Shadowstone, it was still neat and tidy, and was far more flattering on his large frame than on Imogen's short curvy figure. The hair on his jaw was a little longer than it had been before, while all the hair on his head was fastened the same at the back. It had looked a flat, medium brown in the dimmer light of our parlor, but with three windows in my room alone, the scattered rays of the setting sun showed a mix of different tones. There was something powerful about his presence. His muscular size was an obvious reason, yet there was something more about him. Confidence was a good assumption as well, given how he held himself despite his station and all the struggles he no doubt had been through. It was captivating.

Croft moved then, opening a small closet to the left and pointing to the dressers alongside, indicating the clothing that had been procured for me. Then he left briefly, only to return with the small chests I'd packed from Shadowstone.

"My things!" Ivy called out, rushing over to hers and opening it as soon as Croft lowered it to the floor. She grabbed hold of her alpaca and squished it to her face. "Petal! Oh, thank you for bringing her. I missed her terribly."

"You're welcome," I said, watching her joy, then realizing that Clem's and Begonia's chests had been brought too. "Have you seen Begonia and Clem recently?"

Ivy dug through her belongings, then pushed the other chests toward the side wall. "Not for a few days. They don't stay on this side of the castle. They live with the other Clear class in the southeast wing."

"Will I be able to see them, give them their things?" I asked Croft, who had stopped again by the door.

His head pivoted from side to side. *"Maybe. When you see the castle."* His hand moved between us before making a large circle, adding some unfamiliar movements with his fingers in between.

"You'll have a tour like I had! Can I come?" Ivy asked after getting his attention.

Croft shook his head, then pretended to write in a book with his hands. *"Lessons tomorrow."*

"I forgot. Can it be the day after, before induction?" She pouted, her lower lip jutting outward.

He shook his head, pinching his lips together as if repressing a smile at her reaction, then moved his hands like writing again. *"Lessons then too."*

Ivy grumbled and folded her arms.

Unlike Croft, I wasn't able to withhold my smile. Their interaction had me fascinated. Ivy was understanding him nearly as well as me, and she couldn't hear his thoughts. Wait ...

"The induction is the day after tomorrow? Isn't that too soon?" I asked, looking between them both, hoping someone knew the answer.

Ivy started digging into her case again, lifting her few treasures up to inspect each, smiling broadly at some new trinkets Cordelia had added. "You were the last to arrive. They already moved it once. That's what Prince Ren said. They waited for you."

Realizing that there were no more pats from Ivy, Argo stood and disappeared into the sitting room. Croft hadn't moved or motioned at all, letting Ivy explain. His eyes tracked the dog before following behind him. A knock at the main door followed, and I realized that Argo had already known someone was in the hallway.

Induction was in two days' time. My nerves jumped at the thought. Even my skin felt prickly, elation and worry hitting me all at once. I'd find out what position I was to hold, but I'd also be tested in both ways, reading and being read, this time by someone more powerful than Cordelia, someone who might discover I held secrets. There was still a chance my time in the White stone Realm wouldn't be found. There was also a chance I could deny whatever was happening, choose not to do as Sielle said and take whatever position I was given without concern. Why did I need to worry over other things anyway? The Crown was already holding an ongoing trial about the dead and missing Lovely. Why would I need to be involved at all?

Croft returned to the open door with two plants. One a small and bush-like, with dark green spear leaves and soft pink-petaled flowers. My color pink. Oleander. The other plant had dangling vines near double the length of the clay pot, their bright starry leaves twisting together in a beautiful tangle. Ivy.

"We aren't to touch those," Ivy said, getting to her feet with her chest. "Guardian Calla told me that the higher stone classes get their name plant to keep in our room, but you cannot touch because most are poison to us or animals. You're sleeping here, so I get the other room. There's also a bathing room and the room where Croft and Argo will sleep too."

I raised my hairless brows and chanced a look at Croft, but he simply lifted the pots higher. *"Where?"*

"Best to keep them out of reach then? Over the main room's fireplace mantle?"

He replied with a single nod and turned to go place them.

I doubted he knew I could hear his more focused thoughts. He showed no signs of noticing the connection at all. But I needed to be careful around him, especially with anyone else near. If I slipped in knowing something I wasn't supposed to ... Well, then things would get even more complicated.

Ivy carried her chest from the room just as another knock sounded from the outer door. I waited, running my hand over the bedding for a few seconds before entering the main room to see who or what had arrived this time, not entirely prepared to have an attendant doing everything for me.

As I arrived at the doorway, Ivy rushed into the main room. "Dinner!" Her hands clapped, and I knew she was excited to eat more of the tarts she'd spoken so highly about.

"Lovely Ivy and Oleander," Imogen greeted us both, pushing a metal cart to the round table and four chairs positioned along the front wall.

Croft closed the door behind her while Argo busied himself sniffing the air from his side. His nose worked hard, though he stayed in place.

Imogen lifted two trays onto the table and uncovered them, revealing a dark meat roast with herbed potatoes and fresh greens too. I found myself sniffing almost as much as Argo. My mouth watered.

"No tarts?" The corners of Ivy's mouth dropped dramatically. She ducked down for a better view of the cart's lower shelf.

Imogen raised a shoulder with a tiny smirk before lifting one more tray.

"Ooh!" Ivy bounced on her toes.

"You are very lucky that they are the king's favorites too and are made often, but you should not expect them every day, all right? Whether you eat in the gathering hall or here. Go wash."

She darted to one of the other open doors, calling over her shoulder, "All right."

Imogen turned to me next, pausing in place for a moment before her naturally narrow eyes blinked rapidly. She shook her head, looking down at the food and trays and back at her hands.

"Is everything all right?" I asked, seeing her concern. It was as if she'd forgotten something.

"Oh. Well, yes. Apologies. I've been having headaches ..." She rubbed a couple of fingers over her forehead, still looking at the cart, then shook her head again and put on a smile. "No concern. All set."

Croft took a step, holding his hand up in a stop motion.

"Oh yes, the check ... With them also doing them in the kitchens, it's hard to keep up. All the safety measures are important," Imogen added, waiting.

He swung the same hand forward, and Argo moved quickly to the table, which was barely higher than his face. His nose pointed to the first dishes, then he moved around the cart to the other side. He stopped and sat.

Imogen glanced at Croft again. "Maybe the greens?"

Croft stepped forward. Using the extra utensils on the cart, he separated the dishes and stepped back for Argo to check again.

What was happening?

"Argo smelled something?" Ivy gasped as she got to my side. She had already known the process, of course, having been at the castle for a week.

The dog sat again, this time by the plate holding the extra dry seasoning.

Croft lifted the side plate, inspecting.

Imogen peered at it in his hands too. "Mustard seed? Maybe the scent is close to something else."

"Not chancing." Croft set the plate back onto the cart, then stepped away.

"Well, I'll inform the cooks to leave that out of all the Lovely dishes just the same. It's been quite the arrival day for you, Lovely Oleander, so I won't linger," Imogen said, tucking the metal covers into the cart, moving it to the side wall, then grabbing the plate of seasonings and backing up as well. "Though there is still another day to get acclimated, the king and queen thought it best for all of you to get plenty of rest before the induction events. Most meals will be served to you here for the time being, unless you are tasked with work readings prior to being assigned to your position. Croft will direct you where to go in those cases. If you are in need of anything else, let Croft or the outside guard know. Have a pleasant evening."

Before she could get to the door, I whispered, "They were poisoned, weren't they? The dead Lovely." I hadn't thought much about how they'd been killed before seeing the process of food inspection. The truth of why Croft and Argo were with us hit me fully.

Imogen stilled, the door held halfway open. She looked at me, sorrow plain to see in her eyes and on her down-turned mouth. "Yes, they were."

While they offer the most basic
connection to the Realm, Clear stones are
fundamental for entertainment, justice, and defense.
Though plentiful, they are still governed
because of their versatility.
- Anhedral Kingdom Lovely Guidebook

10

"I'm pretty sure you don't know, since you haven't mentioned, but you also haven't asked. Is there a reason?" Kalmia asked as we rounded the base of the lowest floor in the southeast wing. We were three floors underground, past where the other staircases I'd encountered had stopped. Though the natural light from the windows above had disappeared, the pedestal fire basins and wall sconces lit the way well enough.

"A reason? No. I thought inquiring might be rude."

"I understand. You don't know anyone yet. You wouldn't want to start on a bad foot." Her smooth head bounced rapidly as she walked, piquing at my shoulder height with each stride, firelight glinting off the ivory-hued surface. Her incredibly fast pace was to blame, seemingly unnatural for her short stature.

She'd shown up at my door that morning, not long after we'd eaten breakfast and Ivy had left for lessons. She offered Croft and Argo a simple nod in greeting when her own attendant transferred his duty. Then she hurried me out into the hallway and started the castle tour. By the time we'd covered permitted parts of the north hallways—skipping the off-limits royal rooms in the north and northeast wings—and had finished viewing the great hall properly and the main trial room in the south wing, she may have told me her entire life story with bits of castle information mixed in. She was in her thirtieth year, originally from the northern Nursery in Brushland, Opaque stone class, and current lead for the White stones.

She was a talker, words coming faster than her steps, and I struggled to keep up with both. I'd had to stop to look at random hall decorations to catch my breath and try to focus on her words. To be honest, I missed some of the monologue. She was a chattering lilac blur in her flowing purple dress, movements and words blending together soon after we'd begun.

While I hadn't heard Croft's thoughts during the first portion—he and Argo had kept a considerable distance to not disturb us—I saw some of the humored looks he made, though I was unsure if it was due to watching Kalmia's mouth move so quickly or possibly my reactions in response.

Since I'd had hardly any chances to speak, I had been caught off guard at her shifting the focus directly onto me.

"It wouldn't be rude to ask important questions."

"I've been adjusting and settling in, honestly. I figured maybe with the trial, the deaths weren't to be discussed." My words sounded as dry as my throat as we neared two immense and intricate wooden doors outlined with squared blocks of limestone. After seeing the sweeping expanses of the great hall and trial room, I wondered what another grand entrance would hold. My eyes roamed the carved spherical designs while I cleared my throat and lifted my dress's thick skirting, hoping for a little air upon my legs. I'd even chosen one of the plainer options from the day dress selection in my new wardrobe despite the castle being cooler than Anhedral's more temperate outdoor climate. Everything was warmer than Shadowstone. I was glad for the choice, though, since the castle's size was beyond measure and most everyone walked entirely too fast, causing my legs to burn with excessive use. And I didn't even want to think about the blisters forming upon my feet from the pretty flat shoes made of leather stiff enough to resemble slats of wood. I'd have to look for other options.

"Oh," she replied, a lot quieter than she had been. "I understand. Well, it's not a secret, and you should be informed."

"I agree," I managed to rasp in a dull tone.

Argo had moved in front of me, blocking my next step. I turned to find Croft, his body the closest it had been since I'd slammed into him in Shadowstone. My eyes focused on the slim strand of hair that escaped its tie and settled onto his cheek, then they caught with his in a deep exchanging stare. I inhaled, realizing his smell was more than pleasant, with enticing scents of spicy soap and leather. The connecting moment had all of my senses awakening, causing me to shiver.

"Too close." His nostrils flared, then his eyes narrowed and flickered downward as his body leaned back. *"Drink."*

I dropped my own eyes, embarrassed my thoughts had run away and hoping he hadn't read every bit of it upon my face. While I had found him very pleasing in physical appearance ever since my body had collided with his, I had to wonder if our White stone connection played a part.

In his hands was a leather canteen, one he'd donned along with a satchel of items before we'd left the rooms. He'd noticed my thirst?

"Yes, water," I said, taking hold of the neck and lifting it to my lips. I drank several swallows greedily, needing the refreshment. As

I finished, I noticed his eyes on me again, this time my lips as I licked them and said, "Thank you, Croft."

I extended the canteen to Kalmia, but she declined with a placid glance at Croft and Argo. With an appreciative smile, I handed the canteen back, and he retreated several paces without meeting my eyes again.

Kalmia continued our conversation, a little slower now that we had stopped moving. "I'm glad you are smart enough to want to know. Some might choose ignorance, but I feel a Lovely must gain as much knowledge as possible to better serve the Crown." When I only nodded in response, she went on. "The ones who were killed were Dahlia and Nightshade. Dahlia was the Smoke stone lead. Jimson is filling her position unless the king chooses someone else after the induction."

"What is a stone lead?"

Her forehead wrinkled, obviously judging my lack of knowledge in Garden procedure already. "We don't use the same position names as the king's army, like soldier and captain. The lead is someone who manages the tasks and the Lovely who are assigned to that stone division. There are also three stone class heads, above the stone leads. Nightshade was the Eye stone lead, doing the same for those within that division. But he was also the prince's appointed Lovely."

How dim I'd been. I blinked several times, finally making the connection. Of course he already had a capable Lovely appointed to him, likely for years. And now he needed a replacement. It was odd, though, that he hadn't seemed affected at all during his visit or when I'd arrived. Yet, he was the prince and therefore had proper training in most behaviors and mannerisms. It all made me wonder how long they'd spent together and how close they had truly been.

"Then there were the two who disappeared, likely the ones to blame." She frowned but didn't seem too bothered by the idea that two of our own would kill two others. "Blodwyn was the Cloud stone lead. Lantana was already chosen as a permanent replacement because of her experience and skill, so there won't be a change there. Then there was the White stone lead, Tansy. She was—"

I sucked in a breath. "Tansy?" As in Cordelia's Tansy? The youngest of Cordelia's first children group and who smelled of oats?

Kalmia stopped talking, and the golden swirling lines over her eyes pulled together as she peered up at me. "That's right. She came from Shadowstone too, didn't she? Did you know her?"

"No, not really. I was very young when she left. It was before my Name Day."

She pinched her lips together, assessing me. "Well, it's good that you don't. She might very well be a traitor to the Crown, and you wouldn't want to be associated with that when you've just arrived."

"No," I agreed absently, my mind in a spin.

"Anyway, I've been appointed her position unless someone else's skill surpasses my own. I heard you connected with all the stones so far but still need to test with the Eye stone."

"Yes, that's correct."

"True talent. Excellent for you. If you connect with an Eye, chances are you will be chosen to replace Nightshade."

And not take your new position, I thought blandly. Undoubtedly, she was elated to have been placed there, even if it was because two Lovely had died. I couldn't help but feel disgusted, yet also somewhat concerned that I may have acted the same had I worn the blistering shoes for years instead of a day.

She bobbed her head from side to side. "That doesn't automatically mean being appointed as the prince's Lovely, but it might for you. It's because those who connect with all the main stones hold the highest positions. The only left after Nightshade's death are Hydrangea, Hemlock, and Wolfsbane. Hydra's appointed to the queen and is the Clear stone head, while Wolf is appointed to the king and is head of Opaque and all Lovely."

"I'm never going to remember everyone."

"Sure you will," she said with a dismissive wave of her dainty hand. "You said you already met Hemlock, head of the Haze stone class. They comprise the top of our stone council. At the induction, you will meet more of us and understand our positions. Are you nervous?"

"About the induction? Yes, a bit. I don't really know what to expect."

Her lip tugged into a disdainful curl. "Your Guardian didn't prepare you very well."

No, she'd had enough things on her mind. But I wasn't about to share all of that with Kalmia. I didn't know her. And though Cordelia failed to prepare me in the usual workings of the Queen's Garden, she had warned me well enough about people. After being at the castle for only a day, I understood why.

"Shame." Her voice kept its usual girlish pitch, not sounding empathetic at all. She sounded happy actually. "You might need a while to catch up on normal procedures then. Well, I won't go into all the details, but there are four other new arrivals of age who are more than Clear stone capable. Usually, they will be placed to work in the division of their highest stone capability, unless another division is in need. Right now, after losing four, anyone could be moved or placed anywhere. The recent events have caused quite the mess, losing a few who had a high level of skill and experience." She sniffed at the same time her nose actually pointed upward. "Not that it will matter much. I'm certain those of us who have been here longer will be able to teach the newcomers all the essentials."

I nodded and turned my head, faking a look at the decor as I realized this additional information had been more about her than the induction itself. Growing tired of her self-importance, I rolled my eyes to the drab painting of an elder Lovely touching a Clear stone. When I dropped my eyes to really focus on the piece's beauty, I caught Croft's eyes on me.

"Interesting reaction." One edge of his lips lifted the slightest bit.

Heat rushed to my face, and I couldn't help but roll my lips together, mildly ashamed at being caught.

"As for the test ..." Kalmia said with a dramatic sigh, voice louder, drawing my reluctant attention back. "Wolfsbane is typically who reads the inductees with Cloud, sometimes even Smoke if there are any castle safety concerns about fears or desires. Then you will test on your next possible stones, which I hear are all Eye stones since the queen traveled with White. They will assign animals for that. After the tests, division assignments will be given."

"Thanks for explaining ... and for the tour." I was ready to be done. My feet and legs ached worse than they ever had, and my mind was turning into a muddy marsh. If I had any hope of making it through induction the next day, I'd need some rest to reset myself, mentally and physically. There was no sense in worrying about the tests anymore. I'd either pass or fail. I could only hope for the best.

When I didn't offer more praise, simply stared blandly ahead to make my intentions clear, Kalmia said, "You're welcome. I understand the unease. We can move on and maybe cut out the other division rooms so you can rest for tomorrow."

I nearly sighed with relief but managed to hold it all in.

She shrugged and nodded to the guards posted at both ends of the double doors. "I have to check in on the White stone readers in preparation of the induction ball anyway. Many courtiers have come for the celebration, even some foreign dignitaries. They adore vanity readings for entertainment since Lovely are so rare outside of our kingdom."

Of course. I bit down on my tongue.

The guards, who hadn't paid us much mind while we'd stood outside and talked, nodded in return and opened the way.

"I should have mentioned to prepare yourself," Kalmia nearly whispered as we moved forward. "We are walking inside the hollow of a single Needled stone. This is the Realm room, created to magnify any readings done within. It is mainly used for the Clear stone division as they have the integral role of the kingdom's safety by watching over it."

I felt the power as soon as the doors had opened, a soft surge of energy, not quite as intense as the stones that linked directly to the Realm. I still hadn't touched a Needled stone, but it wasn't a necessity. It was the only assisting stone used in conjunction with others to amplify range. However, like the others, not everyone could use it.

"Does it work for everyone in the division? And does it let them enter the same place at the same time?" I asked, looking around. Sielle had used one with the White stone. And even though she had been in the same space as me, she had said no Lovely could. That still confused me.

The doors opened into a dimly lit, wide, circular room. The clear walls reflected the firelight's shine from the surface. Even through the contrast of bright and dark, I noticed the sharp slices throughout, like slivers of metal blades. But it wasn't just the walls. The ceiling and the floors were the same, completely enclosed except for where we'd entered and one other single doorway at the opposite rounded edge. Several long tables butted to each other, end to end, stretching across the length of the space. All had chairs facing in one direction, away from the main entrance. Book shelving lined the side walls at both sides of the table rows. They held no books. Only stone spheres.

"Honestly, you should already know we can't occupy the same space inside the Realm, even if we touch the same stone at the same time." She huffed again. "And no, of course the Needled doesn't work for everyone. But as a whole, it helps boost readings. There are more still buried under the castle. That is why the castle was built here so long ago. It was built around this one to serve a purpose, a powerful amplifier to protect the entire kingdom. Not that we have any current threats since all of our neighboring kingdoms know the power we hold. They have some Lovely, too, a few even gifts from us, but they don't have the numbers we have."

There was no disputing those facts. Anhedral was large. That reality became more clear after seeing much of its land in person during travel. A far cry from studying it on a map. I didn't know the total amount of Lovely we had, but even with those she'd named on the council, it would be an excellent defense.

The doorway across the room opened, and some movement followed. A group of people entered, filing in silently. All of them were Lovely, smooth heads reflecting the soft light in the area. I held still, watching as they split into orderly lines to navigate to the ends of the room. At least half of the group were older children, not yet mature, their heights varying from Kalmia's petite size to taller than my own. All were dressed in white, either plain pants and shirts or floor-length dresses. It was clear the garments differed in small ways, with stitching or panels but not extra frivolous pieces like ribbons, ties, or bows.

They walked along the walls until stopping at their row. Then they reached into the closest shelving, removed a Clear stone, and turned down their aisle. As the closest line spread apart, I spotted two familiar faces.

I couldn't stop the smile or the words that left my mouth. "Begonia. Clem."

Their heads turned with no immediate recognition, until one of Clem's hands lifted with a tiny wave. Begonia's eyes widened suddenly, then narrowed into the more typical glare she'd always cast at me.

I darted back two steps to Croft, not caring about his puzzled expression while I grabbed for his satchel and removed Begonia's pink alpaca and Clem's rolled painting, which I'd asked him to pack earlier for me.

"No, not a good time."

Croft's thought didn't even register as I extended the items outward in their direction.

Begonia's face crumpled. Her eyes darted around at the other Lovely and circled back to me. The biggest scowl she'd ever given appeared before she turned away to face the front of the room. If I had been closer, there was no doubt I'd have seen the reddening of her cheeks. Clem merely shook his head, then turned away too.

What? Were they not allowed their things?

Kalmia cleared her throat lightly at my side. "A session is about to begin. They aren't permitted to interact now. They have certain free times when they aren't on rotation, but I'm not familiar with the Clear schedule. Hydrangea just entered at the front. You can seek her out later, perhaps tomorrow after induction to ask about interactions with them."

"Oh." My hands fell to my sides with the items, unsure how to process it all. They looked the same, possibly a bit paler than they had been, with soft shadows under their eyes. The room's light could have been to blame, though, seeming to cast shadows onto all of them. So many of them. Maybe fifty.

Hydrangea stepped onto a small dais at the front, lifting her already tall stature even higher. She wore a plain dress much like the children, though hers was as black as night with shiny silver stitching—the kingdom's standard. The darkness muted any real distinguishing features from so far away, though her skin appeared to be a russet tone. Her attention was directed to us as she raised her arms and said in a loud and smoky tone, "Stay at the positions assigned to you and keep within your skill range, whether outside the castle wall, the kingdom perimeter, or in between. We must aim for fewer disconnects than your last session. For Realm and kingdom. Let's begin."

All the children set their spheres onto the table in front of their seats, stepped out of their shoes, then slid into the chairs. Their hands placed on either side of their sphere, waiting.

I glanced down, realizing their feet were in direct contact with the Needled stone.

Kalmia grabbed hold of my arm and pulled me backward into her quick strides. With a clumsy stagger, I spun with her as she said, "We need to leave now so we don't interfere with their session."

We cleared the room, and I glanced back as the guards closed the doors.

An odd feeling settled over me, one I couldn't shake away.

Not when I asked Kalmia how often they were in rotation and she assured me that there were several groups that size and four times a week was the maximum amount of readings authorized for any Lovely to maintain a healthy mind.

Not when Kalmia walked me to their group's shared room where I couldn't even leave the items because there was no difference in the symmetrical rows of stacked limestone framed beds or the open closets lining the wall behind them. No numbers. No names. Nothing to show ownership or individuality.

Not when Kalmia's attendant met us by the great hall, and they bid us farewell so she could tend to her White stone duties. While she'd continued to chatter about random castle information right up until the departure, she had grown exhausted by my excessive silence.

Not even when Argo prodded my hand with his snout in demand of a pat before I closed myself into my room.

No, that odd feeling didn't leave at all. It settled in and stayed.

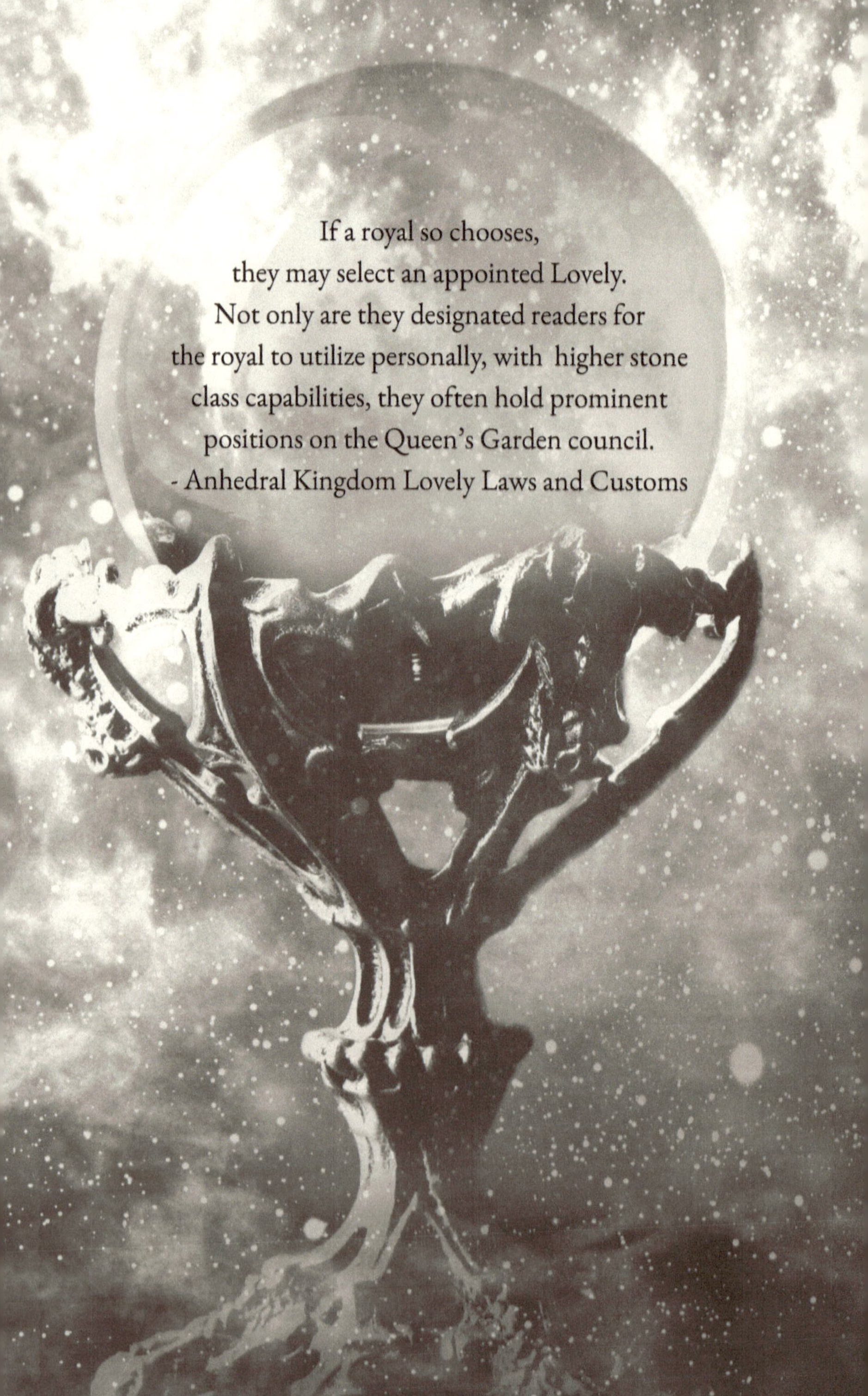

If a royal so chooses,
they may select an appointed Lovely.
Not only are they designated readers for
the royal to utilize personally, with higher stone
class capabilities, they often hold prominent
positions on the Queen's Garden council.
- Anhedral Kingdom Lovely Laws and Customs

11

"That's her. The one who's connected with all so far." While the words were whispered, the volume hadn't been low enough to keep me from hearing over the noise of the gathering crowd. I had an idea that was the intention.

The induction was about to begin in the southern courtyard near the castle's wondrous garden. I, along with the four other new Lovely of higher age and stone class, was waiting to be introduced and seated at the decorated table in front of the tiered platform wall at the garden's entrance. On either side of each place setting lay trimmings or blooms from our Lovely namesakes, much like the plants gifted to me and Ivy in our rooms. And directly across from our chairs, a Cloud stone sphere perched on three rounded peaks of a wood-carved stand. On the garden wall platforms, more Lovely stood near their own seating, separated into stone divisions and flanking both sides of four high-backed royal chairs, one section on the same level and only a few seated on the smaller level up. All were there except Clear stone division. They were in attendance, too, all in simple silver-hued clothing and positioned closer to the castle's rear wall, behind the growing crowd of kingdom guests and court members. And scattered throughout the space, guards took their assigned positions and attendants milled about in preparations.

I thought of Kalmia's council information, but it wasn't difficult to distinguish the divisions. Each member wore garments in the color or accents of their respective stones, some with defining features. A strip of silver lace pinned over blue signified the light shine of the Eye stones. Ruffled and swirling pieces of thin, white or gray fabric were draped over silver garments for Cloud and Smoke stones. Multiple layers of white cloth signified the White stones. Each lead or head also stood out, wearing black with silver accents instead. I picked out those I'd seen or met—Hemlock head of Haze, Kalmia lead for White, and the head of Clear, Hydrangea. They, and the others, stood with their division groups, which ranged in members from twenty to four, the latter being the Eye stones.

Despite having had a full day of rest and choosing my old woolen trial shoes for comfort reasons, my feet began to ache again. I was grateful they were hidden beneath the tiered black ball gown made of lengths of gauzy tulle and silver beading that shimmered like the night sky. The beauty was astounding and far beyond everything I'd imagined wearing. It also fit like a dream, with a lining of fine silk that cradled me closely. But the rough material on the outside that gathered and puffed out from the waist rubbed and scratched with every sway of my arms, like an irritating reminder not to get too comfortable.

The relaxing day had lulled me into a false sense of tranquility. I'd seen Ivy for dinner the previous night, where discussions consisted of a complete summary of her lessons and information about the other small children she'd met, but she had already been gone when I awoke in the morning. Croft had kept his distance after the tour and had also been gone in the morning. Another attendant posted outside informed me that the prince had called Croft away. I welcomed the time alone, surprisingly able to clear my mind before preparing for the induction. I'd also been left a list of procedures to ready myself, including the specific dress to wear and grooming instructions for a proper scrubbing bath, nail trim, and use of skin lotions. The last listed was a selection of designs to be used for correct eyebrow painting. I'd stared into the mirror, holding the tiny brush loaded with black paint aloft, unable to mark my face for several moments. That was when my nerves had returned, the disconcerting feelings seeping back in as I'd looked upon myself, confusion blurring my vision of the future I'd once dreamed of.

The others—three boys, one girl—stood off to my side, awaiting their fate as well. The girl wore the same dress as me while the boys donned identical black shirts and pants with silver buttons and ruffled ties. Two boys chatted quietly to each other, while the rest of us remained silent. I was too busy calming my nerves to speak, to ask them anything about themselves, though I'd heard someone in the nearby crowd list off the town names from where each of us had come. There were only four—Shadowstone, Brushland, Crystal Flats, and Bloodweld. The two speaking had likely come from the same Nursery.

"I like your choice." The third boy spoke beside me, eyes lifting above mine.

I almost wiped my brow, catching myself just in time and letting my hand fall back to my side, dress scratching me once again.

"A thick straight line with a single curve up at the end is pretty bold." His were arrows, points facing inward and feathers out.

"Thanks," I replied, glancing around at everyone still talking, who paid no mind to us yet. "Yours are nice too."

A few seconds passed before he said, "I'm Nettle, from Bloodweld. You can call me Net. You're Oleander? From Shadowstone?"

"Olean. Good to meet you, Net."

"You too." He rocked back onto his heels and also took a moment to glance around. He was my height, with darker umber skin, two divots in his cheeks, and a single one in his chin. "You ready for this?"

"Does it really matter?"

He laughed, the tone deep and melodic. "I wasn't expecting you to be funny."

I eyed him with a small smile that didn't stay long as I thought about some of the other Lovely I'd met. "Right. We all should be too self-important for humor, I suppose."

"I suppose," he agreed, his own smile dropping as he looked upon the other Lovely, most also in discussions while awaiting the royals' arrival, some eyeing us right back. He took a side step closer and lowered his voice. "Did you hear anything about the ones who died ... and the missing others?"

"No, not much."

"I heard that those who died might have been part of an uprising. Allegedly, there's a secret group of Lovely wanting change. Rumors reached Bloodweld months ago. Then some are killed here at the castle? It all seems suspicious."

It was suspicious. I still had a difficult time believing Tansy had a role in it, but I hadn't really known her at all. Not like Cordelia, who had mostly raised her. She might have known if Tansy were the type to be involved. Though things could have changed after she'd moved.

"That's not what's happened," the other girl interrupted, obviously listening in. She had small features, wide-set eyes, and shimmery porcelain skin like the queen and princess. Unlike them, she was nearly my height, with a full-figured frame. "The two who are missing were jealous of the others' positions from what I heard. But they messed up and were too scared to stay, knowing they would be read and sentenced to death."

"That so?" Net asked, doubtful eyes flicking to me briefly. "You're Amaryllis?"

"Yes, from Crystal Flats. News spread to us too, and my Guardian said to be wary of jealousy because there are others always vying for your place."

"Can't argue with that bit," I murmured.

"Of course you can't," Net agreed. "We're all testing on the Eye stone tonight for a last chance to level up in class and division assignment options. But you ... Is it true that it's the only one you haven't connected with?"

"No. I haven't tried Blood or Black either." Maybe he didn't deserve my caustic wit, but I was growing tired of all the talk and gossip already.

"Don't be absurd." Amaryllis huffed, glowering at me as if I had been serious. "One has been lost for over a century and the other hasn't been connected with in almost as long."

I directed my wide eyes and pressed lips at Net, who mimicked my expression conspiratorially. At least he understood my sense of humor.

"There are other possible rumors too, as usual." Net reverted the topic, his eyes grazing over the other Lovely.

Amaryllis shrugged. "There always is. Don't leave us waiting. What else have you heard?"

"That the murders were crimes of passion since the prince was involved with Nightshade and Dahlia too."

"Now *you're* being absurd," she grumbled.

"It's not unheard of. Actually, it's rather commonly known that royals get involved with their appointed Lovely since they know them better than anyone else. That bond is hard to ignore. I, for one, wouldn't mind being appointed, especially to Prince Ren." Net smirked with a wink. "Unfortunately, there's no chance for me. Olean, you might discover the truth soon enough if you get the position. You'll have to read him at some point. It's a crying shame Crown law binds you from confirming or denying any of the sultry rumors."

I remained quiet, considering the implication. While a romantic tie to a royal might be flattering to some, it made me wonder what might happen should a Lovely not reciprocate the interest.

Amaryllis huffed again. "Sure. I suppose it has happened through the years, though I wouldn't assume it to be something normal and definitely not expected. I'm sure there are ... uh, people who take care of other royal pleasures."

Net laughed, likely at her modest explanation, drawing some eyes our way. "Well, I'm certain there are those around the city and castle too. But these are more serious relationships. I've heard tales of the king being intimate with at least one around the time he married the queen. It was quite the scandal. My Guardian said it had the kingdom in upset when those rumors came about. The wedding had almost been canceled."

"That's disgusting. Wolfsbane has been appointed to him since he was a child."

"No, it wasn't Wolfsbane. King Antin was said to have played in the Lovely Garden often when he was younger, and apparently after too."

She shrugged, her attention drifting away, dismissing the conversation.

Croft and Argo had taken position close to the edge of the platforms. They looked even more handsome than they had in Shadowstone, making me think of Ivy, who, like the other young ones, wasn't allowed to attend the induction. She would love to see them dressed in their best again, though. Even Argo had a fancy vest on—black and silver, of course.

Net spun toward where I was looking. "I heard about him. Is he your attendant?"

"The one with the dog?" Amaryllis sneered, rudely leaping back into our conversation.

"Yes."

Amaryllis continued on, "You should request someone else. I heard there's a chance he's involved in what happened. Most everyone they've read for the trial haven't seen anything, and he's the only one who can't be read."

I clenched my teeth just as Croft looked our way and caught my eye. His head tilted a tad, his eyes narrowing.

With an irritable huff, I replied, "He's one of the prince's attendants and was personally appointed to me. Do you doubt the prince's judgment?"

She sputtered and reeled back as if I'd struck her, drawing attention from the two other guys with us. "No, it's not that at all. I only meant—"

"Easy there, Oleander. She's liable to choke on her words before she's to test." Net chuckled, trying to ease the mood. "No one's doubting the prince's judgment, but you can't deny the doubt around an attendant who had access to the rooms where the prince's own Lovely, Nightshade, was found dead."

I sniffed, sneaking a glance at Croft one more time, finding his attention toward the castle. There was no way I'd believe it, unless he'd had cause. Sure, he was on the gruff side, but he was also observant, helpful, and sweet. Perhaps Nightshade and Dahlia weren't victims so much as the ones at fault for something else.

Sielle had told me Croft was coveted and useful to the Crown because no one could read him. If the prince trusted him, it could be possible that someone gave him an order to do something. The reasons for their deaths were endless, and I didn't know nearly enough to speculate. But Sielle wanted me to try to learn the truth. She wanted me to decide that the truth was worth uncovering.

Horns blared to life at the castle's rear entrance, alerting the crowd to the royals' arrival.

"It's time to be as bold as your painted eyebrows," Net said close to my ear as everyone bowed or curtsied.

I smiled dimly. "And to shoot as true as yours."

"Best of luck, Olean."

"And to you, Net."

The horns ceased and a hush settled as the royals stopped in front of their chairs and looked over the entire crowd.

"Welcome." King Antin Vidis's voice boomed over the silent courtyard and around the garden entrance. Everyone positioned themselves to view him and his family. They were picturesque, that much was certain. The queen and princess looked beautiful in gowns that gradually changed color from silver at the top of their bodices to black down at their feet. Their styles differed, however. The queen wore a strapless bell-shape while the princess had chosen a single-shouldered gown that puffed out at the waist much like us female inductees. It otherwise would have been difficult to tell them apart, the queen's slightly more aged appearance not as noticeable at a distance.

I could also finally see how much the prince had taken after his father. At just over fifty years, the king's age was more apparent in his silvering head of cropped brown hair and the deeper crinkling at the corners of his eyes and lips. Those things did nothing to quell his handsomeness, though. Most of his features had passed on to Prince Ren. Strong, angular jawline and plump lips. While I couldn't see his eyes, I could see his straight and somewhat upturned nose. His brow ridge differed from the prince's, though, yet still looked familiar, the prominence setting his eyes deeper.

"We are happy you are joining us for this Lovely induction and wish you all to stay for our celebration ball to follow. Although we are at peace with our neighbors, some of whom are joining us tonight, we've had a few recent losses and trying moments through the year. Any flourishing kingdom doesn't go without struggles. Goals have shifted in my time on the throne, but rest assured, our people are always the priority and what makes our kingdom so marvelous. Along with our powerful army, the Lovely will always be one of our strongest assets, helping to ensure our stability, the unwavering success for our peace, and the continued safety of our kingdom's many lands and waters."

Applause filled the area, and the king lifted his hands with a broad smile. "So right now is the perfect time to celebrate our achievements and bring more power and strength into the fold. Tonight is a special one as we have five new Lovely potentially joining the ranks, one I'm told could very well hold the prestige few others have obtained if she is to connect with the Eye stone." There was no mistaking who he meant, especially when his gaze swept briefly to me, one heavy eyebrow lifting inquisitively. "We also have a little fun planned for our guests. So without any more from me, let us begin with the ceremony. If you have a seat, please take it. Wolf, if you will."

The king's appointed Lovely left his side on the lower platform tier and moved to us as the front part of the crowd took the available courtyard chairs. There were many, but there were at least double the guests. The rest remained standing farther back.

Wolfsbane was indeed older than the king, possibly by a decade. He didn't appear frail, but his tanned skin looked like wrinkled butcher paper, thinned and scarred, with heavy creases and a bit of sagging at his neck. His eyes were wide and clear, white irises vivid even under the growing shadows from the setting sun.

All of a sudden, my body quivered and sweat bloomed upon my skin. If he saw anything ... it would be told in front of everyone.

For some unknown reason, my eyes moved to Croft. In search of what? Safety? Comfort? I didn't know.

And I wasn't sure why in that moment, possibly reacting to my movement, Croft's eyes found me too. My nerves must have been plain enough because he inclined his head and lifted a leg as if to take a step forward. Argo bumped the same leg, and he quickly set it back down as if remembering his place.

"Lovely, as I call you, greet the royal family, then claim your seats," Wolfsbane said, then turned toward the crowd. His orotund voice cut through the air with precision, leaving no concern of reaching all in attendance as he projected, "From Brushland, Larkspur and Hellebore."

The other boys moved quickly, filing one at a time to the royals, bowing low in front of them, then being dismissed to their seats at opposite ends of the table.

"From Crystal Flats, Amaryllis."

She held herself well, head up, with long, confident strides to the royals, gown swaying beautifully.

I felt as though I would be sick. I looked at Croft again and took a deep breath.

"From Bloodweld, Nettle."

"That's me," he said, touching my hand before striding forward.

"And from Shadowstone, Oleander."

I blocked out the stares, ignored the acid taste inside my dry mouth, and started forward. I didn't count my steps or even recall how quickly I'd moved, but I was standing before the royals as though I'd floated. All eyes were on me, the prince's blues catching with mine for a long moment before I dropped into a steady curtsy.

"Your Majesty," I addressed the king, my eyes on the floor.

"Good luck," Prince Ren whispered just before the queen said, "Oleander, how gorgeous. Go take your place."

The king didn't speak. But as I stood upright at my dismissal, my eyes lifted and locked onto a beautiful, shiny pendant hanging from a chain around his neck. It had likely freed itself from beneath his clothing, suspended in the space where the two folds of his formal surcoat met, nowhere near the medals and adornments pinned over the chest. Its silver oval shape instantly stirred my memory, the overlapping letters A and V jumping out easily enough from the swirling background. I had an identical one stashed inside a travel chest in my rooms. I hadn't dared touch it since I'd arrived. His was polished, no dirt to be seen.

I blinked and turned, hurrying to my chair on wobbly legs.

Maybe the pendants were common. Maybe the letters were as well. Yet, I couldn't help to think that they were initials, and, as the A lay above the V, their rightful namesake was Antin Vidis.

Cordelia's lover? The father of her baby? The king.

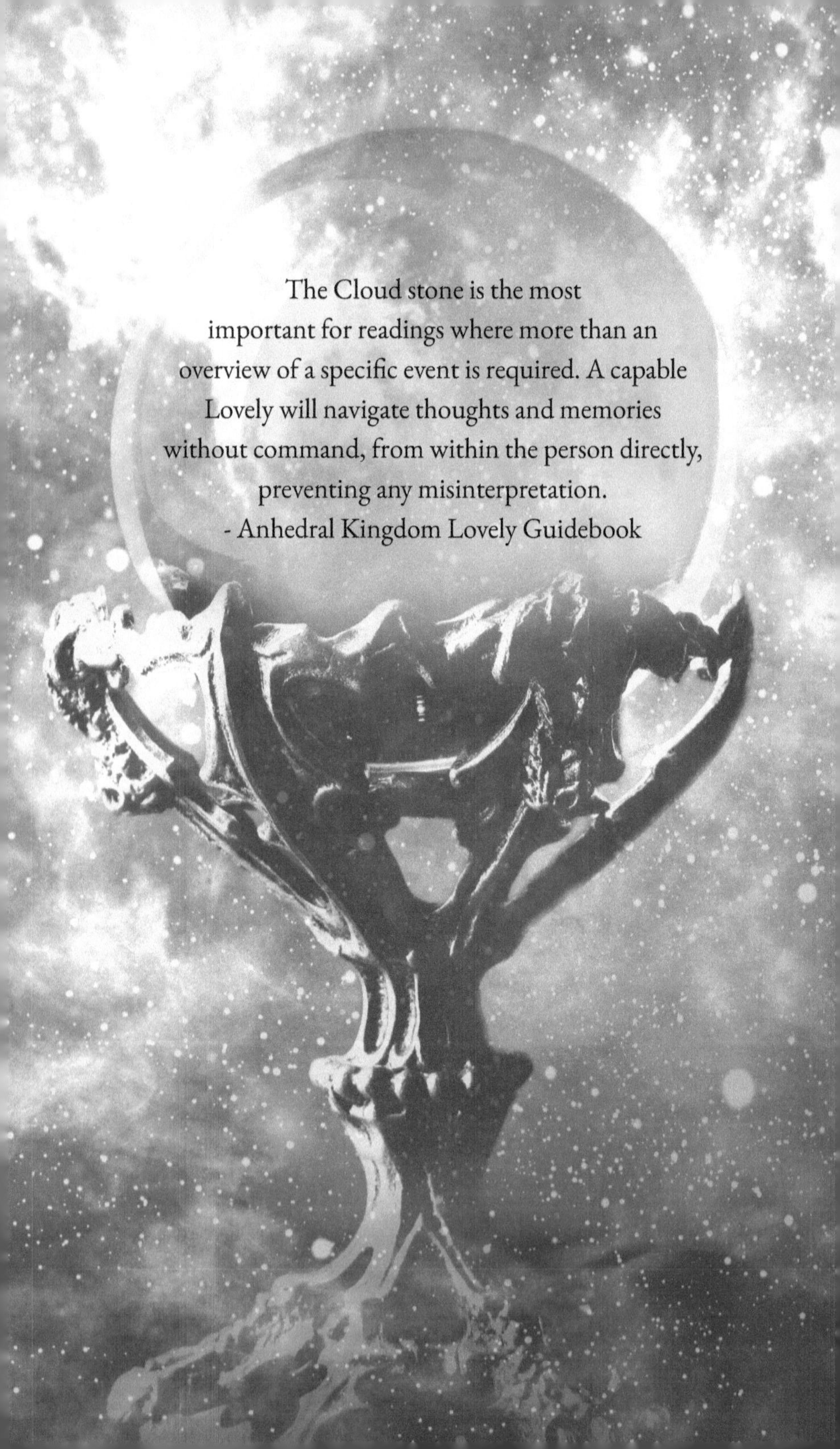

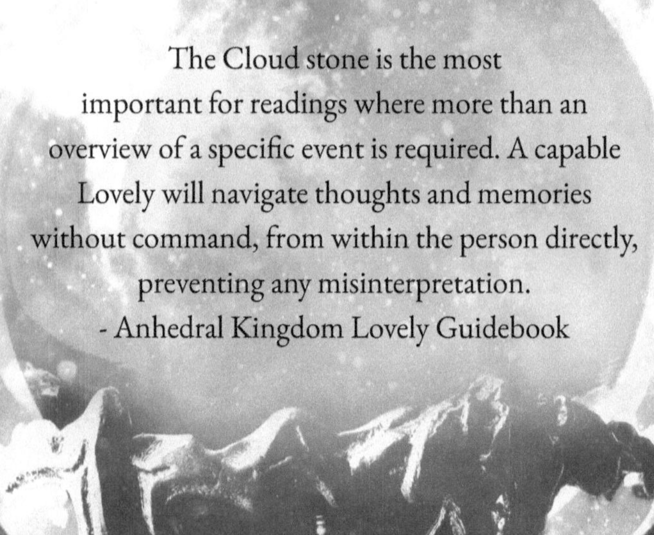

The Cloud stone is the most
important for readings where more than an
overview of a specific event is required. A capable
Lovely will navigate thoughts and memories
without command, from within the person directly,
preventing any misinterpretation.
- Anhedral Kingdom Lovely Guidebook

12

I had to breathe deeply to settle my trembles. The knowledge had my mind and body in a frenzy. It was a struggle to think about anything except what I'd just discovered. Cordelia had been sent away to Shadowstone. The Lovely relation rumors about the king that Net and Amaryllis had just discussed could have been true after all. Having been involved with the new king and being pregnant with his child seemed more a reason to send Cordelia away than if she'd been involved with anyone else. The queen usually acted cold to her on visits, and she also hadn't reacted to Cordelia's reading or her infant's death. She had to have known. She'd simply wanted us to hear it all as well or possibly used it to remind Cordelia of her place. That way she wouldn't protest as we all were taken away.

Why had I pieced it together right before I was due to be read by the most powerful Lovely in the kingdom?

Realm, save me.

"Through the Cloud stone, the Realm provides us Lovely with glimpses into the mind of another. We experience most of the senses and thoughts within the memories, allowing us a clearer representation from their perspective. Now we begin." Wolfsbane moved down to the end of the table as two attendants walked to him, one of whom was Croft. The other carried a chair and placed it opposite of Hellebore. Wolfsbane took a seat while Croft removed a clean cloth and small dagger from a belted sheath, sliced Hellebore's finger, dabbed his blood onto the cloth, and swiped it over the Cloud stone. Hellebore relaxed into his own chair as Wolfsbane leaned forward and took hold.

He didn't need instruction from the king or anyone. He knew what to ask, what to seek. The words came as though he'd done it a thousand times over, which he probably had.

"The castle is bigger than I thought. The food is good. I don't miss the sand of Brushland, always sticking between my toes and fingers. I hope I get into Eye stone division. Princess Naomi is ravishing."

The crowd laughed, and the side I could see of Hellebore's pale face turned a deep shade of red.

"Don't ever think that last bit again," King Antin commented dully, which had the crowd roaring louder.

I fought the urge to turn and witness the princess's reaction while also fighting a smile. Amaryllis hadn't moved a muscle, but Net's chuckle burst out from my other side. The induction ceremony and ball served another purpose, it seemed. I'd thought it was to be more serious, to evaluate our capabilities and our trustworthiness. But I gathered they used it as a connection to the kingdom and a way to make us relatable, since views of us ranged wildly from hatred to adoration. We were accustomed to being used for entertainment. Only this time, it was our thoughts being shared, not someone else's.

Wolfsbane disconnected from Hellebore's stone. He stood upright and nodded toward the king. While the action was a clear indication of his approval for Hellebore's induction, I had a feeling he viewed far more than he'd shared aloud. It was a thorough reading, yet he picked through and vocalized recent and amusing information.

He moved to another place, and the process repeated. First attendant moved the chair, and Croft drew the blade across Amaryllis's finger, collected the blood with the cloth, then smeared it over her stone.

Wolfsbane settled in. *"I should have chosen a better painted design for my eyebrows. I hope tonight's food is good. Last night's fish wasn't as tasty as what we have in Crystal Flats."*

"Someone get me the cooks!" the king shouted, this time a little humor behind his words. The prince and princess even laughed as another roar rippled through the people.

"I'm starving. I should have grabbed one of those berry tarts I saw a little while ago."

And then it was my turn. I hadn't even seen Wolf's nod to the king. Within a moment, he sat in front of me, his large eyes peering at mine intently.

"Finger." Croft's deep, jumbled word was like a calming balm to my panicked mind. His hip bumped against my shoulder, drawing my eyes up to his as Argo sniffed around the base of my chair.

"Sorry," I said, lifting my finger as his scent surrounded me. He smelled good.

The corners of his lips drew downward as he pushed the clean blade tip to the pad of my finger. His eyes fell away from mine as he sliced, seeming uncomfortable with the action. He quickly dabbed the cut with the cloth, then spread it over the stone before backing away.

I took another shaky breath, asking the Realm for a different kind of magic, something to protect my mind.

Wolfsbane grabbed hold of the stone right away. I fought the urge to fidget, to wrap my fingers into the thin tablecloth hanging just over my lap or into the gauzy bunched fabric of my dress.

Some people I'd read with the Cloud stone had known which thoughts and memories I accessed. Not all of them could feel it or see as I searched their thoughts, but a few admitted that it was part of the torture—reliving the worst mistakes of their lives when most had tried so hard to forget them. I'd wondered if it would be the same for us Lovely. The others at the table hadn't shown any indication that they knew what he was seeing, but I felt the strength immediately, and I knew I was in trouble.

He blinked rapidly, something I hadn't noticed with the others. His eyes opened briefly before closing again. Then he started sifting through my mind. Small tugs would trigger my memories, thoughts, and senses, all of it flashing to me as if I were reading myself in a limited way. It was the oddest sensation.

"Croft smells really nice," Wolfsbane said as visions of Croft flipped through my head. In the rooms. With the canteen outside the Realm room. At the Nursery in Shadowstone.

"I can't wait to tell Ivy about Argo's fancy vest." Flashes of Ivy and Argo. At dinner. When we'd first met and he'd licked my face.

"It's a shiny, pretty pendant, the king's." The A and V on his chest. The A and V in Cordelia's hand.

Oh no.

"While there's no harm in coveting a priceless piece that will never leave my neck, I do hope we won't have to hide all the silver," the king quipped behind me, sounding so distant to my ears while more visions flickered in my mind.

Wolfsbane continued on after the wave of crowd laughter receded. *"Lip movement is mesmerizing."* I had become more fascinated with them after meeting Croft, finding myself watching the motion as he did. Croft's lips especially.

Flashes of Shadowstone hit. Touching the White stone. Answering the queen. Then in my room a day later, searching a flower book for a name. *"Sielle has a beautiful name."*

"Sielle?" Croft's voice entered my head just as Wolfsbane released his hold of my stone.

My heart launched into a wild, panicked rhythm, and I forced myself to breathe slowly, steadily, even though my body screamed for me to take large gulps. Wolfsbane had spoken her name. The only good thing was that he'd heard it from my own thoughts after the White stone reading. He hadn't seen our interaction, hadn't heard her speak. My emotions were a mess, unsure how to process everything. Relief and worry tumbled together in equal measure with no clear victor.

Wolfsbane's eyes fell to me as he stood, then he glanced up at the king and gave a single nod.

I was cleared to continue on. Cleared. The knowledge did nothing to calm me because he'd learned entirely too much. He had to have seen all that I had, and that meant he might piece things together.

Croft and Argo moved behind me, and my focus shifted again. Croft lifted a new dagger from his belt and sliced into Nettle's finger.

Sielle. He'd repeated her name, obviously following along with the readings by watching Wolfsbane's mouth. He knew the name, was surprised to hear it from me. He knew her.

Wolfsbane continued on with Net, unbothered by what he'd seen in me. *"There are so many people here. These pants are too tight. They're chafing my ass."*

The crowd exploded into laughter, and Net simply shrugged while somewhat entranced, accepting all of it without dismay.

The entire royal family was laughing behind us. The king struggled as he said, "Someone please see to his wardrobe later."

"I have to find the handsome stable attendant again. I wouldn't mind a position in White stone division. I have to see the Black stone mirror."

A hush settled as Wolfsbane released his hold and stood. The only Black stones remaining were said to be held inside the castle. And the Queen's Mirror was one used by the first queen, the one who started the Garden, promised our safety for servitude, and also rumored to have trapped a Lovely inside a Black stone before her death. We'd learned about it in our lessons, but I always thought it to be a story exaggerated through time like so many others had, something used for a child's cautionary tale about stone addiction over a history lesson.

A murmur rose over the crowd, which was almost completely silhouetted by the dwindling sunlight behind them. Evidently, they'd learned the same story, or a variation at least.

After a single nod, Wolfsbane shifted over to the final place, ignoring the whispers.

Inside another moment, he was seated and placing his hands upon the stone in front of Larkspur.

"Too many thoughts. Think, but don't think too much."

"Off to a fabulous start," the king said blandly, livening the mood and drawing chuckles from the crowd again.

"Smoke division. I want it. Need to start. Desires are incredible. Tempting. And fears. The pain in the reactions. I want to make them beg—"

Wolfsbane disconnected with a jolt and stood.

Larkspur was panting loud enough for me to hear him two places down. I glanced past the back of Net's head to see him. Little drops of sweat shimmered on his forehead. And his expression ... it was one of terror, the look I'd seen so many times on a guilty person's face.

"No, no, it's not what you think," he pleaded low enough for only the table to hear.

Instead of a single nod, Wolfsbane's eyes lifted from him to the king, his head shaking once.

Attendants moved in from this side, took hold of Larkspur's arms, and escorted him toward the castle. He complied, seeming in disbelief as his eyes darted in all directions, looking for help or reason.

"Well, these things sometimes happen," the king announced, taking immediate control of the uneasy situation. "He is deemed unfit to continue in the kingdom's service here. His thoughts are too volatile and hold possible addiction in how the stones and Realm make him feel during sessions. We simply cannot allow any Lovely behaving in such a way to represent this kingdom in any capacity. While this doesn't happen often, the queen will see to it that he is handled accordingly, given help if needed before being released to his prior Guardian for further care. Our priority is our people.

"Now that we've finished the initial readings, we will move on." He clapped twice, but I didn't dare turn to view him completely. After what happened, I didn't want to face any of the royals or the rest of the Lovely. It all seemed too real, too raw. I'd seen enough guilty people and deeds to last a lifetime, but none had been a Lovely. Net grimaced in my direction, seeking my reaction. I lifted my painted eyebrows with a small frown before promptly looking forward again.

Four soldiers of the king's army, wearing black battle leathers, decorative silver armor plating along their chests and shoulders, and short swords at their sides, walked up the center aisle of the crowd, each holding a lead of a collared wolfdog. They looked nothing like Argo except in their tall, broad builds. While his coat hair was short and smoothed over his muscular frame, these had thick, scraggly lengths of fur with mixed coloring of slate gray, black, and chestnut brown. The breed was the product of a shepherd dog and wolf mixed together. The Crown raised and trained them through the years, using them for patrol and battle missions.

As each soldier and wolfdog took a position in front of our table, facing the crowd, eight attendants came from the pathway of the castle, half carrying spheres within their gloved hands. All moved to our settings from the front, and after the empty-handed ones took possession of the Cloud stones, the others placed the new spheres upon the small stands. The polished stones resembled the darkening night sky, a coloring of blue-black with a continual streak of hazy light upon the surface as if the moon's reflection were ever-present.

Wolfsbane—now at our backs—cleared his throat. "It's an honor to enter the Realm in any capacity, but being granted access into a living being's mind is a privilege not to be taken lightly. And what's more, with an Eye stone, it's not simply looking through one's mind to recall information. This stone allows us to take over control completely. As most of you know, it mainly works with mammals of a certain intellect."

"So no flies on walls or snakes in the grass." The prince was the one to chime in this time, his voice more jovial than dry as the king's had mostly been.

"No, but perhaps mice in holes," the princess added in, sounding as though it were a reminder and not a game.

Grumbles of both displeasure and intrigue rose up from the people.

"This is true," Wolfsbane admitted. "And that's why the use of this stone is limited for specific duties and purposes, such as essential missions for the kingdom, in war or peace, and in ceremonies such as this, to test connections of our new members. The four here have already proven themselves capable members of the Garden and have made their vows to the Crown and kingdom. They will be given their division assignments soon after this test, so let us see if they will take on another stone ability."

A different attendant walked to the wolfdog in front of Hellebore first. She drew a small dagger and nicked a place above the collar while the soldier maintained his lead. The well-trained canine sat on its haunches without movement, without a sound.

The attendant then took a cloth to collect the blood and carefully wiped it along the stone's surface.

Hellebore glanced over his shoulder just as the king said, "Proceed."

With shaky hands, Hellebore reached out and took hold of the sides, only to deflate when nothing happened.

Instead of walking to the next in line, she skipped over Amaryllis and me both, and stopped at Net's wolfdog and soldier to repeat the process. I wasn't sure what to think of that. Boys first? Then I remembered I was the only one to connect with the rest. I was being saved for last. The induction culmination. No pressure.

Having heard the king's mild impatience before, Net didn't look at anyone before taking hold of the stone.

The canine on the lead shook its head, then gave a loud bark.

"Excellent." The king's tone lightened, sounding pleased. "Now for a little fun, yes? There are a few things hidden among the guests tonight. The handler will walk to the back of the crowd and give Nettle his orders. Please stay in your place and don't ruin the fun."

The soldier moved with the lead, struggling to get the canine—Net—to follow. He spun and jumped, then tugged at the end, not listening. Then the soldier bent and spoke, and Net's actions instantly changed. I was willing to bet that he had reminded him of the royals and what might happen should he get too rowdy.

His eager behavior made me smile, though. Excitement bubbled inside as I considered for the first true time the possibility of connecting to the Eye stone too. Ivy had shown such happiness after she had, and I knew I would as well.

They walked down the edge of a main garden pathway, farthest from the castle. Net stopped a couple times, his nose pressed firmly into the packed dirt bordering the cobbled stone. They disappeared behind all the standing bodies. After several moments, Net broke through the people, nosing around all of them. There were yelps of protest from some unprepared people as he bumped against their limbs or shoved his snout to their rear ends.

Along with the rest of the crowd, the royals and Lovely were all chuckling, clearly enjoying all the entertainment as well.

Net barged his way in and out of the rows without care and finally found what he was seeking. His sleek body dove beneath a chair and pitched upward, throwing the gentleman seated there to the ground. He sprinted toward the garden entrance, then stopped alongside the row of massive pots lining the castle walkway and proceeded to pee on one. Then he continued on, leaping onto the garden wall lower platform to Wolfsbane, extending whatever was clenched inside his mouth.

This time, I had turned to watch the progress. The din of voices and laughter was so loud, Wolfsbane didn't speak as he held the leather pouch aloft then opened it up to reveal a small cut of meat. As the noise quieted, he said, "That's all, Lovely."

A pitched whine came from the wolfdog. A moment later, the wolfdog sat back calmly, watching Wolfsbane. "Good, Shadow." The treat was given just as the soldier appeared to collect him.

At the same time, Net's head shook at my side, then he promptly leaned over and retched onto the ground. I leaned away, grateful that he hadn't been facing me.

"Wolf forgot to mention that the Eye stone can be disorienting," the king said dryly. "And you will be cleaning the piss off the queen's garden pot yourself."

Net sat upright again, wavering a bit. Although he appeared ill and unfocused, a smile curved his lips.

Through the years, many living
beings have been tested with the Eye stone.
While some avians are susceptible to Realm influence,
only mammals are able to endure the rigorous strain
in the mental capacity required for the bond.
Those with proven logical skills fair the best.
- Anhedral Kingdom Lovely Guidebook

~ 13 ~

The attendant passed me again, stopping in front of Amaryllis, and I knew I'd been correct.

They held me for last. The induction grand finale if I were to connect. Nausea bubbled in my gut and sweat formed along my palms and forehead. This was like a fever dream.

Blood from another wolfdog was collected and smeared, and then Amaryllis reached forward. As soon as she touched the stone, she let out an angered groan.

"Easy now," the queen said, finally speaking. "Don't forget your place."

If anyone else found it odd that she had only now spoken, no one said a thing. She was in charge of the Lovely, but I supposed that never superseded the king's authority.

Amaryllis had the good sense to look chagrined. Even though night had settled in, attendants had already made their rounds during the events, lighting the numerous lanterns and metal fire basins along the perimeter of the castle and walkways. The blotchy flush in her cheeks could be seen clearly enough.

While the other soldiers and wolfdogs filed out, leaving one pair remaining in front of my place, something had me seeking out Croft and Argo. I wanted to know they were there, close. Maybe because I needed someone with me, despite the connection. Begonia and Clem were in attendance too, somewhere at the back, mixed in with the Clear stone division. And that helped a little, soothing my unease even if they didn't care at all about me or the induction. It still wasn't enough, though.

For the first time in a long time, I needed someone.

Croft and Argo had positioned themselves behind the far end of the table, just below the entrance platform. I didn't have to turn around completely, only twist my head and peer over a shoulder to see the ripples of light and shadows dancing over their still bodies. The simple view of them calmed my breaths. Croft had been studying the crowd, but at my movement, his focus changed. Those amber eyes almost glowed in the firelight, the depth of them enthralling. Even through the expectant, sweeping silence of the crowd, I couldn't hear him. I wanted to, especially after he'd repeated Sielle's name.

The attendant moved a few steps, stifling my wandering thoughts. I closed my eyes and inhaled, blocking everything and everyone out, needing to find balance before a possible connection. My mind had to be as clear as possible, my focus on the link between me, the stone, the Realm, and the wolfdog.

As soon as I opened them, she had nicked the back of the canine's neck for its blood.

Like the others, there was no announcement or preparatory speech this time. She smeared the blood over the blue stone and stepped away. I leaned in close, watching the streak of light stretch and shift with my movement. Along with the usual pull in energy, the visual movement brought its purpose to life, making it the most alluring of all the stones. Splaying and lifting my hands, I reached forward and took hold.

There was a surge inside my body, stretching then contracting. Like the lesser stones, I couldn't see the transfer or navigate the connection. Everything had been dark as it occurred. And suddenly, a soft whine rose in my chest before my vision cleared, revealing a soldier's pant leg and an applauding, seated crowd.

"It's official. We have another to add to the prestigious class of Lovely who have connected with all viable stones. Oleander! Now, let us see what she's capable of inside one of our finest and have a little fun too. Just not as much as Nettle, hopefully."

The laughter blasted into my sensitive ears, which twisted in all directions, trying to decipher information from all angles. It was altogether strange being inside something other than human. My skin itched, my body warm, my vision somewhat bright despite the darkness. All colors had muted, some turning gray completely. I also had to pee, immediately making me understand why Nettle had relieved himself—or rather, the canine. My nose acted freely, sniffing the air for information and separating it all into groups in my mind. There wasn't much of a struggle to distinguish what the sounds and smells were so far as if the link between us could decipher the differences and render them recognizable to me, which was a pleasant surprise.

"We're following the same path." The soldier leaned over to speak to me, his voice commanding and familiar even though I'd never met him before. "I will give your order and cut you loose at the back. Let's go."

And so we did. My legs shuddered some, adjusting to walking on four legs instead of two. I stared at the ground, step, step, stepping. Several paces later, we turned the corner at the pathway and different scents hit my nose, unlike most others hovering around the induction ceremony and all the people.

It was subtle at first, quelled due to distance and something else. My nose twitched, eager to find whatever it had locked onto, eager to solve the mystery. When we closed the distance, I realized why they weren't so clear. They were buried under the soil along the pathway. It was exactly where Nettle had stopped briefly too. Hints of leather came first, with other smells inside.

Stones. There were stones buried below, wrapped in leather pouches, like the one secured to the soldier's belt. They held their own specific scent that I could distinguish, the link inside my mind connecting them to what I hadn't been able to smell as a human and adding more from what the wolfdog had already known as well. It was potent, though, as if they'd been ground into powder.

I reached out, a single paw scraping at the ground where another print had been. It was a spot where Net had stopped for sure, with a lingering straw scent of the other wolfdog I inherently knew to be a brother of my own. The smell from below, though, was seawater, salty and crisp. Clear stone.

I wasn't told to dig, and I wouldn't have had time anyway because we had barely stopped, only slowed. The next came. Cloud. Another Net stopped for. Fresh like rainy cold air in Shadowstone. And with another step, it was Smoke. More potent than from the blazing fire bowls, with a sleepy, dense fireplace smell that would make most eyes water. My nose dipped closer to the soil in another spot, discovering something warm and spicy, like seasoning on dinner but sharp like ... Needled.

Continuing on the path, we could have been finished. But more scents came halfway down, about where the rows of seats ended. I hadn't seen Net stop later because I'd been seated. I glanced backward, still able to see the garden entrance platforms and all the royals and Lovely there. The king had remained standing.

White might have been difficult had it been buried in the center of a forest. Luckily, the woodsy plant smells were strong enough to decipher through the dirt. A paw spot there and another a few steps down showed where Net had also touched. Eye stone. Musky and pungent, not unlike a matted alpaca in need of a bath.

I choked, a gruff hacking sound exiting my open mouth as we walked on. A floral smell hit my nose next, much to my relief. I hadn't seen or touched the Black stone, but it had to be part of one. It was delicately sweet, much like the many fragrant pots of flowers placed throughout the castle, only more powerful.

The soldier kept moving, encouraging me on. I went along several more paces until another stench hit me harshly, demanding my attention. My neck pulled to the side as the lead yanked the collar at my throat. The soldier stared down at me, irritated at my sudden disobedience. I ignored him, dipped my head, and crouched to the side of the path, my nose leading the way again, following the new stinging metallic smell of iron and rust. The odor bit into the inside of my nose. It was as if a decaying iron box or chain had been buried inside a leather pouch.

I moved on, realizing a few steps later what it could mean. There had been two more inside the leather like the other stones. Two I hadn't known. Two, not one. But there was only Black remaining.

"All right. I'm releasing you now," the soldier said, unhooking the collar. "There are hidden items with closely related scents to confuse you. Your order is to seek out the one that smells of black powder. It doesn't matter if you've never smelled cannon fire or a musket shot. Arjun—the wolfdog—knows. That should mean that you do as well."

I opened my mouth to tell him it had already happened, and I actually said, "Bark bark ruff."

His dark eyebrows lifted. "Right, well ... Off you go."

And I went, weaving into the standing crowd, trying hard to tune out the loud chatter and excited pitchy screams from the younger Clear stone Lovely. Before I set off on the main goal, I recognized a few other smells and pushed through the bodies with purpose, finding what I wanted right away.

Begonia and Clem. They no longer smelled of Shadowstone's crisp mountain air and wet mud, but whatever had been natural to them called to me nonetheless. Mixed within the center of so many others at far taller heights, they couldn't have been able to see anything. I bounced excitedly and nudged into Clem first, making him chuckle before his hand came down on my back for a swift pat. I did the same to Begonia once, hearing her protest softly among the laughs and cheers. Stopping with a quick glance upward, the hesitant lift at the corners of her lips was plain enough for me to see.

The thrill from that alone had me overjoyed. As I took off, weaving through the people, sprinting along the outside rows at some points, my joy turned into exhilaration and then appreciation and respect for all dogs and their abilities. All my other Realm connections had been filled with negative emotions. Even the lighthearted vanity readings about love interests or family life had been mostly rooted in anger, jealousy, or dismay. Within the White stone, I'd been pensive. This was the first true time I'd been able to experience elation inside the Realm.

A coal smell had my nose to the ground, only to abandon, knowing it was pure. Then there was a whiff of sulfur with a spoiled taint, which had to be a rotten egg. Finally, toward the very front, I picked up on the definite mix of black powder. Locating the spot, I lifted my head, looking past the last few rows of seated people at the table, where my body sat utterly still, a shell unprotected. Though it was a usual occurrence, we rarely saw it. This time was different than the White stone too, in that I wasn't floating closely above but completely free of my body. It made me pause, realizing the detriment of physical distance more than ever.

Shaking myself, I refocused and began to dig. The powder had been contained inside a usual rifle pouch. I grabbed hold and leaped into a run.

Everyone was cheering again, but my eyes and ears were set on the king, who was on his feet again, beckoning me to him with a wave of his hand. Not Wolf.

"Excellent. Excellent." The king's voice quieted everyone else.

The other royals and the Lovely had remained seated but were applauding like the crowd. I was grateful for the different body, unsure how I'd handle such praise being so close to all of them.

The king grabbed hold of the pouch, took an exaggerated look inside to confirm the contents, then held it aloft. His voice lowered. "Well done, Oleander. I will have a meeting with you soon for special discussions, but you will report to Wolfsbane tomorrow for your assignment briefing. For now"—his voice rose again—"enjoy the evening ball with everyone else ... after you free the wolfdog and allow yourself a small respite, of course."

Without the pouch of black powder beneath my nose, that same bitter stench from the soil spot drifted to me. Metallic. Decay. I was too far from the spot, so there was no way the scent spanned the distance. It was physically closer. My head swung around as I sniffed, but it was difficult to determine the source. I moved a few paces to the side of the platform wall where attendants were gathered with food trays and drink carafes, losing the scent.

"No sense dawdling, Oleander. You'll have plenty more time in the Eye stone soon," the king said, his high spirits continuing as he lifted a silver eyebrow at me and took his seat again. He beckoned to the attendants gathered near the slate steps and more near the castle. "Bring the wine! Let us all toast to the night and to our new Garden members!"

I turned, peering down at my motionless physical body, then at Croft and Argo still in the same place they'd been. Croft's eyes were already on me, nowhere else, as if waiting for me to leave the wolfdog. He'd been watching the king, following along with what he'd said. As I readied myself to disconnect, I caught another smell. From the ground step, Imogen handed two carafes to another female attendant behind me on the lower platform. As she took hold, I instantly stiffened.

Imogen remained in the same spot, her eyes blinking rapidly. She shook her head and glanced around, appearing dazed.

The scent hadn't registered to me right away, but the wolfdog knew it, had been trained to detect it. And in its mind, it was deadly.

Without another thought, I turned and leaped into the air, colliding with the attendant pouring the wine into the queen's goblet. Chaos erupted as the wine sprayed all over the royals.

Screams echoed around the grounds. Everyone's eyes were on me, angry and hostile. Croft and Argo were at my side in an instant, standing just ahead. Guards rushed forward with swords drawn, while the soldiers climbed onto the platform too, their wolfdogs immediately sniffing the remnants, then each sitting and looking at their handlers.

"Your Majesty?" Wolfsbane's voice broke through the screams.

King Antin's eyes widened as he stood and dropped his silver goblet. It smashed against the slate-covered platform and clanged into the now silent air. He grabbed his throat. "Wolf. Who? Who?"

Queen Reina shrieked, lunging forward as the king's knees buckled and he began to cough and sputter.

Falling alongside her mother, Princess Naomi called out, "For Realm's sake, someone get the doctor!"

"Wolf!" the prince screamed, eyes frantically taking in all the people. "I want whoever did this found! Soldiers and guards, lock the castle down. Gather everyone out here. All Lovely are to be on duty. Everyone will be read. I don't care how long it takes!"

My focus shifted to Imogen, who hadn't moved during it all. Her body stood utterly still as she took in the surroundings.

Croft noticed my attention, and Wolf had as well. "You saw?" the latter asked.

I dipped my head with a pitiful whine in reply. It was the truth, but ... Something was off.

Wolf moved swiftly, telling the closest guard and soldier to take Imogen into custody. "She's priority. Lock her alone. No one speaks with her until His Royal Highness or I say so."

A wail came from the queen and the entire courtyard went eerily silent. All the canines seemed to understand immediately, releasing soft yips, then longer, mournful howls. Even Argo.

Wolf leaned down closer to my ears, and I could smell the salty tears on his cheeks. "Change now, Oleander. You've done well, but you won't be of use to us anymore tonight. Croft will see you back to your rooms."

A moment after, as soon as I could focus, I was back inside my body. Reentering myself was disorientating, my senses readjusting with a dizzying effect. It was manageable, but that didn't matter. Combined with everything else, I still had to drop to my knees under the table and retch.

Any discovery of a Blood stone, whether
whole or in pieces, requires immediate disclosure
and surrender. If found in possession without cause,
the offense is punishable under Crown law.
- Anhedral Kingdom Lovely Laws and Customs

14

A pounding sound woke me. Three hard knocks exploded through the dark, silent room. Ivy lay snuggled into my side, having climbed into bed with me during the night. She'd been asleep in her own room when Croft, Argo, and I had returned, with a guard posted outside in the hall since she'd been alone. The shock of what had happened, plus being physically exhausted after my first connection to the Eye stone, had stolen all my energy. There was so much I needed to consider, but I couldn't even process my thoughts correctly. Wolf had been right. I would have collapsed where I'd stood had I stayed in the courtyard any longer.

I rolled the six-year-old over to free myself from the bed, then moved into the main room, finding Croft asleep on the long settee in front of the fireplace. Argo, already alert, had used his head to nudge Croft's shoulder. I watched the exchange in the soft glow of ember light, wondering if I should wake him. He must have decided resting in the main room was better than behind another door.

His choices didn't go unnoticed. They made me curious if anyone else saw the same thoughtfulness, if his courteous actions extended past the usual duty requirements.

"Please let me in," a voice spoke lowly from outside, far weaker than the knocks it followed.

Prince Ren's voice. The new king.

Croft sat upright, unfocused eyes landing on Argo first in understanding before his face turned to me. He still wore his nicer attendant clothing, though the black shirt was unbuttoned and heavily wrinkled by sleep. The dying embers of the fire gave his skin a warm glow, also lightening the strands of loose hair along the sides of his head.

I cleared my throat and spoke while pointing to the door. "The ... king, I think. He's asking to come in."

His eyes widened, and he stood with a nod. *"All right."*

I moved to answer, checking over my thin nightdress, only then realizing I'd been standing in front of Croft in the same thin material.

As soon as I opened the way, King Ren staggered inside, his body losing support from the door.

"Olean. I ..." He walked right into me, his weight and momentum strong enough to force a few backward steps. His arms engulfed me immediately, his face burrowing into my neck. I felt the wetness along his cheeks before feeling the vibration of his chest and shoulders.

He sobbed against me, and I was a statue, unsure what to do.

"Whoa." Croft had redone his shirt and had moved to our side.

I stared into his eyes, seeing the emotion there, knowing that while he was only a castle attendant, he had been here long enough to hold empathy for the royal family, possibly even deeper feelings.

"He's gone. He's gone." King Ren's words pitched and dropped inside his breaths, and I knew he hadn't had any sleep since the late king's death.

My hands lifted around his back, patting him gently there, hoping to give some comfort. "I'm so sorry."

"You saw. You saved us. Whoever did it … it was meant for us all. Thank you. Thank you."

There was no appropriate way to respond given his father had just died. I hadn't been fast enough to save him, but I wasn't about to add my own regrets to his grief.

His body shifted, his mouth too. Hands slid down my back, lower and lower, arms tightening their hold. My eyes snapped wide when his lips met my neck, kissing my skin there gently, then licking.

"What is he doing?!" Croft's eyes met mine as my body stiffened.

"Your High—Majesty." My plea came out strangled.

As I wiggled in his hold in an attempt to push away, Croft stepped in, tugging the new king back, freeing my body from his. *"No."*

"Sorry. Oh, Realm, I'm sorry," the king mumbled, his eyes wide as they flitted between Croft and me. "I'm not sure what I … I thought you were … But Nightshade is gone too. I couldn't sleep. I didn't have anyone … to see or talk to," he rambled on, trying to apologize, to explain.

"I understand," I admitted, having seen enough grief and loss through the stones to know most weren't of sound mind after such a loss, especially if they hadn't slept and had had too much wine to drink. I had a feeling he was being honest, that he wouldn't try anything again. So I pushed past the uncomfortable incident. "You can stay ... if you'd like. Sit. Maybe we can have some tea?" I took a seat, and he followed without protest.

Croft watched me closely, lips pressed together tightly, jaw clenched. *"Mmggrrr."*

That wasn't a word. Had he growled in his mind? My eyes widened, but I was quick to correct my expression.

Croft's eyes narrowed a bit, then he nodded once and turned to the fireplace to stoke the fire and placed the kettle inside.

King Ren sat silent for a few moments, elbows on knees, head hanging down. He lifted up and rested his chin on his folded hands. "I don't know what to do. I'm not supposed to be ... king. It's too soon. There's too much to know, to learn. If I were more confident in Naomi's abilities to rule, and not her lusting for a taste of power, I'd probably abdicate."

"Abdicate and hand rule to Naomi? No. You can do far better than her, and him as well if you learn from his mistakes. There were enough." Croft continued with the fire but kept moving his eyes to us, following along with the conversation.

Croft's words were coming in longer strings and clearer than ever. Perhaps it had less to do with the connection between us and more about his personality. He might ordinarily be less expressive, considered a quiet type whether vocal or not. His comfort around me could have changed given our living situation, or the night's events had disarmed us all.

"This place is falling apart, even before the deaths. My father was obsessed with finding a Blood stone. Spent so much time and money, killed towns by digging away the foundations, collecting any stones left within the ground to be sure no one else had access. I think whoever the traitor is knew his priorities were skewed. And they're still out there, creating dissension ... maybe a revolt. Killing ... Oh, Realm. They killed him. They killed him." He dropped his face into his hands and wept.

I laid a hand on his back and rubbed a circle. My eyes were on Croft, who retrieved the room drink cart and began preparing tea. He had Argo sniff everything thoroughly—the leaves, strainer, and all the settings and silver. Argo finished and lay down closer to the fireplace, still on guard.

"The late king pulled too many back from the borders, even after hearing threats. He was neglectful. Was ... Now ... Queen Reina and council advisers along with Lovely will aid the new king until his official coronation, whenever that may be. But will they move quickly enough to prevent further problems? Will they find if this was connected to the other poisonings? I should discuss with Wolf."

His lengthy thoughts had me entranced. He wasn't simply an attendant at all. He had paid close attention, likely in a good portion of the king's meetings, the prince's, and others as well. I had no doubt about the knowledge he held. It was no wonder they considered him so valuable, especially with his mind being blocked from Lovely access.

Croft served the cups of tea, and I lifted mine under my lips, still staring at him. "Thank you."

He nodded once as he placed the other on the tea table in front of the king.

"Please drink some," I said after a sip of the calming lavender and mint. "It might help you rest."

He did, lifting it for a temperature test at his lips, then drinking it down in one gulp. In a placid, almost disassociated tone, he said, "Wolf told me you pointed out Imogen while using the Eye stone."

"Yes."

"They are holding her tonight, and anyone else they were unable to read right away. I'm not certain when we will question her, but I would like you to be there."

"Of course."

"Croft." The king placed his cup down, seeming more in control than when he'd entered. "Thank you too. You are to stay with Olean, only leave her when told to by myself or Wolf. I can't seem to trust anyone else right now, not until they've been cleared."

Croft nodded.

"Olean? Croft?" Ivy's voice came from my doorway. She peered out at us, rubbing her eyes.

"Yes, Ivy. I'll be there in a moment," I replied.

"Oh, well ..." King Ren stood, adjusting his shirt, still a little unsteady on his feet. "I should ... get back. I'm sorry again for ..." He motioned absently toward the center of the room, embarrassed by his previous actions. "And I will see you both soon."

Croft walked with him to the door, making small hand gestures toward where the guard was posted outside.

"Ivy, go back and lie down, yes?" I asked, seeing her in the doorway watching. "I promise, I'll be in there soon."

"All right," she conceded and disappeared inside the dark room again.

I moved the tea things back onto the cart and pushed it to the side wall.

Croft closed the main door and approached, pointing to me and moving his lips. *"Are you all right?"*

It was the first time I'd seen his lips move to assist with communication. I stared for longer than I should have because he took another step forward, seeming concerned. At last, I sputtered, "Uh, about ... the new king? Yes, sure, I'm all right."

He waited a moment as if deciding to believe me or not, then nodded and pointed to himself and the cart, and finally to my room. *"I'll get the rest. Go to sleep."*

There were thoughts I needed to share that couldn't wait, so I held up a hand for a moment to draw his attention back. "I need to talk to you, tell you some things."

He let go of the cart as he focused on my lips.

My eyes fell to the ground, unsure how to start and what to tell him. I needed to confide in someone, and he was who I trusted the most. His feet were bare like mine, and I wasn't sure why, but it felt more intimate than when I'd stood less clothed with Jonah. It took me another moment to lift my eyes to him again, curbing the tiny smile that wanted to form on my lips.

His lips twitched, and he lifted an eyebrow, a single one, in question. The shape of it, with the jut of his heavy brow line, had my mind shifting thoughts again, recalling something from before. A single eyebrow lift ... It made me think of the silver one that had lifted at me only hours ago, following the test. The late king's eyebrow.

Croft pointed four spread fingers upward on one hand, tapping the first in the straight line to his chin. *"Talk?"*

The vision of the late king had my thoughts scrambled again. I tried to concentrate. "Yes. I trust you. And I know maybe I shouldn't trust anyone. At least that was what Cordelia told me before I left, that I shouldn't even trust the Lovely that I don't—"

Croft's fingertips touched my jaw, turning my chin back toward him. I hadn't even realized I'd looked away. Nervousness had crept in and made me ramble through the words.

The touch of his hand, the warmth from the contact of his skin to mine, traveled down my neck and made the rest of my body shiver. He had moved closer, close enough that his head had tipped down some as he stared at me. Those captivating eyes, like delicious honey, flicked between my mouth and eyes.

"Sorry I turned away from you. I'm just ..." I licked my lips and saw the moment he noticed.

His hand dropped from my chin. He backed away a step, and his lips pinched together. *"Too close. What am I doing?"*

"No, no, it's not about you. Oh, I'm making a mess of this." A chuckle burst from me before I wiped my palms down my face. I made sure to look right at him as I started again. "I shouldn't trust anyone here, but I feel like I can trust you. And I really need someone to confide in. Something isn't right about the king's death. Especially with Imogen. She looked confused after. Unfocused. Like she didn't even know what she'd done."

He thought my words over, then he mouthed the words and thought them, *"Maybe not."*

"It's possible. And I suppose they'll determine more from her reading. But I have the strangest feeling she wasn't in control of herself." There. I'd admitted it out loud. He might not believe me, but it needed to be said. All the pieces had connected for me, and I couldn't simply deny them or forget. This had to be investigated.

His eyebrows lifted. *"Blood stone?"*

There was no way I'd admit to hearing him yet. Telling him about that would have to be an entirely different conversation.

First, I needed him to believe this, if even a little bit, because after learning about his thoughts, he may never want to be near me again.

"If you're thinking Blood stone, that is exactly what I mean. I know it's said to be gone, but ... The first night I arrived, Imogen brought dinner, remember?"

He nodded and waited for me to go on.

"Before you had Argo check the food, she paused a few moments. She got this blank look in her eyes, like she disappeared in those seconds. Then she blinked a lot, refocusing. I asked her if she was all right and she said that she'd been getting headaches. At the induction, after I'd noticed she'd been the one to hand the other attendant the wine then smelled it and knocked her over, I looked back at Imogen. She hadn't moved at all. She stared straight ahead like she didn't know what was happening."

His gaze was intent on me, taking my words in, considering it all.

"There's more, though. King Ren just told us how focused the late king was on finding the Blood stone, and that made me realize what happened last night. There was more to the Eye stone test than what everyone witnessed. After the soldier led us to the pathway, I believe there was another hidden test that maybe the king only knew, perhaps someone else too, but he knew about it for sure. There were stones or fragments of them buried under the soil, each contained inside a leather pouch. We weren't meant to dig them up since we weren't told to do so, but because we were in the wolfdogs and could smell scents more clearly, we identified them out of curiosity. The king watched."

"I saw that too." Croft nodded and moved a hand in a pawing motion.

"Yes. It wasn't random smells. At first, I thought it was only ones I'd seen and connected with before. But then, I got to the end, or what I thought was the end stone. It smelled like flowers, so I assumed it was the Black stone, even though I've never seen one in person or connected with it. That should have been the last one. Several paces later, away from the others, there was one more. It had a sharp metallic scent, like rusty iron, with a foulness of decay. I didn't focus on it much, assumed it could be something else buried there inside leather. Then, after I was up on the platform and the king had taken the black powder from me, I smelled it again. I couldn't locate the source, but it had to have been a Lovely. No guards, attendants, or soldiers were close enough. That was right before everything happened."

I let out a long breath, relieved to have told him.

Croft stared at me, his expression so intense I prepared myself for a rebuttal or a rejection.

Instead, he inhaled deeply and let out his own lengthy breath with a nod. Processing it some more, he walked toward the fireplace. As he looked around, he stabbed his fingers into his hair to brush it back, then moved a hand to his jaw, scratching the scruff there.

I waited, watching him think, unsure what else I could say.

After a glance at me, he disappeared into his room. He returned a moment later with a paper and ink pen, sat on the settee, and used the tea table to write. *Wolfsbane can be trusted. Him alone. He was the king's closest ally and knows that there was more involved with the others' deaths and disappearances. I'll be with you when you speak to him.*

He handed the paper over, and I took a seat at his side and read what I'd already heard him think. I touched my fingers to my mouth, then stared into his eyes. Despite all the dread of having to discuss this more and find whoever killed the king, the relief of having him believe and support me was overwhelming. I choked back a sob and let my hand fall to my lap. "Thank you for believing me, for helping."

His hand reached out, covering mine softly. He nodded. *"You're welcome."*

My affinity for him felt so real, so honest. And for the first time in my life, I felt as if someone could see me beyond being a Lovely. I wasn't naïve. Chances were good that he would have helped anyone else, but I did doubt the extent. There was something more between us, and I hoped it went beyond the connection from the White stone.

I looked down at our hands, and when he didn't immediately remove his, I smiled and looked up. "I should get back to Ivy. We all need sleep before tomorrow."

Then he did remove his hand, taking hold of the paper and tossing it into the fire as we stood. He nodded again and mouthed, *"Good night, Olean."*

"Good night, Croft."

When I entered my room, I glanced at him one more time, finding him watching as I closed the door.

Do not assume the Realm to be finite.
It presents differently for
stone classes, types, and sizes.
A Lovely's personal ability can also have an effect.
- Anhedral Kingdom Lovely Guidebook

15

Death and wolfdogs plagued my dreams, making for a fitful sleep that bled into a rough morning. Ivy had overheard too much during the new king's visit and knew the late king had been killed. Understandably, she hadn't wanted to attend lessons. After giving in to her demand of knowing the details from the induction while we ate breakfast, she hugged me, Croft, and Argo closely before going with Guardian Calla. As much as I didn't want to leave her, I knew she would be safe with the Guardian and other smaller children.

Overall, the castle's daily events seemed to be running along as usual. Attendants moved through the normal routines, though the number of guards and soldiers with wolfdogs had increased drastically. Croft led me to the south wing of the castle where the trial hall and most of the other reading rooms were located.

We found Wolfsbane inside the Eye stone division room along with Net and a few other Lovely. They all greeted us as we entered. Despite the other attendants being posted outside, waiting to escort their Lovely, Croft wasn't asked—nor did he offer—to remain in the hallway with Argo. No one said a thing, either knowing his position with the royals or afraid to question anything after the king's murder.

The Eye stone room was less than half the size of the Realm room. Darkened walls held numerous paintings and sketches of animal anatomy, displays of written scrolls listing attributes and weaknesses of each, and even some memorial plaquettes casted with replicated animals' portraits and their individual names.

"You have your assignments," Wolfsbane said to the room. "Report to your areas after dinner. If you're here, check in with me to see if we've moved on from guest readings. Now, go get some sleep."

All of them looked exhausted, with heavily bagged or drooping eyes, and their painted eyebrows now smeared from sweat and wear. They also still wore the previous night's clothing, including Net, though I noticed he had found a better fitting pair of pants.

He waved, keeping his hand low as he followed the others to the door. I replied with the same, feeling a closeness to him after testing together.

"We should walk," Wolfsbane said when it was only us remaining. His eyes were as bad as the others, no longer as bright and clear as they had been at induction.

We didn't speak until we exited the south side of the castle into the courtyard and walked to where the back of the induction crowd had been. I looked straight ahead at the garden entrance platforms. The grounds had already been cleaned of chairs and any mess caused by the ceremony. Anyone who hadn't been in attendance during the late king's death wouldn't have noticed a thing out of place. But despite the pristine topiaries and perfectly symmetrical outer pathways lined with flowers, it all appeared duller under the cheerful morning light.

As Wolfsbane stared on in silence, Croft and I turned away from the view with Argo happily sitting between us.

"He wasn't the greatest this kingdom has seen," Wolfsbane said, eyes still on the garden entrance. "His father was difficult to follow, having overcome war and garnering all the glory after. Antin had an easier reign. There are many things he could have done differently, but he did care for most of his people. We can hope the prince does better. It will be difficult. This is not the way anyone wishes to take the throne."

"No, surely not, Wolfsbane," I agreed, hearing Croft echo much of the same in his thoughts.

"You're welcome to call me Wolf," he said, turning to us and assessing me and my plain black house dress, more with curiosity than judgment.

I didn't wish to wear any of the fancy things in my closet and my old dress had been removed, so I chose the simplest available—a black single layer dress with silver bits of lacing around all the edges.

"The Cloud stone showed me some things last night," Wolf went on. "You were raised by Cordelia. I knew her years ago."

"And the late king? Did he know her well too?" I asked boldly, wanting to confirm my assumptions. He'd been with the king for years. He would know. And I couldn't ignore my curiosity.

"Yes." The word was somber. "The pendant you have was a gift to her. They were together once, though he was to be married to the princess of the Jewel Isles, an arrangement between the kingdoms after years of war. He loved his queen, but she was not his first love. Not long after the wedding, Cordelia was sent away to Shadowstone."

That had been much more than I'd expected. Hearing the rumors from the others at the induction, I had almost written their connection off as trivial, possibly holding a far deeper meaning to her than to him. But hearing Wolf's admission and knowing that Cordelia had only spoken of love to one person, it would mean that the baby she'd had was the king's. And if the timeline of her leaving was correct, she'd been pregnant before the king's wedding.

I debated sharing the truth, knowing that it was not my story to tell. But as I needed to be open with him in hopes that he would believe everything else, I decided it was better to share.

"She was sent after she had a child. The boy was dead at birth. Ivy's Name Day reading was of Cordelia with the Cloud stone. We all heard the memory of her labor before her mind collapsed into exhaustion."

Wolf's face seemed to pale. "I didn't know. The king didn't either. I would have seen … in all the years of his readings."

"That is tragic." Croft shook his head with the thought, crossing his arms over his chest. He'd been there too but had no idea of the connection.

"The Lovely aren't fertile." Wolf shook his head too, either in denial or surprise.

"We aren't supposed to be, no. I can tell you honestly that the queen hadn't reacted during the reading. It was like she had already known."

"She pushed for Cordelia to be relocated. She knew of their love, knew having her here in the kingdom wouldn't be good for her union."

We were all silent for a time, letting this information settle. Croft was who tapped Wolf's arm, drawing his attention.

"Yes, let's discuss last night." Wolf's gaze shifted to me. "I would like to know more about what transpired for you. So you're aware, you will be called soon for a reading in the trial hall for someone to confirm the accuracy of your memory of events. Was there more that you needed to share with me?"

I proceeded to relay all the details. Croft added what he could, but he hadn't chosen to bring paper, and I guessed that was as much for our safety as his own.

Wolf listened without interruption, nodding in certain instances. Finally, when I finished, he summarized, "You believe someone has a Blood stone, is capable of using it, and possibly used it on Imogen?"

"Yes."

"Hmm. I've known them all for years, trusted them. But after the recent events, I'd suspect anyone." He thought for a few more moments. "The stone burial test is true. Of course, it's only used on Eye stone capable Lovely, which means it happens less frequently at induction ceremonies as the other tests. The main stones are sometimes buried in different locations, and we never leave them there. Even though they're smaller stones, they're still to be protected. However, the remnants of the Blood stone have remained buried in the same place for years because it contains less than a finger worth of pebble and dust. Antin didn't want to raise suspicion should anyone keep tally on the number of bags and get too curious. No one has ever shown signs of locating it, not even the wolfdogs by themselves. Only a Lovely who might connect with the individual stones should have the ability to find them, and even then, only inside an animal with a superior sense of smell."

"So I was the only one to locate it?" I asked, hoping for a different answer.

"Yes. And I saw the king's reaction. It may not have been noticeable to anyone else, but that was always his focus. If the kingdom had a Lovely with a Blood stone ability ... Well ... he was determined to find a stone. As soon as that happened, he planned to let the world know."

"He wanted to meet with me soon," I offered, recalling the late king's words.

"Of course he did. The prince was right. The late king would have let more houses crumble, more lakes dry up, and wrecked more lands with mines if he had the Lovely to find and wield that stone. When you have the protection in place, the priority should be the people and the lands. There has to be balance." Croft's thoughts were angry. His passion for the kingdom and its people had me feeling mad too. How could a king be so single-minded?

I struggled with Croft's thoughts in my head, barely managing to listen to Wolf at the same time.

"Locating a stone would have been your primary assignment," he said flatly. "It didn't matter that we are in peace times. He wanted other kingdoms to fear the potential weapon, to ensure none would act aggressively for years to come. Having a Lovely with the ability to use a person's mind and body would ensure that. After last night, we can see why. If word of this were to spread ... There's no real way to know what could come to pass since we don't even know who's behind it. A Lovely of ours could be to blame, but are they working with someone else?"

I frowned at the realization. "They had to have known how valuable they would be to the king and that didn't matter to them.

That carafe was for all the royals to drink. Will they try again for the others too?"

"What about Imogen?" Croft moved his hands, and I realized Wolf understood some of his movements well enough.

"Imogen?" Wolf confirmed. After a nod from Croft, he said, "I believe she was questioned and read after the Lovely deaths and had no involvement, but she hasn't been read after last night. We had everyone possible on Cloud and Clear stones to sort and release all the guests first. We also cleared several attendants, soldiers, and guards, but not all. Many were held overnight. The Lovely are all on sleep and reading rotations, working through all who are left. So she will be read after more information is collected. Your reading will happen beforehand too, Olean." Wolf gave a nod, then looked toward the sun creeping higher into the sky.

"Do you think whoever did it knows I located the buried Blood stone?"

"Possibly," he admitted. "They could have been busy using the test as a distraction. Hard to know for certain. Hopefully, the other readings will give us more information."

"Hopefully before my reading too."

"Yes." He nodded. "It's better if this doesn't get around until we know more."

"Will you tell the new king?"

"No, not yet. It's a risk either way, but I think if he's told, the responsible Lovely might realize our awareness. Right now, they only know we suspect Imogen, which they should have accounted for already. They have to be Eye stone capable. That's nine of us now. Not including myself, or you and Nettle as new members, it narrows it down to six. Four in the main division you saw earlier—Titan, Wisteria, Azalea, and Yew. Then there's Hydrangea and Hemlock, the other stone class heads on the council aside from myself. We all have a higher influence, so they could have the reading delayed or try to manipulate who's assigned to the trial. I'll get as much information from the readings as possible. If I don't find you first, come to me soon."

"Oleander! There you are!" Kalmia yelled from across the pathway at the castle's back entrance. She grimaced when she noticed Wolf behind Croft. "Sorry, sorry. I was told to fetch her. Everyone else is tasked or sleeping at the moment and the dowager queen wants Olean for a White stone reading ... She's hoping to speak with the late king."

"Oh. All right," I sputtered, shocked.

Croft and Argo turned and started toward her, but before I could step away, Wolf touched my hand to halt me. He turned, purposely facing away from them.

"There was something else concerning inside your mind," he whispered. "You're connected with him somehow?"

My heart pounded so loudly that I had trouble hearing his last words. There was no reason to ask who he was referring to. "I, well ..." With a glance past Wolf, I noticed Croft had stopped to wait, watching us curiously. His hand patted Argo's head absently at his side.

"I'm not sure how, but I heard his voice in you. He isn't aware, is he?"

I shook my head, knowing there was no way to deny the truth.

"We like to think we know everything about the Realm and what it allows, but that's far from true. The Opaque stones are especially powerful, and not all of that power is beneficial. Be careful. I would suggest you sever that link soon because whatever I saw could be seen by others."

I nodded in agreement, but before I could turn away, he added, "And, Olean? You would be wise to tell him the truth and hope his kindness toward you keeps him from requesting a formal trial."

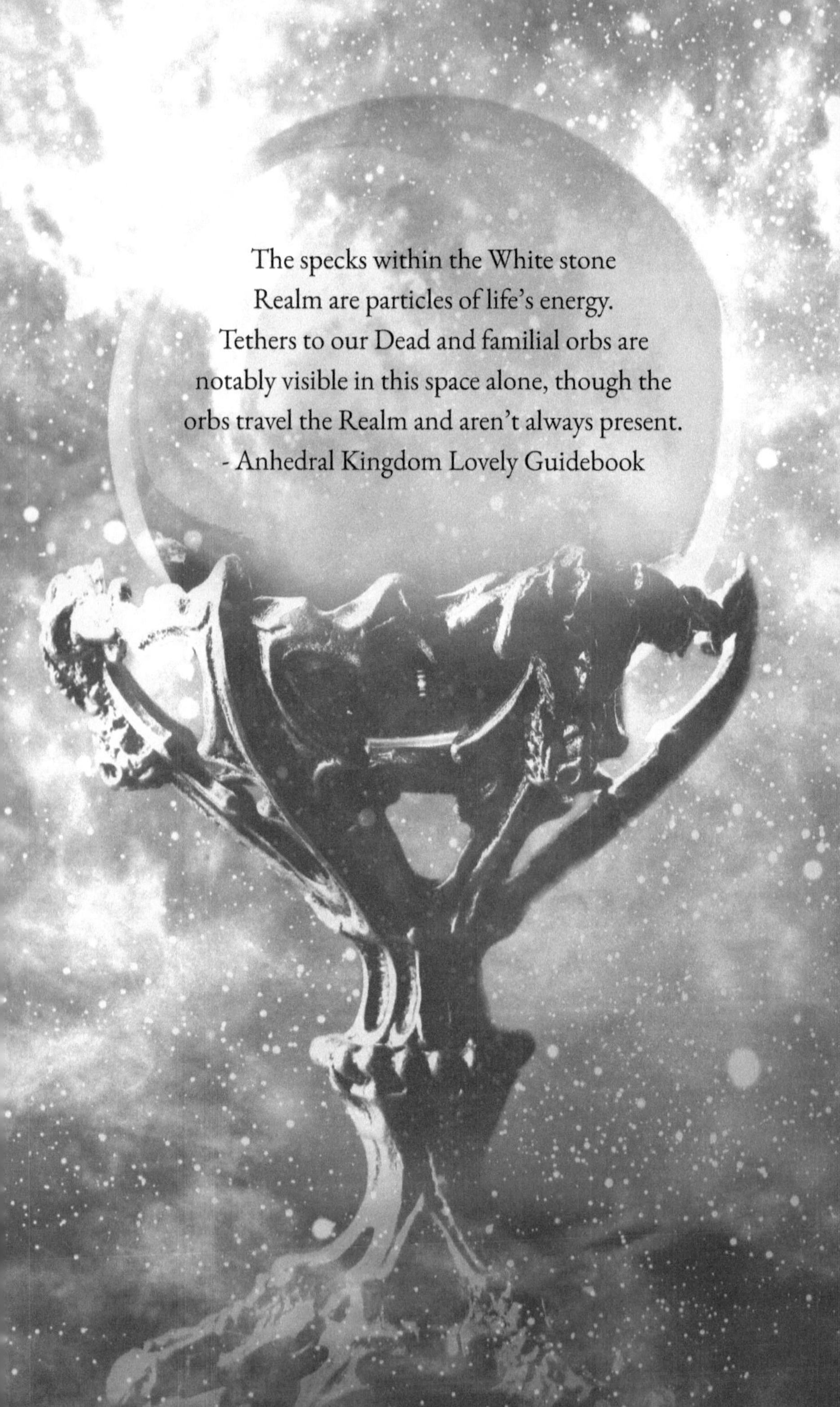
The specks within the White stone
Realm are particles of life's energy.
Tethers to our Dead and familial orbs are
notably visible in this space alone, though the
orbs travel the Realm and aren't always present.
- Anhedral Kingdom Lovely Guidebook

~ 16 ~

"I'm the White stone lead. I don't know why she would choose you," Kalmia said as we neared the north wing and the king's and queen's personal chambers. She'd done well at staying quiet during most of the walk through the corridors and stairways, but the need to speak had become too overwhelming, apparently. "I told Hydra that I'm well rested. I had the shortest Cloud stone readings before being dismissed last night. They were for guards and attendants posted inside the castle, not even outside at the ceremony. And I've already slept some too. Not as much as you, I suppose, but I am far more experienced."

Her pitchy, irritable tone grated on my tired mind, adding to a dull ache already there. The sore spots on my feet had begun to hurt again, too, so I'd maintained my own pace, forcing her to slow hers. And though I may have been offended by her blatant assumption and dismissal of my abilities, I found her points somewhat valid. Pleading her case in order to remove myself from the reading was tempting, since the idea of having another White stone reading with the dowager queen almost made me sick, especially when the grief of loss was so new and emotions could become volatile. Yet, the chance of speaking with Sielle again was what ultimately kept my mouth closed.

At least Croft and Argo had stayed with me. Kalmia tried to insist they leave and have her attendant escort us to the dowager queen, but Croft gave them both a look so cold it had me questioning the warmth he'd shown me, while also making me shiver at his protectiveness. Because I'd heard his thoughts as well, and I wouldn't forget them and how they made me feel for a long time.

"Not even if I were dead."

He wasn't a guard, but he sure was acting like one, and even more assertive. As much as my heart leaped at the thought that his fierceness could be something more, King Ren had ordered him to stay with me. I was his job. Nothing more.

Wolf had been right, though. I had to tell Croft. My intrusion on his thoughts had been a serious mistake and an unforgivable personal intrusion. Hearing him hadn't aided me in learning more about the other deaths like Sielle had wanted, only that he could know Sielle. He might offer some insight about her if I'd asked, though I had my doubts he would after I told him the truth. Given how much I already knew of him, how proud and honorable he was, I feared he'd never want to see me again.

Numerous guards and soldiers lined the hallways leading to the royal chambers. Two soldiers had their wolfdogs circle us, then two guards outside the queen's room opened the way. An attendant made us wait inside a great room until permitted entry. He returned to escort us quickly, allowing me only a short time to admire the velvet furnishings, a few of the lifelike portraits on the walls, and the sparkling diamond-shaped chandelier hanging from above before walking us to a small parlor.

Two soldiers and wolfdogs posted at opposite sides of the room along with another guard and the attendant. Queen Reina sat utterly still on a tufted black chaise, her back flush along the high end. Her stare remained forward, blank and focused on nothing at all.

"Your Majesty," Kalmia said, and we all bowed or curtsied with her.

"Thank you for coming," she replied, her tone flat. Her hand lifted from her lap in an almost imperceptible wave for us to come closer.

I eyed Croft and Argo a moment and waited for Kalmia to approach first. There were two chairs and two settees around the tea table in front of her chaise. A White stone on a plain wooden base stood alone atop the table.

"Your Majesty, sorry we were delayed. We were updating King Ren with the latest findings." The smoky voice came from Hydrangea as she and Hemlock entered the room behind us. She moved fast, sweeping into the area and curtsying as low as her impressive height allowed. The lines in her square face were more visible than they had been in the darkness of the Realm room and at the induction ceremony. Like Wolf had been older than the king, she too looked older than the queen, which made me wonder what her position had been prior to the king and queen's marriage.

Hemlock followed along with her, bowing to the queen, his movements slower, his rounder cherub face looking far younger. There were dark circles pressed below his eyes, though, showing that he'd had little rest following the king's death. As the primary for the trial council, he might not see a good night's rest for weeks to come.

Hydrangea took a chair closest to the queen's side, a place she was likely accustomed to as her appointed Lovely. Hemlock sat in the other chair, so Kalmia and I sat in the settee opposite the queen. Croft and Argo remained standing behind the other settee to our side, not at the door or outside with the others.

"Would you like an update as well, Your Majesty?" Hydrangea asked after a brief glance at us.

"No," the dowager queen replied, turning her upper body to face the table. "Ren will brief me later when we discuss the formal announcements, the burial arrangements and invitations, and start the plans for his coronation. For now, I only wish to hear from my husband."

"Your Majesty, if I may," Kalmia began, her petite body leaning forward. "I believe I would be most prepared—"

"I don't care what you think," Queen Reina interrupted in the same lifeless tone, her eyes on the White stone.

Kalmia gaped like a fish out of water for a moment, gasping one single tiny breath, then remembered to close her mouth.

"Your Majesty," Hemlock said, his throaty tone unnerving as it cut the awkward silence. "I believe you mentioned Oleander having a breakdown after her White stone test. I'm certain one of us could do this reading to a far greater extent if you'd like to wait—"

"There will be no waiting," she replied, swollen eyes meeting mine and no one else's. "Olean, if you'd please."

I nodded. "Yes, of course, Your Majesty." There would have been no argument, even if I wanted to recuse myself for any reason. Her eyes held a haunted, empty look that pierced right into my heart. There was no time to consider all the things that could go wrong, no time to worry about having to enter the Realm when two of the Lovely present could have been involved with killing the late king.

After a deep breath, I reached forward to pull the stone's base closer, then took hold.

Air whirred and whistled around as my consciousness entered into the Realm. All motion halted in an instant as it had before, leaving me suspended above my physical body and the others below.

The space appeared the same, hazy and indistinct, only in a different setting. Ribbons of speckled light trailed throughout the room, their brightness and beauty reducing the vibrancy of all other things. The endless sky replaced the ceiling of the queen's parlor, dark and infinite. The queen's first words came in slow, stretched tones, so I took the time to let my eyes wander and reacquaint myself.

Several light clusters floated around her as they had previously. Brighter ribbons and wispy trails wrapped closely to each of the Lovely, including myself, stretching out in all directions. A few spheres of light gathered near the soldiers, guard, and attendant, but the lengthy trails hadn't. As I'd noticed the first time, they wound closer to the Lovely, typically one main wisp identifiable as a tether.

With a turn of my hollow form, I glanced at Croft and Argo below. Croft's and my connection was obvious, like a string of light between his head and mine. Relief flooded me. If the dowager queen had requested one of the other more experienced readers to try immediately, they would have seen the link and known something was amiss. Deciding not to dwell, I studied the rest of the area.

The parlor in the queen's quarters was double the size of the one in Shadowstone, which made the difference between the two stand out immediately. We all had been positioned more closely there, the light streaks more plentiful in such a confined space. It was the reason I hadn't thought much about the light around Croft then, why I hadn't even questioned connecting with him by touching the light around his head. I trusted that Sielle had known something that I hadn't, that perhaps I'd misinterpreted the streaks altogether.

Croft hadn't had an orb near him in Shadowstone. One drifted near him now, yet not directly at his side. There were a few orbs beside the soldiers, attendant, and guard. Though no trails surrounded them the way they did Croft, the way they did all the Lovely.

The dowager queen's request processed in my mind, forcing me closer to count and confirm the orbs nearest her. I replied as Sielle had told me, thinking as if I'd wanted to speak.

My focus returned to Croft. How had it been possible? His mind being blocked from readings could have something to do with the lights wrapping near him, but there was also a thinner wisp coming from the vast sky above and stopping before reaching him. Spinning around, I took a moment to look over my own body and then the other Lovely, spotting the thinner wispy streak of light, seeing how it actually connected with us. Tethers had been my assumption the first time, and that hadn't changed.

Queen Reina watched me closely as I spoke, new tears spilling into a leisurely trail down her cheeks.

"Sielle?" I asked in my mind, hoping for her to hear me. I needed answers to the growing number of questions I had, including help with separating Croft and me as Wolf suggested.

No response came.

The dowager queen asked me to speak with the orbs. I did as she asked, repeating their information to her, recalling the same names as those in Shadowstone. No King Antin. As my body slowly recited my words to her, I tried to refocus.

Everything I'd seen identified Croft as a Lovely. There was no denying that. But how? He had hair, and his eyes ... his beautiful amber eyes were most definitely not white.

"It's the reason you were able to connect with him in here." The low echoed voice startled me as it had before.

"Sielle?!" Shock and excitement had me calling out her name as I would vocally. I knew the instant I'd made the mistake, but there was no way to take it back. There was no stopping it from following the other words I'd spoken to the queen.

"How?" I asked inside my mind quickly, not knowing the time we'd have left after my error. "And how do I separate myself from him?"

"Some Lovely are not born the same and can look like regular people. They are the ones who usually die."

"Die?" I nearly gasped. "You mean ... the twin? Our tether to the Realm?"

"Yes. Some live."

"Instead of the Lovely?"

"Sometimes."

"Croft?"

"Yes. He doesn't know he's one of us. It's why his mind's blocked from readings. All Lovely young are blocked until they touch their first stone on their Name Day. It's not well known because there's never reason to read a child before then. And if any young ones are in the area when a White stone is used, they look relatively the same with the lights around them. The Lovely doing the reading wouldn't think twice unless they had a reason to look more closely at a child."

"So he's never touched a stone? Never made the Realm connection? How can that be possible? As an attendant, he wears gloves when carrying stones. But he's been read before. That's how they all knew his mind was blocked." I eyed the thinner wisp close to him, stretching into the sky with no attached orb in sight.

"He's served the Crown for years, likely was read several times over early on. When nothing changed, they stopped trying, knowing he wasn't a threat but an asset. They wouldn't have allowed him to wipe his own blood onto a stone as an attendant, so no contact was made."

The information had me questioning all my knowledge as a Lovely. The Dead could live instead of us and connect to the Realm? I'd never heard anything about it. But it didn't feel like a lie. How else could I have connected to Croft? We connected with a person's mind through certain stones, but it wasn't the same. The Realm linked us briefly, and it was direct, with a specific purpose that we couldn't change. Not the same as hearing strong thoughts outside the Realm.

As I heard Sielle's name leave my mouth below, I watched everyone's reaction closely. Kalmia, who had held little interest until then, glanced at the dowager queen. Her gaze seemed more hopeful about a potential failure rather than curious about the name. Hemlock eyed Hydrangea, but her focus remained on me, attentive.

"Sielle." The name repeated back to me slowly. Croft. His side view of my face allowed him to watch my mouth as I spoke to the queen.

The queen asked me who I was speaking of, and I lied to her, explaining another orb had answered. It didn't explain the intensity in my tone in reaction to Sielle's voice, but it would have to suffice.

"I need to know how to fix it," I said to Sielle, trying to prioritize my questions to her.

"He'll have to touch a stone and connect to the Realm. That'll end your link and connect him with his own."

As much as I knew I had to tell him the truth, explaining it all and having him connect with a stone added another level of concern. He could very well reject the idea entirely, not believe a word I said. Yet, at least I had the answer.

"I heard him think your name. During induction, Wolf read me with the Cloud stone. Croft repeated it as if he knew it, and he just did it again now. You know him. Tell me how. And what do you know about the murders? Have you heard that the king is dead? I'm here with no idea of what to do with any information. At least one of the Lovely is involved, not the two who fled after the other murders. But I can't tell anyone anything because I don't know who else to trust. Your lack of information and direction has made this even worse."

"I'm sorry," she whispered, the echo of her voice barely heard. "I couldn't explain then. Too much information would have overwhelmed you. There was a chance you wouldn't believe me if I had. And it would have brought more trouble for you here if someone found out."

"Well, that might still happen. I'm due to be read soon, to verify what happened at the induction." I paused a moment, letting the worry go. There was more I needed to know. "So how does he know you?"

"I grew up near the castle. That's how I know of Croft and probably how he's heard my name too. I also know the ones who left ... Blodwyn and Tansy. They were part of a group who wanted to end the indenture."

"The king's opposition? I heard rumors that they might be involved in the murders."

"No, that's not true. They aren't exactly an opposition. They'd planned to approach the prince and possibly the king, to begin discussions about a different future for the Lovely. Nightshade and Dahlia knew as well. They were all friends. They didn't kill them, but they were the ones who found them and knew they would be blamed or be the next to die. So they left, went into hiding. With no access, we haven't been able to find out the reason for the murders. If anyone there had decided they were traitors, they would have had a trial first. But now that the king is dead, it's possible that someone had hoped to frame them. They don't know who or why. It's why I connected with you."

"Whoever killed the king tried to kill the entire family. I was connected with a wolfdog and smelled the poison carafe meant for all of them. The king had some before I reacted."

"Someone wants the throne, the kingdom," Sielle stated. "Are the others safe?"

"Everyone has escorts, and there are more guards and soldiers with wolfdogs, checking everything."

The queen had finished her new request, wanting me to speak with every orb in the area.

Her desperation caused Hydrangea to lean closer to the chaise and whisper softly.

Despite the unease of having to talk to all the orbs and how long it could take, I felt no hesitation. If it would help soothe the queen's sorrow for a little while, it would be beneficial.

I moved my echo form to the next closest orb to the queen's chaise, the one nearest to Croft.

A thought occurred to me, one that made my stomach flip nervously. The first time Sielle had connected with me in the White stone could have been coincidental, hoping to find someone. But … "How did you know this time? If you have no contacts in the castle, how did you know I would be connected to the White stone right now?"

"The Needled stone. Since it acts in aid of the others and doesn't have a sole Realm purpose itself, we are able to maintain contact without the worry of addiction. With its indirect Realm connection, it allows me to sense when you are using a stone."

"But how? I don't understand how we can talk in here. Lovely can't occupy the same Realm space even with the same stone."

"That's mostly true, yes. I don't fully understand it all either."

Her words came slower, more thoughtful, not like her usual tone and speed. It was as if she were hesitant, or not telling me the full truth.

Hydrangea had spoken louder, pleading with the dowager queen. I moved again, trying to focus on what I needed to do even though Sielle's words had given little reassurance on how our ability to speak may or may not make things worse when I was read next. I could only hope Wolf would do the reading again.

I spoke to the orb, asking for its name.

"Antin Vidis," it replied, making me gasp. I knew everyone would hear my reaction soon enough, so I'd wait for the queen's direction.

"The king?" Sielle asked, her echo a soft whisper.

"Yes, but ..." I stared at the orb, wondering why it wasn't closer to the queen.

"What?"

"Is there an order to how the ordinary dead align themselves here? Where their orbs tend to be? The only ones I've spoken with have been the queen's relatives, all elder." Though I'd seen the one close to Cordelia's stomach and it made me wonder if it had been her child.

"I'm not sure. I've never seen it, only sensed."

"What do you mean you've never seen it? Were these your first times touching the White stone too? Surely you have other people near you?"

"No, I can't see anything with the White stone, and probably others. I'm blind."

Hydrangea's voice broke through, telling me to end the connection. My gaze moved to the dowager queen, watching her hunched body heave and shake, emotionally breaking down. Even if they'd heard my gasp, there had been nothing to indicate they knew I'd found the king.

I couldn't hold on, couldn't argue. The dowager queen would only endure more sorrow if I pushed her to listen, and if I took too long to release the stone, I'd surely be questioned by Hemlock and Hydrangea.

"I have to go," I said to Sielle. "I'll try to connect again, or find you some other way."

"It won't be safe for you to look for me outside the castle. Stay and find out who's to blame."

I disconnected right as everyone's eyes had started to shift my way, noticing my delay.

While my physical body jolted, accepting my presence again, an attendant helped escort the queen from the parlor.

The recovery hadn't been as bad as when I'd first connected with the White stone, those issues likely caused by the initial link with Croft. There was a slight dizziness, but I breathed through it as everyone else stood to leave.

Hydrangea looked between Kalmia and me. "Although we are in mourning, we still have duties to attend to. I know you spoke with Wolf earlier. Did he inform you about our usual procedures for new members?"

"No, we mostly discussed what transpired last night and the readings to follow," I admitted, leaving out the other details.

She dipped her elegant head. "Yes, there are still many to be read. You as well because of your direct involvement while in the wolfdog. But as we are sorting through it all, we need to continue on. It's customary for new members to join others in all different divisions, to see normal procedures of stone classes despite the position you may be assigned. Tomorrow, you will join Kalmia. We have a pregnancy nearby, close to term. We always travel to them to ensure the safety and acquisition of the future Lovely, no matter how far away. Fortunately, this one's in the city. You will have escorts for safety, of course."

Before I could respond, Kalmia did. "It'd be our honor. Are there any others joining us?"

"The others from the induction will also attend as they need to learn the same," Hemlock added with a bland look.

"Are we to take a White stone to confirm it's a multiple?"

Hydrangea looked us over once more before walking to the door. "Do we need to assign someone else to lead White stone? You don't sound confident."

For the second time, Kalmia gaped. She recovered quickly, uttering, "No, of course not. I've attended many birth meetings, so I'm more than capable—"

"Good. Rest well this evening. Wear plain travel dresses for the visit and report the findings to me tomorrow. And, Olean, be sure to paint your eyebrows. It is a daily requirement." She didn't even bother looking back as they left.

Lovely are required to present themselves
in a respectable manner at all times by
following all laws and customs set by the Crown.
Appearance and attire are regulated to reflect
cohesion, not individualism, and to show proper
respect to the Realm and the kingdom.
- Anhedral Kingdom Lovely Laws and Customs

~ 17 ~

We went our separate ways after leaving the queen's rooms. As he did throughout the day, Croft needed to take Argo outside. Instead of allowing another attendant to escort me to my rooms, though, they walked with me first, then had someone else stand watch outside until they returned.

A midday meal arrived with them. After Argo cleared the food, I took a seat at the table, ready to devour the savory smelling cut meats and cheeses and sweet-scented berries. The White stone reading had been tough, the discussion with Sielle the most exhaustive part. My thoughts had become endless, trying to navigate all the information about the murders, about Croft being a Lovely, and about Sielle herself. A blind Lovely, unable to see what the Realm showed her. I would have never imagined.

Croft had taken a few minutes to clean up in the bathing room. When he returned, he helped himself to a plate of food and positioned himself to stand near the cart to eat. Despite my offering a chair at other meals, he'd always declined, either taking the same standing place or sitting on the settee by the fireplace, not wanting to disrupt Ivy and me.

With a wave of my hand, I drew his attention. "Please sit with me?"

His lips pursed in contemplation for only a moment before he took the seat across from me, the one usually left empty since Ivy would sit right at my side. He nodded, stacked a couple of cheeses, and tossed them into his mouth. Argo let out a long sigh near the fireplace and settled onto his wool mat.

I smiled and took a few bites of blueberries, puckering at their tartness. The questions tumbled in my mind, wanting to ask him about everything I'd learned. And while I'd also wanted to tell him the truth, I struggled with how or when the best time would be. As frustrated as Sielle made me regarding her lack of information, I found myself understanding her reasons. What I needed to tell Croft would be overwhelming. It wasn't my place to determine what he could handle, but I knew it would be a lot to take in all at once and there was no way to explain everything he needed to know in smaller increments.

"Can I ask some questions?"

"Sure. I guess we need to discuss some things," he thought but simply shrugged, lifting a single eyebrow that sent my mind in a different direction once again. That eyebrow ...

I refocused, taking a drink of water. "Will you go with us tomorrow?"

"Yes." He answered physically with a nod.

"You probably hate not being with the new king. You're his attendant, but he's stuck you with me. Sorry for that. I'm sure you'd be of a lot more use to him, especially right now."

He chewed down some meat and a piece of bread, his eyes watching me intently as he shook his head. The stare told me more than the simple movement, even before I heard his thoughts. *"No. He needs space right now. I'll help him soon enough, if he rises to his position. But you ... You're more important. And I'm not sure if I know why. I just know."*

I coughed a little, emotion catching in my throat. "No, huh? All right," I said as if I hadn't heard a single thought.

He stood fast, then moved to the tea table and retrieved more loose paper and the ink pen he'd used after the king had left.

As soon as he sat again, I said, "Sorry if I'm asking too much."

His lower lip pushed outward before his mouth formed a tiny smile and he shook his head. *"I don't mind. I like what I hear from you."*

What? Before I could even think, I asked, "Can you hear anything at all?"

He used a finger and thumb as if he were pinching something before writing on the paper exactly what he thought. *"A little bit. Loud sounds, certain tones."*

"Loud sounds, certain tones." I smiled, plucked up more berries, and placed them in my mouth. I knew that to a degree already. It matched the way he thought of words—unclear, missing pieces. His eyes never left me, watching as I chewed. While I enjoyed the direct attention, I needed to refocus. "Did you have any feelings about today? Hemlock? Hydrangea?"

He busied himself with a couple more bites as well, taking time to consider my words before writing. *"I don't trust either. Never have. Hydra uses her position with the queen well, questions Wolf's authority often. And since Hem oversees most of the trials, he has an inflated sense of worth."*

I chuckled. "They don't hide much then. What about the others who died? Did you know them?"

He flipped the top paper over for blank space. *"I thought so. Nightshade was close with Ren. He was with him before I was placed as a royal attendant several years ago. He and Dahlia were more humble than others. Same with Blodwyn and Tansy. They never acted more important than guards or attendants."*

"Do you think they are to blame for the murders?"

"I don't think they are. They acted like friends."

"Did you ever see them discuss changes for the Lovely with Prince Ren or King Antin?"

"No, I don't believe so. What's this about?" His eyes searched mine.

I sighed, knowing I needed to tell him more. I'd hoped to keep his involvement minimal since he was already linked with me. But I trusted him and needed him to trust me too. "What if I told you I believe they didn't kill the others, and that whoever killed the king was responsible? None of those four were plotting against the king, but they did want a better life for the Lovely. They had planned to speak with Prince Ren and King Antin, hoping to allow Lovely more freedoms."

He scratched at his scruffy jaw as he continued to study me, then wrote, *"How do you know this?"*

I pinched my lips together, deciding total honesty was best. I had to trust him fully and give him the truth ... At least some. The truth involving him would have to wait. "I've talked with someone ... inside the Realm. They live close and know the others in hiding. They want me to help find the truth and are helping me do the same."

"You trust them?" He barely looked down while writing.

"I do. She's helped open my eyes even before leaving Shadowstone. I understand now that Cordelia could only offer so much information, not wanting to hurt our chances by tainting our minds with her own experiences. I can't help but feel some disappointment, though. My only goal had been being a member of the Queen's Garden, to be placed in the highest position I could, to serve the kingdom. I guess in some ways, I didn't care to understand there would be more things involved, more issues to navigate. And that's not including the murders. So yeah, I trust that she is helping, that she wants to find the truth too."

"She? She's a Lovely, but not here in the castle." His fingers wrote slowly before lifting away to show me the paper.

"Yes, she's a Lovely but doesn't have a normal Lovely name. Her name is Sielle." I watched his reaction, knowing he had heard the name before and wanting to find out why. If he knew her, we might be able to learn even more working together. "Have you heard of her?"

His gaze fell to the table, eyebrows pulling together. *"A child at the school. But it couldn't be her. A Lovely?"* When his eyes lifted, he shook his head and wrote a single word. *"No."*

"No?" I confirmed, my trust plummeting with his lie. I'd offered so much information, and he wouldn't share what he might know. Why?

He shook his head again, eyes drifting away.

Despite my disappointment, part of me understood his hesitation. If he did know her, maybe he felt compelled to protect her. Given that he was unaware of her being a Lovely, he could want to find out more on his own. I couldn't exactly fault him for keeping something like this to himself when I was hiding so much from him.

"Shame. She might be able to get more information from the others, help figure out who's using the Blood stone," I admitted when he looked back at me. After some silence, I took a sip of water and changed direction. If she was a Lovely and he hadn't known, and she said Croft was a Lovely who also didn't know, there had to be a connection. He'd mentioned a school. "I want to know more about you. Did you grow up here? What position did you have before being a royal attendant?"

He pointed to himself with a shrug before taking a drink of his own. His sudden playfulness following the avoidance should have surprised me. But I realized it was a more natural reaction than my original assumption to his gruffness when we'd first met. More and more of his personality emerged with each of our interactions. He fascinated me, maybe more than he should. I found myself not caring to hold back, though, even if the complexity of the situation might bring more problems between us.

"You want to know about me?" He scribbled the words and kept his amber eyes on me. They were disarming, truly. People often said a Lovely's eyes could pierce through their soul, more often the reaction to the unusual white color. I'd never thought much about it. But Croft's seemed to do the same to me, holding something more than just the beautiful color.

"Yes," I said, finishing off a piece of bread, then leaning forward, resting my folded arms onto the table.

"Why?" He only wrote a question mark.

"Why not?"

"Not important," he wrote flippantly, sloppily.

"If you'd rather not tell me, that's all right. But I can see you. You're definitely important."

"You are too," was what he thought, which had my heart pounding and my breath hitching. He dipped his chin, gave me a half smile, and wrote instead, *"I grew up in the city, at a home for orphans that was also a schoolhouse for impaired children. Got a job at the castle as a laundry hand first, then main attendant before this."*

A schoolhouse for impaired children. Sielle was blind. That was the connection.

"Do you enjoy this work?"

His head leaned to the side as he glanced around the room. He took his time eating another large bite of cheese and meat before changing to a new piece of paper and writing, *"There are days I feel as if I could offer more. I see some of the problems in this city, this kingdom, and it frustrates me that there's nothing I can do."*

My brow line rose, surprised by his honesty. "Have you said anything to King Ren? You are his attendant. He seems to value you."

"Valued as an attendant, yes. Mostly one with a protected mind." The thought was dry as he wiped his mouth with his napkin, tossed it onto his plate, then picked up the pen again and furiously wrote. *"I've mentioned some things to him, but he was never serious enough about his future role. He passed a few ideas to King Antin. Most were ignored. Why waste time and energy on older building restoration, public health, or our ailing farmlands? Why be concerned with prevention and preservation since nothing has truly fallen apart yet? When nothing major has happened to the kingdom in years? But*

now, something major has, and who knows what the outcome will be."

As soon as I finished reading from the paper, I looked at him. *Really* looked at him. His entire body had gone rigid with intensity. His convictions and knowledge of the kingdom had me amazed.

"Well," I uttered, bemused. "If you were this vehement with the prince, it's no wonder he ignored you. He probably couldn't read this scribble."

Croft's lips parted as he stared at my mouth, processing. Then, suddenly, the largest grin spread over his face, and his breath released in a whoosh as his body shuddered. He pressed a hand to his stomach and smacked the table with the other, causing the plates and silverware to jump.

I couldn't stop my own laughter from taking over, letting it out without restriction while falling against the back of the chair. It was complete possession. As my body shook, my stomach cramped and tears stung the corners of my eyes. The happy, unbridled emotion came over me like a heavy mountain storm in Shadowstone. Fast and wild and free. I'd never needed something so much—the release like a balm for my soul.

As my laughter settled and my gasping breaths calmed, I finally opened my eyes to Croft. His humor had disappeared completely. His intensity had returned, though this time his focus and thoughts were entirely on me, not the kingdom he obviously cared so much for.

"Beautiful."

I felt the flush rise, starting at my belly and climbing all the way to my face. It felt so wrong to hear the thought, something that should have been private. But even if I hadn't heard it, it wouldn't have been hard to discern. His gaze was fiery, capable of melting me on the spot, and most definitely telling of his thoughts. I was almost certain he could read mine as well, see how I noticed all the intricacies of his handsomeness, like his strong, capable hands and muscles, his taunting lips, and the way his hair tempted my desire to feel its soft waves daily.

His eyes stayed locked on me, and he leaned forward, resting his arms on the table.

The tension grew, the silence adding even more as the air around us became dense and hot. I coughed lightly and took a drink of water, escaping into its coolness. When I finished, I said, "See, you are important. And I'm sure the new king will listen if he wants to know what's good for this kingdom."

That made him smile, the corners of his eyes crinkling. After a moment, he picked up the pen. *"Tell me more about you."*

"Why?" I asked, repeating his unwritten word to be clever. He scowled playfully, making me smile in turn. "I'm rather dull. You already know where I'm from. What I do. There's not much else to say."

He pursed his lips and wrote, *"Tell me something else. What do you like? What don't you like?"*

"All right," I answered. "I like this room even though I feel I don't deserve it. I like sharing it with Ivy and hope I can keep helping her learn about being a Lovely. I enjoyed using the Eye stone at the induction, the experience of being inside a wolfdog. But I know it's a privilege to be taken seriously. Otherwise, I could cause them harm. I dislike having to read criminals with the Cloud stone. Their thoughts and memories ... they're awful, difficult to forget, and invade my dreams." My mood soured, my mind instantly flipping through different victims and all they'd endured.

His hand reached over to lie on top of mine for a moment, then he flipped the paper and wrote more. *"You are stronger than so many for helping their victims see justice. Tell me something else good. What is your favorite thing?"*

I was grateful for his kindness and assurance. The good in what we Lovely did often got lost in the turmoil inside our own minds. "I'm not sure I have a favorite thing."

"No?" He licked his lips as he wrote again. *"Food? Book? Pleasure?"*

Heat surged through me all over again, meeting his eyes. There was no way I was telling him about my stolen moments with Jonah. I almost laughed at the thought, wondering what his reaction might be. Instead, I answered, "I liked cooking for the others with Cordelia. I enjoy fruits the most ... and pies. Though the fruit tarts here are good too, almost as good as Ivy thinks. Books? Hmm. The stories about the marsh goblins and the cloud gods were always my preference. And the soap here is my favorite."

"Soap?"

"Yes. The soaps in Shadowstone were bland, no added scents. I like the delicate floral soaps here most, jasmine and rose, I think." I laughed when he smiled and thought of the way he smelled. "And the spicy ones too."

The door opened then, cutting through the conversation as Ivy rushed inside the room, yelling, "Goodbye, Guardian Calla. They're here, so you can leave!"

"See you tomorrow," Calla said and left after her ruddy face peeked around the door to make sure we were in fact there.

Ivy rolled her eyes as she walked to the table, standing between Croft and me. "What's funny? Oh, you've been writing?"

Croft crumpled the used papers before Ivy could read anything, then stood and walked to the fire, tossing them inside.

"Ivy," I admonished. "Stop being so curt with Guardian Calla. And it's rude to assume you can read someone's conversation."

"Oh," she said, eyes wide and smile falling with understanding. "I'm sorry."

Croft was still turned away at the fire, not seeing.

"You need to apologize to him too."

Ivy moved to the fireplace and gently tapped Croft's hand to get his attention. When he pivoted toward her, she said, "I'm sorry for trying to read without asking."

Setting the fire poker down, he mouthed and motioned to her, slicing one hand over the other. *It's all right.*

She smiled and skipped back to me, her extra fluffy dress floating all around her. "Are you staying here?"

"Yes, I believe so, for the rest of the day."

Her little body bounced onto the tips of her toes. "That means we can play some?"

"Sure," I answered, standing with the empty plates to clear the table.

Croft had finished poking the paper to ensure it had burned fully. He noticed my movement and waved his hands at me to stop. I placed what I'd held into the cart, then lifted my own hands in surrender.

He walked over and pushed at my arms in jest while Ivy made her way to Argo to pet him.

"All right. I'll stop," I said to Croft, biting my lip as he scooped the remainder from the table, watching his body move so fluidly.

Dangerous. The attraction between us was growing stronger, and I didn't think I could stop it even if I wanted to. His charm had me ensnared, and there was no way to ignore his thoughts and actions toward me either. But I knew it might all change when he found out the full truth about our connection.

And yet, I couldn't tell him. Especially since he'd lied about Sielle. I needed to know more, needed to find their link, needed to find her. Maybe after that the answers would come.

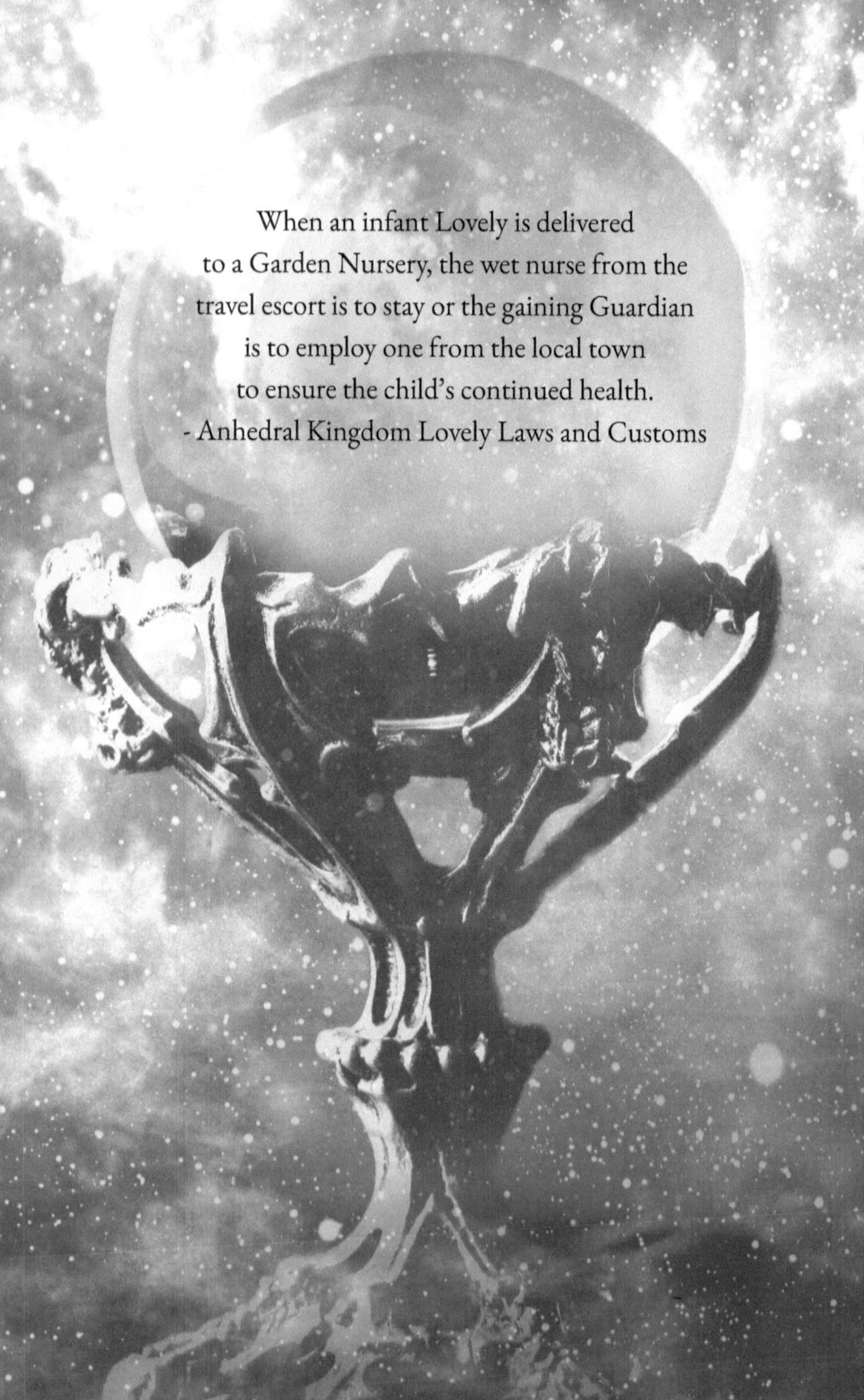

When an infant Lovely is delivered
to a Garden Nursery, the wet nurse from the
travel escort is to stay or the gaining Guardian
is to employ one from the local town
to ensure the child's continued health.
- Anhedral Kingdom Lovely Laws and Customs

We took three coaches the following afternoon, departing the castle to travel into the city and visit the pregnant woman said to be carrying two. Nettle, Amaryllis, and Hellebore were all called upon to attend as well. With each having their own attendants and additionally four soldiers and wolfdogs joining us, our group amounted to fourteen plus the four trained canines and the best one of all, Argo.

I pushed for a seat nearest to a window, but Croft blocked my effort, taking it for himself with the single thought, *"No."* Being denied a view of the streets and people had me annoyed, especially when the others appeared to have better views and excited smiles. It wasn't until after we'd departed the castle's courtyard and passed the gatehouse that my pouting ceased, realizing why Croft had denied my attempt.

A few cobbled streets into the packed city, some of the residents tossed—not so nicely—all kinds of food items and maybe some other things at our travel line. The coach's window shuddered under the assault while Croft held the internal drapery closed, peering out occasionally. As something bigger slammed into the frame overhead, the horses neighed, the coach jerked about, the soldiers yelled to the outsiders, and Croft's arm wrapped over my shoulders, pulling me against his side. Argo barked a few times before settling down at our feet. While I wasn't overly frightened, I found myself curling against Croft all the same, accepting the protection easily.

As the threat disappeared with calmer streets, his arm went back to his side and the tension in his solid body eased into a relaxed posture.

"What in the Realm was that?" Nettle asked from the forward seat of our coach, his face turning sideways to look at his attendant and Kalmia. They both sat in his row, while Kalmia's attendant had the other window in back with Croft and me.

"The crops have suffered this season. People are growing more restless," Croft thought.

Kalmia peered out her window hesitantly. "We aren't supposed to talk about the king's death while we're out today, but some have probably heard by now since the induction. They must be upset."

"Upset the king is dead and throwing food? It's a wonder she manages to dress in the morning."

Two bursts of air slipped past my lips, and the small shudder in my body drew Croft's attention. His head twisted, and his eyes narrowed as he peered over at me.

I hastily wiped under my nose as if something had made me itch. After a sniffle, I asked, "We aren't supposed to talk about the late king? What if someone asks?"

"I'll handle it," Kalmia replied. "Until the dowager queen sends out the official word, she wants everyone to maintain silence."

Avoiding Croft's gaze for the remainder of the trip, my eyes pinned onto the side of Nettle's bald head as if it held the answers to all my current problems. I struggled with finding solutions to everything. Croft's truth, finding whoever was responsible for the deaths ... it was all stacking up and had the potential to topple.

We arrived at the family's house after a lengthy maze of condensed buildings and marketplaces. Fortunately, the house was near the center of a quiet street, surrounded by other homes, not an angry lettuce-throwing person in sight.

I stayed with Croft, waiting for all the others to follow Kalmia. "Have you been to one of these before?"

He shook his head as we entered the house.

The large sitting room felt cramped with us inside, even with leaving two soldiers and their wolfdogs outside to guard the entrance.

"Hello, Family Haprone. I'm Kalmia. The newest members of the Queen's Garden are also with me to observe our meeting today. Nettle, Amaryllis, Hellebore, and Olean," Kalmia said in greeting, nodding at the male and female sitting on the long settee pushed against the opposite wall. There were minimal decorations on the walls and a small table, plain and charming.

"Hello," the pale man replied nicely enough, though his eyes were attentive and his arm protective around the woman's back. "I'm Jaman and this is my wife, Hepma."

"It's a pleasure," Kalmia said, walking closer. "I'm sure you know why we are here, as you've likely spoken to someone from the castle already regarding your pregnancy. We are here to confirm and nothing more, so it shouldn't take long."

"And if it is confirmed?" Hepma asked, eyes brimming with tears, though she was able to keep them from spilling over her rosy cheeks.

"Someone will come closer to your due date and help plan your birthing process to ensure it will be as easy and as safe as possible."

"And take my baby away?" Hepma said, losing control of her emotions, tears finally spilling over. "You will take the one who lives. That's how this works."

"Hepma," Jaman said in a whispered plea. "They will help you. If it means that you survive …"

Oh, Realm, I had not been prepared at all. My knees shook as realization hit me. I hadn't thought about the birthing or what occurred after, which was entirely foolish. Why hadn't Cordelia told me? Why had I never truly asked? My main assumption had always been that my family had died. The other was that I'd been abandoned or offered up, same for the rest of us, because we were so different from ordinary people. But no, we were taken from them. Taken from our families after our births. They were left to grieve two children, one dead, one living. And we were placed in Nurseries to be raised by Guardians. This was the reality of the indenture? I felt ill.

"We only wish to help make the process easier, to help you and both children as best as we can." Kalmia approached the couple and got down on her knees across the table from them. "We will do this fast to ease your stress. Alve, the White stone, please."

Kalmia's attendant carried a box to her, removed the White stone and its plain wooden base, and set it onto the table. Kalmia reached forward and took hold.

She didn't require any questions, which made me understand that most of us held the same control while inside the White stone Realm.

"You have many family here with you. They will help guide this birth. There is a great bundle of wrapping lights around you, nested at your stomach. That is indication enough that you are carrying a Lovely since people do not have the same presences, only cluster orbs of family."

The couple held each other tightly, quietly accepting Kalmia's words.

Croft grabbed my wrist, drawing my attention to him. His gaze was locked on our hands, mine shaking in his grip. His eyes lifted to me, understanding held inside their amber color. My breaths were unsteady, and I wasn't sure how long I could control myself in front of anyone.

As soon as I looked at Kalmia, I realized she had already withdrawn from the stone, but her focus wasn't on the couple or even the others in front of us. It was on Croft and me, confusion in her stare.

"Is that all for now then? My wife needs rest," Jaman said, helping her to stand.

"Of course," Kalmia replied, also getting to her feet. "Many thanks for accommodating this visit, and we wish the best for you all."

I wasted no time leaving, pushing through the door to escape. It was all too hot—my body, the house. I fought for composure, hearing Croft exit behind me as I gulped large lungfuls of cool air and leaned over.

"What's wrong with you?" Nettle asked from somewhere behind me.

No answer came from me, but from my periphery, Croft ushered him away. *"Leave. Now."* The others got the message, disappearing back to the coaches without another word.

Croft's hand pressed against my back, and Argo bumped against my leg, giving a soft whine.

"Are you going to be sick?" Kalmia asked after the others had gone.

"I don't ... I'm not sure."

She scoffed, and a growl from Croft followed closely inside my head. "You didn't react this way yesterday. Is this what happened when you first tested on the White stone? That was a smaller house as well, right? Is there something wrong with being too enclosed?"

"Maybe. The room felt too cramped. I couldn't breathe."

Kalmia's white flat shoes came into sight as she moved to stand in front of me. "Well, something is most definitely wrong with you. It could also have something to do with what I noticed in there before disconnecting. Some of your light reached outward. It was touching Croft, oddly enough, probably because you were standing so close."

"What?" Croft's thought was loud.

I coughed, choking on air as she spilled the information as if it meant nothing. Had she really no idea? She'd taken the lead White stone position, but maybe she hadn't seen anything like it before. Maybe she didn't know as much as Sielle had told me.

"I may be broken," I uttered in a frail attempt to deter her thoughts. With a deep inhale, I stood upright, placing my hands on my hips, thinking of another way to distract her from reaching the truth. During the queen's session, there had been something that niggled at me, something she might know easily enough. "I do have a question for you about the White stone, though. You mentioned their family, that they might help them along."

"In Realm support, of course," she said dismissively. "It's a genuine, comforting thought, especially knowing at least one will join those who have already passed."

"Of course," I agreed. "But my question is about the order of family, their light clusters. Orbs. I've only talked to the queen's, so I'm not as familiar with it as you are. Is it only blood relations who tend to stay near a person? Is that why I didn't see …" I lowered my voice. "Him?"

"Oh." Kalmia turned her head to look around, not bothered to have Croft still beside us, though he was watching our every word. "Yes, most likely the reason. A couple can stay with each other if their bond is strong, but the orbs tend to be closer to blood relations. Parents. Siblings. Extensions of those. It's why Hydra had the queen stop because he could have been anywhere. She might have had you looking for hours, possibly summoned King Ren and Princess Naomi to join us, in hopes he'd be near them."

"So … a parent?" I asked, finally understanding as all the pieces joined together. The late king. His prominent brow. The single eyebrow lift. The slightly upturned nose. And Croft. Croft, with those exact features, though different skin tone and a broader body frame.

"Yes," she confirmed. I gasped in response, causing her to sneer. "I'm not sure what's wrong with you, but we need to leave now. There's no time to dawdle in the city. We have to report our findings to Wolf and Hydra."

My head pounded. It was hard to think. Croft's hand pushed at my back, guiding me down the row to the final coach. The coach door opened, and Argo barked. Loudly. The sound pushed its way into my already crowded head, demanding attention.

I hadn't thought much of it, hadn't even lifted my eyes to the door before something shoved my arm and body hard, throwing me off balance, knocking me off my feet and flat onto my back. Argo's barks were more insistent, angered and violent. A sharp burning pain registered in my arm just as Kalmia screamed. I lifted up into a seated position, trying in vain to understand what was happening.

Croft's body was pitched forward, lying on top of someone else, wrestling them. Argo had a hold of a leg as it kicked and kicked, a feeble attempt to shake him away. When their bodies shifted around, I realized the person was Alve, Kalmia's attendant. Kalmia stood frozen in place, hands covering her face, watching everything unfold the same as me. Two of the soldiers rushed over, their wolfdogs joining the fight.

"Knife!" Croft's thought rang like a bell.

A knife was knocked away from Alve, clanking against the cobbled stones. Before anyone else could grab hold, Alve had it again. But to everyone's utter shock, instead of fighting on, he twisted the blade and stabbed himself in the neck.

Croft scrambled off him, arms spread wide as he backed away. The soldiers and wolfdogs all stepped back as well, stunned.

Kalmia cried out, and two more screams echoed from within the coaches, the others having seen the ordeal too.

I couldn't move. My focus locked onto Alve, watching the life fade from his skyward stare as it turned cold and blank. It was the very first time I'd seen it with my own eyes, not through anyone else's.

Death. And he'd done it to himself.

"Olean. Olean." Croft had moved to me in an instant, his body crouched before me, his hands searching. He stopped moving, his eyes staring just above where his hands gripped my lower arm. The burning pain pulsed above my elbow. *"Blood. You're injured."*

"Oh, Realm!" Kalmia cried. "Alve!"

The soldiers urged her inside the coach protectively.

Croft's fingers directed my face to his, alert and determined eyes meeting mine. *"You're all right. You're all right. I have you."*

I nodded in a daze, still processing all that had happened. Finally, I looked down where he had started ripping away the base of his undershirt beneath his vest, confused as to why. Then I looked down at myself and noticed the blood running down my arm in a steady stream. Red spread over my skin, soaking into my plain gray dress.

Croft wrapped the strip around my arm, adding pressure that made me scream. He gritted his teeth. *"I'm sorry. I didn't see. I'm so sorry."*

"Not your fault," I admitted, staring at him as he bandaged me.

His eyes lifted when he finished, a slight tilt in his head. *"Let's get back."* He got to his feet, but instead of grabbing hold of my hands to help me stand, he crouched close, slipped his arms under my back and legs, and lifted me against his body in a cradle.

He maneuvered us into the coach while the soldiers tended to the others. One stayed behind with Alve's body as the horses started to move.

The aftermath silence hit. Everyone was too stunned to speak, and I was glad for it. Enduring a verbal clash of information from everyone recounting all the details right away would have been torture. Croft didn't move me from his lap. So I stayed there, pressing my face into his neck, closing my eyes, and allowing the smell of him to smother all my other senses, easing me into calmness. My heart. My breaths. At some point on the return journey, I'd fainted or fallen asleep, exhaustion overtaking me.

All Lovely past their
Name Day are to be included into
Nursery rotation duties for age-appropriate trial
and vanity readings. Regular checks are required
to help prevent addiction or madness. If a child is
found unfit, the Crown requires immediate
notification and will determine the best remediation.
- Anhedral Kingdom Lovely Laws and Customs

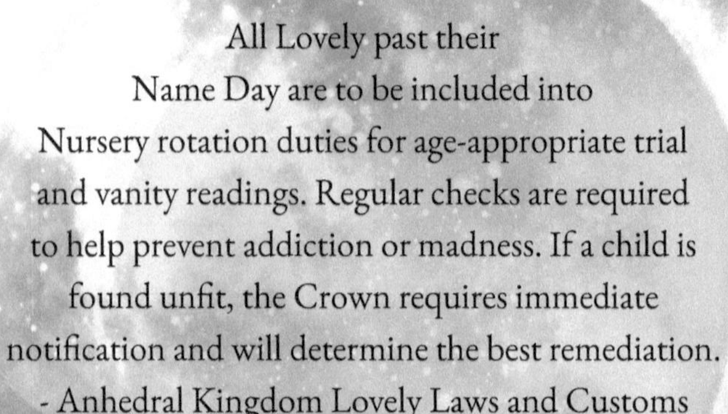

~ 19 ~

I woke for a second time in the evening before the sunlight had fully faded through the windows, the most delicious scent of roasted beef and vegetables spreading through the air and into my sleep. Dinner had already been delivered, and Ivy and Croft sat at the table in the main room. Croft rose as soon as he spotted me in the doorway, and I waved him off, noticing my arm bandage had been changed sometime after our arrival to the room.

I'd woken first when we'd returned to the castle. I argued with Croft, insisting on walking to the rooms myself, only succeeding the first part of the trip. Weakness had me abandoning the fight when we reached the stairs, so he'd carried me the rest of the way. I'd drifted off again as soon as I'd lain down on my bed.

"Olean," Ivy said, rushing over and crashing against my body. She wound her arms around me and pressed her face to my growling stomach. I hugged her close. "I wanted to come in and lie with you, but Croft told me to wait. He said you needed to sleep."

Argo bounded over from his bedding by the fireplace excitedly, curious about what Ivy was doing. His tail wagged as he sat beside her, and he licked a kiss on my hand.

"Thank you for wanting to check on me," I said, lifting my eyes to find Croft watching us. The intensity there caught me off guard, almost making me lose my smile as I wondered what was wrong. I mouthed a "Thank you," to him.

He nodded once, but his face still looked far too serious.

"Does your arm hurt? Croft told me what happened. It's all so scary."

"It does hurt some." I touched the bandage covering my upper arm. "And, yes, it was scary."

Ivy pushed away, tipping her head back to see me. "I'm glad you're safe now."

"I'm glad everyone is," I said, the word everyone catching a little as I thought of Alve's lifeless eyes. He hadn't been safe. Why hadn't he been safe? The only logical answer made my stomach turn.

"Come eat. I'm almost finished, but you need some." She walked to the table and delved back into her food.

"This looks like entirely too much. Way more than usual. I don't think we can eat this ourselves."

Croft watched me closely as I sat and began dishing some food for myself. I ate gratefully, humming in pleasure as my stomach settled.

A few minutes passed in contented silence. Even Ivy was too busy eating to tell any tales from her daily lessons. We shared warm glances and no sounds aside from chewing until a knock had Argo barking, and Ivy and I looked at the door. Croft stood, letting his napkin fall to the table. I wasn't sure who I expected to see in the doorway. Maybe Wolf. But I hadn't expected Begonia and Clem to step inside, seeming shy as they glanced at Croft and then around the main room.

"Begonia! Clem!" Ivy stood and rushed at them, knocking into both with a fast, hard hug that neither seemed to mind. Their clothes were patchwork shades of white, with no accents or frills. They looked gaunt compared to when I'd seen them last, though I'd been looking through a wolfdog's eyes in the beginning of the night. Dark circles pressed below their eyes, showing their lack of sleep.

"Hi, Ivy," Clem replied, patting her on the head and giving her a soft smile, then turning his focus to the table and food.

"Hi," I said to both of them, standing and watching Begonia continue her perusal of the room.

She looked even more pale, no color at all tinting her cheeks. Even her freckles had faded.

I held myself together, feeling a rush of emotion hit. Their appearances and sullen demeanors ... I knew without asking that it wasn't only about the readings for the king's murder. It was evident after I'd seen the other Clear class that they were connecting to the Realm often. And by how both of their eyes moved to the table, I could see that wasn't the only form of neglect.

"How are you both here?" I asked, honestly shocked they'd been allowed to visit.

"Because we shouldn't be here?" Begonia's sharp tongue showed itself, becoming defensive immediately.

"No, that's not at all what I meant," I said as she scoffed and crossed her arms over herself, looking smaller than ever. "I wanted you here before. I had asked and ... After I saw you in the Realm Room, I wanted to give you your things and see you again." My words were a rush of apology and emotion, nearly cracking.

"Someone sent for us." Clem's eyes went to my arm. "They told us about today and said we were allowed to come see you. We're glad you're all right."

"Yes. Glad you're all right," Begonia said, her lip quivering the tiniest bit.

That was when I realized why she had started fighting right away. It was her standard reaction to most things she found irritating or angering. But this time, she was scared. And maybe that fear wasn't strictly about today or about my injury at all. Maybe it was about being here, having the dreams of what her life could become shattered by the truth of what our life really entailed.

I pushed around my chair and walked purposely to them. "I've missed you both terribly. I want you here with us, and will try my hardest to make that happen. I'm so sorry it took me this long to see, to realize ..." My voice did break then as I pulled them against me.

There was no hesitation from either. They fell into me as Ivy always did and began to sob silently. Ivy joined us, squeezing her small body in between us all. I turned my head and met Croft's eyes, seeing instantly he had been the one. He'd gotten them to come and had ordered more food than usual, knowing they would dine with us.

He dipped his chin, then disappeared into his room to give us some privacy.

After a few minutes allowing them to break down when they'd been showing such strength for so long, I felt their shuddering bodies relax and pulled back. Their gazes were timid, unsure. Clem hastily wiped under his eyes with his sleeve, and Begonia did the same with her hand.

"Croft got all this food for dinner," I said, pointing at the chairs. "Let's eat."

We didn't speak about the castle, the readings, or the royals. The conversation went back to Shadowstone, staying safely away from our current issues. I told them a less emotional version of how much Cordelia had missed them in the few days I'd stayed behind. Then we discussed the weather difference, how fresh the mountain air felt compared to the city's drier, temperate climate. Talk led to the townspeople we grew around, and that led to giggles over certain vanity readings we'd been through—if Mr. Stalp would still be searching for love, and if Ms. Trefind would learn to mind her own business instead of her neighbor's. And then we talked about the farms and how much Ivy missed the alpacas the most, which had her remembering that she had their things in her bedroom and dragging them in there to see it all.

I started to clean the table, sorting the completely empty plates and bowls onto the cart. Argo—who had stayed put while Begonia, Clem, and Ivy had given him hugs on the way to the room—lifted up from his position as soon as I walked the cart to the door. Always watchful, always protective. It only took a moment for Croft to appear, obviously having kept an eye on Argo's position through his room's open door.

He held up a hand to stop me, insistent on doing his duty. I watched him move, observing the tasks of a position he'd taken so much pride in. There were many things I admired about him. His kindness alone made my heart race. And after what had happened in the city ... the way he'd protected me, defended me, fought for me ... I understood more about emotional depth than I'd ever had. Seeing things and experiencing them from an outside view with a Clear stone, or even from inside someone else's thoughts with the Cloud stone ... None of it compared. I'd never been closer to someone, and I knew that wouldn't change at all after the link between us was broken. I felt everything for him.

When he'd finished pushing the cart outside for another attendant to take away, he closed the door and turned to find me watching. His eyebrows tugged together in a questioning look.

"Croft." His name left my lips in a choked whisper. My eyes watered, the entirety of the day's events slamming into me all at once. I couldn't hold it all in anymore. "I'm not … I can't …"

His body moved to mine as my first tear escaped, lifting one hand to look over my bandaged arm while the other cradled my face steadily, thumb wiping the tear from my cheek. He held my face angled toward his, peering down into my eyes. *"Pain?"* He mouthed the word, and I shook my head. *"Tell me."*

The sobs started, and I struggled to keep them under control so the others wouldn't hear. "I'm not sure how I can thank you. You saved me. But you shouldn't have fought him. You could have been hurt. And I … I couldn't even move. I was so shocked. So scared and useless."

"No. You were frightened." His head shook with the thought, eyes flitting between mine and my lips. *"I'm sorry. I have the training and should have seen it sooner."*

My body trembled. From all the emotion. From his comfort. "After seeing the couple. Seeing what actually happens. I didn't know. How could I not have known? I always wondered about my family, wondered if they'd died or had given me away. I had no idea that we're taken away and placed in the Nurseries. They don't even have a choice, do they?"

He frowned, processing all the words I'd spoken too quickly. It took him several moments, but he simply shook his head.

"And then, seeing Begonia and Clem ... They look unhealthy. Starved for food. Stripped of what little individuality they had. They're grouped together, the Clear stones. I understand why it might be that way, but I had no idea they are treated so differently than everyone else. They don't even want to discuss what they've experienced, but it's nothing like what they'd hoped for after leaving Shadowstone. How can they be treated as lesser when they're integral to the kingdom's safety? I'm so confused and frustrated and ... sad. I'm so sad about it all. I don't know what to do."

I moved my limp arms up and around his waist, clutching his strong back, needing that support that had soothed me earlier in the day.

"Olean." His other hand lifted to my face too, wiping more tears. The sorrow in his amber eyes changed while we were locked, a fierceness entering them as his brows dropped and his lips pursed. He slid his hands down my neck and over my shoulders, abandoning our eye contact in exchange for pulling me close against his chest. His grip tightened as much as mine had, giving me the strength to hold on while I continued to shake.

"You're all right. I have you." He held me, and held me, and held me more until my tears dried. And when the thought of Ivy, Begonia, or Clem exiting the room had me pulling back, he tightened his grip for several more moments as if he knew my retreat was reluctant and too early. I would have continued on, soaking up his warmth and smell, losing myself inside it all, but I knew it was bordering on inappropriate. He was caring for me, being nicer than he needed to. And though I heard and understood some of his thoughts, I still wasn't sure how he truly felt. If I

was only part of his job, or if I was something else. Because I was starting to feel more for him.

The truth needed to come. All of it, including what I'd finally realized at the couple's house, what had had me dazed. He was the late king's son.

Argo stood upright in our periphery, staring at the door. A knock followed a second later, and Croft pulled back, eyes still on me. After brushing his thumb over my cheek one more time, he let me go and answered the door.

Worried about who it might be, I wiped my hands down my face to clear the tears away fully. The brows I'd painted on before the trip into the city were of no concern. They had already disappeared, having smeared off onto my pillow while I'd slept.

A short female attendant moved forward to enter, but Croft blocked her way. *"No."*

The attendant stepped back with a nervous smile and a blush in her cheeks. "Sorry, uh, Croft. I'm so used to everyone always saying enter." While I looked at her toothy smile from behind Croft's large body, giving her my own soft smile, I could see from the side of Croft's stern face he didn't bother reciprocating. He was back to his usual gruffness, pleasantries long gone. Though after what had happened in the city, it was perfectly understandable.

The smile wilted right off her face. "I was sent to deliver a message from Wolfsbane. He will speak to you and Olean tomorrow morning. You are to meet him in the prison early. Imogen is to be read."

Croft nodded once to show his understanding. When she didn't move right away, he took a step forward, forcing her to take a step back. Then he closed the door.

He lifted his eyebrows at me in obvious question. *"You get that?"*

I nodded with a chuckle. "I heard her. And you were awfully curt."

He stalked the few long strides to me, his body large and formidable. It was no wonder the attendant was intimidated. Though whether her reactions were due to attraction or fear, I had no idea. For me, it was most definitely the former.

He stopped a pace away, looking into my eyes, and thought, *"Not risking anything. I was too trusting before. It won't happen again."* Instead of mouthing the same or grabbing paper to write out the explanation, he merely shrugged with a long blink and a quirk in one side of his lips.

Well. That made my heart kick.

The others came out into the main room again, and Ivy called for me to show Clem and Begonia my room. I uttered, "Yes, go ahead," and hoped they hadn't noticed how difficult it was for me to look away from Croft. Especially when his mouth stretched into a full smile, noticing my hesitation to join them.

Finally, as he inclined his head toward his room to show that was where he would be, I pressed my lips together and tore myself away.

Despite how stifling I'd imagined it would be trapped inside my rooms with an attendant watching my every move, it had turned into our safe space. Having Ivy and Croft with me was like a spring day inside a winter storm, comforting and refreshing. And with Begonia and Clem also with us, that feeling only grew, giving me more to prepare and fight for, come whatever may.

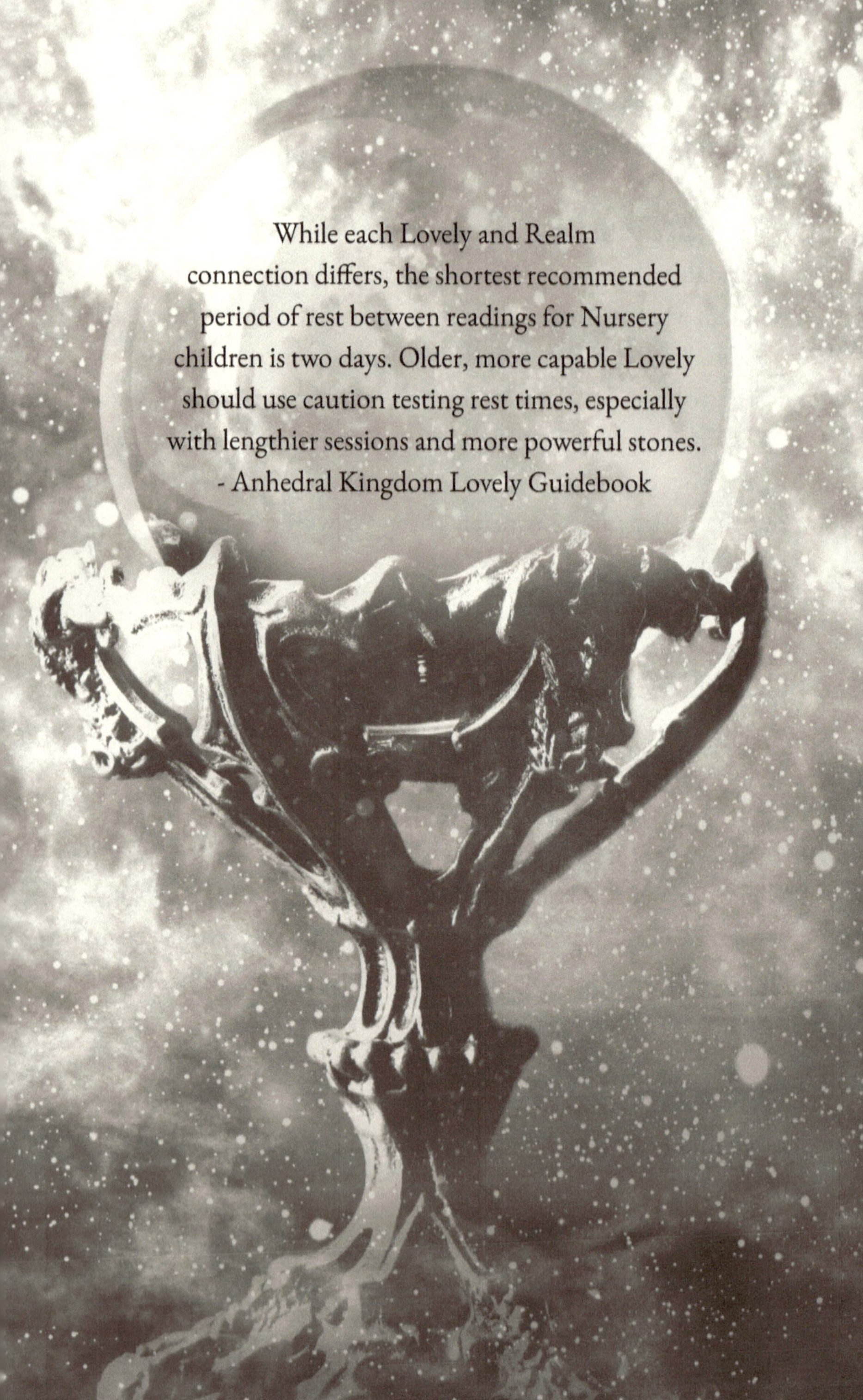

While each Lovely and Realm
connection differs, the shortest recommended
period of rest between readings for Nursery
children is two days. Older, more capable Lovely
should use caution testing rest times, especially
with lengthier sessions and more powerful stones.
- Anhedral Kingdom Lovely Guidebook

The next morning, Wolf stood at the entrance of the castle's prison located three levels below ground in the south wing, much like the Realm Room in the southeast wing. He looked a little more rested than he had the last time I saw him, his focus noticeable.

I found myself feeling the same after the previous night, getting more sleep despite extra restless bodies in my room. With no one showing up to try to reclaim Begonia and Clem, they stayed with us. We'd never shared rooms in Shadowstone, but Ivy had asked Croft to help move her bedding into my room so they wouldn't have to be alone. Part of me wondered if Begonia and Clem agreed to join us only to appease Ivy. Yet when everyone settled, I realized it had been a collective need. I'd reluctantly sent them back to their Clear stone class duties after breakfast, knowing that keeping them away would do more harm than good. Refusing their assignments wouldn't solve the issues immediately. Among all the other problems, that one had to be dealt with more delicately and in due time, especially since Hydrangea was the Clear stone head.

"Croft. Olean. I was sorry to hear about yesterday, and I'm glad you both are all right." His gaze swept between us. There was a bit of detachment in his words. Not that he hadn't meant what he said, but that something else had taken precedence over any other thought.

"Hello, Wolf," I replied, my stomach twisting. Something had happened. I looked around the dim, empty hallway. The stretch leading to the stairs appeared like most others in the castle, with intricate trim and finished walls holding sconces and lavish paintings. But the single wall of the prison's entrance had retained an older facade, vertical iron bars buried deep into granite to create the prison entrance, closing off the tunnel disappearing into darkness behind it.

Croft motioned to Wolf while thinking, *"Will it be here or the trial room?"*

Wolf sighed, having understood enough of the hand movements. "I planned for us to meet here, to read Imogen ourselves since her official reading kept getting delayed by the dowager queen and lack of official orders from the king. But when I arrived, they were already carrying away her body."

"She's dead?" I asked, horrified.

"How?" Croft mouthed the question and also cupped his hands, with bent fingers, tips all pressed together, and made a forward semicircle.

"She used her dress. Hung herself from one of the overhead iron bars anchored in the rock." Croft motioned something too quickly for me to see and Wolf replied, "There were two attendants, two guards, and a solider posted outside here. I read them all already. All told the truth."

"So she did it to herself. Like Alve?" I asked.

"Exactly." Croft's thought was in agreement.

"Yes. And we can guess why." Wolf glanced around, making sure no one could overhear. "Whoever we're searching for is covering up their mess. They knew if Alve or Imogen were read, we would see the evidence. There's no way to know if we could have seen who's behind it, but we might have proven a Blood stone had been used to control Imogen and Alve through their readings."

"Now they both seem guilty, and we have nothing," I said, piecing it together.

"But why try to kill Olean?" Croft moved his hands to signal the same to Wolf. His thoughts were almost too angry for me to decipher, the tones even more jumbled than usual.

"We'd wondered before if they watched your test closely enough to see you scent the Blood stone. I think the attempt on your life confirms that they did. They know you are the only other Lovely who could know what really happened."

"They will try again." At my side, Croft's entire body turned rigid.

"Yes," I agreed to both of them, no longer able to dismiss Alve's stabbing me as simply being a close enough target.

Wolf shook his head and began to walk, waving for us to follow. "We need to see the king, inform him about everything. Unfortunately, his time for mourning is over. He has some decisions to make."

Breakfast had already finished, so we passed many attendants moving carts and goods along the trip to the king's royal study and meeting rooms in the northeast wing. Guards and soldiers with wolfdogs stood watch at intervals along every hallway as they had since the late king's death. Though, as we neared, they were grouped closer together. Armed, alert, and prepared for an enemy we'd yet to determine.

We were permitted entry quickly and ushered through several spaces to reach a stately room filled with tables overflowing with all kinds of intricate items. Maps. Small lifelike carvings of other castles in other countries. Compasses. More maps with lines, marks, and Xs inked over the surfaces. There were also shelves of books along each wall, a few settees and chaises, and a grand desk positioned in front of the far window. And beside the expansive fireplace was an oval mirror as black as night, framed in a strip of solid, dark stained iron and wrapped in swirling filigree. It was beautiful. It was *the* mirror. The Black stone mirror.

"Your Majesty," Wolf called loudly, drawing my attention back to the reason we were there.

A loud thunk and clanking glass had us all looking in that same direction, toward the mirror, the tall fireplace in the corner, and the one settee that faced away from the entrance. King Ren stood upright from where he had fallen from the settee, clothing rumpled, shirt untucked. He wobbled on his bare feet, using the seat's back for balance. Several carafes and bottles perched on the tea table next to him. All open and empty.

"What is it?"

The skin on Wolf's face had many lines and some places of sagging skin, but those did nothing to disguise the clench of his jaw. "We need to discuss some things without the ears of others. Sit." He pointed to the chair behind the massive desk. "Guards and other attendants can wait outside."

The king huffed a breath, his flickering gaze stilling on the desk. The frown on his lips and close of his eyes said more than words could. He walked slowly toward it, steady enough not to stumble.

As everyone else cleared the room, we approached and stopped behind the guest chairs in front. Argo followed, taking a seat at Croft's other side.

Wolf went on, ignoring the king's emotional struggle. "If you haven't been informed, some of the Lovely were attacked in the city yesterday. Oleander was hurt, but Croft prevented much worse from happening."

King Ren's eyes left the desk, and he looked me over, noticing the bandage on my arm. His full lips parted, and he took a single step in my direction. "Olean."

Croft matched his step with one of his own as if to come between us. *"Don't."*

The king noticed, halting in place. A moment of clarity hit him, recalling what had happened the last time he'd touched me. His eyes went wide. "Sorry." He relented, moved around the desk, and sat down in the chair, surprisingly keeping his focus on us, eyes flitting back and forth. "I'm sorry that happened to you and thankful it wasn't more serious."

"It could have been," Wolf added, obviously having been briefed more extensively by someone the previous day. I'd imagined it was the soldiers or possibly even Kalmia, though she had to have been distraught about Alve.

"Well," King Ren said with a dip of his chin. "Whoever is to blame, we will have them stand trial immediately. They will suffer the worst punishment imaginable."

"It was Alve, the attendant assigned to Kalmia after the king's death. And he can't suffer anymore as he's already dead," Wolf noted.

"Mighty fine job, Croft. Your training with the soldiers met all expectations. Excellent," the new king said, looking purposefully at Croft. The words were genuine but also stilted, indicating the discomfort of sitting in his father's chair—possibly for the first time—along with his stiff posture and jittery hands.

Wolf crossed his arms and released a frustrated breath. "Your Majesty, while Croft did an excellent job of protecting them all, he didn't kill him. Alve killed himself."

"Why would he do that?"

"Why, indeed," Wolf said. "And why would Imogen kill herself this morning as well, right before she was to be read about her involvement in the king's death."

"What?" That information had managed to clear a path in his head through the wine and sorrow.

"It's true," Wolf said, eyes finding mine.

It was time. We had to tell him and hope that he was sober enough to comprehend it all.

"Your Majesty, I discovered something at the induction that we need to discuss. You told me that your father was obsessed with finding the Blood stone. I believe another Lovely has found it and used it to kill the king, had Alve and Imogen kill themselves, and possibly is to blame for the other murders as well."

The placid look upon his face changed at my words, upper lip lifting, eyes narrowing. He turned to Croft, then to Wolf. "You're serious? Imogen wasn't to blame then?"

Croft huffed an annoyed breath and thought, *"It's time to pay attention."*

Wolf nodded. "Imogen was surely the one to hand the wine off, possibly the one to add the poison, but she was being controlled by someone else."

"How do you know this? No one has seen a Blood stone in years. Why wouldn't my father have known?"

"I'm the one who knows because I scented one during my test," I answered somberly.

Wolf continued with the information, filling the king in on the events of the induction, how he knew about the buried pieces, vouching for my story, and why I'd suspected Imogen had been controlled.

"Why wasn't I informed right away?" King Ren leaned over, his face pointed to the desk, which made Croft shift his weight from foot to foot.

I'd noticed he reacted that way occasionally if he was unable to read someone's lips. Annoyance and frustration at being disregarded.

I turned my face toward him when I replied to the king, "I debated telling you when you came to my room that night, but you didn't appear to be in a condition to listen."

The king cleared his throat uncomfortably, recalling the night he'd visited again. "No, I wasn't," he admitted, wiping a hand over his mouth then over the back of his neck before straightening upright. "I'm listening now. What happened to Imogen?"

Wolf recounted the morning's events, noting that Imogen's reading kept being put off and it could have been because of the Lovely we had suspected.

"I feel as if I'm already drowning. I have to lay my father to rest. My mother wants a celebration, to call a full court gathering, use everything we had for the induction ball plus add more to properly see him off while possibly holding my coronation. I need to speak to his advisory council regarding all the army posts along our borders and inland, and dig into all the things he had woefully ignored." He sighed and looked at Wolf, defeated. "And this ... An enemy within. I won't pretend to know how this should be handled. What do we do?"

Wolf glanced at us, raising his eyebrows, the simple thick lines of black paint lifting in high arches.

Croft grabbed a piece of paper and pen from the desk and started writing. He handed it over for me to read. "Imogen wasn't questioned, but Olean can be read. It should be in front of others, to inform everyone so there's no question of the truth. We should also question all the Lovely. They weren't read after induction because no one believed there to be a reason. And if they were read about the other murders, something could have been missed, misunderstood, or covered up, especially if more than one are working together."

"Yes, I agree that will be the way to determine things, but we still don't know who's to blame. If we don't have more details pointing to the specific Lovely, they'll feel more threatened, which might make things worse," Wolf answered.

Croft wrote, and I read, "They're already threatened. They attacked Olean because they know she can find the Blood stone. They want to cover it all quickly. Could have been what happened with Nightshade and Dahlia. Maybe they found something out."

"Possible," Wolf agreed.

"Actually, they tried to attack me when I first arrived, before the induction," I recalled. "I'm not sure why, unless they just wanted a distraction. Imogen brought dinner, and Argo scented something. She acted confused that night, said she'd been dealing with headaches. That confusion is how I made the connection at the induction. She was staring at nothing after it happened, not understanding what was going on around her."

"Right. The spices," Croft thought.

"And in the city, they waited to attack," I added. "Alve could have stabbed me several times over while he sat beside me in the coach. But it didn't happen until after we saw the couple. Maybe they had to wait for some reason. Or whoever used the Blood stone had to be close by?"

"Could be. It'll be a challenge to determine everyone's schedules or ask whereabouts without raising more suspicion. Did you happen to notice anyone else around at either time?" Wolf asked.

"No. I'd been inside my rooms before dinner that night. And in the city ... I don't recall seeing anyone after we left the couple's house." I hadn't exactly been thinking clearly at that time, but I wasn't about to bring up why. Croft being the late king's son was a whole different issue I would have to admit soon enough. Especially if he was the eldest son, which I hadn't really considered. He was an orphan, but when had he been born? He and Ren certainly looked close in age.

Wolf rubbed a hand over his smooth head and started to pace. Everyone thought silently for some time, then Wolf stopped in front of the desk again. "Olean can scent the Blood stone. No one else can." His face turned to me, his eyes apologetic. "If I could, I would. So it has to be you. You'll use the Eye stone again, this time without anyone outside this room knowing you're inhabiting a wolfdog. You'll search the castle alongside one of the soldiers who have an active post, assigned to walk the grounds and check rooms. That'll give you more access. Whoever's using the stone either has it in their possession or has it hidden close."

"Should we inform the soldier?" The king inquired, his eyes somber but clearer than they had been. "It might be difficult otherwise."

"Yes," Wolf agreed, looking at him. "We can screen one this evening. You'll have to decide whether or not to inform the dowager queen."

The new king scrubbed both hands through his thick, short hair, letting out an exasperated sigh that seemed to come from his bones. "I'm not sure that's a good idea if the Garden's second-in-command and the trial council primary are two of those suspected. My sister and mother are naturally close to their appointed Lovely."

Croft wrote quickly and handed it over to me. "Don't. Given her current emotional state, a possible betrayal from someone she trusts will not be taken well, whether or not she chooses to believe it. Either way, her reaction will be unstable."

"I agree." The king stood with an overhead stretch. "Croft, please continue on with Olean. I've been covered well enough, and the threat against her is more imperative. You've done very well with everything. Olean, you haven't said much. I know it's your duty and you've taken a vow, but are you feeling up to this task after all that has happened?"

"She's more than capable. Stronger than most I know." Croft's thoughts had me coughing as I tried to inhale, making me look far weaker than his very questionable praise gave me credit for.

"I believe I can do this, yes," I replied.

"You'll have to try to be as efficient as possible. There's a lot of ground for you to cover. With no help, you might need to conserve your stone contact time so you don't encounter any setbacks with your mind. Wolf, you'll have to check in with her daily, yes?"

Wolf nodded in reply, confirming the concern.

If I was to connect daily, there were many risks involved, including addiction and mental strain. It would be more time than I'd ever been in the Realm consecutively. Cordelia was always overly cautious with our rotations in Shadowstone, especially after rough trial readings.

"Good. Well, if there's nothing else. You may go to rest for the evening. Report with Wolf tomorrow."

As Croft moved to turn around, I spoke again, needing to make sure one more thing was settled before I started the assigned task. "I do have something else. A request, if you will. The others, my … Nursery mates. Clem and Begonia. May they stay with me like Ivy is? I understand that Clear usually are housed together, but they are not doing well. I believe it would be good for them, and me, if we are permitted to stay together."

There. I'd done it as tactfully as I could, even though I'd wanted to report my thoughts on how all the Clear stones were treated. I'd managed to keep all the rest to myself. At least for the time being.

The king stared at me, his focus intense. "You're unhappy with how they are placed?"

Croft had repositioned himself at my side again. Watching. I wasn't sure he'd caught all that I'd said, but his eyes were set on King Ren's reply.

I took a deep breath, preparing myself, not willing to lie. "Yes. I didn't want to bring it all up in discussion because of what else is happening, but yes. They haven't been here long and it's obvious that the Clear stones aren't treated as favorably, or possibly endure a continued lack of consideration. They've lost weight. They look excessively tired. I understand that they were worked hard after the induction in order to sort through all the attendees, but it seems to be more than that." I couldn't look at Wolf. The fear of overstepping had me only staring at the king, hoping I hadn't leaped over some kind of council command order, or undone what trust I'd started to build by doing what I believed to be the right thing.

King Ren rolled his lips together, looking around his father's desk. He nodded once. "Yes, well, there are many things that are in dire need of change, as I mentioned earlier. And while I hope to address them all, the priority is finding whoever murdered my father first."

"Of course," I admitted, my voice nearly a murmur.

"But I do not wish for anyone to go without, or be worked into exhaustion. So they may stay with you if you feel it will help. I will discuss the Clear's routines and quarters with my mother and Hydra, regardless of what else is happening."

I nodded with a small smile. "Thank you, Your Majesty."

"You're welcome. After everything you have proven so far, I believe you will find the evidence we need. If that is all, I wish you all the favor of the Realm in the days to come." When I curtsied, and Croft and I turned to leave, he continued to speak with Wolf. "All right. Let's decide on the soldier and wolfdog. If we need to speak with Commander Tromlien to find the best on the rotation, let's do it."

To receive eternal protection,
the Lovely pledged their servitude to
Crown and kingdom generations ago.
Should a Lovely break their vow or any law,
a trial will determine a punishment
ranging from dismissal to death.
- Anhedral Kingdom Lovely Laws and Customs

~ 21 ~

The afternoon following the meeting had been mostly quiet. Croft and I had returned to the rooms, lost in our own thoughts regarding all that had been discussed with Wolf and the new king. I took most of the time to rest, knowing that my upcoming Eye stone connections would be taxing. When I came out into the main area for the midday meal, I caught Croft's eyes on me, seeming worried or curious. I'd stolen glances at him as well, wondering how he would take the news about his father, if he knew who his mother had been before he was orphaned, and if he was the rightful heir despite being illegitimate.

We exchanged some thoughts about the mission while we ate, like what the best order of search was and how much ground I should aim to cover during a single connection in a day. We decided it best to check the personal rooms first as it would naturally be the easiest and most accessible place to conceal a stone.

But it could be anywhere, and that thought already had me tired and discouraged.

Ivy had returned from lessons a short time later, and Begonia and Clem weren't far behind, having finished their Clear stone duties and released back to my rooms. They hadn't been questioned or stopped, which was reassuring and also unnerving, knowing that Hydra had been informed of the change.

Though her personality suggested a deep-rooted sternness for upholding the Crown rules, I had to wonder if as a Lovely she might welcome a change for the betterment of our people. Except, of course, if she had been involved with the murders. Then she was likely opposed.

No one else could know about my assignment, but I had to at least warn the others to use caution while they were outside of our care. Before they all left the following morning, I chose to tell them to guard their blood and to be wary of anyone, including the Lovely. Begonia and Clem accepted my lack of information well enough, understanding that their safety would be at stake if we were to disclose more. Ivy, however, fought us for a few moments, not fully grasping the need for secrets. She finally relented and agreed to be extra careful around everyone and to not tell anyone what we'd discussed, even Guardian Calla.

Then it was time.

A soldier knocked on the main door, and Croft answered. Nearly as broad and tall as most male soldiers, with well-defined musculature under the plain battle leather uniform, tightly braided and wrapped golden hair, and a friendly smile, she introduced herself as Willa in a firm, professional voice. She carried the usual short sword and side dagger like all the others on inner castle patrols. We invited her inside, and she handed a wooden box to Croft. Then in a slightly more adoring tone, she introduced her female wolfdog as Mais. "She placed first in the most recent wolfdog challenge, which tests in agility, scenting in multiple divisions, and detainment. She's been tasked in many Eye stone missions, all of which have been successful and without issue."

"Impressive," Croft thought, eyeing Argo while setting the box onto the table. *"Don't feel bad. You're important too."*

"Thank you for that information," I replied, keeping my tone steady despite wanting to laugh. While Argo was very disciplined, he was still curious, sniffing the air in her direction without leaving Croft's side. Mais, however, couldn't have cared less about his presence, barely sparing him a glance. "I will treat her with respect and try my best to live up to those standards. Though I wish I had seen some of her normal training to match your procedures."

"That's no problem. I'll guide you along the way. Since we will be indoors, you will not be restrained. They heel on the right side and don't move ahead unless told to. If you scent anything, you can whine, give a single bark, or paw to give me direction. I will talk to you whenever it's necessary or if we're alone, but I will remain mostly silent so that no one, especially other soldiers, notices a difference."

"All right. That sounds manageable. They didn't give you any other directions?" I asked, to be sure.

"They mentioned you and Croft could determine the route since I'm currently on a roaming rotation, but also recommended starting with the rooms first."

"What we thought as well." Croft nodded and handed her the paper we'd used earlier to outline the day's course.

Willa took a quick look. "Right. We'll stay in this wing first and move on depending on how you're feeling. Since this is only your second time using the Eye stone, we should track time closely for safety as well. I'll update you on that since I've heard it's difficult to recognize while you're in the wolfdog's focused mind. They also said that no one is to deny us entry even if a room is occupied. I have the king's signature card if anyone questions us, explaining that all rooms are being searched by his order. We are not to answer questions, only defer to him."

"Good." Croft crossed his arms over his chest with the thought. *"That should keep the guilty from assuming the purpose too quickly."*

I breathed deeply and looked toward the settee. "If there's nothing else, we should get started."

Croft grabbed the wooden box again and moved with me. As soon as I was seated, he removed a large Eye stone, and situated it in front of me on its square iron base. The streak of light curved along the blue surface, entrancing me again with its beauty, this time in the daylight. Croft removed another stone with a wrapped wire base and placed it directly behind the other. A Needled stone, meant to amplify my range.

When I lifted my eyes, his were there to catch me. That single eyebrow pulled high in question before his thought even registered. *"All right?"*

"I'm ready," I said with a reassuring smile.

He stared at me for a few seconds, then pointed to himself and to the ground. *"I'll be with you here the whole time."*

My smile grew, touched by his concern. "I know. Thank you."

He nodded, then turned to Willa and Mais, drawing his slim attendant's dagger. Willa instructed where it was best to draw the blood, and Mais didn't even flinch when Croft did. He used a cloth to collect it, then smeared it over the stone.

After another deep breath, I reached forward, extending some fingertips to the second stone, and let the Realm welcome me.

Darkness consumed everything as my mind swept away in a constricting, twisting motion once again. The transition was even easier than before, and in only an instant my vision brightened to a view of Argo's large gray head and floppy ears beside Croft's waist. Like before, most colors had dulled, but my vision remained sharp.

Mais accepted my presence nicely. I opened my mouth and gave a quick bark.

"Wonderful. Shall we go?" Willa asked.

I looked at the settee, seeing my body in its immobile state, my hands on the stones. The sight never failed to evoke an array of emotion—awkwardness, fear, happiness. The experience of separating from your own body unlike anything else.

Croft's eyes shifted from me to my body, noticing my pause. *"I have you."*

I heard him! The night of the induction, there had been too much commotion while inside the wolfdog, and he'd been too far at the start. His thoughts came clear now, possibly from being so close.

I barked one more time and turned toward the door.

All the Eye stone capable Lovely were on our list of personal rooms to check. First, Hydrangea. Given that her duties as the dowager queen's appointed Lovely and head of the Clear stones presumably kept her away from her rooms for a majority of the day, we naturally started there.

None of the hallway guards questioned our appearance or our entering her room with a master key. That had me considering the protection of any room. Though, I should have known that a Lovely's space wasn't really protected, no matter our deemed level of importance.

Mais's body moved quickly, efficiently. Her feet soft and quiet, her ears sensitive, and her nose skilled enough to detect the closest guard's recent meal—spiced beans, buttery bread, and smoked chicken.

Paintings, plaques, furniture, sculptures, and other decorations filled Hydrangea's main area, which was the same size as my rooms only more cramped with piled possessions from years of service. Four doors could be seen as well, though she likely lived alone or with a single attendant. Several namesake shrubs resided on ledges or in larger pots throughout the space, offering a variety of rippled blooms from the palest whites to the darkest grays and blues—though there were likely shades of pink I couldn't see too. And their honeyed scent was ... nauseating.

The canine nose knew to stay away.

Dresses upon dresses filled the closets, armoires, and dressers in all the rooms. One room stood out to be what she used for sleeping. While the others appeared rather stale in decor, hers held personal goods and more tailored fittings. Books took up some space on the small table near the wide bed. Floral-patterned drapes with golden stitching hung over the three windows, so different from the standard black and silver of the kingdom's colors found in the rest of the castle.

I moved with purpose around it all, not wanting to waste time while still being thorough. Willa continued to keep silent in the room, likely using extra caution in the chance someone came too close to the outside door and could hear.

Nothing stood out. No poisons aside from the plants. No metallic decaying scent of the Blood stone. As I turned to leave her main bedroom, a different scent from the base of the wood armoire hit my nose, a tiny glimpse of something through the honeyed cloud blanketing the entire space.

Willa moved with me, pulling the front doors open and pushing the dresses around inside like she had in all the others. Shoes lined the bottom section also, but this one didn't only smell of musty feet sweat and stale floral perfume. Strawberry. The smell wafted up, and I lifted a paw at the base.

"Something?" Willa asked, crouching down to search through the shoes. She lifted a brown leather satchel from the back, and I whined to confirm. Her fingers moved fast, opening the top and removing the contents. A brush with several long black hairs. A glass perfume decanter of the strawberry scent. Cheek and lip stain. A silver handled mirror.

"Well," Willa said, eyeing me. "I'm guessing this is the dowager queen's. It wouldn't be hidden unless it either wasn't appreciated as a gift or not gifted at all."

I dipped my head.

"I was told we aren't to take anything that isn't linked to the Blood stone. We must leave it, to not panic anyone and cause more turmoil. If stealing from Queen Reina is her only offense, she'll be dealt with later."

As she placed everything back into the rightful place, I walked to the door and waited to move along.

Hemlock's quarters had the same amount of rooms and smelled of decay, but not the metallic rusty kind I'd hoped for. He harbored scraps of food in many different places around his rooms, some I doubted he recalled since they'd been in various states of decomposition much like the compost stations we used to maintain healthy garden soil in Shadowstone. And it wasn't only my dog nose that could smell it.

Willa opened a dresser drawer and gagged. "Does he not allow attendants in here? It smells worse than the wolfdog kennels. This has to be unhealthy."

I agreed but didn't bother barking. The search had to continue on. Hemlock's namesake plant gave a majority of the main sitting room's overall bad aroma, adding a musty and bitter animal urine scent that had to be the true kennel connection for Willa, even though she wasn't as aware of the main source. I wasn't all too surprised when I sniffed out a more pleasant scent coming from one of the extra rooms. We opened it to find items gathered on the bed, also things stacked on the two tables, and an empty easel standing in the corner by the single window. Unable to see clearly, I had to lift on my hind legs, setting my front paws on the bed's edge to see what items were there. Sketches littered the bed and the tables. Stacks of paper too. Uncountable pieces of charcoal in different sizes spread across it all. It was messy, much like his main rooms. But the pictures ...

"Amazing," Willa said, lifting one. "He's truly gifted. And maybe obsessed."

They were all the princess. In various poses and level of dress. I moved to the table and stood to see more. All her. The thick and thin strokes of charcoal held so much depth in very few lines. He captured her in all manners, all emotions. They were beautiful.

"He's deeply in love with her. I hope it's reciprocated because otherwise, this could be a clue to his involvement."

It was true. Even though we hadn't found the stone, both rooms had possible hints of involvement. Hydra having stolen from the queen could easily mean she envied her position and wanted the same power. And Hemlock's drawings could very well be unrequited love, which often ended badly. I'd seen it enough times to know, the last time being the worst, with the Shadowstone's chancellor and Countess Ashboard.

We covered four more personal rooms before Willa declared us finished for the day. Titan, Wisteria, Azalea, and Yew all had Eye stone capabilities, so their rooms had also been at the top of our list. Titan's room was the only one concealing anything important. A dresser drawer smelling of fresh sea water revealed a pendant with a clear stone much like the one Cordelia had given me. His didn't hold the late king's inscribed initials, though. None of the rooms smelled like the Blood stone or held anything more than items from their individual hobbies and fancy clothing.

A few hours had passed since our start, which was a long duration itself, never mind for only my second time connected to the Eye stone. Willa decided it was best for me to disconnect without returning to my room to keep her and Mais's visits there to a minimum. Connections would also be done at a distance to prevent unwanted rumors by the guards and attendants. She informed me where she and Mais would be at ten the next morning, so I wouldn't be too disorientated when we began the next session.

After I bowed my head with a soft whine, I forced myself to leave the Realm.

A gasp left my mouth as the room spun upon my return. The dizzying sensation hit me harder than the first time, likely because of the duration. I instantly saw Croft seated in the chair he'd positioned beside the fireplace and across from the settee. He jumped to his feet in response to my movement.

My stomach churned, unwilling to wait for my feet to move me to the bathing room to be sick. There would be no holding it back. I leaned over, readying to vomit all over the beautiful, intricately knotted rug. But I noticed an emptied fireplace bucket right at my feet just as the contents of my stomach came up.

I remained hunched over for a time. Embarrassment shouldn't have been an issue given what I had been doing, yet I couldn't help to feel that way as I watched Croft's legs and feet move around the floor in front of me. His hands came into view too, placing water and a dampened cloth onto the table. I could sense his nervousness as he waited for me to sit upright.

I took hold of the cloth first, making sure to wipe my face and mouth clear before finally lifting up.

His eyebrows dipped, and he mouthed, *"Are you all right?"*

"Yes," I croaked, the nausea settling, the room stilling. "I'm so sorry you had to watch that again. Thank you for the bucket. I'll clean it all in a bit."

He waved his hands low. *"Don't be sorry. It's no problem."*

"I'll tell you what happened. I just need a minute." I stood and shuffled to the bathing room to clean up and take a moment to breathe. When I returned, Croft passed me with the bucket and cloth to take care of the mess. I let out an exasperated sigh and sat on the settee again, my body and mind fatigued beyond belief.

As soon as Croft reentered the room, I stared until he noticed my irritation. "You should have let me do that."

He rolled his eyes and shook his head. *"No, because if that bucket had sat for even another minute, I would have added more to it."*

I chuckled and dropped my eyes to my lap to be sure he didn't know I'd understood. After a moment, I looked back up and started in on the information, recalling all Willa and I had found and all we hadn't.

Croft grabbed some paper from the tea table and started writing. *"So nothing too telling in the rooms. What are your thoughts?"*

"My ...?" He wasn't only wanting the facts but how I interpreted them. I had to smile at that. As a Lovely, our thoughts after a connection weren't regarded. We were there to state the truth. Relay the information. Our opinions never counted. Sure, the new king had asked how I felt about doing the mission, but that wasn't the same as wanting my thoughts on the topics. Croft was different, though.

His eyebrows went up and his lips scrunched in an adorable, mocking gesture. He wrote, *"Having problems reading my scribble?"*

I laughed and shook my head. "No, it's just ... It's not a question for us usually. Our thoughts. Only facts. Truth. We give the reality of what the Realm shows us, other people's thoughts, not our own. I'm not used to it."

He nodded, then used a hand to comb the strands of loose, wavy hair away from his face. There were pauses while he wrote the next words. *"Get used to it. You're important, Olean. In so many ways.*

Right now, you are this kingdom's biggest asset, the most valuable, and not only for your Realm ability. Your intelligence, strength, and honesty are what this kingdom needs."

All of those felt like a kick to my stomach, especially the last. Honesty. I was not being honest with him, and he had done nothing but protect me and treat me kindly since I'd arrived. I dropped my face, not wanting him to see the turmoil stirring inside. How could I tell him?

His fingers touched beneath my chin, lifting my eyes back to his. He stared at me, the intensity building. Once again, it was as if he were diving into my mind, my soul, trying to see it all.

I felt like a liar, knowing there'd never be a good time to admit the truth, especially when I needed him to continue this Eye stone mission with me. I couldn't do it without him, and he would surely leave if I told him everything.

I chuckled and licked my lips nervously to hide my discomfort, then said, "That's very kind, but I'm only doing my duty, as so many others are."

His fingers fell away from my skin, yet his eyes continued their infinite exploration as his thoughts ran and ran and ran. *"You are so much more. To them. And to me? I shouldn't want you the way I do. You are a Lovely, and I am an attendant who's been too close. I should have fought harder to give you more space, to be sure this proximity isn't to blame. But I can't deny what I feel, or what I see in your eyes when you look at me. I wish I could speak these words to you because I don't think writing them will ever suffice."*

I wanted to melt. To cry. To tell him I'd heard every word. To kiss him that very moment. Because I had never experienced an emotion so bone deep before, like so many mixed into one, digging into every part of my being and staying until my final breaths. I should have been rejoicing, but it only made me feel worse.

A few hard knocks on the outside door startled me and Argo too. He woke up with a bark, and sat upright by the fireplace.

"Food," Croft wrote. *"Hopefully, you can eat some before you rest."*

He got up and moved to the door, and I was glad for the reprieve because I was moments away from falling apart in front of him.

He deserved so much more than being lied to.

While people and animal deaths
have occurred during Cloud and Eye
stone connections, via injuries, accidents, etc.,
there has been no recorded instance where
the connected Lovely died as a direct result.
- Anhedral Kingdom Lovely Guidebook

22

Days proceeded the same. Not long after Ivy left for lessons and Begonia and Clem went to their duties, whether for their own lessons or Clear stone readings, I would connect with the Eye stone, using a cloth of Mais's blood. Wolf had brought a small vial the first night he checked in so Willa and Mais wouldn't be seen too often around my rooms. Though, he stated one of the old cloths would work in a bind. With some water added, the dried blood could be smeared over the stone, but the connection usually wasn't as strong. It was good information to keep in mind, and it made me wonder if whoever had used the Blood stone had needed to do the same. I doubted Alve or Imogen had willingly offered their fresh blood, unless under control already.

Willa and I moved throughout the castle without issue. Some other soldiers would stop her to talk about their posts or ask about her assignment, but there were no other disturbances. We'd searched rooms while other Lovely were present or passed them in the hallways. Even Wolf and King Ren had walked by us, neither talking or even sparing a noticeable glance to ensure the secrecy of our search.

I connected for longer periods each day, faring no ill effects mentally or physically, aside from vomiting, which had stopped altogether after a few days. And as always, Croft had been there, waiting and watching over my physical body, ready to give me anything I needed. We'd been closer than ever during those times, in the brief periods alone before Ivy, Clem, and Begonia returned to the rooms.

A week and a half had gone, the time seeming too fast and too slow at once. I'd taken only one day off during that, Wolf insisting on it despite his acknowledgment of my good mental state. That day had been almost entirely sleep. Mais had also had a checkup. She was good as well, having no issues stemming from my mental intrusion and readjusting quickly after each session. We'd made some progress, searching several main rooms including the kitchens, pantries, great hall, formal throne room, Realm room, Clear stone quarters, and guards and attendants quarters. We'd found nothing.

We switched the time to see if it would help at all, later than usual, nearing dinner. After finishing the lower level of the south wing in the prison, we ascended and moved toward the southwest wing, an area I hadn't visited. We passed Kalmia as she left the White stone room with several other Lovely, possibly from a division meeting or session. Her petite body and drawn face looked forlorn and a little dazed. It made me wonder if she had been tasked by the dowager queen to continue seeking out the late king. It was possible. I hadn't known much of the happenings around the castle aside from things Ivy, Begonia, and Clem shared and information Wolf offered during his visits. Nothing else unusual had occurred since Alve's death. The king had met with his council to begin accepting his new role. The princess had been spending much of her time with the dowager queen, isolated in her rooms.

And an official notice had been sent throughout the kingdom to announce the late king's death and give news about the memorial ball Queen Reina had requested to be held after the funeral. It was to take place in four days, which made our search even more important and stressful. Each new day brought more activity throughout the hallways in preparations. Another reason we'd opted to try a later time.

With the White stone room cleared of occupants, we searched quickly. The room had paintings of past kings and queens as well as their ancestors, their portraits a reminder of those who might be seen when accessing the Realm. Everything else resembled an ordinary space compared to the other stone rooms, though the elaborate tables and tufted cushioned chairs looked the most comfortable of them all.

"Nothing?" Willa asked as I dipped low beneath the shelving, letting my nose be my guide, sorting through whatever scents were buried inside the thick White stone aroma of mint and forest wood and grass.

There was nothing.

I shook my head.

We descended to another lower level at the next stairway. Very few sconces flickered with flames along the separate hallway. Shadows spread into near darkness until the very end where one door stood, isolated much like the prison. My canine eyes adjusted well enough, picking up the subtleties in the dimness I knew I wouldn't ordinarily be able to see.

"Black stone room," Willa commented after trying the door and finding it locked. She removed her master key and pushed inside.

"No reason to keep it open if no one can use it, or could die if they tried."

She wasn't wrong. All who had through the years either died immediately because their brain could not handle the power or died by being trapped within, unable to break free of the Realm to rejoin their bodies.

I couldn't stop the shudder that spread through the wolfdog. There was no way to know how truthful all the old fables were. Stories often stemmed from reality, bent and twisted along the years, ripped and sewn together with new pieces to suit whatever need, but most still held some foundation of truth. The bits of truth were often the most difficult part to accept.

For the Black stone, it meant the unknown. The vast, untraveled, and unbridled division of the Realm, or possibly the full entirety. And that was terrifying. We had very little knowledge of what was possible within. Most assumed it showed everything the other stones could. Some thought it showed the future, something elusive to the rest, something desired by so many in the goal of ultimate power.

If King Antin had seen promise of a Lovely connecting to the Black stone, he might have obsessed over it as well, especially since he already had a collection said to be all that remained of them. There was a chance in the moments after my induction test, that he had an idea I'd connect to the Black stone as well as Blood. Because he had watched the detection test he'd buried below the soil. And I'd scented both for sure.

The confirmation of that hit me even before Willa pushed through the solid door, little whiffs of scent leaking from underneath. But as soon as it opened fully, the air within flooded my nose. Its stagnant smell of delicate flowers was both powerful and smooth. It made my wolfdog nose twitch.

"I see nothing," Willa whispered into the darkness. The dim light from the hallway added very little to the blackened room.

As Willa backed into the hallway to retrieve fire from the nearest sconce, I remained still, letting my eyes adjust and take in all the details. The view confused me at first. Though dots and streaks of the dim light mimicked a starry night, some stretched in an arch in the center of the space, bending, as if it were being pulled deep into a sky at the center of the room. Halfway up from the floor, though, it disappeared.

"Here we are," Willa said, stepping into the room with a burning wick. She moved around the room, lighting both the iron sconces on the walls as well as the four basins on pedestals.

I hadn't moved an inch. And as I stared downward at Mais's wolfdog front paws, lifting one to take the first step, I halted in place.

Black stone. Most all of it. The polished floor. The uncut boulders comprising the walls, stacked all the way up to the limestone ceiling. The carved pedestals with hollowed fire basins. And one massive half-sphere at the center of the room that left very little space to move around it.

"Realm. Now I understand why it's always locked. Others have said it holds all the Black stones, and it does."

Not all, I thought, an image of the mirror in the king's study coming to mind.

I set Mais's paw back down just behind the line in the floor, the division from slate to Black stone.

Noticing my hesitation, Willa said, "You're in another body. Do you believe something will happen if you make contact?"

A whine escaped me. There was no way to know for sure.

"Probably safer to assume so. There's a shelf behind here that you might want to check, though. Here, let me ..." She strode over and, with no struggle at all, she lifted me into her arms and carried me around the space, careful not to touch anything.

Viewing it from her hold, I could see that the half-sphere had made a circular table, platform ... or a bed. The story of Evil Queen Rose's Lovely being trapped within the Realm had me wondering if this was where the Lovely's body had been placed. Inside this room. Alone and detached, unable to escape.

A shelf had been carved into a boulder at the back of the room, holding a single smaller sphere cradled inside a cast iron display stand. There was nothing else. No other scent triggered my nose. And while the room wasn't exactly like the Realm room—made from a hallowed out individual stone—the strength of it was unmatched. Even inside the wolfdog, the power of the Realm pulsed to me as if to draw me in. There was a chance I could connect. I'd scented it after all. But there was no way to know if I would die or be trapped.

Willa circled around the half-sphere and set me back into the doorway.

"Let's lock up and quit for the night. Your dinner is probably waiting. I'm sure Croft is too." She chuckled with a head shake when I glanced up at her. "Apologies. I'm taking the liberty of being honest with you when you can't even reply. I've only seen you together once and it was enough. If anyone looks at you that way, like a favorite dog does, as if you are the center of their world, there's no reason to deny it. Unless, of course, you don't feel the same. But I could plainly see that you do too."

I retreated into the hallway with a small yip, glad I wasn't able to respond with words because there was no simple way to reply.

"We've been given clearance to start the royal rooms tomorrow. Let's go early shift again, yes?"

I nodded and calmed myself to disconnect.

The main sitting room spun into focus as my hands fell from the Eye stone onto the settee cushion. I gripped the material for balance and the world slowly settled.

When I looked up, I found Croft's eyes on mine already, as they had been all other days. The amber color like dark honey and as sweet too. The look they held was as Willa had said. Thoughtful and adoring. And also concerned and alluring. If she had seen it only once, maybe it had been foolish of me to question my own sight over and over again.

"You all right?" His lips asked the question as he reached out and touched the top of my hand.

The action and the contact of skin grounded me back into the space, reassuring and calming. A wave of nausea rolled through me but passed quickly.

After a moment of looking at his hands, I answered, "Yes. Where are the others?"

He inclined his head toward the rooms just as I heard Ivy's and Clem's distant chuckles.

I glanced briefly over my shoulder at the table, spotting the dinner I had obviously missed. "They ate?"

He nodded, then stood and took a few steps toward the table. I moved to go with him, but he waved in a downward motion, his mind set. *"I'll get it for you."*

I didn't argue, my feet still unsteady.

He returned with a full plate and goblet of water and set them on the tea table. He'd chosen a cut of boar meat, small bites of peppered cheese, the end of a bread loaf, and a blackberry tart.

"Did you have to fight Ivy to save that tart for me?" I asked, smiling as I lifted the plate onto my lap.

He shook his head and the corners of his eyes crinkled with his amused smile.

I glanced over at Argo, noticing red stains near his paws at the front of his wool mat. "What happened?"

Croft looked, then wrote with a frown, *"I haven't let him run enough, so he needed his nails cut. I clipped one too short. He's all right."*

"Guess I shouldn't ask you to do mine then," I teased, drawing another charming smile from him.

As I ate, I filled him in on the evening's events. He wrote what the others had discussed after returning from lessons and duties.

All three ventured out as I finished eating, picking through what remained at the table before joining us near the fireplace.

"We were told that Cordelia is on her way here for the funeral. Everyone has been invited," Begonia said, being sure to look at Croft when she spoke. In all the days that had passed with them staying with us, she and Clem both had regained the weight they'd lost and looked far less tired.

"I'm glad," I replied, thinking of how Cordelia might feel knowing the king had died. He may have been her one true love once, so I was certain there was a fair amount of sorrow even if they never were to be.

"Will she stay with us?" Ivy asked as she reached over to pet Argo lying beside her. He lazily rolled over in demand of belly scratches.

"I don't know. Maybe."

"I hope not," Clem said with a yawn and stretch, drawing gasps from the girls. "What? If she stays in the rooms, Croft, Argo, and I will be outnumbered. Plus, all the beds and settees are taken except this one."

Croft pointed to the settee, then wrote something and gave the paper to Ivy to read, "She can use our room for the visit. Argo and I will stay out here."

"I guess that would be all right. It'll be nice to spend time with her again," Clem admitted, leaning back and closing his eyes.

"Go to bed," I said with a chuckle.

"But we didn't spend time today," Ivy whined, her eyes drooping. "I know you can't tell us everything, but I wanted to hear about your reading. You were twitching a lot when we ate dinner."

"Tomorrow we'll spend more time. And was I really twitching? It must have been the fleas."

She giggled, then promptly yawned. I stood and helped her up, hugging her to my side as we walked to our room. She'd already been staying with me before they had moved in, but Clem and Begonia had officially taken over hers, rotating their nights between the bed and the extra settee Croft had gotten from someone else's quarters.

"Good night," Begonia said after I emerged from the room. While she still kept some distance between us, her old irritable attitude lingering, we were closer than we had been. I accepted it gratefully and hoped one day things might be even better, possibly when and if something changed for the Lovely and she felt even more free to accept herself.

"Sleep well," I replied with a smile to her and Clem before their door closed.

Croft had already moved the dinner cart into the hall, leaving me to stare around the space. He drew my attention, walking toward me from the door. He nodded toward my room. *"Bed?"*

"No. I'm not too tired."

"Pain?" He pointed to my arm, which no longer needed a bandage to cover the thickened scab of skin. It remained tender, though, still healing beneath the surface as well.

"It's good." I touched it reflexively and moved back to the settee to sit and drink more water. As soon as he could see my lips again, I said, "Tomorrow are the royal rooms."

He took a seat in the chair next to me, grabbed the paper, and wrote, *"I'd hoped you'd find something by now."*

"I had hoped, too. With everyone coming to visit ... I fear something bad will happen again. They have to know they will be questioned soon. You heard Wolf yesterday too. Hemlock and Hydra are the only ones left for questioning. All the others were cleared."

"King Ren shouldn't have allowed the delay, should have insisted they be read immediately."

"I know. I'm not sure why he'd let that happen. He knows what's at stake."

Croft wrote more furiously. *"Because while the new king is finally acknowledging his role, even in a time of mourning, he's still backing down from his mother and sister, who are both influenced heavily by Hem and Hydra. And while Wolf also has great influence over the king's decisions, he knows he can only insist so much before possible repercussions or interventions by the king's council. And he's not willing to risk his position with everything that's happening. If he's taken out of his place, the others would scramble to be his replacement, leaving us all worse off than now."*

I let a long breath out in a sigh, thinking of Croft's own potential place and all the truth I needed to disclose. Maybe it would never be the right time. Maybe I needed to tell him, be brave and hope he would forgive me. Because his rightful position, if it was correct, could affect everything. And while I'd wanted to confide in Wolf about it all as well, I knew that would be another violation of trust, another reason for Croft to hate me. He needed to hear it first before anyone else. He needed to hear it from me.

"You're so right," I admitted, biting my lip as I considered how to tell him. "You would be a great leader, you know? You have so much knowledge of the kingdom, so much to offer."

His eyebrows bunched together. A burst of air escaped from his incredulous smirk. With a head shake, he wrote, *"Me? I'll never lead anything. But I try to help."*

"You do more than help. I think you'd be truly remarkable. You're intelligent, honorable, gracious. You know this kingdom's issues, probably what steps to take in order to solve them. And if you didn't, you would seek out those who do, and do what needs to be done for the people here because you care so much. I can see it. You're passionate and kind. And I'm saying this because ..."

"You are being kind. I can say all the same about you as well. You haven't been here long, but you've already given so much of

yourself." He shifted closer and laid the paper on my thighs to read, his hands staying there, fingers cupping under my knees, thumbs resting along the top.

Warmth spread all over, even though my dress was a barrier of fabric between our skin. I lifted my eyes to his after reading, needing to convey the truth. I took a deep breath, readying myself, anticipating his reaction and how much it would hurt. Tears welled in my eyes, my emotion becoming too strong to control, knowing that he would walk out of the room when I finished. "You've given so much more. You're brave and true, and honestly the best person I've ever known. I want to be as brave."

As I spoke, his hands lifted to my neck, fingers slipping below my ears to cradle my face, thumbs wiping at the tears that had escaped down my cheeks.

I pressed on, not wanting to delay any longer, my breaths erratic between my words, breaking them all apart. "I wish … I want to tell … you everything. There's … so much to say—"

I didn't get the chance to continue. Croft leaned up and out of his chair in an instant and pressed his lips to mine, stopping my words, my breath, my heart. The kiss was tender, exploring as he waited for my reaction. And I gave up the fight and gave in to him without hesitation, needing to feel all he wanted to offer. My arms reached up and around his back, to hold on and take more. He shifted out of his crouched position, twisting to my side to sit on the settee. And while his lips stayed on mine, keeping us together, his hands dipped down to my waist and he drew my body onto him, my legs spreading over his lap.

It was my turn to take hold of his face, my fingers touching the scruffy hair along his jaw, then greedily moving into his hair to feel the silky, wavy strands I'd been dreaming of touching. I sighed as his tongue licked my lips, then dove inside my mouth for a deeper kiss, pulling me closer to him, holding me fiercely.

I was weak. A simple fool for his touch. Because despite wanting to tell him everything, I couldn't bring myself to end our connection, to tear away from how my body felt pressed against his. He cradled me powerfully, one arm and hand around my waist, anchoring me to him, while the other reached higher, fingers splayed at the back of my neck and head in both a possessive and cherishing grip.

"These lips. You are a gift. A treasure. For me. I couldn't fight this with all the strength in the world. But I will fight anyone, everyone if needed, to keep you, to protect you."

Oh, Realm. The words running through his mind were the most beautiful I'd ever heard. They made me cry harder, feeling more tied to him and also more heartache for what might come. I didn't want to lose him.

My body shook as I sobbed, and he pulled back, concern written all over his face. His eyes wide. His nostrils flared.

"I'm all right. I'm all right," I whispered after his eyes searched mine and fell to my lips. I dropped my hands, letting one rest upon his chest, feeling the heavy, fast beats of his heart.

"All right." His concern eased, eyelids lowering as though he understood. And maybe he did to some extent, knowing that my soft smile meant I was not in physical pain. Maybe he assumed my tears were joyful, though that was only partly true. And maybe he knew I needed to stop before things went any further, which was definitely true, as I would never be able to live with myself if I continued on without him knowing.

One hand wiped at my tears again while the other moved to my upper chest, splaying to mimic my hand on him, feeling the beat of my heart. He released a long breath and pulled my face to his, our foreheads touching.

He closed his eyes, content. I did the same, absorbing the rhythm and feel of him, his breath, his life.

It was a connection unlike any other, one I wanted to keep forever, one I hoped was stronger than the lies that could certainly rip us apart.

Queen Rose's fable has been shared
through the generations. Despite all the variations,
one most important fact remains.
Should a Lovely touch a Black stone, they will die.
- Anhedral Kingdom Lovely Guidebook

23

Willa and I searched the late king's rooms first, then moved on to the dowager queen's. Her attendant and the guards had questioned Willa, doing their job to protect their queen well until they viewed the signed order from the new king. We moved through all her spaces quickly and quietly, trying to be as efficient as possible and not cause her more distress.

Queen Reina sat motionless in the same chaise as she had been during the White stone reading. Her long black hair fell unbound around her shoulders, no longer holding a sleek shine. The simplest dress I'd ever seen her wear draped over her frame like a thin black sheet. Her eyes cast down to her lap, barely noticing our arrival or caring to acknowledge us, even when Willa had formally addressed her with a soldier's bow.

She hadn't fared well in the time following the king's death.

In the chair beside her, Hydra sat stoically, watchful eyes observing our every move as we searched in and out of all the spaces. No unique smells registered to me. When we finished the parlor area around them both, Hydra got to her feet. From my point of view, she and Willa appeared to be the same height, especially as Hydra leaned in closer, keeping her voice low to speak.

"Now that nothing's been found, please report back to the king and tell him that this was highly unnecessary." Her husky voice held no ire but was nonetheless sharp.

"Apologies, but it wasn't unnecessary at all if the king ordered it to happen. However, I hope that our disturbance did not ail the dowager queen in her time of mourning." Willa's reply was simple but firm. She wasted no time turning toward Queen Reina with a departing bow. "Your Majesty."

Hydra's boxy face dipped downward during Willa's bow, the lines at the corners of her eyes deepening as she assessed me. I diverted my gaze, staying at Willa's side as Mais would. Not a shake or a whine came from me, no indication at all that I was something more. But ... Her stare definitely told me she assumed as much. To be the queen's appointed Lovely, she was intelligent. She hadn't seen me in two weeks. Not even in passing. There was no doubt in my mind that she knew something was happening, even if she'd been spending a majority of her own time locked away with the dowager queen.

We left right after, disappointed and disheartened once again.

As we neared the princess's rooms, I halted. Willa stopped immediately, eyeing me first then where I focused. In the center of the long hallway, the door to the princess's quarters was unguarded. Only a drink cart stood outside. Even the guard usually posted at the corner of the hall was gone.

Willa pointed silently to the door, still several feet away.

I dipped my head and took a single step closer, listening to the voices on the other side.

"No, no. You are not listening to me." Princess Naomi's soft tone traveled out to my ears, though it wavered.

I took another step, assuming she might be in duress. She sounded flustered.

"We are wasting time. There is no point in waiting any longer. The earliest guests are due to arrive tomorrow."

My feet remained in place, my head tilting. She was not in duress. Willa kept watch, head turning back and forth to be sure no one entered the hallway.

The next voice that came was almost too soft to hear, several words indistinguishable. But it was recognizable, as there was no mistaking Hemlock's throaty pitch. "If ... hasty ... could ..." I stepped closer, needing to hear more clearly. Willa stayed in the same spot, probably to prevent any accidental sound.

"I really don't care," Princess Naomi replied. "I told you what needed to happen. You've stalled this long enough."

"It's been ... risky." His voice remained cautious. I took another step. "I will handle the reading. I've learned to control what others can see of me well enough. Nothing will come of it, but something will if we rush. Naomi, please."

"Don't you dare assume to call me that, especially when you haven't held up your end of this deal. My brother is growing stronger, not weaker. And you come to me now for more time? No. You will do your duty, or you will find yourself in a cell quicker than my father's last breath. I know what you keep in your room. If I ran to him crying, all my brother would need to see would be those pictures. There would be no reading."

A stuttered coughing sound followed, loud enough for Willa to turn her head. "Your Highness. I will not break my vow to you. Give me until this evening. I will return here, this time with a better prospect to use the stone."

I lifted a paw and whined softly. I had heard enough to incriminate them both, with or without the stone.

"Yes?" Willa asked and the voices on the other side disappeared completely.

I barked, and Willa took two more steps to the door and knocked loudly.

Princess Naomi answered it herself. "What is it?"

"Your Highness," Willa said with a bow, then extended the signed order.

The princess took it with a huff. "What is this? My rooms? Ren has no right to do this. I need to speak with him right now!"

Willa extended an arm, preventing her from leaving. "Sorry, Your Highness. The orders state if you are in residence, you need to stay for safety reasons while I check. Whoever is with you must also, including any guards"—she looked around, lifting her eyebrows—"and attendants." None were around.

Hemlock cleared his throat. "I don't see why this would be relevant to a search. I'm the trial council primary. There's no reason for me to—"

"Please read the order if you like, but you need to step inside. I would hate to report the trial council primary to the king and his advisory council for failure to follow the king's directive."

Princess Naomi huffed and handed the paper over for Hemlock to read. Both stepped farther inside and began complaining as we entered. Willa lifted an arm forward in a point, telling me to search without her, knowing she needed to stay with them.

Except for a slightly foul smell coming from Hemlock's clothing as I moved past them into the area, everything smelled of vanilla, sweet and pretty. Four separate rooms were filled with possessions—different kinds of artwork, clothing, and jewelry, some things truly unique in appearance and style, made from foreign places. Her sleeping room had the most open space, with a writing desk and bookshelves. What was most surprising, though, were the maps similar to those in the king's study. The night of King Antin's death, King Ren had told us he would have considered abdicating if Princess Naomi hadn't been so lustful for power.

With what she and Hemlock had been discussing, it all made sense. She had wanted Ren to abdicate, had been plotting with Hemlock to make that happen. They seemed an unlikely pairing, but he was her appointed Lovely. I supposed if his obsession was real, he probably told her what he could do and promised whatever she'd asked.

Frustration made me huff, taking a longer amount of time on my own when my nose failed to scent anything we needed. There was enough on their words alone, but finding the stone was what we wanted, what we needed.

Then I thought about it more clearly and padded back into the main room where Hemlock and the princess stood brooding. Willa's lips turned down, seeing that I carried nothing in my mouth.

"What's it doing?" Hemlock said, straightening up as I moved directly to him. His hands shook at his sides. Guilt or fear? Despite the odor of his clothing, I nosed closer at his waistline. "Get away. Call your wolfdog off!"

"I can't do that." Willa watched attentively as I continued.

"This is preposterous," Princess Naomi said, upper lip rising in a sneer. "You're allowing this animal to assault him."

I pushed against his loose pant leg, digging in for a whiff at his pocket, then promptly sat and let out the loudest single bark filled with both joy and disgust. It was faint, but there was no mistaking the metallic stench of the Blood stone. It managed to sting my nose despite whatever had muted its smell.

Willa's eyes widened. "Yes?"

Their reactions were fast with the realization of being caught. Hemlock lunged for the door while the princess spun around and ran toward her room. Hemlock managed two steps, his body passing through the open door and out into the hallway before I bit down hard on his ankle. He kicked at me, but he wasn't strong or fast enough to keep going because Willa had used her entire body to slam into him, knocking him onto the ground.

"Good work," she said with a smile. She repositioned herself so her knee pressed into the small of his back, then dug through his pocket and lifted out a stuffed leather pouch smaller than her fist. "Let's see what we have here."

"It wasn't my doing. You need to let me go. I'll speak with the king myself." He tried to protest and squirm beneath her, but she leaned harder onto his back, knee digging into his spine. He released a startled cry and went completely limp, giving up the fight.

Willa pulled another pouch from inside the first. And then another. And another. Each smaller in size than the one before. The total count was eight. From inside the last, Willa drew out a tiny iron box.

A female soldier and a male guard appeared from the hallway corner. As soon as they spotted Willa, they rushed over.

They began asking questions, which she didn't bother answering. She withdrew the king's order and held it out for them to see. "One of you hold him. The other, restrain the princess and bring her out. They need to be escorted to the prison by order of the king."

They didn't argue. As the guard took hold of Hemlock, Willa remained in a crouch, holding the box between us, allowing me to watch as she lifted the top portion. Inside, on a silk cushion meant for a jewel, sat a stone barely the size of a silver coin, its deep shade of green speckled with dark red and orange.

I felt the intensity despite its small size. It was powerful. But like Cordelia had said about the pendant of the same size, there was a limit to access the Realm. Hemlock couldn't have been far away when the murders had happened. Though we'd find out all the truth soon enough.

"Is that ...?" the guard holding Hemlock asked.

Willa's eyes met mine. I dipped my head, acknowledging that our assignment was finished. We'd found what we'd needed.

Hemlock began speaking again as the soldier and princess emerged from her rooms, the latter already yelling her anger about the situation, trying to intimidate the soldier. When they passed the doorway, Hemlock also became her target.

During the chatter, Willa patted me on the head and scratched around my ears, as she would to Mais for a job well done. She leaned closer and whispered, "I have them and will report to the king immediately. You should go. I'm sure you will be summoned for questioning soon."

I barked once, then calmed myself and disconnected.

In a rush, I was back inside my room, sitting on the settee. My arms dropped to my sides, and I fell back into the cushion until the spinning ceased and the nausea quieted. With my eyes closed, I smiled. We found the Blood stone and the two responsible for the murders. The relief was beyond compare. But it was still hard to believe. Hemlock and Princess Naomi ...

I opened my eyes to the ceiling first, then sat upright, expecting to see Croft's eyes on me already, as they had been every single time I'd returned.

But he wasn't in his usual chair.

I glanced at the goblet of water on the tea table, puzzled.

"He's not here," Begonia said as she appeared from her bedroom doorway, wearing one of the plainer dresses from my closet. She'd been doing that while staying inside the rooms, choosing anything else but what had been given to her to wear as a Clear stone class, a subtle way to protest her position.

It was early still, before lunch, which made her statement more confusing. She and Clem had a day off from their duties and had been in the room when I entered the Realm. But so had Croft.

"Where—" I cleared my throat and took a quick sip from the goblet.

She didn't wait for me to finish the question. "He left a note there in case you returned before he did, though he said he wouldn't be long. Mentioned something about needing to go into the city, visiting with someone. He had the midday food brought and checked before he left. It's on the table if you're hungry."

Visiting someone?

I reached for the paper beside the water and read it in a whisper. "Two guards are on watch outside. They know, aside from me and the king, no one is permitted entry. I will return before Ivy's lessons end and hopefully before you even read this. Croft."

Begonia ran her fingers along the side stitching of the dress, possibly feeling some awkwardness since there was no one else in the room with us like usual. "Are you all right? Did it go well?"

Oh. Maybe the fidgeting had been some concern too. "Yes, thank you. It went well."

"Good," she replied, not bothering to ask if I could tell her more. She already knew I couldn't yet.

As my eyes roamed the room to regain my focus, my thoughts drifted to Croft again, wondering about his visit into the city, who he was seeing. The two stains at the front of Argo's empty mat drew my attention. They had darkened to a deep wine coloring overnight, nearly black. Dried blood.

Before I could change my mind, I stood and grabbed the wool, then returned to my seat. I dumped some water over the stone and used the other side of the wool to wipe the surface clean.

"What are you doing?" Begonia asked, walking to the settee and propping a knee onto the cushion, eyeing me with suspicion and disapproval, given the scowl that formed on her lips.

As I rubbed Mais's blood streak from the stone, I said, "There's a lot I wish I could tell you, but I can't right now. I expect to be summoned for questioning soon. That's how well today went. But as for this ... I believe it might be more pieces to the mysteries of not only the murders but possibly about who Croft really is."

"What do you mean 'Who Croft really is'? Is he hiding something?"

"No, well, not exactly. There's something about him that I don't think he even knows yet."

"And you know? How?"

"I just do, and I need to find the other links to know for sure. But I can't really explain right now. There's not much time. How long ago did he leave?"

"Maybe an hour. He thought you'd be gone for at least four."

"Right. Well, I need to do this now because with everything else happening, I might not get another chance."

Begonia took a seat at my side, staring at me with wide eyes. She looked six again somehow, in that time around her Name Day, right before she started hating me. The freckles were so clear all over her pale face while sitting so close. There was concern in her eyes for sure now, but she didn't speak or act on it in any way. No tentative touch of her hand on mine. No whispered questions to ease her thoughts. But that was all right. I understood.

"I'll be fine," I promised. "Do as Croft asked. Don't leave and only answer the door for him or the king. All right?"

"Yes," she agreed, rolling her lips inward as she eyed the stone. "I don't think this is a good idea, Olean. Aside from not having a direct order to do it, Croft will be really upset with you doing this to Argo without him knowing first."

I sighed, understanding that it was one more thing I would have to confess. But if it led me to more information, it needed to be done. "He's going to hate me soon enough, even if I don't do this. I have to, though."

She frowned, seeing my resolve. "All right. Be safe."

The corner of my lips lifted, and I covered her hand with mine, needing to reassure myself as much as her. After a nod, I spilled a couple of drops of water onto Argo's blood stain, waited a moment, then smeared it across the clean Eye stone.

Without another thought, I reached forward for the second time that day and touched both the Eye and Needled stones, hoping it wouldn't be the biggest mistake of my life.

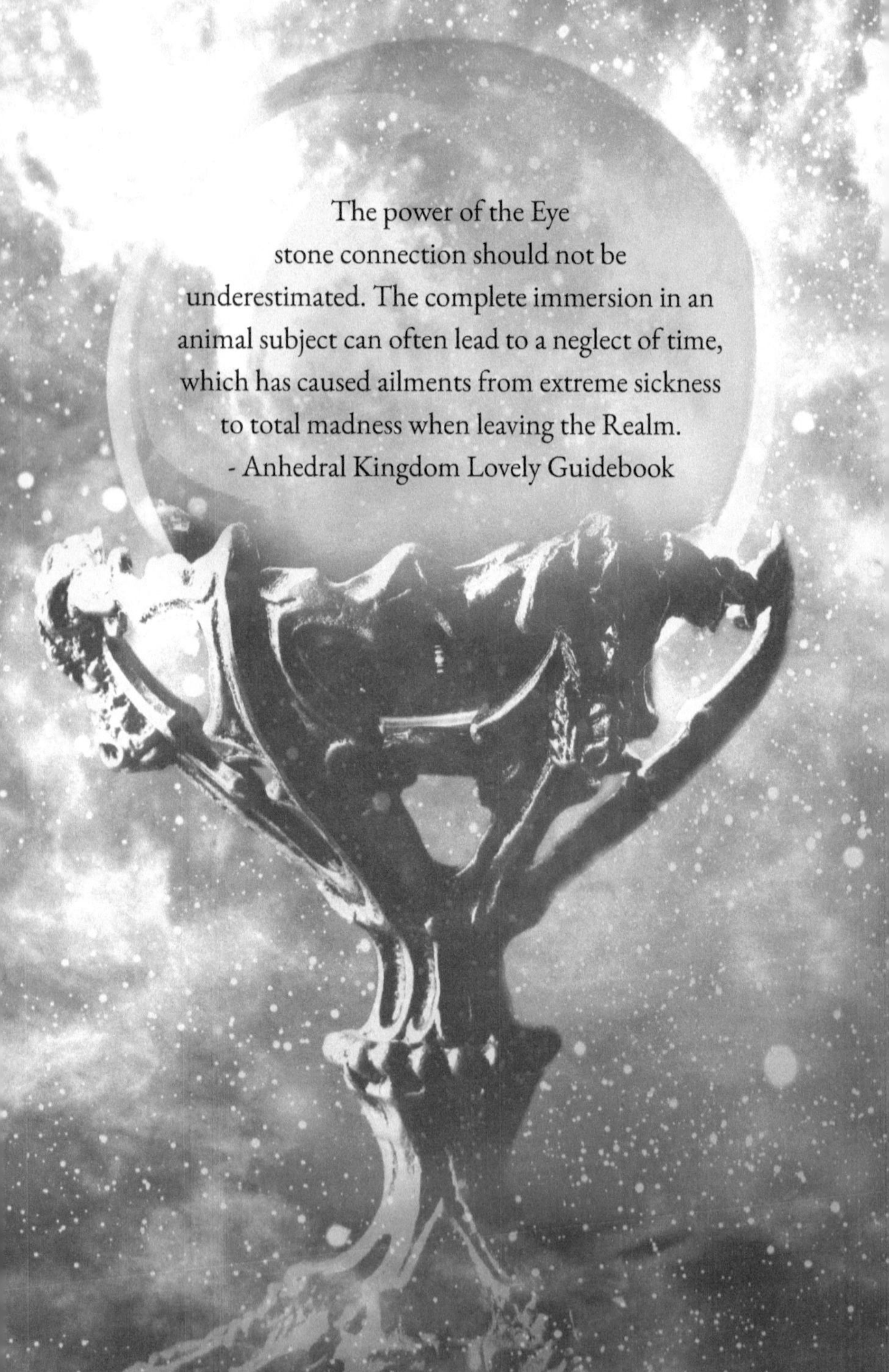
The power of the Eye
stone connection should not be
underestimated. The complete immersion in an
animal subject can often lead to a neglect of time,
which has caused ailments from extreme sickness
to total madness when leaving the Realm.
- Anhedral Kingdom Lovely Guidebook

~ 24 ~

The whine that escaped my mouth couldn't be controlled. After spinning into the Realm's darkness, I felt the same but also entirely different. A bright light nearly blinded me as my vision cleared. The sun was high in the sky and beaming down onto the cobbled road. The day was hot, warmer than I was used to, having been inside the castle for days.

I was also in Argo's body, with deep blue-gray fur. And even though his hair was shorter than the wolfdogs', it still covered most of his body. I could sense the heat releasing from the pads of my feet. My open mouth also gave some relief too.

People milled around us in groups, some under tents, others walking along the street. Croft stood at my side, wearing a set of light gray pants I'd only seen him wear off duty in the room. He also had on a loose white shirt, possibly to keep from being recognized as a castle attendant. There was no telling what might happen if he had been dressed in the usual attire.

Lifting my head, I eyed the table he stood in front of and sniffed the dense, warm air, realizing that Argo's nose was similar to the wolfdogs' and likely had the same things memorized from his training as well. There were many scents lingering along the table, and I realized why when Croft lifted a bar of soap under his nose and took a deep inhale.

"Rose. This one is good."

I heard him. I'd heard him that first time inside Mais, but I'd wondered if it was because I had been close to him, both inside the dog and also my physical body. With my body back at the castle, that couldn't have been a factor now. It could also have to do with the Needled stone. My range of use was far, despite using older blood. I just hoped it continued.

He took the bag that was offered and let it fall to his side as he dug into his pocket for coins to pay the outstretched hand. I sniffed at the bag, smelling the delicate floral scent of rose and also a spicy peppered scent too. He'd bought new soaps. For me? He'd asked my favorite things and I'd told him ...

He stowed the bag into his satchel and, after a quick glance down at me, started walking.

It took me a second to realize that I hadn't moved, watching him walk away while I considered his thoughtful gift. I realized my error as soon as he made a turn and looked back over his shoulder, only to find me running to catch up.

His head twisted in all directions, looking for ... danger? He swiped his free hand through his hair and looked down at me when I heeled properly at his side. His eyebrows dropped lower in concern or confusion.

I panted harder. While I'd watched them interact and understood their usual movements together, there was a possibility I'd do something incorrectly and he'd know. I still needed to take the risk. I needed to know where he was going, who he was seeing.

He reached down, patted my head, and waved low as he started walking again. I let out a sigh through my panting, relieved that he'd chosen to ignore my delay.

We walked steadily for several more blocks, past another market with merchant tents that I assumed displayed a variety of bold and bright colors, though I only saw an array of yellows, grays, and light blues. A row of connected stone houses followed on the next block and that continued on to local storefronts with baked goods, furnishings, and a tailor shop.

The building at the end had two extra levels up. Its larger size became clear as Croft navigated the narrow pathway at the side, between it and a small apothecary.

Croft knocked on the side door and waited patiently.

The door swung wide inward, revealing an older woman in a simple full dress and stained apron. A knot of silver hair sat atop her head like a ratty bird's nest, with pieces sticking out in all directions. She was larger framed, though short in height, with wrinkled skin darkened by the sun and speckled with brown and white spots all over.

"Sorry, no solicit—" The cordial, flat greeting died on her lips as she saw Croft, then glanced down at me. She instantly beamed, down-turned lips lifting into a radiant smile, narrow eyes twinkling. "Croft!"

Croft tucked the bag beneath his arm and motioned to her with two hands. *"Hi, Ms. Pearla."*

Pearla? Had I heard his thought correctly? *Oh, Realm!* The name from Cordelia's memory. It could be common enough. Yet the piece fit too well to be an odd coincidence.

She motioned back to him, clearly understanding the words he spoke with his hands, while also saying in a ringing voice, "It's so good to see you!" She hugged him immediately after, pinning his arms to his sides, making him look like a child despite her shorter stature. She backed away after a second and eyed him up and down. "Come in, come in! Let me feed you."

Croft shook his dropped head, letting me see the full grin upon his face too before following her. He closed the door behind me and moved into a cramped kitchen and pantry, then through another doorway into a longer dining room filled with multiple tables and chairs.

Ms. Pearla patted a firm hand to my head and scratched behind my ears quickly. "It's lovely to see you too, Argo." Her hands lifted and motioned to Croft more while she spoke. "It's been too long, but I imagine you have been busy."

Croft's response looked the same, both hands in motion while his thoughts helped me follow along. *"Yes, it has. I'm sure you've heard about the late king. I can't really speak of much, but we're hoping to settle things soon. There's a Lovely…"*

"Is there now?" Pearla replied with a soft chuckle. "You know, I am proud of all you've chosen to do, but I still think you need to take care. There are many things with the royals and their Lovely best left alone."

Croft nodded, eyes moving between her lips and hands. He took a moment to reply. *"I knew you'd say as much. Unfortunately, I'm more involved than ever, but I feel I can help make things better for everyone."*

"Of course you do, and I'm certain you can." She sighed with a knowing smirk. "Who is she?"

His body shook as air escaped his mouth in a silent laugh. He wiped a hand down his face, which had turned a little pink. *"All right. Oleander. Olean. She's intelligent and ..."*

"Not like the others," Pearla filled in, giving him a wide-eyed teasing look.

I wanted to cry and be sick at the same time. While my heart was absolutely filling from his admissions, the guilt from overhearing the private conversation was a knife in my stomach.

"Yes," he admitted. *"She wants change too, could possibly make things happen with the power she has. She's from Shadowstone. Actually, there was something I wanted to tell you ... I traveled there with the queen and I think I met someone you know. The Guardian there was read with a Cloud stone. There was a memory and your name was said. I thought I'd tell you that."*

"Shadowstone?" Pearla asked, cheerfulness instantly gone, replaced with a stolid expression and subdued hand motions. "Cordelia?"

"Yes. So it was you? You know her?"

"Yes, I knew her." It was a short answer, but her flat tone told so much more.

Croft obviously saw her unease too. *"All right?"*

Pearla pressed her lips tightly together and looked around the room, at the table and all the settings. She made eye contact with him again. "Was she well?"

"Yes, well, saddened, I think, because all four of her Lovely came to the castle with us."

"All?"

"Yes. But I think she is on her way here to attend the funeral, so she will see them again."

"Oh, her heart. She lost so much before. And they took even more." She clucked her tongue and shook her head before continuing, "I've told you since you were small that there are times when information is good and times when it does you no good at all. It's safer not to dig. I kept you safe here along with others who were in need under that same reasoning."

So it was true. He'd been raised here. By Pearla. And Sielle had told me Croft was a Lovely, that sometimes our Dead didn't die. Sometimes they lived instead.

It all fit. He was the late king's child ... and also Cordelia's.

"What are you saying?" Croft's demeanor changed now too, not quite understanding what Pearla meant. But I knew. She'd kept a secret, one possibly no one else knew.

She smiled and waved her hands together. "Nothing. I'm only wanting you safe, as always. It was my honor to raise you, you know. I'm happy with the man you've become, even though you left me too early and chose to work at the castle."

Croft's eyebrows remained lowered, studying her. He didn't move his hands, but his thoughts were loud. *"What aren't you telling me?"*

Pearla reached out and squeezed his arm, then moved her hands and spoke. "Do you want to eat? You can sit and tell me all the news, or is there another reason for the visit?"

Croft glanced down at me, seeming to collect himself. He motioned back to her. *"I need to ask about a girl who came for your lessons right before I left. Blind. Brown hair, I think. She had a home, so she was only here during the day. I never saw her again when I visited. Her name is Sielle."*

Pearla thought a moment. "Yes. Sweet girl and fast learner. I've seen her around the markets. She doesn't live far. Several blocks east. Why?"

"A friend mentioned her. Do you have the information?"

"Sure," Pearla replied and walked into the parlor area.

We followed, watching her go through a shelf filled with papers. "Here it is. Last I have for her was house number fourteen on Coin Road. Cross road is Trellis."

"Thank you."

"No time to sit and eat then?" she asked with a knowing smile.

Though he returned a smile, it wasn't nearly as excited as it had been. *"No, not this time. Soon."*

"All right. You take care, Croft. And good luck with your Olean."

"See you again soon." He motioned but didn't offer another embrace, only turned to leave.

I followed behind him, exiting the same way we'd come, keeping my head up with difficulty. He'd only felt a sliver of dishonesty from her and it had affected him enough to shut down his happiness. He barely knew me in comparison to the woman who had raised him, yet I feared my deception would hurt him worse.

Sielle, I reminded myself. She had been my goal, the reason I was risking so much by using the Eye stone on Argo. I'd already discovered so much, learning that Croft was not only the late king's son but Cordelia's as well. He hadn't been born to another woman after all. I didn't know all of Anhedral's laws, but I knew that an illegitimate birth was still valid for the throne. Which meant since Croft was older than Ren, he was the heir apparent, the rightful new king.

I didn't know Pearla's reasons for lying, aside from her wanting to keep him safe. It was obvious that Cordelia didn't even know about the other son born. Recalling the memory from the Cloud stone, she had given birth to the first baby, the Lovely who had died. But she'd lost consciousness after the guards had entered. That meant she'd delivered another, one Pearla took to keep safe, knowing that he would have been taken away otherwise. Or worse, killed.

The sun had fallen halfway between its midday point and the horizon, and Croft moved at a faster pace through the streets, understanding his trip into the city was nearing an end. I trod along the thin strips of grass at the sides of the roads whenever possible, avoiding the overly warm stones so as not to hurt the pads of Argo's paws. I felt nothing of his cut nail from the previous night and hoped not to make things worse.

Croft spun in circles at some corners, taking in the road names and making the necessary turns. The city seemed to expand and breathe farther away from the castle. The areas weren't as cramped. Homes and storefronts spread wider apart. It was the same with the roads. More trees. More stretches of grassy fields.

A lightness began to form inside my chest and head, my eyes starting to lose focus. I blinked, which seemed to help. But then I felt it again, the roads blurring, my mind shifting focus.

Finally, we arrived at Coin and Trellis. House number fourteen stood at the corner of the quiet road, with a large field at its back. Like the others in the surrounding distance, it was built with stacked tan stone bricks and a slightly pitched roof. Ivy vines rose up to the top of the second level, sprawling out over an entire corner.

Croft scrunched his lips, then took a quick look at me and the position of the sun before knocking on the front door.

No one answered. But a sound caught my ears. It was distant, not directly inside but at the back of the house.

I whined and pawed at Croft's leg, drawing his attention. As soon as he looked, I ran, taking off around the front garden, passing the ivy-covered corner. His clapping followed behind me, demanding I return. There was no way he could press for an answer at the door. It would be difficult for him to do so, not having a voice to announce himself in the usual way. So I knew I had to be the one to make them see us. I would not leave after coming this far. There would be no other chance.

I slowed around back, entering a small cobblestone courtyard with a fountain at the center. The rear entrance had two doors set inside an archway. One of the doors was open. I listened, and padded closer. Voices filtered outside. Female and male. Croft's footfalls neared, alerting whomever was inside to our new position, silencing their voices. They had obviously not wanted to answer the front door, and I wondered why.

My vision blurred again, this time darkening too. I was losing time. I'd been connected to the Realm too long, and with the greater distance from the castle and my physical body, my connection was weakening. I had to act.

"Argo! No!"

As my vision cleared, a motion behind the door made me leap into a run. I felt Croft's hand at the back of my neck as I lunged, his fingers slipping away from my fur with a failed attempt to stop me.

The door shifted forward to close, the motion fast but not fast enough. I jumped into the air, slamming into it before it could latch, knocking away any resistance and bursting through into a beautiful dining area.

I barked and barked, pleading for attention, though I'd already gotten quite a bit. The backs of two bodies ran toward the front of the house as the smell of oats caught my attention.

Oats.

I hesitated as my mind registered what it could mean.

That pause was long enough for Croft to come from behind me and grip me hard at the scruff of my neck so I couldn't take off again.

"Croft?!" a male's voice called out. "And Argo!"

Casting my eyes upward, I saw it had been a male and a female who had run. Both were almost as tall as Croft and wearing loose merchant clothing with wraps of silk to cover their heads, everything in shades of gray to my canine eyes. Him with darker skin, a crooked nose, and young features. Her a golden tan, a pointed chin, and streaked marks for eyebrows.

Croft stopped moving behind me, releasing me not long after feeling me still. I glanced up, seeing when he noticed who they were. His head jerked backward, and his mouth opened with shock.

They both slipped their wraps off, revealing their bald heads. Blodwyn and Tansy. The missing Lovely. Sielle had said she knew them, that they hadn't been at fault. Had she been keeping them safe?

My vision went out again, and I whined softly. It wasn't my whine, though. It was Argo.

"What's wrong?" Tansy asked, stepping forward. "Did he get hurt on the door?"

Croft leaned down and looked me over. The haze cleared, and I gave a shake of my body, not wanting them to lose focus.

"What are you doing here? Are there soldiers with you?" Blodwyn asked as Tansy gave me a quick pat on the head. She and Croft stood again, both sharing courteous smiles. Blodwyn repeated his question, realizing Croft hadn't seen his lips.

Croft motioned for paper, and Blodwyn went to the writing table near the kitchen's entrance and brought it over for Croft to use on the dining table instead.

They both read what Croft had written, which I hadn't heard in his thoughts fully. The words had been erratic. Though I knew the cause was not his fault. It was my weakening connection.

Blodwyn let out a relieved sigh, wiping his shaky hands on the stomach of his shirt. "So you aren't here for us?"

"Sielle! It's all right to join us. It's not a soldier as we thought. Croft's here to see you," Tansy called out, being sure to face Croft.

My vision went in and out again, part of my focus seeming to see the inside of my room at the castle, the fireplace across from the tea table. And I thought I heard Clem's voice.

A figure of a girl emerged from beyond the kitchen doorway, her long, ruffled dress a black, blurry haze like a cloudy night. As she came into focus, I saw she wasn't a little girl, but my age, and the same height. She held a thin stick in one hand, sweeping it back and forth as a guide. The other hand at her side clutched something small within her fist. Long, straight strands of light brown hair hung over her shoulders, continuing past her full chest, the ends nearly touching her wide hips.

And then my heart stopped altogether.

Because as I looked upon Sielle's dark honey skin and oval face, I noticed several more things. Pointed chin. Round lips. Freckles stretching across her small, fleshy nose and out over her high cheeks. They were the features I saw daily within the reflection of a mirror or the surface of a shiny stone.

But her eyes ... Her eyes were the darkest brown, so beautiful. They stared blankly ahead, unseeing.

"What is happening?" Croft had taken two quick steps backward, covering his chest, startled the same way I had been.

My sister. My twin?

I whined, then barked, thoughts screaming inside my mind. How was it possible?

"We're right here," Tansy said, guiding Sielle, who turned her head toward the sound, toward us, stopping only feet away.

"You said it's Croft who's here," Sielle said, her low tone exactly as it had sounded within the White stone, only without the chasing echo. "I remember you. It's been years, though."

"You look ... so much like her." Croft stayed where he was, arms limp at his sides. *"Those years ago ... You looked different. I would have recognized the resemblance otherwise. How is this possible?"*

Tansy lifted a hand, drawing Croft's attention. "Would you like me to read something for Sielle?"

"Yes." Croft took the paper and wrote fast. *"You look ... I ... understand ..."*

Everything faded out again, images dimming, sounds jumbled.

I whined again and barked, both Argo and myself seeming to take up space within his body.

Croft's blurry figure looked down at me. I could feel his confusion even though I couldn't hear him or see his features clearly.

My view focused again, only not fully.

"Yes," Sielle replied to whatever Croft had written. "Olean is my sister. No, I didn't know until recently, when I discovered my own connection to the Realm. I've talked to her there, through the White stone. But with this"—she held out her fist and opened it, revealing a Needled stone—"I've been able to feel when she's connected to different stones, even if I've never touched some of them. Like right now, she's connected to the Eye stone. I can feel the changes in her through our link."

"Yes." Croft wrote more, his breaths heavy as he processed it all. *"Searching for the one who killed the king."*

"She was," Sielle replied after Tansy read Croft's words. "But now she's here."

"Here?" Croft's eyebrows lowered and he pinched his lips as he watched her, possibly worried he'd misread her words.

"Though ... you're losing connection, aren't you?"

I barked, sitting fully as the room spun, growing darker and darker.

Croft's gaze dropped fast, eyes no longer confused, their amber color like the start of a furious wildfire I'd never have the chance to see extinguished. Everything behind him disappeared into blackness, and then he did too.

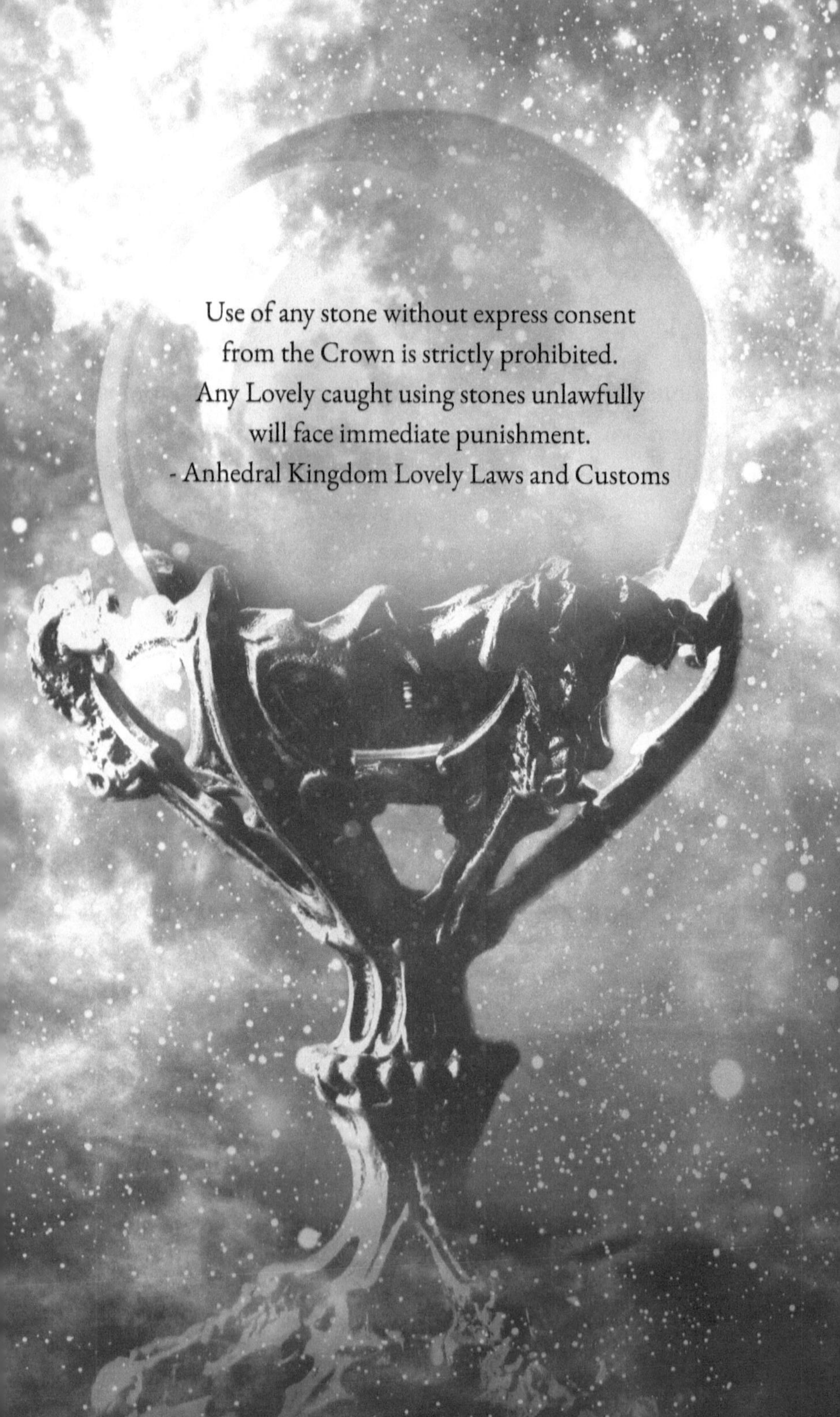
Use of any stone without express consent
from the Crown is strictly prohibited.
Any Lovely caught using stones unlawfully
will face immediate punishment.
- Anhedral Kingdom Lovely Laws and Customs

~ 25 ~

My connection ended. Despite the weak link to start, with using Argo's diluted blood, I'd traveled far outside the castle with Croft, well into the city. And I'd gotten to see what I'd wanted. Sielle. My sister. I had a sister!

I'd also learned more. Croft was heir apparent. The rightful king.

I held no reservations with the truth after all I'd learned. He would know everything as soon as he returned to the castle, even if he decided to hate me after all I'd kept from him, after using Argo without his knowledge. He needed to know. So as soon as I'd seen Sielle, had realized who she was, and she'd confirmed knowing of my presence, I'd stopped the fight and disconnected.

The whirling effect of returning to my body hit harder than ever. The reason could have been the distance or the length of time, as I'd been connected twice in the same day for the longest total period. Nausea and fatigue overpowered me, my arms falling to my sides, their weight having been suspended so long they felt deadened.

"Olean, you're back!" Ivy's voice pierced through my head as my body tilted with the room, forcing me down onto the settee.

"Ivy, give her space. Clem, grab the ash bucket," Begonia said, her voice softer, closer.

As soon as my face shifted over the cushion's edge, I retched, hoping they had the bucket in place. It was one time I was grateful my stomach had been practically empty, having had nothing to eat since breakfast.

A hand pressed against my back, rubbing calm circles.

My thoughts started catching up. Ivy had spoken?

I coughed to clear my throat, then took a wet cloth Begonia's hand offered to wipe my mouth. After a moment, with my arms braced on the seat cushion, I pushed upright and asked, "How did Ivy get in the room?"

"I let her in," Wolf said, startling me. He sat in the chair near the fireplace, eyes staring pointedly. "Where were you?"

I grabbed for the small cup of water on the tea table and drank it down, my throat incredibly dry from lack of fluids. Swallowing thickly, then setting the cup down, I admitted the truth. There would be no hiding anything now. "In the city. I was with Croft. In Argo."

"And did Croft know?" Wolf repositioned himself, crossing one long leg over the other as he watched me.

I couldn't tell what he was thinking. His stoic features gave nothing away, which wasn't surprising. Lovely were usually good at controlling their emotions, and he'd had years of experience. "Not initially. He had already gone when I returned from my assignment with Willa. I'm sure he knew it was me before I disconnected."

He nodded. "So you chose to use Argo's blood without consent from the Crown or a direct assignment from me or any other lead Lovely?"

I hung my head, staring into my lap. "Yes. I acted myself, without anyone's approval. And I believe something I learned to be vital information for the kingdom."

His thinly painted eyebrows rose, and he uncrossed his legs again to lean forward. "Really? If that's true, then we shall see when you are questioned. So your questioning won't only be to verify what you and Willa discovered and confiscated earlier today. I came here to collect you for that and to congratulate you on a job well done. And while that is all still true, I am now obligated to report your infraction of unsanctioned stone use to the king, and you will be questioned to the full extent for breaking the law."

"I understand." There was no argument, no excuses.

"She's in trouble?" Ivy's voice pitched with worry. I glanced over to see her perched at the other end of the settee, Clem standing behind her, his hand on her shoulder. She wiped at the tears slipping down her cheeks.

Wolf's gaze softened as he turned toward her. His lips pulled up into a small smile. "Yes, little one. But if she did have cause and found important information as she claims, then I believe the punishments won't be severe."

He would know soon enough that whatever punishment I'd receive wouldn't compare to what I anticipated from Croft. It all would be deserved. I'd crossed too many lines.

"I hope not. Olean has been working really hard every day. And her mind has been so strong." Ivy wrung her hands on her lap.

I had to smile at her conviction, but there was nothing I could say to comfort or assure her. I had no idea what my fate might be, and I didn't want to give her false hope.

"Begonia, bring Olean something small to eat, please." Wolf waved a hand toward the table where dinner had already been delivered, then focused on me. "I'll allow you a few more minutes to regain enough energy to walk, as we need to report to the trial room right away."

When Begonia brought me a plate of only breads and cheeses, assuming what would keep my stomach calm, I told her thanks and started to eat.

Wolf watched for a moment, then said, "The princess and Hemlock were already questioned in front of the king and dowager queen. They are both being charged with treason and murdering King Antin."

While the others in the room gasped loudly, hearing what had happened for the first time, I merely kept eating, starved for food.

Wolf didn't pay mind to their reactions. "They are responsible for Alve's and Imogen's deaths as well. Though there was nothing from them in regard to the other Lovely. They are currently being held in the prison and will stay until the king decides their fates. I read Willa immediately after to see her account as well. We knew you might need some time to rest, so we agreed to reconvene after dinner for your questioning. Since we got all the information we needed for their convictions, your questioning was to be a simple matter of procedure. Until now ... Is there anything I should know before then?"

I finished off a large portion of bread and drank down the remaining water, processing his words. I didn't want to worry the others with too much information, especially before my questioning. It would only upset them more while I was gone. They would find out everything soon enough.

"You are already aware of some information," I admitted. "What you advised me to tell Croft ... He still doesn't know. And there is more to his story than I or anyone could have imagined. You and everyone else will see it through the Cloud stone, but it is best that you do know one thing first, to prepare for what will come. This also has to do with the pendant and the two people connected to it."

I saw the moments he both understood exactly what my few words meant, and when he knew what that truth meant. His eyes widened briefly, then widened even more, and his body eased backward into the chair. He sorted through the connection and implications, attention retreating inward. As his eyes lifted to the ceiling, then dropped to the floor, then moved to the fireplace, the others turned to me, confused by our cryptic conversation.

Begonia sneered as I knew she would, Clem rolled his eyes, and Ivy frowned.

"I'm sorry. You'll know soon enough, I promise. But you—"

"—don't need to know right now," Begonia finished sharply. "Honestly, I'm so sick of being left out in the pasture like some brainless goat. I'm old enough to hear whatever's going on. I've seen plenty enough."

She had a point. She wasn't much younger than me and old enough to understand most things. Had I been left out at her age, I would have felt the same. I instantly felt bad for treating her like a child after they'd moved into my rooms. I'd only wanted to protect them all.

"You're right. Wolf? Can I make a request?" I asked, watching him recapture his focus.

"Within reason," he replied.

"I would like Begonia to attend my questioning."

His lips dropped at the corners. "I don't think that—"

"She's old enough," I pressed, eyeing Clem and Ivy to be sure they understood why I hadn't said them as well. "I'm requesting her as an observer, if one's permitted."

His eyes scanned over her. She'd been standing off to our side the entire time, not bothering to sit while I'd eaten. Even with having had the day off duty, she had applied her painted eyebrows in her preferred single-stem flower design and still had on the simple gray dress from earlier in the day.

"I'll allow it," he said, standing. "Now we must go."

Begonia's tiny smile was both happy and sad, knowing that while this was a testament to her growth, it also meant she might witness my prosecution.

I'd walked through the trial hall in the south wing a couple of times since I'd arrived—while touring and while searching. There was nothing too significant to its appearance. It served a purpose without decoration and reminded me of a cleaner, better furnished version of Shadowstone's town hall where all our criminal readings were held. Several rows of walnut benches occupied the back half of the room for any necessary audience. Beyond that, a round table made of the same wood was positioned alone on a dais, with two chairs on either end and a Cloud stone in the middle. It was the reading table, the focal point. Along one side of the room, a thin table stood with notebooks for record keeping. On the other side, a split-level bench. And positioned at the back of the room, close to the dais, there were two intricately carved thrones and a few other high-backed chairs.

The king sat in the tallest throne, the dowager queen at his side. They wore no crowns, no fancy formal clothing, only simple black attire. Hydra was seated beside Queen Reina, maintaining a supportive presence as her appointed Lovely. All were motionless, as if they were still coming to terms with the truth about Hemlock and Princess Naomi. Along the split-level benches, more Lovely were in attendance, to bear witness as a council. I noticed Net as well as Kalmia, both watching me move down the center aisle. Willa sat in the front audience bench row, Mais at her feet. There were also a few guards and attendants, plus another Lovely I wasn't familiar with sitting at the record table, tasked with keeping detailed reports of the readings.

"Your Majesty," Wolf greeted for us all, bowing while Begonia and I curtsied behind him. "I, Wolfsbane, have brought Oleander for questioning in regard to her role in the Blood stone search. She's requested Begonia's presence to observe."

"Granted," King Ren replied, his tone flat. Being closer, I could see the reddened skin around his and the dowager queen's eyes. They both had listened to memories from the princess, heard that she had been at fault for the late king's death in her goal to obtain the throne. They had endured so much within such a short period of time, and I was about to deliver more upsetting information.

My arms shook as Wolf motioned for Begonia to sit with Willa and Mais.

"I also need to add that this reading for Oleander will not only be for her role in the search for the Blood stone and its discovery, but also for her own offense of using the Eye stone without express permission from the Crown."

"What?" King Ren straightened, his attention clearing with Wolf's statement. His emotional daze vanished inside a second. "What's this about, Wolf?"

"When I arrived at her rooms earlier to retrieve her for questioning, I discovered that she was still using the Eye stone. Though she was no longer connected on the assignment with Willa and Mais but using it for her own reasons."

"And what exactly was she connected to?" His voice dropped as anger took over.

"She stated that she was connected with Croft's dog, Argo, and that she had valid reasons for doing so in order to retrieve vital information for the kingdom."

"Is that so?" He sounded enraged, and I could hardly blame him. Too much discovered deception in one day would infuriate anyone, turn them into the biggest skeptic before hearing any explanation. "What say you before we begin, Oleander?"

I swallowed thickly, hoping for the best outcome the truth could deliver, even if it meant a punishment for my breaking Crown law. Everyone deserved to know. "While there were other reasons for the use, I did discover something important. And though the information may not be well received, Your Majesty, it's something that needs to be brought to light. On my vow as a Lovely, I'm sharing this truth as it was revealed by the Realm."

As Wolf pointed to the chair on the opposite side of the round table for me to take, the main doors opened behind us.

I glanced back as I walked, seeing Croft and Argo enter, the latter showing no outward effects of my connection. There was no controlling the sudden emotion that burst inside me, escaping in a soft whimper. I held the rest in, clamping my mouth closed, squeezing my eyelids together as I sat down in the chair. I wanted to disappear, to not watch what was about to happen, but I had to open my eyes and face it all.

"Croft," King Ren called out, waving him forward and pointing to the front bench to join the others. He then turned and asked me, "Is Croft aware of this?"

Croft sat beside Begonia, positioning to see everyone's mouths clearly. As soon as he understood what the king had said, he looked directly at me. Though not into my eyes. The direction of his gaze was lower, only to my mouth.

My chest hurt, and I struggled to take a breath. "I believe he is aware I used the Eye stone unlawfully on Argo. But he is not aware of the information I discovered about him."

His eyes lifted then, finally connecting with mine. That fiery anger still lingered, not entirely gone, yet I could also see interest inside the hurt. He was taken aback, not fully understanding the reasons I was being questioned.

"All right then. Let's proceed." King Ren relaxed back into his chair. "Wolf, start with the Blood stone searches to get the confirmation we need for record purposes. Then move on to her charges and this information she insists is vital."

"Yes, Your Majesty," he replied as an attendant walked to my side.

Queen Reina hadn't moved at all. I wondered if she'd even blinked since I'd arrived. She was but a shell, filled with only sorrow.

Willa and Begonia both eyed me with concern, their trust in me holding out regardless of my wrongdoing.

The attendant drew a blade, quickly sliced my finger, dabbed a cloth, then smeared it over the Cloud stone.

Wolf didn't hesitate, taking hold and starting in on my mind, my thoughts, my memories.

Views from the induction and King Antin's murder came first. He repeated it for all to hear, confirming how we'd discovered the use of the Blood stone at the start and going on through the events to follow. Then came the searches. My thoughts from Mais's wolfdog body. All the different people, rooms, and scents. He repeated all I had overheard from Princess Naomi and Hemlock, then discovering the stone.

Queen Reina cried softly, staying in her chair despite having to hear the betrayal from her daughter all over again.

"Good," the king called out. "Let's move on. Find the information she wants to share, Wolf."

Knowing what he knew of my ability to hear Croft and understanding what I'd insinuated in my rooms only an hour before, he delved further into my mind, farther back in memories, searching for the link.

"Ivy's reading Cordelia for the Cloud stone. She gave birth before coming to Shadowstone. Queen Reina had no reaction. She knew."

Gasps sounded all around, most of the Lovely reacting to the news about one of us having had a child.

Wolf continued, rushing through all the memories, images flickering through my mind so quickly it was hard to keep up. *"Cordelia gifts me a pendant, one holding a Clear stone, one with the initials AV. Croft is now my attendant at the castle. Sielle was right. The connection I made to him in the White stone worked. I can hear his thoughts when we're close. The king's pendant is the same as Cordelia's. They both have the king's initials. Wolf tells me that they did love each other before he married the queen. Sielle spoke again in the White stone. She said she knew of Croft. That he is one of us, one of our dead who lived instead. A Lovely. That's how the connection worked. The king's light orb hovered close to Croft, not the queen. Croft tells me about his youth. He lies about knowing Sielle. Croft is gone after I found the Blood stone. He went to the city. Argo's dried blood works on the Eye stone. Pearla raised Croft as an orphan. Pearla was Cordelia's nurse maid when she lost her Lovely baby. Croft is the king's first child, the first heir."*

The room was utterly silent. Tears leaked from my eyes as the last few visions flipped through my mind. Since no one stopped him after that truth, Wolf spoke again. *"Someone's hiding in Sielle's house. I can't wait for another time. I need to find her. Tansy and Blodwyn are here. And Sielle is ... she looks just like me. She's my sister."*

When he finished, the trial hall went silent again. No one dared move, dared breathe, after his words. I looked at Croft as tears spilled down my cheeks. His attention remained on Wolf, his eyes wide.

Wolf disconnected. "That's all, Your Majesty."

I couldn't take my eyes from Croft, not caring what the king or anyone had to say. It took several moments, but then the king spoke. "Wolf. I will speak with you and the council in my study. Please send soldiers to collect everyone else involved in Olean's memories. They are to be questioned as well."

"Ren, I didn't know another lived," the queen said weakly, drawing my attention to them.

His messy hair stuck out at the top of his head as if he'd been pulling at the strands. He turned to her with a blank stare and no reply, so she stood with fresh new tears in her eyes and left the room through a side door. Hydra followed close behind.

My focus went right back to Croft, finding his stare already on me. His lips pressed together and his jaw clenched, making the muscle there flex.

"As a reminder," the king said. "Olean has proven herself as an asset to this kingdom, finding the Blood stone and those responsible for the most recent murders. I will need to consult with my council over this new information and question all others involved. However, she also broke the law."

His words barely registered as I watched Croft's expression. I'd wounded him. No matter what else had happened, I'd betrayed his trust. As much as I knew this would happen, it still hurt to see the emotion in his eyes and not be able to take it all back. I loathed myself for causing him pain.

"Croft." My voice was a whisper, but he watched my mouth move. "I'm sorry, I—"

Before I could mouth another word, he stood, turning away from my words and walking to the door with Argo following.

"Croft!" Wolf called, motioning to the guards to stop him.

"Let him go," King Ren called out, and the guards halted their movements and let Croft pass, leaving us all behind. "He needs time ... like the rest of us."

"Croft," I mouthed again, getting to my feet, this time not able to be vocal as sobs broke through. My body shook. It took every bit of strength I had to remain standing.

"Lovely, go back to your assignments. Guards and soldiers, to your posts." King Ren stood. "Since Olean broke Crown law, she is to be detained in the prison until further notice. And because Croft and his dog were who the offense was against, he will help decide on the punishment after everything is sorted. Wolf, escort her if you wish." He stood and left by the same side door his mother had taken.

"No!" Begonia called out, her words drawing my attention.

"It's all right," I said quickly, wiping my face as Wolf gently took hold of my other arm. "I will be fine. Go back and stay with Clem and Ivy. Keep them safe and calm. Cordelia should arrive soon and help you."

"Wolf, please, ask the king ..." Begonia pleaded with him as he moved me past her and Willa. She lunged forward, but Willa wrapped an arm around her, keeping her in place, which I was thankful for. I tried hard to hold myself together, to show her some version of strength through a forced smile, but as soon as Wolf and I moved to the stairway and descended to the lowest floor where the prison was located, I couldn't contain my emotions anymore.

I fell to my knees at the prison entrance, my breaths fast and rough through my sobs. "I hurt him, Wolf. I'm so sorry that I hurt him."

"I know you are," Wolf replied, helping me back onto my feet. "It might take him some time, but he will realize that you are sorry. And if I was correct in what I saw ... how he truly feels for you ... He will understand why you did it too."

He checked in with the posted soldiers, and we traveled through the first barred entrance, then walked the cold hallway deeper into the cavernous prison. Much like the Realm room, it had been carved out into the stone foundation of the castle, deep underground. The air was wet, clinging to my skin and making me shiver. Wolf announced us again to two guards at the next barred doorway.

"She'll be right in here," one of them said, showing Wolf the cell to lead me into.

I walked slowly but willingly, accepting the punishment even though the offense had been justified.

Wolf released his loose hold of my arm. It may have been procedure as an escort, but I believed he'd done it more to lend support than for any other reason. And I was appreciative.

He watched the guard step back to his post. "I realize you aren't focused on what your punishment may be for this, only concerned by the harm you've caused Croft. But I can tell you that it shouldn't take long. The king summoned everyone. As long as we can get confirmation from their readings, and everything is in order ... well, we know what should happen. If Croft doesn't go to the king soon, he will be summoned too. They will sort it all and find that while you did use the stone without consent, you used sound judgment for the kingdom to do so."

I listened as I turned in a circle, taking in the small enclosure. There were no windows underground. A small pallet of bedding lay to one side along with a bucket. That was all there was. I nodded at his words, numbness already starting to take over.

"What I saw of Sielle ... I'm not certain what to think of it. But I don't pretend to know all the capabilities of the Realm. All the revelations from your memories are difficult to believe, most of all that Croft himself is a Lovely. Though, with his mind being blocked, it makes more sense than anything else."

"It does," I agreed, knowing there was so much more to tell Croft. Now that he was aware of our link, I had to tell him how to sever it. If he ever chose to speak with me again. But if he decided not to, I would still pass on the information. That way he would be completely free of me.

"One more thing before I leave for the king's study," Wolf said, staring down at the bedding with a frown. "Sielle had been with Tansy and Blodwyn. If she was harboring them, there's a chance she could be charged with a crime too."

"Harboring?" I asked, suddenly alert. "They did nothing wrong. She explained that they had been friends with Nightshade and Dahlia. That they had fled the castle, worried that whoever had killed the others would try to kill them as well. All four had planned to speak with the king and prince about lessening Lovely restrictions and they believe that might have been the reason. They couldn't stay to be questioned. They were too fearful of losing their lives."

He nodded and looked me in the eyes. "All right. I hope when they are questioned, that is the truth."

"Me as well. They didn't seem hostile when Croft and I—Argo arrived. I'm still very confused about it all and surprised that the princess's and Hemlock's readings didn't show their involvement."

"I was also." He stepped back through the slim cell entry and pulled the barred door closed with another frown. "I'll update you as soon as I can."

"Thank you, Wolf. Apologies to you also, for my dishonesty."

"No need, Olean. I'm glad for it and hope that Croft comes to terms with his new history soon, to accept what is rightfully his." After a reassuring smile, he left.

And I was alone.

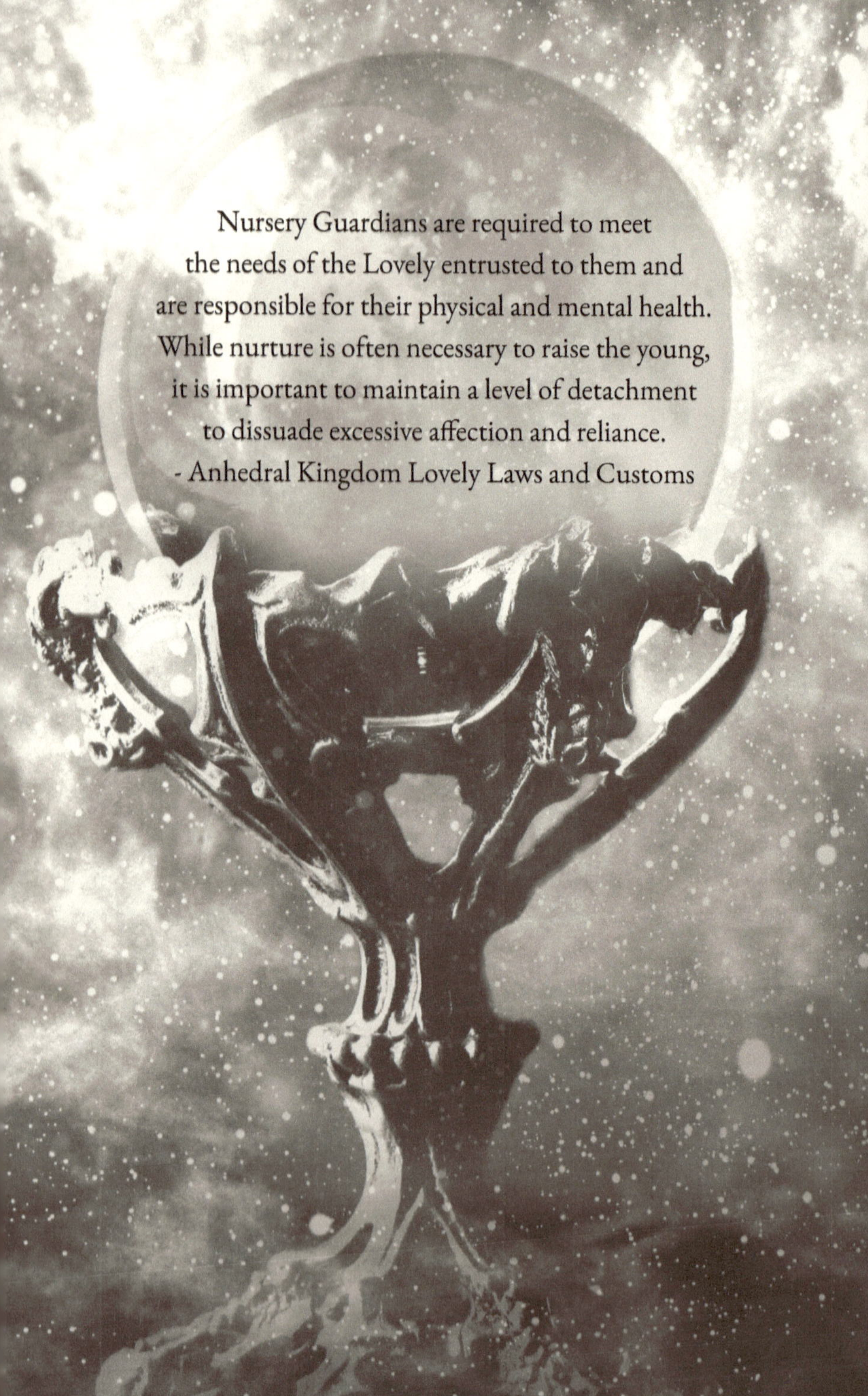

Nursery Guardians are required to meet
the needs of the Lovely entrusted to them and
are responsible for their physical and mental health.
While nurture is often necessary to raise the young,
it is important to maintain a level of detachment
to dissuade excessive affection and reliance.
- Anhedral Kingdom Lovely Laws and Customs

No one had visited, and I was glad for that. Begonia, Clem, and Ivy didn't need to see me locked away. It was far better for them to imagine what a castle cell to be than to see the depressive cage firsthand. I hadn't tried speaking with any of the guards during their rotations or the soldiers who would often walk through the prison for their checks. But I did overhear some of their conversations regarding Hemlock and Princess Naomi, who were being kept in the lower level where more mortal offenders were contained until they met their final fate.

I did wonder if they would be killed for their roles in the king's death and the others. Alone with my thoughts, I also wondered how they hadn't been involved with the Lovely deaths. While it was possible for Tansy and Blodwyn to have lied to Sielle in order to gain a place to hide, I refused to believe that Sielle was directly involved. She would have had no need to contact me through the White stone otherwise, aside from simply discovering my existence.

Time drifted into the next day, and the guards brought me small rations of food and water only twice. The hunger served as a reminder, though. I had done what was right for a cause. Cordelia had told me before I'd left Shadowstone to remember what was really important. Croft was important to me. And he was also important to the kingdom. His ideas, his knowledge—it needed to be used and shared. He would make a fitting king. If what I'd done made that happen, then I wouldn't be sorry. I'd offer my apology for hurting him but not for helping this kingdom.

Another day passed, and my body revolted. The cold was bone deep, and the straw bedding base and two thin blankets did little to help comfort or warm me. I imagined many of the prisoners went insane before dying in their cells from the shock of solitude and the bitter cold.

"Olean," a distant voice called my name, waking me from a foggy dream state. With the constant light from the closest flickering sconce flame, it was growing difficult to determine the hour. Even the guard rotation had been unreliable, as the length of time always differed. The two meals weren't consistent either. Anyone could lose track in a short span. One more turn of the world would set me fully adrift.

"Olean!" The voice came again, waking me altogether. It was familiar. Abrupt but smooth.

"She's in this one." One of the guards came up to the cell door, and to my surprise, unlocked it.

As soon as he pulled it wide, Cordelia appeared from around the rock wall.

The tears in my eyes were immediate. I stood on shaky legs, the cold and weakness wanting me to fall back into what little comfort I'd found.

"Olean," she said again, rushing forward. Her fresh, soapy scent wrapped around me before her arms did, the smell and feeling overwhelming and almost too much to handle.

"Cordelia," I cried into her shoulder. I'd thought I'd been regaining my strength and sense of self, that the prison cell had tested my determination yet also fueled my convictions. But all that crumbled in a blink, surrendering to emotion. That was when I understood something real. I didn't have to be so strong all the time. Sometimes, I even needed help. I'd gotten my first true experience of that with Croft, leaning on him when things had become too painful. And as soon as I thought I'd lost him and that support was gone, I automatically felt I needed to recover, regain my power to fight off the emotion. But it didn't have to be that way. There was strength in accepting emotion, and so much growth too.

"You're so cold. Come. Let's get you back to your rooms and into a bath." She cradled my arm, supporting me as we walked to the door.

"I'm allowed to leave? What's happened? Wolf never came with an update."

The guard said nothing as we passed, simply closed the cell door behind us.

"He sent me as soon as he got word to release you. They've been busy with questioning and council meetings ever since your reading. I was filled in on everything. You are so brave. I am so proud."

"No, not brave. I'm a coward for not telling Croft immediately. I don't regret what I did. It was right and important, but I regret the way it happened. I don't think I've ever been so conflicted."

"You care for him?" she asked, squeezing my arm as the outside guards opened the way for us to exit the prison.

I inhaled deeply, the heat slowly coming back into my body as we moved. "Yes. And I ruined it all. Did Wolf or Begonia tell you what happened?"

"They both told me things. I want you to know that everyone makes mistakes. I've made so many myself, including not being honest with all of you and choosing to remain bound by my grief in Shadowstone, not fighting for what was really important—all of you. But we learn and hopefully make changes for the better."

I remained silent for nearly the rest of the walk, understanding her even more. When we entered the northwest wing and the hallway to my rooms, I asked, "Were you questioned?"

"Yes, by the Cloud stone lead. They searched much of the same, but went further back to see my relationship with King Antin before he wed and through my pregnancy."

"You know about Croft then?"

She smiled as she glanced at me, her pale white eyes gleaming. "That he's my son? Yes."

"How do you feel? I mean ... are you all right?"

"I am. I was able to speak with Pearla after her reading. She told me what had happened after the first baby was born, how Croft had come while I'd fallen into exhaustion, my body continuing through labor. She acted fast, asking a nursemaid in the city to keep him safe while she helped me recover. It was a difficult decision for her, but she knew if I or anyone else discovered the truth, his life might have been in danger. As much as I mourn the years I lost with him, I am grateful that he had her to raise him, to teach him."

We passed several guards posted in each hallway and a fair amount of soldiers with wolfdogs patrolling too. With the threat of the Blood stone and those who used it locked away, I would have thought the added protection would have diminished.

Both of us were crying as we entered the room, and more tears came as Begonia, Clem, and Ivy greeted me too, with hugs, and food, and questions I was finally able to answer.

As soon as things began to settle, Cordelia told the others to ready for bed and instructed me to have a bath. I sighed, already anticipating the pleasure of the warm water.

"Ivy had me sleep in your room with her. Would you like me to take Croft's room instead?" Cordelia asked, watching me move my night clothes into the bathing room.

Begonia had said all his things were gone when she'd returned from my reading in the trial hall. He hadn't stayed with them while I was gone. That saddened me more, realizing he had needed to get away from everyone in order to process everything.

"No, you can stay in there. I'll take his room." A bag of soap lay beside the small water basin. I didn't open it, already knowing it was what Croft had bought from the market, the rose and spiced soaps smelling so lovely. Moving back into the main room, I asked, "Have you seen him?"

"No," she replied, standing from the cushioned armchair and walking the used tea settings to the dinner cart. She shuffled the dishes around, preparing to push it out into the hallway for an attendant to take. "Pearla told me he'd come straight to her place for answers but left just before a soldier arrived with her summons. And Wolf said he returned to the castle last night for a discussion with the king and his council. But no, I haven't seen him."

"And the others? Tansy, Blodwyn, and Sielle?"

She smiled broadly. "He said they were here today, read by others, and cleared. I didn't see them either, though I am so happy that Tansy is not involved with the deaths. I'm also very happy for you. To know that you have a true sister here is wonderful."

"Yes, it really is. I'm excited to meet her properly, when I don't have a tail and can speak without barking." We both chuckled. "There's so much to discuss."

Sometime later, hours after my bath, I lay inside Croft's room, in the bed where he'd slept. It was just as comfortable as the one I had, arguably even more so because it was his. An attendant had changed the linen and blankets, but the scent of him in the space lingered, calming me.

Yet I still couldn't sleep, my mind replaying all that had happened, and anticipating cold dreams of the prison.

A knock on the door had me rushing from the room to answer, to stop the others from waking. Hope flooded my chest despite what little chance there was for it to be who I really wanted to see.

Cautious even though a guard remained posted nearby, I unlocked and opened it a crack.

"Olean." Wolf's tired face came into view, his eyes half-lidded, brow without paint.

I opened the way for him to enter. "Wolf, come in. The others are asleep."

He sat with me at the full table near the door. "I apologize for the hour and for not visiting earlier. Cordelia ensured me she would get you from the prison."

"It's all right," I replied, anxiously folding my hands together.

He glanced around at the dying fire, the light in the room dim, with only two main wall sconces lit. "I wanted to let you know personally that all the ordered readings to verify your information have been completed. All were favorable."

I nodded. "Cordelia said that Croft was back and in meetings. How is he?"

"No longer in denial. He didn't attend any other readings but was briefed of the findings. He and Ren met with the king's council, which took some time to gather and then to go through the old laws to confirm terms of the heir apparent. They were in discussions alone for several hours after that, because while it is true that Croft is the rightful king, he was not raised to be as such and has every cause to abdicate. With all that has happened, they both have much to consider, and I believe they will come to the best decision for the kingdom. They won't have to announce anything tomorrow if more time is needed."

"Tomorrow?"

"The funeral and ball. With many of the court and other guests here, there was no option to cancel. They will announce whatever they find best to inform the kingdom about all that has happened."

That was why the guards and soldiers were still in place. The funeral and ball. I'd forgotten completely.

"I was released, but had there been a decision regarding a punishment? Am I permitted to attend?"

He rubbed a hand on the back of his neck, pressing hard at what I imagined to be soreness from a long several days. "After the readings were concluded and Croft had been informed of their findings and of your confinement, he chose not to give any extra punishment, so it all was dismissed. If it's of any consolation, I need to note that he was very distressed to learn you'd been in the prison. He hadn't been aware until today."

He hadn't. Of course. He'd left before I'd been taken there. And though he'd had reason to hate me forever, knowing that he had some reaction did make me feel comforted. It opened the door for a chance, a possibility of forgiveness or at least no lingering hatred. "It is. Thank you for telling me."

At the thought of forgiveness, I asked, "And what about Sielle, Tansy, and Blodwyn? How were their readings? You said Croft didn't attend?"

"No, he didn't. The queen also didn't attend any after yours. She is suffering extensively over the princess's betrayal. Two other Lovely handled the remaining readings. And while I trust the findings and am happy to know Tansy and Blodwyn had nothing to do with Nightshade's or Dahlia's deaths, I am left perplexed. Unless, of course, it was done by their own hands ... We'll have to reconsider some things." He paused a moment, his contemplative frown turning into a soft smile. "But I did read Sielle, and it was a pleasant surprise. She is similar to Croft. While we've heard about rarities like them before, no one has seen it recently. I suppose there are reasons these instances occur, like the Lovely sent to confirm the childbirths leave after discovering the Lovely infant has died, not waiting to witness the other child's birth. It's also quite possible some know and decide to ignore it anyway." He gave me a pointed look, showing me that he understood more, that it could happen purposely to be kept from the Crown.

"For Croft's case particularly, he was kept hidden for the reasons we know now," he continued. "As for Sielle's reading, her questioning involved Tansy and Blodwyn. We had to check your connection memories as well. We couldn't see the White stone interactions, only what you and she recalled after disconnecting.

The reason you two can speak there is rather difficult to understand, since no Lovely are able to access the same Realm space at once, even if they are touching the same stone. Did you figure out why you can?"

"No, I didn't understand it at all. I was hoping to speak with Sielle more about it," I admitted.

"After first reading you, I thought about it often, trying to understand. While a sibling Lovely might have the ability because of the relation, two sets of Lovely from the same family but different births has never been recorded. And even if both from the same birth lived, like if Croft's brother had, then there would be no Dead tether to the Realm at all. No access through the stones. But after seeing Sielle and reading her, all the pieces came together. You were born a set of three."

I gasped, touching my lips. "I hadn't even ..."

"Thought it? No one else had. It's something else that's never been recorded in our history, in any of our books. Though it's possible it has happened without notice for the reasons I mentioned. Also, the other sibling might never know of their abilities without access to a stone. Sielle only recently found out too. But unlike Croft, she touched a stone and discovered her tether and its link to you as well."

"I'm not sure what to say. I want to speak with her, to finally meet and thank her." It seemed unbelievable, yet it made the most sense. We were born a set of three. Three.

"You may have that chance tomorrow. Your sister's been invited to attend the events." He stood, tapping his fingers to the tabletop.

"My sister." The words were a whisper in an effort to control my excitement, to not wake the others. I stood and moved with him to the door. "Thank you again for coming to talk with me. I appreciate all you've done. And if you see Croft, could you tell him …" I stopped, unsure of what I wanted to say to Croft. He was the first one I wanted to tell about Sielle, but I knew he probably didn't want to speak to me. And if he did, I would apologize over and over before anything else. If only he'd listen. "Could you tell him I was truthful with everything else? That I was honest about him. That he will be a remarkable leader."

Wolf nodded as he opened the door. He turned before leaving. "I think so as well. Good evening, Olean."

The dead are never truly gone.
Their life energy continues on within
the Realm, creating the connections and
allowing the Lovely many views of the world
through the use of different stones.
- Anhedral Kingdom Lovely Guidebook

~ 27 ~

The funeral took place after midday in the royal cemetery, deep inside the expansive main garden. Mausoleums made from limestone, slate, and granite spanned outward in a spiral, the very first king to reside at Anhedral Castle positioned at the very center. Several remained nameless and empty, having already been constructed, awaiting embellishments to suit whoever would be laid to rest within. King Antin's—which would eventually hold the dowager queen as well—was refined with pillared corners, a spired roof, and inlaid jewels along the single doorway's arch. For the ceremony, black and silver banners draped across the front. Though the late king's body had been interred in the days following his death, the funeral ceremony was an honor to pay homage and recognize his entry into the Realm.

Clouds streaked the sky, preventing the day from turning unbearably hot. It was a gift from the Realm with everyone dressed in black and silver to pay their respects as a kingdom. The attendance exceeded that of the induction, people spreading outward from the front of the mausoleum, stretching well into the sections of the garden's flowering plants. Only the royals and dignitaries were seated in two rows at the front. Everyone else stood for the service, which a minister of the Realm faith led.

The late king's advisory council and Ren also spoke words and remembrances, while the dowager queen remained still in her chair. Unmoving. Unreceptive.

Though there had been no official directive, most Lovely with roles in the main Garden council were positioned behind the royals. The Clear stones had gathered behind everyone as usual, making me wonder if they had been instructed to do so beforehand or if it was an unspoken rule to be adhered to at all events. Cordelia and I kept Begonia, Clem, and Ivy with us, off to one side of the center. I'd been prepared to argue with anyone who instructed otherwise, but luckily, no one had seemed concerned. Could have been because we'd chosen to stand nearest to Willa and Mais too.

Notably missing were Princess Naomi and Hemlock. Murmurs were heard prior to the start of the service, people who hadn't yet been informed realizing and speculating on the obvious absences.

The morning had crawled, everyone in the rooms determining what we would wear and waiting for word on when to leave for the service. I'd pushed for our early arrival, watching for any sign of Sielle or Tansy and Blodwyn, who we'd heard had been welcomed back to the castle the previous night. None had come. Even though I'd been disappointed, I had hope Sielle would accept the invitation and attend the later event.

And as much as I fought to stay focused, to keep my mind from wandering away from the dedication to the late king and his achievements, my eyes searched for the only other person I wanted to see. Croft. He and Argo had arrived later than most, choosing to remain near the garden's entrance until just before the start of the ceremony. Cordelia had grabbed hold of my arm, physically stopping me from going to him. She'd whispered that it wasn't the right time or place. I didn't fight, knowing that well enough. I also knew that while I wanted to be close to him, I couldn't be the first to approach. It would be yet another invasion to hear his thoughts again.

He hadn't interacted with anyone that I'd noticed, except for Wolf in a brief exchange. He chose a spot on the opposite side from the royals, though not taking a seat. It was a default choice in a usual place for an attendant, standing at the edge of the row. He didn't blend in as he normally might, and it had nothing to do with his and Argo's position. It was his clothing. He hadn't worn his formal attendant attire, with the silver-lined black shirt and neatly tailored pants. Instead, on the day of his father's funeral, he donned a royal suit. The tall, shiny black leather boots. The tight and trim black pants. The full black surcoat with an intricate silver tapestry design, which spread from the high waist front down to a split tail at the back that hung lower than his knees. The similarly designed silver vest peeking out from below. And finally, the black undershirt buttoned to his neck.

He'd chosen to accept his new identity, proudly showing who he was while also paying respect by allowing distance.

I thought he couldn't be any more handsome. I'd been so wrong. Between him showing his royal claim and the stately clothes fitting him better than anything else could, he set my heart into the wildest rhythm imaginable. The impact was very close to that of him relaxed in my rooms, in night clothing and bare feet, his arms around me, and his lips pressed to mine.

My mouth had gone dry the instant I saw him and remained that way throughout the funeral. I was lucky to be alive from the amount of times I'd held my breath and looked his way, begging him silently to see me, to come find me and speak to me. But he had never once looked, never once torn his gaze from the front mausoleum step and whoever was speaking.

King Ren's words of his father had been concise, listing his most notable accomplishments and recalling favorite memories of a man whose life was taken too soon. In the end, there was no announcement during the service, which was understandable. Discussing the people responsible for his death as well as introducing another heir would only soil his memorial.

People dispersed quickly. Some gathered at the garden entrance as well as in the great hall inside, staying for the life celebration ball. Others with close accommodations left to discard their funeral attire and don more appropriate clothing. We did the same, retreating to my rooms to dress for the second time. The dowager queen passed us on the way inside the castle, Hydra leading her along with a few guards. Queen Reina still had a blank stare, as if she didn't know where she was or where she was being led. Hydra kept hold of her arm, but the dowager queen tripped over something, falling to her knees. She'd been the only one wearing a crown, and it nearly slipped from her head.

"Your Majesty." The concerned words came from everyone near. We all leaned closer, trying to help her recover.

"Ouch," Ivy said from behind me, sympathetic to what had happened.

"She's all right. I have her," Hydra said with a curt smile, carrying on past us, her arm bumping against mine. The guards took more care to create a path through the other people, making me wonder why she hadn't gone a different way from the start.

I tried my best to stay positive while changing for the evening. The gown I chose was the fanciest of all those hanging within my closet. Layers of pale pink tulle twisted around the front, leaving the side of one leg partially exposed. The bodice folded over as well, with the gauzy fabric draping off the shoulders, wrapping over my chest, then cinching with a thin tie at the waist. The pieces over the shoulders and down onto the bodice were decorated with delicate lace shaped to form flower blooms and petals. It was a gown made specifically for my namesake and was the most beautiful thing I'd ever worn.

Everyone else had already finished and were waiting in the main sitting room.

Begonia and Cordelia both gasped when I entered from my room. Ivy was less subtle, screaming, "You look so pretty!" Her bright, toothy smile showed the growth her two bottom teeth had made during the past weeks.

"You forgot to paint your eyebrows," Clem said, rolling his eyes and falling back onto the settee, not caring to wrinkle his fitted white shirt and black pants. While he also had on his ruffled black tie, he had left the surcoat in the room.

"I didn't forget," I said with a shrug.

Cordelia narrowed her eyes, and I thought for a moment I was about to hear her clipped tone, like so many other times I'd bent the rules in Shadowstone. Not seeking any new clothing during her stay here, she'd chosen to wear her favorite golden lacy dress, which made us all feel more at home.

After a moment when no irritated reply came, her lips lifted in amusement and she moved to the bathing room.

Begonia and I glanced at each other, puzzled by her reaction. Begonia had chosen a fancier gown from my closet as well, hers a vivid emerald green that made her pale skin luminous. She looked older and ... happy.

When Cordelia emerged with a wet cloth and proceeded to wipe the painted brows from her face, Ivy let out a shriek that changed halfway through, going from alarm to elation. She ran over to Cordelia, green gown decorated with Ivy leaves flowing out behind her little body. She giggled as Cordelia turned the wet cloth on her and wiped away the thin vines and leaves she'd painted on minutes before.

Begonia rolled her lips.

"You don't have to do the same," I assured her. "But I think something like this ... it's another thing we should be able to choose for ourselves. We shouldn't have to paint these on in order to make others more comfortable with our presence."

"I agree," Clem said, standing and moving to the bathing room to remove his own.

Ivy giggled and made a turn in her gown, excited to be part of something we were all doing together even if she didn't fully understand why.

"Ivy ... did you get hurt?" Cordelia asked, wiping at the back of Ivy's arm with the cloth and lifting it up to show a tiny dot of blood.

"Yes, before we came back into the castle, when the queen fell. I think I scratched my arm," she said, making me realize her sympathetic comment hadn't been that after all.

Begonia's lips leveled out as Clem flopped onto the settee with his legs draped over an arm, the painted slashes over his brow wiped clean. Then, with determined steps, she walked to the bathing room to remove hers too. When she came back out, she flashed a smile. "Do you think we'll get into trouble?"

"I really don't care," Clem noted, eyes closed and feet kicking absently.

"You should care," Cordelia replied, which grabbed his attention. "I think something small like this is a good way to start challenging our restrictions, to start fighting for change if that is our intention. Today has been busy and emotional for everyone in the kingdom. The royals and many others are still in mourning. So while I doubt anyone will make any fuss about our little rebellion, we should still understand and care about their reactions in order to properly express our reasons. That way they can understand why this affects us and why it's important."

I nodded, considering all the steps to take as time moved on. If Croft became king, I knew many changes would come, including for the Lovely, regardless of him being one of us. He had seen many things he disagreed with long before we arrived here. And if Ren continued on as king, I still believed he'd hear the Lovely's concerns regarding our indenture. He had taken suggestions from his advisory council and from Wolf, so he was open to what decisions might be best for the kingdom.

While the others fell into chatter over what food would be served at the ball, I went into my room to retrieve something I should have returned days ago.

Cordelia moved to me when I waved to her. She eyed the pink line on my arm where the scabbing from the knife wound had fallen away. "How are you feeling?"

"I'm all right, I think. Well, nervous, hoping to see Sielle, and hoping Croft might speak to me," I admitted, blowing out a breath. "But I wanted you to have this back. I didn't end up wearing it at all."

Her finger touched the edge of the pendant I held in my palm before covering it with the cloth it lay on. "I gave it to you. I have no use for it anymore. Haven't for a long time. It's up to you to keep it or give it to someone else who may want something of the late king's."

Croft. I smiled with understanding.

We left the rooms not long after. Nervousness and excitement bound through me at an even greater amount than the morning. My mind frantically moved through possible interactions with both Sielle and Croft, unable to focus, unable to settle. The bond with my Nursery mates had grown stronger than ever, and nothing would ever replace them, but I was desperate to meet my sister. And though I had hope Croft would speak to me, my heart felt the dread of never being forgiven.

People already filled the great hall. There were also some lingering outside in the courtyard, both areas serving for the large celebration. The amount had lessened from the funeral, some having chosen to forgo the event after a mournful day. I understood well enough. It had felt odd, but the dowager queen's wishes had been upheld. She had planned for the ball to be a celebration for King Ren, but that was prior to the recent revelations. They probably should have called it off. However, it was arguably the best time to make any announcements.

I left the others in the hall, in need of fresh air, my emotions reaching an unbearable level with all the people around.

A cool breeze greeted me as soon as I passed the doorway into the courtyard. Pink and orange colors streaked through the clouds above, the last little bits of light pushing out from the distant horizon while darkness settled in along the grounds.

"Oh, she's over here, by the door. Olean!"

I turned to see Tansy in a black gown moving toward me, leading Sielle at her side.

"It really is something to see," Tansy said as I met them halfway. "You do look identical."

Sielle smiled brightly, her large deep brown eyes staring in my direction, though not in my exact place. Her layered lilac-colored dress fluttered like flower petals in the wind, soft and beautiful.

"Hi," I breathed the word, and her face and eyes turned toward my voice.

"Hi," she replied, lips curving into a full smile.

Tears came from both of us, an instant response. Joy flooded my entire being as she opened her arms. I did the same, stepping into her slowly, letting her feel my presence. Then we were embracing fully, arms around each other, holding on tightly.

"If you are both all right, I'm going to see Cordelia," Tansy said, and I nodded as she left us.

"I'm so happy to have found you," Sielle said.

"I'm so happy you did too." I breathed in, loving the smell of her unbound hair surrounding us.

"You smell good. What soap do you use?"

I chuckled and pulled back a little. "I was just thinking the same about your hair. I like the flower scents and spices too. This one is rose."

She laughed softly, her deeper tone not much different than my own. "I like the florals as well. Here, can I ...?" Her hands lifted from below my arms up to my face.

"Yes." I leaned in, letting her lay her palms on my cheeks, her fingers moving to explore my eyes, ears, and nose.

"It really is hard to believe," she said, gently touching my bald head.

"Wolf came to see me last night. Told me how we were three, which had allowed us to be in the same Realm space together."

"I didn't understand immediately either. My first stone connection happened when I went into Father's room ... Oh! Our father! We have a father. He's visiting other family in Bloodweld right now. But you can meet him when he returns. He's going to be so happy."

"We have a father?" *Oh, Realm.* I was having trouble breathing, overwhelmed as her hands dropped down to my neck and then to my shoulders. "I would love to meet him. And ... our mother?"

Her head shook and her lips tipped down. "No. She passed a few years after our birth. I don't remember much of her, only what Father tells me."

"I'm so sorry," I replied automatically, feeling the pain she must have felt as such a young child.

"I am also." After a moment, her hands returned to her sides. "About the stones ... Father had procured both sometime in my youth, even though personally owning them is discouraged. I believe it was his way of grieving, possibly hoping for some kind of connection to our mother since he wasn't permitted to discuss the birth with anyone else. Having signed the indenture documents from the Crown and receiving the payment they deem acceptable for taking Lovely away, he upheld that law and never spoke of you or our dead sister.

"A few years ago, he traveled without me for the first time, leaving me to stay in the house alone with an attendant to visit daily. That was when I discovered the stones locked away in his room. I had gone into his closet for something but felt a difference in the air, felt the power stemming from a trunk buried beneath several others. That was when I connected with the White. I am blind inside the Realm there, but sensed and spoke with our dead. They shared names if they had them and some memories, nothing to help me better understand why I was able to connect. I knew enough about the Lovely from attending school, knew I shouldn't have been able to connect at all.

"Not long after, I did the same with the Needled from another trunk, but I realized it didn't have the same Realm link. I learned more about all the stones, about the history of the Lovely, growing curious. After more research on the Needled stone, I realized my connection to it felt different than had been described. That was when I discovered you. Certain times when I touched the stone, I felt you through it and realized you were inside the Realm with a different stone. It still took a long time to understand our tether there, that we had another sister, and that our link is through her, allowing us to be in the same Realm space."

I took a deep breath and let out a long sigh.

She sighed too. "I'm sorry for not being honest with you from the start, for not telling you everything as I was learning it myself. I should have."

"No. I understand why. And you were right not to. I would not have been driven to know more about the deaths. I might not have even connected to Croft, which I don't regret despite hurting him."

"There's been a lot of new surprises."

"Yes, that is very true," I admitted. "Thank you for coming here. I understand even coming for questioning was a risk. So thank you."

"I'm not bound by the same laws as our father. I never signed anything." She smiled slyly, making me laugh. "And besides, though the king and all the others were shocked by the truth, he released me without issue and without a discussion about being a Lovely. Tansy and Blodwyn had even been surprised as we expected the king or dowager queen to demand my indenture, given that I have the ability to connect with the Realm."

"I think they've been overwhelmed with everything. The murders, the trials, the funeral, and this celebration ... There might be an announcement regarding Croft happening tonight. We should probably join the others so we don't miss anything."

"Good idea. Would you mind leading me? Tansy took my cane."

"Of course."

Others moved aside while we walked into the south entrance from the darkened courtyard. Some had been staring the entire length of our discussion, noticing our nearly identical appearances. None of them approached, though. I was grateful for the time alone as our first introduction, to begin our friendship.

"I bet we are a sight to see. There are so many whispers around us."

"Yes, we are a confusing sight. But I'm not certain what's causing more of a stir, our likeness or my lack of eyebrow paint."

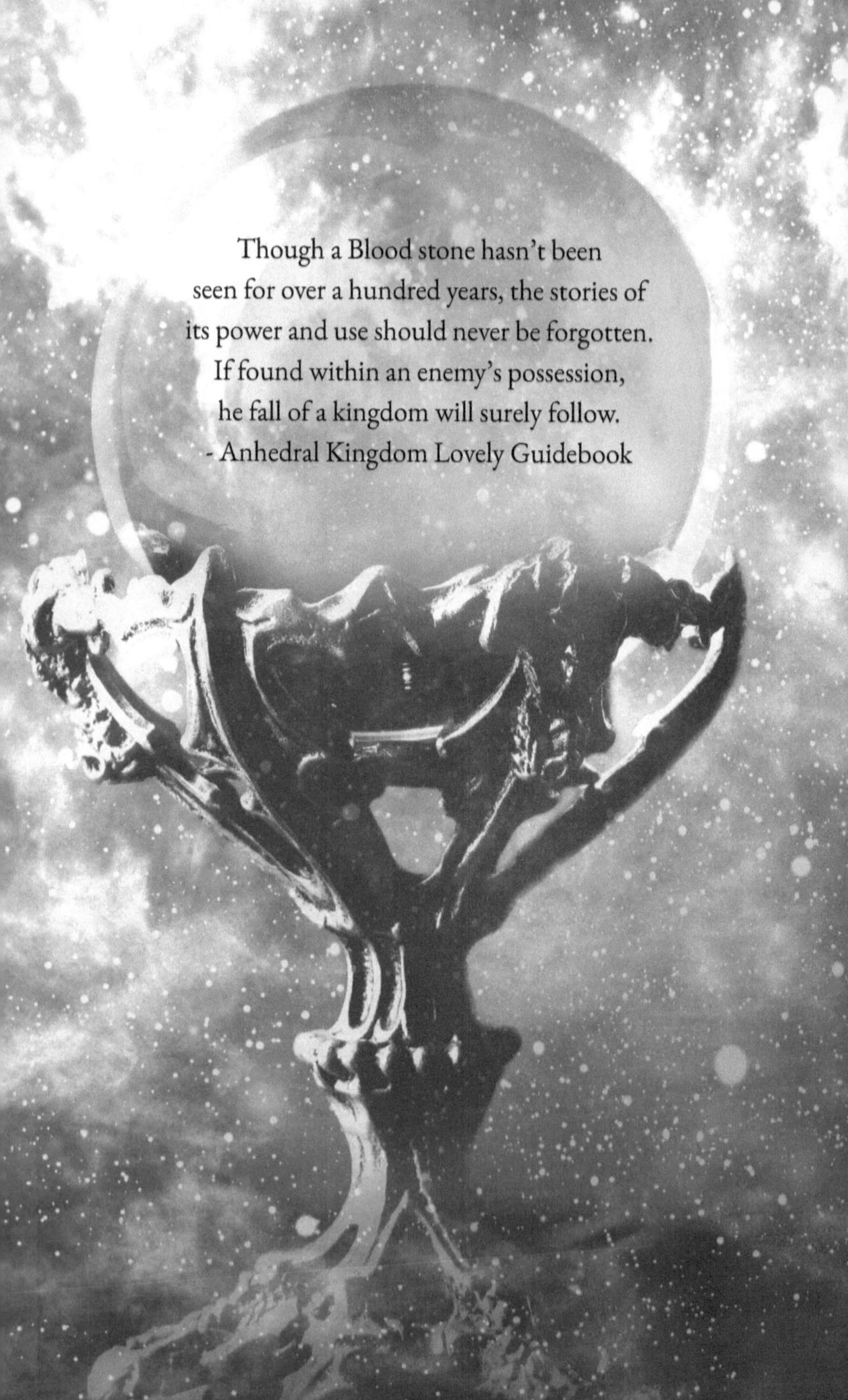

Though a Blood stone hasn't been
seen for over a hundred years, the stories of
its power and use should never be forgotten.
If found within an enemy's possession,
he fall of a kingdom will surely follow.
- Anhedral Kingdom Lovely Guidebook

~ 28 ~

The others had been thrilled about meeting Sielle, gushing over her and her dress, enthralled with the tale of how she'd discovered the stones in her home and how we'd been able to talk within the Realm. She hadn't minded retelling all we'd already talked about, humoring Begonia, Clem, and Ivy with all the details.

Cordelia was especially happy, having finally reconnected with Tansy. After they discussed what might have happened to the others Cordelia had raised, they'd fallen into tales of Tansy's time in Shadowstone. We joined in as well, recounting stories of our time together.

However, my thoughts began to drift pretty quickly, letting them continue on while my eyes roamed the great hall for Croft. Drinks and food were brought out to the side tables, and people continued to gather and chat. Nettle made sure to come over and say hi, expressing his concern for all that had happened while also satisfying his curiosity about my sister. Kalmia had stopped as well to introduce herself to Cordelia and to find out whether Tansy would be reappointed as the White stone lead since she had returned to the castle and had been cleared of any crimes. No one knew what the orders would be, though.

Kalmia fluffed her white gown, having worn the stone class color because she hadn't been instructed otherwise. Her face had to tip upward to speak since most of us were far taller. "They haven't called a proper meeting for the Lovely council in well over a week. Wolf has been busy with the king. Hydra has been spending all of her time with the dowager queen, having someone else lead the Clear stone readings for the kingdom's perimeter patrols. The rest of us have been going on as usual, trying to hold everything else together." Her voice pitched extra high with concern.

"I'm sure we will get more direction soon," Tansy assured her. "You should get something to eat and drink. You look paler than your dress."

Kalmia's eyes widened, looking down at herself, affronted. "I ... do feel a bit weak."

Tansy nodded in encouragement. "Get some food so you don't collapse and miss anything."

She gave us all a tentative smile and moved in well-practiced steps as if she were floating along the floor to the side of the hall.

A hush came over the room, then murmuring took over, voices rising again.

King Ren and Croft appeared at the main doors, splitting the crowd. Argo had spotted us off to the side, breaking his duty by stopping briefly. Croft's head swept in our direction, his beautiful amber eyes locking with mine for a single moment between strides before facing forward again. They walked fast to the far end of the room where the dais held the thrones at the center and other high-back chairs. They remained at the edge and turned to address everyone, Argo heeling correctly. Wolf followed closely behind, the long tail of his gray surcoat swinging until he stopped at the very front and stood off to the side, below the steps of the dais.

Everyone instantly quieted. No speaking. No eating. No movement at all.

King Ren and Croft both hadn't changed after the funeral. His attire was a near match to Croft's—black pants, silver accented surcoat, silver vest—though his undershirt and ruffled tie were white instead of black. That had me curious if he had lent Croft his own clothing, having so little time for a tailor to make something new for Croft. The fit looked nice, even though Croft held a bit more size in height and musculature.

I breathed deeply, calming myself for the information they planned to announce. At my side, Sielle took my hand, grasping it gently, following the sounds and silence well enough to know what was occurring. I gripped hers in return, thanking her silently.

King Ren lifted a hand to ensure complete silence before he spoke, his voice loud and direct. "Thank you all for staying or returning for this celebration. With all that has happened, a ball didn't seem the best of ideas. We discussed canceling. Ultimately, we thought it wise to continue on and celebrate King Antin's life."

He took a moment, wiping a hand over the hair that had grown along his jaw, then back through the mess on his head, which he appeared to have already done many times in recent hours. "The day has been difficult for most of us, having to say farewell to my father, a king who departed not by way of age or even illness, but by the hands of his own blood. This might come as a shock to some of you, but we've discovered through questioning and many readings, that my sister, Princess Naomi and her appointed Lovely, Hemlock, were responsible for our father's death."

Gasps echoed to the ceiling, and he held up a fast hand to keep everyone's focus. "I don't wish to shed light on the details, as they are of no importance to this event tonight. We collected the evidence we needed and they will be dealt their punishment soon enough. Following such a great loss to our family, this has impacted us even more so. But we will not let the kingdom suffer for it. We will not allow that."

His face turned to Croft for a moment, who had kept focused on him throughout it all, reading his lips. Then his gaze traveled around the hall. "There was another discovery made at the same time. This one a welcomed one. As you can plainly see him standing at my side, as he has for quite some time. Croft has been a loyal attendant of ours for many years, starting first as a laundry hand when he was younger, then becoming my own attendant in recent years. But he is not who we thought. Or who he thought he was himself. He is my true brother, born half a year before me, and thus the eldest child of Antin."

Unrestrained voices rose all around us, people understanding exactly what that information meant. King Ren silenced them again, swiping his hand through the air in a faster, impatient movement. "We've done extensive questioning through many readings to confirm this truth as well. And we found it all to be valid. Since then, we've met with the kingdom's council regarding our laws and what that means for the throne. Anhedral asserts that the first born child in the royal line, no matter the gender or marital state of the reigning monarch, stands as the heir apparent."

He waited, allowing everyone a moment to process all he'd said before pressing on. "With never knowing his true self, never knowing himself as a prince, and finding himself in this sudden new role, Croft needed time to consider what this meant for him and the kingdom. He has learned many things through the years and was often council to both my father and myself, with ideas to make our kingdom better. So together, over the past days, we've explored what our kingdom needs moving forward after our father's death. All the issues building from lack of concern and neglect will be addressed. We will take action to bring our land back to its previous health and vitality, work for the equality and unity of our people, and maintain peace. More changes will come, but I can assure you it will be for us as a whole, not the Crown alone. And while I will continue with the duties I've come to revere as a prince, I will also aid Croft in his new role as our king."

The attendants and guards were the first to cheer and applaud, but everyone followed along quickly, accepting what Prince Ren had said. Begonia, Clem, and Ivy screamed with joy, even bounced in place. Croft's hand lifted to cover his heart before he dipped his head in a bow, a silent vow.

Tears came again, leaking down my face as I watched him proudly. When he lifted his head, his eyes found mine and held. The corners of his lips tugged into a soft smile that had me sobbing openly.

Everyone dipped into bows and curtsies, accepting him as their new king.

I almost couldn't take it. The emotion was strong, my heart wanting to burst with pride and with my love for him. And though a little smile could mean so many things, it didn't seem to mean what I wanted it to at all. Because as everyone stood again, his eyes were gone, that smile directed to Prince Ren as they shook hands, and then down to Wolf, who reached up to him to do the same.

Prince Ren waved into the air. "All right. All right! Croft requested that I tell you all that he understands there may be trepidation about him accepting the throne due to his deafness. But he and I both want you to know that he is more than capable and will work diligently every day to prove his worth, his loyalty, and his honor. His official coronation will be planned soon. As for now, he will assume his role, and I will stand behind him always. That is all for now. Please, have a wonderful evening."

Croft's eyes came to me again, and my knees shook at the new look there. Intense. Determined. Happy.

I touched my lips, ignoring all the movement of people around me. Before he looked away, I mouthed, "I'm sorry."

His head tilted, eyebrows drawing together. Prince Ren came to his side, patting a hand to his back before stepping into his view, severing our contact. He guided him to the side of the dais, where people had started to gather to speak to them, Wolf included.

"Well, that was thrilling," Cordelia said, her smile brighter than the sun itself. "I wasn't sure if Croft would reject his birthright. Were you?"

"No. I wasn't certain either," I admitted sadly. We hadn't interacted in days. The looks he showed me could easily have been a reaction to the happiness he was feeling after their announcement. There was no way to know for sure. But once again, I had to stop myself from moving toward him. I couldn't be the first to approach. Especially at the ball, with so many people wanting to meet with him. No. Any interaction we might have wouldn't occur tonight.

Music started to play, capturing our attention. Several people with bow-drawn string instruments had entered the hall and took seats at the front, on the other side of the dais. As they played, others spread away from the center of the expansive floor, clearing space for dancing.

Watching him had quickly turned into torture. Sweaty hands. Shaky legs. My excitement had me wanting to stare all night, but the longer I did, the more my heart began to hurt.

"Where did Ivy go?" Begonia asked, peering around all our bodies.

"She said she saw Guardian Calla and wanted to say hi," Clem said, eyeing the food tables.

"I don't see her," Cordelia added, turning in a circle.

"I'll go look outside." It was the escape I needed. I touched Sielle's arm and said, "I won't be long."

"All right," she replied, smiling brightly, reflecting the energy from all around us.

"Are you hungry?" Tansy asked her, leading her by the arm toward the tables. Clem happily tagged along.

Cordelia stood onto her toes, eyeing different areas of the room. "I'll search here."

I nodded in reply and moved toward the door, sparing one more glance at Croft, whose eyes spotted my movement and watched as I walked away. The back of a green dress caught my eyes, and I followed, only to lose sight before reaching the doorway.

With the end of the announcement, many wandered the hallway and moved out to the courtyard. I picked up on people's words, noting both positive and negative responses. Even some Lovely seemed confused, unsure what to think about such a change. I overheard two soldiers talking when I stepped outside, the delight over Croft becoming king plain to hear in their tones.

Ivy was nowhere to be seen in the courtyard. She also hadn't strayed farther down to the garden entrance, where only one couple had gone to disappear into the dimmer torchlight to steal a moment, their mouths pressed tightly together, too focused on themselves to notice anyone else. I didn't bother to disturb them, especially when I recognized Nettle's dark bald head and what looked to be a stable attendant's clothing.

I went back to the castle, knowing Ivy wouldn't choose to be outside so late, even if she had found Guardian Calla. Avoiding the great hall, I moved in the other direction, passing the trial hall and stairway to the prison. A scattering of people roamed the area, discussing the announcement and other things, taking a respite from the crowded great hall.

Not too far along, getting complimented on her beautiful green dress by a few guests, Ivy stood. Guardian Calla was nowhere in sight.

"Ivy!" I moved to her as the other people smiled and offered hellos before leaving us.

"Olean! Everyone loves my dress," she said, pulling the material outward at her sides and twirling around, making it fan out wide.

"I heard. What are you doing out here alone? Clem said you wanted to see Guardian Calla?" I glanced around again, seeing no one else except another straggler coming from the closest bathing room.

"No. I only wanted to get away from there and all the talking. I hoped you'd notice and follow because there's something I want to show you."

The way she spoke made me pause a moment. But before I could even think more about it, Ivy took off at a run, her dress flowing wildly behind her. She passed the White stone room and disappeared into the far stairway quicker than I'd ever seen her move.

"Wait, Ivy!" I called out as I gave chase. A smile took over my face. The idea of chasing her around the castle felt daunting, but it also was the best distraction I could have asked for. Yet it was wise to let someone know first. "Stop a moment! We can play, but we need to let Cordelia know what we're doing."

My shouts down the stairway got no response. I breathed hard and fast, my chest and legs already tiring. What little physical endurance I'd built since moving to the castle had nearly vanished after spending so much time in the Eye stone and contained inside my rooms. The days confined inside a prison cell hadn't helped either.

Arriving at the bottom, I glanced around. Firelight from two sconces flickered dimly. I realized immediately where we'd gone, too deep in thought to have considered it beforehand. Isolated much like the prison, only one door stood at the end in near darkness. Ivy was already standing outside of it.

"Ivy! We should not be down here, all right? Let's go back to the ball and have some food," I urged. "We'll eat and then we can play a game in another place."

Knowing the door was locked, I didn't rush forward when she took hold of the handle.

But I'd been wrong.

The door offered no resistance, and her arm disappeared as she pushed forward.

"Stop!" I screamed, fear forcing me into a run. "It's the Black stone room, Ivy. Don't go inside!"

"I'm not going to, foolish girl," she replied, her voice still girlish, though the words too mature.

"Ivy?" I stopped just before reaching her.

She spun to face me, hands behind her back. A toothy smile formed on her angelic face, the bottom gap making me question what I'd thought she'd said.

"I know you want to play. And we will, but we need to tell Cordelia where we are first. Everyone was looking for you."

Her hairless brows lifted. "They'll find me soon if you cooperate."

"What?"

"Honestly, you are not as intelligent as I thought you to be if I need to explain everything."

My mouth opened, not quite understanding what was happening. "Ivy, who—"

Suddenly, her hands came forward from behind her back, one hand holding a dagger, the dim light making the edge of the blade glint.

"What is ..."

"Does this make it easier to understand?" she asked, lifting the blade and pushing the tip to her dainty throat.

I lunged forward on instinct, arms outstretched, wanting to save her from ... herself.

It hit me then, the truth like a cannonball to the chest, large and impossible to miss. I had been a fool. How had I not realized sooner? *Oh, Realm.*

"No, no," Ivy said, her innocent voice lifting with mockery, making me want to vomit. She pressed the tip in farther, tilting her head back for me to see clearly. "Unless you want me dead, I'd step back."

I did what she asked, holding my hands in the air as my stomach clenched and my body shook. Ivy had been scratched or cut after the funeral, when Hydra and the dowager queen were beside us and the latter almost fell to the ground. Ivy's blood had been taken to use with the Blood stone.

"Tell me what you want, Hydra."

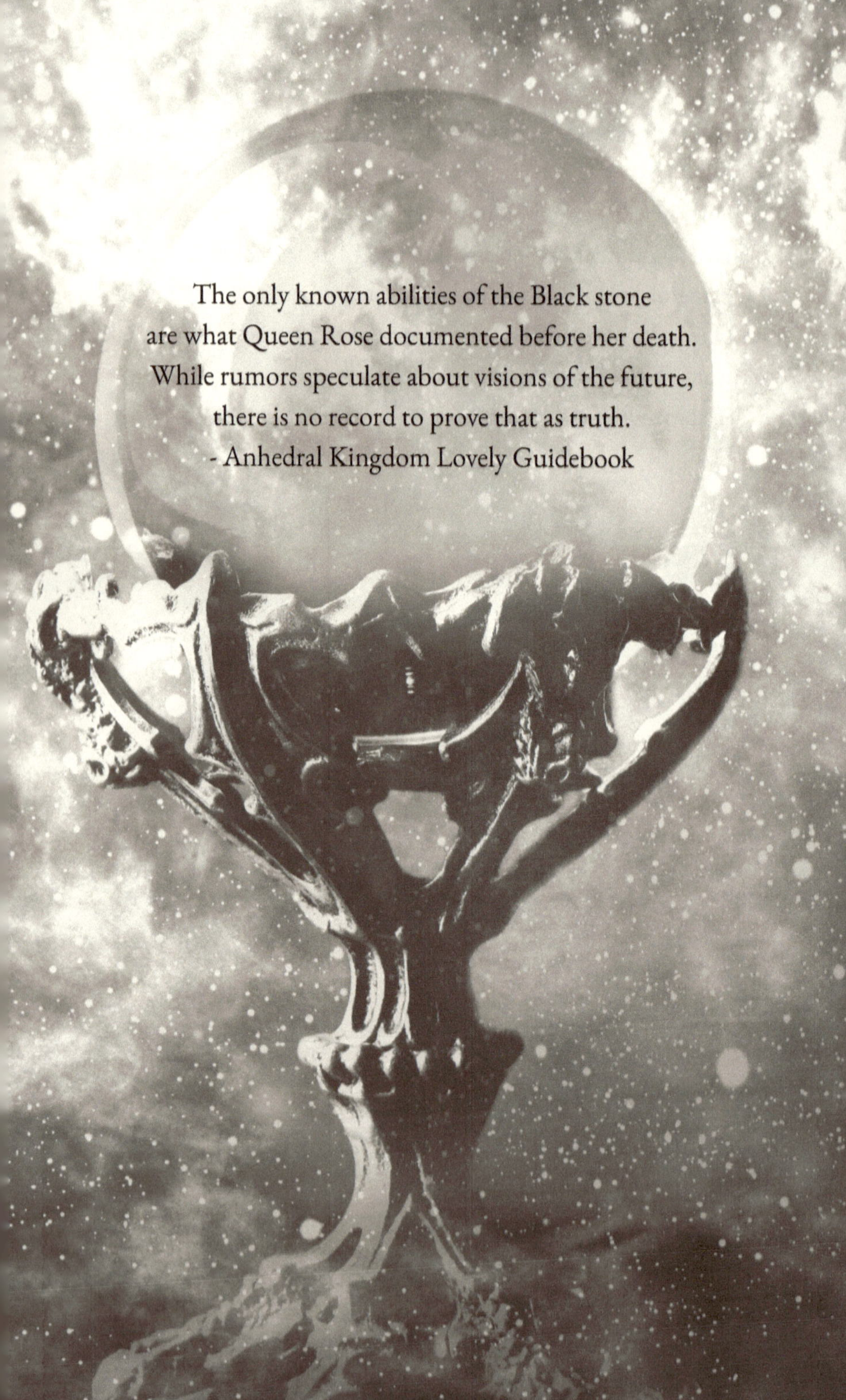

The only known abilities of the Black stone
are what Queen Rose documented before her death.
While rumors speculate about visions of the future,
there is no record to prove that as truth.
- Anhedral Kingdom Lovely Guidebook

I vy's small, beautiful face smiled brighter. "All hope isn't lost for you. You had me concerned with that bewildered look on your face."

I grimaced, watching the point of the dagger press against the delicate skin of Ivy's throat. There were no guards posted at the stairway or hallway, no soldiers patrolling. There could have been some moving upstairs, but there was no hope of getting their attention while Hydra had control of Ivy's life.

After a hard swallow, I repeated, "What do you want?"

"What do I want? Well, there are many things I want, and I may share with you. But first, you need to move into this room." She shoved the door wide, then her little body took a few steps backward, staying safely out of my reach while I did as she asked.

The Black stone room appeared the same as when Willa and I had searched, though I was not seeing it from Mais's eyes. I also couldn't smell the stagnant floral scent as I had with the wolfdog's nose. The iron sconces and four fire basins had already been lit, casting reflections off the numerous facets of the boulders stacked against the walls.

I took in the surroundings with a quick glance, not wanting to turn my back toward her. Though I had a feeling it wouldn't have made a difference if I had.

She stepped into the doorway without crossing into the room.

"Please don't let her touch anything," I begged in a whisper, trying to control all my emotions and stay strong for Ivy. Knowing that Imogen would have told someone had she remembered being controlled by the Blood stone, it was likely that Ivy wouldn't know this ever happened. That was my only solace. If she survived, she wouldn't recall a thing, even if I died.

"Of course I won't. There's a chance that she's strong enough, but I'm not willing to risk that when I have you now. I've waited a long time."

"A long time?"

"The searches around the castle were so predictable. It was amusing that you all thought Hemlock was the only one Blood stone capable. He wasn't alone in keeping his full abilities a secret from King Antin. I discovered mine even before Antin took the throne. Later, when he became obsessed with searching, hoping someone would catch a scent despite no one passing his buried stone test, I'm the one who found a Blood stone large enough to use while traveling on a canine mission in Crystal Flats.

"Hemlock did a fine job of keeping his secret too when he arrived after, likely for the same reasons as me. If we had shown the king what we could do, we would be viewed as nothing else. I was perfectly content with things as they were, knowing Antin would go no further, do nothing significant in his rule. I was happy serving my queen the most, though, willing to do so until the end."

"Then why kill Nightshade and Dahlia?" I asked. "That was you, yes? They were friends, and not troubled from what I learned. One wouldn't have killed the other and then themself. And Hemlock and the princess weren't involved. They were questioned and cleared."

Ivy's shoulders lifted in a shrug. "I hadn't planned to kill them at all. But they were insistent about change, about making life better for us Lovely. They had all these plans they wanted to persuade Ren and Antin with. They were trying to alter the procedures here."

"And you don't want that? To be treated more fairly, to be given a choice in how we live our lives?"

The scowl on her lips told me enough, but she explained more. "Not everyone deserves that, no. Most Lovely are not worthy of that at all. We have roles here. Direction. Purpose. Order needs to remain in place or some will decide to revolt, which will only make the kingdom suffer. Like you," she said in a huff, lifting her finger to point at my face. "You don't think I've noticed your disregard for rules, refusing to paint your eyebrows? And then having those other little weak ones staying with you instead of in the shared Clear stone quarters? That type of behavior creates dissension, and that is not good to fester amongst us when our kingdom's defense is at stake."

"So you want to keep things the same? To have Lovely contained by this indenture forever? Taken away at birth, to never know their families at all? Why then allow the king's death? Did you not know Princess Naomi and Hemlock planned to kill him and the others?" I wasn't sure what to do other than keep her talking. While it was good to understand what her reasons were, my main defense was time. Cordelia's concern could push her and the others to come look for us. It was the only option because I wouldn't risk injuring Ivy with an attempt to knock away the dagger. I would never forgive myself if I took that chance and something happened to her.

"No, I knew." Her lip curled. "By that time, I had already decided I'd waited long enough, that it was *my* time. See, I planted the stone long ago for someone to find. Wolfsbane might have been Antin's appointed Lovely, but he's never sensed the other stones. Hemlock found it soon after he arrived at the castle. Then I waited. I wanted to see if he would use it, wanted to see if he would tell anyone. It took years for him to finally test it—the coward—which he did on his beloved princess. He felt guilty after and ended up telling her of the stone, but not confessing to the use. I didn't mind waiting through all of this because, aside from being content with my position under the queen, my focus was to study him, to know if his mind was strong or weak. But his readings proved quite dismal, unable to stay connected for long periods of time and not sorting things for himself while inside the Realm. So I decided to keep waiting."

"Waiting for what?"

"For you," she said, her voice so low I almost hadn't heard.

I glanced over my shoulder, realizing exactly what she meant, why she had been waiting. There was a cloth draped over one side of the half-sphere's top, a knife placed at the very edge.

"Yes," she said, louder now, smiling. "I would never risk myself. And while Hemlock seemed to have the ability to connect with all stones, he's weak. I refuse to risk all my efforts on someone who might simply die as soon as he touched the Black stone, like so many others have. Had I been linked to that, the casualty could have been my banishment or maybe my own death."

"But you're risking it now with me?"

Her arm shifted, the dagger point dropping a little but not fully. "Are you really asking me to list your attributes? You haven't touched the Blood stone, but you scented it *and* the Black stone in Antin's test at induction. I watched that myself. And in the searches, you stayed connected to the Eye stone over a period of several days, for hours at a time. Not once did anyone question your mind. That isn't easy. Hemlock would have gone mad."

I glanced behind her, past the door, seeing a small shift in the shadows in the hallway. It was enough to distract her. The dagger dropped a bit more as she turned her head a little, trying to see what had drawn my attention. I hesitated for a second, telling myself again that it wasn't a good risk to take, but I couldn't not try something.

I lunged forward, only to stop short as she took a quick step backward and lifted both arms into the air, one swinging the dagger into the other. The blade drew across Ivy's pristine skin, cutting into her flesh.

"No, no!" My cry echoed all around, my shame at taking such a risk hitting me again and again. Blood dripped from Ivy's arm onto the hallway slate below.

"Do not move again or she will get worse."

"All right. I'm sorry. I won't." The words came hard and angry, pushed through my clenched teeth with ragged breaths as tears streamed from my eyes.

She appeared shaken too, feeling the injury herself. Her chest heaved as she slowly, silently recovered.

"How ... how do you even know what might happen when I connect to it? How will you even use this for yourself?"

She shook her head at me, agitated. "I'm sure you heard of Queen Rose and her Lovely. She successfully trapped him and used the connection until her untimely end. But he wasn't her first. She tested many. Some of her notes survived the years, kept within the castle as a caution to the new royal line, to prevent history from repeating. I found them very informative, with enough details to help me understand how it can be done with success. But ..." She flicked her wrist, pointing the dagger behind me. "I've told you plenty. With all the years I've waited and all I've done to get here ... Well, I thought offering some of my journey might ease your mind before your connection. Now, though, it's time for you to get on the stone. Take the knife near the far edge, cut yourself, and add your blood to mine in the center. Use the drape to climb up so you don't touch the stone until you lie down fully."

"But maybe this isn't the only way," I insisted. "Maybe there's a way for you to talk with Ren and Croft. They could—"

She laughed, the girlish giggle coming from Ivy's mouth like the cruelest dream. I thought I'd seen most all wicked things through the years of using the stones and viewing inside other people's minds. This was something different altogether, the combination of sweet and monstrous beyond unsettling.

"There is nothing they could do. I only need you. So do what I tell you or she dies. And don't assume hers is the only blood I collected after I retrieved the Blood stone. If she dies, others will follow, until you do what you're told."

My entire body convulsed, with refusal, with terror, knowing I was out of time. There were no other options, nothing else I could say that could change her mind. I was either going to die immediately or very soon. And I hadn't been able to give Croft a proper apology. I hadn't told him how I felt. I would never know if he felt the same for me. He would be free of my connection, though, with me gone completely. That was some consolation. If they moved past this, found a way to stop Hydra, he could continue on and lead the kingdom as a true king. He would be wonderful.

Reluctantly, I turned, eyeing the rest of the room. There was something missing from when Willa and I had searched. A smaller Black stone in a cast iron base had been perched on the shelf cut into a boulder. It was no longer there. Taking in the half-sphere, Hydra had lain a drape of cloth at one side. The knife was on top, its blade smaller than the dagger she held to Ivy's throat. The silver surface showed it had already been used, the edge streaked with a red tint. That led my eyes past the drape, to the uncovered stone. While it was as black as a starless night, firelight shined along the surface, curving over a rounded edge in the middle instead of streaking across a flat one. A circular puddle the size of my palm lay suspended in the center. Blood. It was hers. She'd prepared this room, all of it before connecting with the Blood stone and taking control of Ivy.

"Do not stall any longer. If I must, I will start cutting more of her."

"No. No, I'm doing it," I assured without looking over my shoulder.

I lifted the blade and gritted my teeth. A shadow of pain spread through my upper arm, memory from being stabbed by Alve. Pushing aside my fear, I swiped the blade's edge across my lower arm in one swift motion. The pain took hold immediately, making me cry out.

"Hold it over the top. Add it to the rest." Ivy's tiny voice instructed, making me cry harder.

Blood leaked from the wound, steady drops joining with the thickened puddle below.

"That's enough. Now the rest."

Staggering to the end, I placed my hands on the fabric. Then I leaned forward, letting my hands and arms support my weight as I shifted my lower body onto the top. It took careful, small movements to adjust, positioning onto my backside right in front of the blood puddle.

"Don't leave her here," I pleaded. "Please. I don't want her to wake up and see this. Please. Take her upstairs before you leave her."

The huff of breath from her lips almost had me looking her way, but I couldn't bear that either. I didn't want to see Ivy's face with Hydra inside anymore. I replaced the image inside my mind, thinking about her smile earlier in the night after she'd dressed for the ball. Happy. Joyous.

"All right. I will grant you this as a last request. I will not leave her here but at the top of the stairway to be found. She'll join the others just in time for all the fun to begin."

Again, I hesitated, clenching my eyes and my fists. I had no idea what was about to happen, if anything at all. But she wouldn't tell me even if I asked.

I took my calming breath, for the first true time completely unsure if it would be my last before entering the Realm.

Oh, Realm, if I'm to die, take me however you must. But please spare everyone else.

"Go now!"

Slowly, I leaned my body down, feeling the blood seep into the fabric of the gown before making contact with my bare upper back. Then as soon as my skin touched the stone's cool, wet surface, the force of the Realm pulled me flat, pinning me down. All my breath rushed from my mouth and nose in one big burst as the pressure expanded, my body unable to fight, unable to move in any way. It took one moment of confusion and fear before my vision went black and my mind followed.

While the stones allow Lovely
to access the Realm, the tether is the true link.
They are always connected.
- Anhedral Kingdom Lovely Guidebook

~ 30 ~

Stillness surrounded me. No whirling sensation. No one else's visions or thoughts. No voices. Nothing.

The blackness remained, like an endless void. Hollow and cold. Silent and grave. I thought for a moment that perhaps I had died. That I had met my end. Hydra would continue on if her efforts with me and the Black stone were never discovered. There was a good chance they wouldn't be. She'd prepared everything so well, so it was likely she had prepared something to conceal the truth if I should die. Maybe she'd arrange the room to appear as though I'd decided to attempt a Black stone connection myself. Or she could dispose of my body or relocate me to another place to create some other plausible story. For me the details didn't matter. After all, I was dead.

Though that dense stillness began to move, opening into a recognizable scope of land and sky. Anhedral stretched out around me, from sea to sea. The view was astounding. The city sat below, so many lights flickering into the night. And at the center, the castle. The expanse of empty land around it was quiet and dark, but the outer wall, gardens, and lighted pathways twinkled with life.

The imagery reminded me of the White stone Realm, though there were no lengthy streaks or heavy clusters of light. No orbs. I was seeing the world as it was from above.

Without direction, the image narrowed, my presence floating downward to the castle and then through. Suddenly, I was above Ivy at the ground floor of the southeast stairs. She turned in a circle, observing her surroundings with confusion, blood leaking down her arm. As she realized where she was, she ran through the hallway, passing a few people, the White stone room, and then the trial hall before reaching the southern entrance and the open doors to the great hall. Her little body moved between the larger crowd, searching until she found Cordelia.

I felt something stir inside me even though my physical body was trapped in the Black stone room levels below. Relief. It swelled within me, giving me hope that this Realm didn't mean complete detachment from life and emotion. No, I could still feel it all.

"Where have you—What happened to your arm?" Cordelia rushed with her, heading toward the tables and attendants along the room's side, grabbing some water and cloths to clean the cut on Ivy's arm.

"I'm not sure. I think I got lost. I remember being near this door, then I—"

"Oleander," a voice called out, resonant and assertive. It was not Sielle's deep tone that echoed from inside the White stone. This voice was smoky and curt. It took me a moment to place Hydra's true voice, as only minutes before she'd been speaking from within Ivy. "You've connected. You're alive."

Her joy sickened me. I tried to focus on disconnecting as I had with any other stone, but it did not work. There was no shift in the Realm, no feeling of separation. I was trapped.

A daring growl ripped through my chest, to let her and the Realm hear my anger and frustration.

"Well, with that reaction, I can see that the process was successful. I did everything correctly, and you are connected to me. Come to where I am."

There was no thought and no control in my movements. Cordelia and Ivy disappeared as I floated up and up, through the hallways, to the north wing, and into the queen's quarters. The dowager queen appeared in one room, asleep. She hadn't attended the ball, hadn't heard the announcement. She'd isolated herself again following the funeral. And unbeknownst to her, Hydra had been committing high treason.

Hydra sat behind a desk in the queen's study, which wasn't as grand as the king's but far tidier, containing books, paintings, and a few fire basins atop pedestals. Only one was lit. On the desk lay a stack of journals and loose papers. The missing Black stone sphere with the cast iron base was there too. That's what had Hydra's focus, her eyes peering deep within. She wore the same black layered gown she had for the funeral, with long sleeves and silver lace trim. The silver paint she chose for her high-arched eyebrows glittered in the low firelight against the deep hue of her skin.

"Are you here now? Show me."

It was a demand like before. A command, I realized. And when she gave one, I followed. Even though I hadn't been told to answer her question, I replied anyway as a test for my own knowledge.

First, I responded in thought only, as I had with Sielle in the White stone. But there were no words, and she didn't acknowledge at all. Then I replied as I had when I wanted my body to speak outside the White stone, and I heard the words come from the sphere, "I am here." At the same time, the image of my view of her reflected within.

The Black stone plainly had an opposite response to the blood smeared onto it. While most of the other stones used blood to designate the target's mind, the Black stone used it to designate who had the power to control the one connected with the Realm instead. It was a way to anchor and manipulate the Lovely held inside.

Her enthused smile was unnerving. I could feel the energy surrounding her, heavy with arrogance, greed, and malice. "Excellent. Now we work. Show me the fair Ren, son of the late King Antin."

My presence swept away from the room, tugged backward and dragged through the castle, into the great hall. Her seeking Ren had my mind racing, wondering why. Then I thought about the announcement. She hadn't been there. She also hadn't attended the other trials after mine. She knew about Croft's birthright, though, and about my sister to some degree. But in all her preoccupation with the dowager queen and preparation to trap me, there was a chance she didn't know Croft's decision to take his rightful place as king. Regardless, there was no clear way to determine what she might do. I could only hope for a way to intervene, despite her control.

Prince Ren and Croft stood near the center of the great hall, engaged in more conversation. Some people danced around them.

Others ate. Croft's eyes wandered toward the door, where I noticed Clem, Tansy, and Sielle. The others were nowhere in sight. Were they looking for me? Was he?

"Run. Leave," I attempted to scream, willing to try anything.

Hydra laughed cruelly. "Oh, you foolish girl. They can't hear you. Unless maybe I tell you to speak to them. We will see if it's possible with all the Lovely soon enough. Right now, we will have a little fun and test the control over lesser beings. First, call out to all the Black stones still untouched deep beneath the castle. There are many that were left alone to preserve the castle structure, and they will react to your energy inside the Realm. Then call to the insects, rodents, and any snakes, lizards, and toads inside the castle walls. Tell them to attack the people."

I had no power. No voice. Whatever she wanted to happen, happened without my consent or involvement. It was as if her words made it occur through me. My presence shuddered with a surge of energy, rattling my mind and the surrounding air. The castle began to quiver, little tremors causing people to step off balance and let out gasps of surprise.

The screams started right after as the floors shuddered more violently. Loose items on the tabletops fell, goblets and plating crashing to the floor, ceramic and glass shattering as the hall erupted in chaos.

Then the insects came en masse, escaping from the widening cracks along the stone floor, from corner wall gaps, and dropping from the ceiling. Some as large as a hand, others so small they appeared like specks of ground spices, gathered and moving together. Out of their safe places, they scurried along the floor or spread their thin wings and flew. People swung their arms, swatting all they could, and kicked their legs to stomp and squash them under foot.

Mice and rats followed as quickly, rushing forward, climbing up pant legs and the bottom fabric of gowns. People screamed louder, watching the rodent bodies trampling through the streams of insects.

Then more came, slithering snakes, leaping frogs, and running lizards. Some had their direction and intention clear, going right for the people, while others were easily tempted and distracted by the chase of their prey and a catch of an easy meal, snatching up the rodents and insects and chomping them down.

Hydra's laugh rang through my mind, thoroughly entertained. "Look at everyone around him. They have no idea what this means."

Her view remained on Ren, even though I wasn't entirely focused on him. I had some freedom in my vision.

Attendants, guards, and soldiers weren't certain what actions to take, as confused as everyone else and simply trying to avoid getting bitten by anything along the ground or in the air. All the dogs barked, even Argo, who remained at Croft's side. He snapped at the rats, biting the air aggressively to warn them away. Prince Ren and Croft both ushered people toward the door, realizing fast that inside wasn't the safest place to be.

"He's moving. Follow Ren."

My focus shifted. The prince had rushed ahead, exiting the great hall, leading others toward the doors and out into the courtyard.

Tansy helped Sielle, Clem, and Ivy outside, all of them screaming and slapping at the swarms.

"They bite!" Clem yelled, stamping the ground, crushing as many as he could.

"Sielle," I thought, hoping against all odds that our connection might be stronger than Hydra's control. "Can you hear me? Please hear me!"

There was no reply, no reaction as they continued to move farther outside. Tansy helped her, patting down her own gown then Sielle's too. Of course Sielle couldn't hear like she had before. She wasn't connected to a stone, couldn't sense me at all.

"Enough with the little things," Hydra snapped. "Let's move on to something ... more."

She didn't tell me to call them off, but some started to disappear, abandoning people's feet, seeking the closest place to hide or fleeing into the gardens. Most people stopped moving, glad for the reprieve while also stunned by the occurrence. Their wide eyes scanned the area, meeting others' shocked gazes as they sought confirmation and reassurance that they hadn't experienced it all alone, that it hadn't been a fevered dream.

"Everyone, stay calm! Guards, attendants, soldiers, do your best to extinguish these nuisances," Prince Ren called out through the crowd. "Let's check in, make sure everyone's—" His voice cut off as Hydra spoke.

"Larger animals. I need to look over what Queen Rose wrote again, to be certain," Hydra said, seeming to go through the notes she had spoken of before. "We are going to test this stone's link with the wolfdogs. Then we will move on to all the Lovely. Yes ... here it is. All Lovely with a Realm tether can be controlled. The Realm holds the link between them and their Dead, so the Realm can control it. She was wise with all her trials."

I watched the others from above, terrified of what was to come, what *I* would make happen to them. There was nothing I could do to stop it. I'd never felt so helpless in my entire existence. Powerless. I was useless. I could feel the sting of new tears in my eyes even though my presence would not physically create them.

"Oleander. Call to all the canines. Tell them to obey you alone."

The surge of energy built up again, shaking the air around me before bursting outward in splinters, like lightning within a violent storm.

While some creatures continued their direction, the canines below suddenly stopped. The barking ceased. Their fearful fits calmed. They all sat as if they'd received the command to. Their soldiers reacted first, giving orders to move or walk, pulling their leads, trying to follow Prince Ren's words to help the people.

But the wolfdogs didn't move.

"This is phenomenal."

Other people started to notice, Prince Ren and Croft especially. As Prince Ren stared on in question, Croft's focus locked onto his own dog. Argo had sat back onto his haunches, waiting.

Oh no.

Croft patted his head, trying to gain his attention. There was no response, no acknowledgment.

"Good, good. Now, call them to attack the soldiers."

"No!" I screamed, only hearing Hydra's laugh before the energy fired out from me.

In an instant, all the wolfdogs had turned on their handlers with fierce snarls. Then they all dove forward, some locking on to lower legs immediately while others gave chase.

"What is this?!" Prince Ren shouted while others started to scream again. He stumbled around, then grabbed hold of a wolfdog latched onto a soldier's ankle.

"I ... I don't know," Wolf replied to him, trying to render aid as well. His arms wrapped around the back of the wolfdog as it jerked forward again and again to get to the soldier. It didn't care that they were there. It had its order and wouldn't be dissuaded.

"Mais!" The name drew my attention around. Willa stood in front of Mais, holding her hands out in a silent command as Mais inched closer, teeth bared as she growled. "Down. Down, I said. No!" Mais leaped into the air, hitting Willa in the stomach and knocking her onto her back. Willa held firmly under Mais's chest while the wolfdog snapped her teeth again and again, closer to Willa's neck and face.

Argo ran past their scuffle, stealing my focus while Hydra's excited laughs continued on inside my mind. He'd darted away from Croft, chasing after a soldier who either wasn't in the canine division or had managed to escape his own wolfdog's ire. Argo nipped at his heels as they ran down the length of the castle wall, disappearing into the darkness.

Tansy was moving Sielle and the others back inside, seeking shelter to avoid any wolfdogs. No one knew the canines' order had only been for soldiers. But I was glad to see the others searching for a safe place.

Croft stood completely still for several moments, shocked by the confusion and devastation all around. As Wolf lost his grip on a wolfdog and it bit down on the soldier's arm, Croft jumped in to help alongside the prince.

"They don't care about us," Wolf commented, getting to his feet.

"What?" Prince Ren shouted at him.

"They couldn't care less that you are holding them or hurting them in the process." Wolf's gaze swept around the courtyard, absorbing the situation. "They are only targeting the soldiers."

A yelp came from nearby. A soldier was pinned to the ground, flat on his back. His wolfdog stood still on top of him, stopping its assault after the soldier's dagger had pierced its front leg. The soldier let his head fall to the ground, relieved the wolfdog had stopped after the shallow wound.

"I know what this is," Wolf said.

"What is it?" Prince Ren yelled, he and Croft still struggling to keep hold of the wolfdog.

"The Black stone. Someone has connected to it, is using it."

"I should have known it wouldn't take him long to figure it out," Hydra said, seeing what had happened clearly, the view still focused on Ren. "Let's move on then before he can share any ideas. Call all the Lovely."

Convulsions took over me entirely, pulling more energy from everything around and beneath the castle. It twisted inside, spinning and stretching me out. The stagnant scent of flowers invaded my mind as if I were smelling the Black stone room with Mais's nose again. The force of the Realm was too strong, more powerful than it had ever been before. Every part of my ethereal presence strained under the force, under the constraint.

The terror I felt inside had me thinking of all the faces of all the people I'd read with the stones. Though my body was in the Black stone room, still and quiet, I imagined my face to show the same terror as theirs. Because I was as close to death as they were. My life about to collapse.

"It's working!" Hydra's voice rose above everything else.

Then the twisting pressure unraveled, discharging, releasing all the strain and torment like ribbons streaking through the sky.

As my presence settled, I looked over the grounds. The wolfdogs had ceased their attacks. But the Lovely had stopped moving completely, standing in place, their white eyes pointed toward the sky, toward me.

Croft hadn't stopped, though. He was a Lovely, but he hadn't stopped moving like the rest. Then I realized why. He had never connected to the Realm himself, had never touched a stone. He still had never connected with his own tether, his Dead. So the Black stone couldn't control him.

"Wolf?" Prince Ren said, he and Croft releasing their hold of the wolfdog and getting to their feet. "What's this?"

He grabbed Prince Ren's arm to catch his eyes, mouthing and thinking, *"Black stone."*

I'd heard him. I hadn't earlier, but with the Black stone connection, Hydra's voice, and everyone else's too ... It had been too much, or maybe I hadn't been close enough. It seemed that the Black stone hadn't broken our connection, though, allowing me to hear inside his mind. Which meant those thoughts were also safe from Hydra.

"You've been stronger than I expected. I may be able to keep you going for some time," Hydra said, breaking through my thoughts. Unfortunately, she hadn't succumbed to the command as a Lovely. Her blood link to me and the Black stone kept her in control. "But this is what I'd hoped for, your connection to the others. It's exactly what I wanted. I take the throne and the other Lovely will follow. Those who don't, die."

Using the Lovely had been the plan, a good way to gain control. She knew from the start, likely reading what could be possible within Queen Rose's notes. Though I could tell she was fearful of what might follow, whether I died or not. There was a chance the notes didn't tell her how to keep the control after procuring it.

"Let's not waste any more time with frivolity. Tell the Lovely to kill the royals and anyone who stands in the way to protect them."

The Lovely moved immediately, heads leveling, seeking out their victims. Others exited from inside the castle's doors. Cordelia, Tansy, Sielle, Begonia, Clem, and Ivy were among them, and the dread was like ice forming in my bones. Sielle moved in the correct direction, but she still couldn't see. Her body bumped into someone else, then tripped over the stone edging of the courtyard, falling down onto her knees.

Wolf shifted toward Prince Ren. He wasn't fast, merely determined, reaching out as Prince Ren staggered back. Then he took a swipe at Croft, who dodged the efforts as well, stepping out of reach. Though he was capable, Wolf was older. His body had to be lacking the energy and muscle it would take to kill either of them. But the others were younger, and they were moving fast.

"Soldiers! Guards! Detain the Lovely! Do not kill them." Prince Ren shouted loudly, watching as the ones who hadn't been seriously injured by the dogs took a moment to absorb the change in threat, then shifted into their duties and rushed forward to follow the orders. They moved quickly, aimed to halt them all, one hitting Blodwyn from the side and knocking him to the ground.

"Croft," I cried out inside my mind, my heart hurting as I watched the Lovely draw nearer to them.

Croft stopped abruptly. His feet. His head. Everything stopped moving.

Had he ... heard me?

Croft's head turned around with his body, searching, looking ...

His mouth moved with his thoughts. *"Olean? Olean!"*

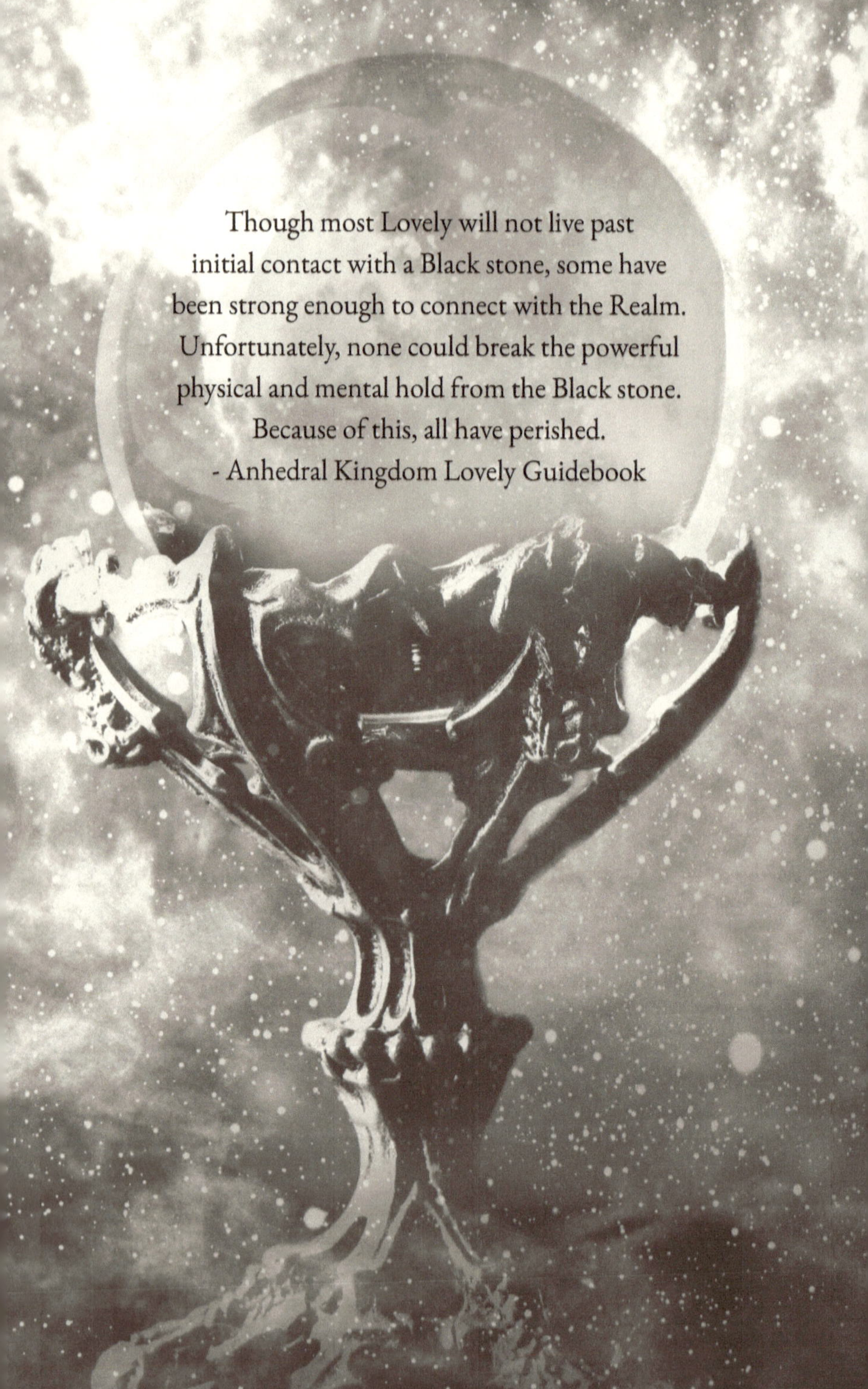
Though most Lovely will not live past
initial contact with a Black stone, some have
been strong enough to connect with the Realm.
Unfortunately, none could break the powerful
physical and mental hold from the Black stone.
Because of this, all have perished.
- Anhedral Kingdom Lovely Guidebook

~ 31 ~

Croft locked eyes with Prince Ren, mouthing the same thing. My name.

"I don't know," the prince replied as they both ran toward the garden entrance. "I haven't seen her all evening."

I thought harder. Concentrating on what I knew. The Black stone not only allowed me to hear him without a physical body being close, but it let me push my thoughts to him through our direct connection. He had told me that he could only hear some tones. But the chance of him understanding whatever I tried to explain without seeing me, my lips, was almost impossible. I needed to think images. Show him. Because no one else knew what to do, where to search. Wolf might have if he wasn't being controlled.

"Why aren't they moving faster? Tell them to move faster, use weapons, use the guards' and soldiers' daggers." Hydra's smoky voice wavered with anger.

More Lovely came from the castle, all stone classes, all ages. I watched Ivy run, her little body tripping over her gown when she took a sharp turn. Clem was fast, but a guard got to him before he caught Prince Ren, swiping his legs out from under him.

Images. I had to think images. *Hydra. Hydra with the Black stone. Hydra in the queen's rooms. Hydra seated beside the queen.*

Croft's steps stuttered, his eyes unfocused. *"Hydra."*

"Hydra! Yes! Croft!" I cried out inside my thoughts again, thrilled that it had worked.

His eyes widened, then he smacked Prince Ren's arm as they turned in the other direction from the garden. He pointed to his head and mouthed, *"Olean. I hear her."*

Prince Ren's eyebrows lifted as a few Lovely neared. A soldier had gotten to them too, taking one of the Lovely down as the other two locked into their own fights. Croft's fist punched against one's stomach. And when he didn't fall from that hit, Croft hit him in the face. Prince Ren did the same, jostling around to avoid falling. The Lovely wrestling with the soldier on the ground managed to free the sword. He thrust it into the soldier's chest.

There was no remorse, no moment of clarity for the Lovely at all. He kept going. Though Croft and Prince Ren had managed to knock down the others, the one with the sword swung it toward them. Another guard arrived right on time, blocking the Lovely's attack with his own short sword, letting them get away. The fight had delayed them, though, and more Lovely had caught up.

Hydra. Queen's rooms. Black stone. The only possible way to stop it all would be to kill her. That could end her connection to me here, end her control, and her commands. He needed to know.

"She's with the queen." Croft's thought was clear. He'd understood me.

He pointed to the castle, letting Prince Ren know there was a goal, a direction to take to bring the chaos to an end. The prince nodded and kept running.

Begonia and Cordelia had managed to cross into their path. Croft slowed, eyeing Cordelia in an almost conflicted way. She was his mother. As far as I knew, it was the first encounter between them after the discovery, though she was not controlling her own mind. He and Prince Ren both chose to keep moving straight for them, purposely colliding into their sides, throwing them off balance, causing them to stumble and fall. Croft gripped his side with one hand as they went on, breaking away from all the rest. My view shifted to Cordelia, noticing a dagger near her in the grass.

"Close the doors behind us," Prince Ren called out to everyone inside, attendants, guards, and soldiers alike. "Some stay here to keep them out. The rest of you come with us to block whoever's inside."

Croft's hand lifted from his side as they entered the castle, coated with red blood.

My stomach rolled. *Cordelia's dagger.*

"What's wrong?" Prince Ren stopped, realizing that Croft had fallen behind. "You're injured?"

Croft waved him away, dripping some blood to the floor as he pointed toward the hallway leading north, mouthing, *"Hydra."*

"She hasn't been around either. I thought she'd been acting suspicious and too overbearing with my mother. Also skipping her duties. So ... my mother's rooms?"

"No!" Hydra yelled. "Where are the others? Someone stop them!"

They made it to the north stairway just as more Lovely arrived. Guards shattered the blockade attempt, fighting them off, then impeding several younger Clear stone class by ramming their bodies into one another.

Even more guards and soldiers reached the queen's rooms with them, helping to open the lock, then shoving through the barricaded doors.

Hydra sat on the chaise in the parlor, Black stone sphere on the tea table in front and the dowager queen at her side. Queen Reina looked more alive than she had in days, completely aware she was being held captive. Her eyes were wide and alert despite the darkened circles beneath them.

"Hydra, I trusted you. All these years ... I cannot believe you would do this to me after all we've been through," Queen Reina said, her voice flat, emotionless.

"Honestly, my goal was to give this kingdom what it's needed for a long time. Competence. Someone who will use any method, any means, not simply focus on continuing the same gutless path for years to come."

"I'm not sure how you imagined this working out," Prince Ren said, shaking his head as he approached.

Croft walked the other way, moving slowly around the settee and chairs.

Hydra sneered coldly, lifting her hand a small amount to show the knife she had pressed to the dowager queen's side. "I find it amusing that you feel this is the end."

"Isn't it? It doesn't seem you have many options left." Prince Ren stopped beside the tea table, paying no mind to the guard and soldiers who had entered behind them. The sight of them was for Hydra to take in, to know that she'd been bested.

"Don't I? Well, the Lovely have killed a few already. But I suppose I could have them do better should you decide your mother's life is of little importance. How about this kingdom without any Lovely at all?"

"What?" Croft thought as he stopped at the other end of the table, watching Hydra's movements closely.

"What are you implying?" Prince Ren asked, not taking his eyes away.

"Don't play the fool with me. Though you've been lazing at your duties, not wanting to rule at all, I do know you possess the intelligence to understand well enough. You move any closer, you risk your mother and the lives of all the Lovely throughout the kingdom. While you've seen those here react to the orders they've been given, it's not just them. No. We are connected to all in the Realm. So if I were to give the command to kill themselves ..."

Though my heart was located in a room many floors below, I felt it stop. All the Lovely. Gone. Dead. Panicked, I yelled, "No!"

Hydra laughed through everyone else's silence, eyeing the sphere with amusement. They hadn't heard my yell, couldn't see whatever she could inside.

But Croft could if I thought to him directly. There was nothing I could say, though. No information I had would help stop her.

More fighting could be heard in the outer main room and hallway. Lovely had arrived inside, battling their way in to attack the royals.

"You are right about me. I've failed enough times in my life, enough people," Prince Ren said, shaking his head. His demeanor had shifted, choosing to indulge Hydra's words. "I refuse to let this be another. We will not—"

Queen Reina moved before he finished his words, lifting her arm in a fast motion and twisting her body, which forced Hydra's knife hand toward herself. Croft and Ren both seized the opportunity, rushing in. Queen Reina grabbed hold of the knife too, battling with Hydra for control while still seated.

"Call the Lovely to kill themselves!" Though Hydra's words were grunted, they were effective. The energy burst forward again, pouring from me in waves, the force stripping pieces of me away.

All the Lovely fighting to gain entry outside the parlor stopped to process the command.

Prince Ren leaped forward, diving into the struggle. As soon as his hands landed onto his mother's, the additional force pushed the blade into Hydra's stomach. Croft had gotten there too, his hands pinning Hydra's shoulders to the back of the chaise to control her body while Queen Reina removed the knife, uncertain whether or not to strike again.

The Lovely moved, searching for weapons or any means to do what they'd been told. The need to check on everyone was strong. As much as I wanted to pull back from the scene, to observe the entire castle and make sure all the others were safe, I couldn't. I needed to see this through to the end.

Hydra laughed at their hesitation. Her black gown darkened even more at the center of her stomach, blood slowly spreading into the material. But it wasn't enough.

"She has to die or the others will," I thought, feeling weaker, hoping Croft would understand.

Croft knew, even before I could think of the image of the Black stone. He grabbed hold of the base and tossed the sphere into her lap. She thrashed, only for the queen to grab her hand and press it down onto the stone's surface.

I saw the moment it happened. The Realm opened for her the instant her skin touched. Her body went still, her white eyes pointing toward the ceiling, lifeless. Her soul entered like a swirling storm, particles of light twisting upward and scattering into the dark beyond. The sphere rolled from her lap and dropped onto the floor.

The Lovely halted again. This time, though, their eyes blinked, their focus returning. They turned their faces, discovering where they were, confusion setting in. Their voices filtered into the parlor while Queen Reina, Prince Ren, and Croft stepped away from Hydra and the Black stone.

"Croft," I thought, feeling overjoyed that it was over and that he hadn't accidentally touched the stone. But I was still connected. Still inside. And feeling lucent and frail.

"Olean?" he thought, frantically searching, then peering down at the stone by Hydra's feet.

"Someone is connected?" Queen Reina asked, her eyes tired and sorrowful as she noticed where Croft had looked. "That's how Hydra did it all."

"Yes," Prince Ren confirmed as Croft nodded. "Olean. She'll be in the Black stone room then, if ..."

Croft motioned as he thought, *"She's still alive. I can hear her. Feel her."*

"We should go, and find Wolf too," Prince Ren replied, understanding at least some of what Croft had motioned to him. "He might know how to help."

A hollow sensation tugged at me. The Realm. It felt bigger, unbound, infinite. I wondered if not having Hydra as a connection, not having her command, meant I would be lost inside until I died.

Maybe there was more information, a chance for me to return. I thought hard. *Notes. Table. Queen. Study.*

They had already moved to the main room's doorway, when Croft turned around. Prince Ren answered questions from some of the people gathered there, waiting for Croft to return. Moments later, he did, carrying the journals and loose old papers. He began reading through them, then passing them off to Queen Reina as they hurried down the hallways.

Cordelia, Sielle, Wolf, and all the others weren't far from the great hall. Everyone had been talking, trying to discern what had happened. As soon as they saw them, Prince Ren began the explanation.

He addressed the attendants and guards. "Begin a search. Take everyone in need to the doctors to be seen right away. Gather all the other Lovely. We need to figure out how to save Olean from the Black stone."

While they left with their orders, Wolf stared at the prince and Croft. "You will not be able to physically remove her from the stone if the stories are correct. Not until she has died."

"No. There has to be a way." Croft scowled at him before glancing at the papers in the dowager queen's hands, his eyebrows low and nostrils flared in frustration. He turned and rushed down the hallway, not caring who followed.

But they all did. Cordelia tried to have Ivy stay with Begonia and Clem, but they refused. Tansy guided Sielle, who had remained silent after hearing all the details from the prince, though her eyes brimmed with tears. Scratches marked her arms, face, and neck, injuries from her following commands without seeing, without having a guide.

They rushed to the Black stone room. Queen Reina handed the notes to Wolf as she and Prince Ren strode in. Wolf kept close to the doorway.

Cordelia grabbed hold of Croft's arm before he could step beside Wolf. "Please be careful. One accidental touch of a finger could kill you."

"Right," the dowager queen agreed. "None of you should come any closer. Ren and I will try to move her." They did, grabbing hold of my shoulders and pulling me, grunting with the effort.

The stone kept its grip. Though I couldn't physically feel it, the pressure at my connection didn't relent. I attempted to concentrate, calm my mind as if I were connected to another stone, try again to separate myself. Nothing happened. The only difference I could feel was the energy within the Realm. It was dissolving.

"This can't happen," Ivy cried out from outside in the hallway. Begonia was quick to embrace her, holding her tight to give as much comfort as she could.

Wolf's eyes were on the book and pages in his hands.

"Olean. What's the answer?" Croft shifted from foot to foot, looking everywhere around the room.

I couldn't form a reply. There was no answer for me to give.

"There's blood here beneath her. A knife at her side. Her lower arm is cut." Prince Ren walked around the half-sphere, searching.

"It's her blood and Hydra's too," Wolf said, eyes still on the pages. "That's how Hydra had control of her while she was connected."

"It's how Queen Rose did as well," the dowager queen stated. "I've read those but never fully understood her ramblings. There was no real need. We didn't want any Lovely risking their lives by touching this stone."

"We risk our lives even with lesser stones," Tansy said from out in the hallway. "Too long of a connection, too many connections—we can lose our minds. Things need to change."

"They will. They are," Prince Ren replied. "But now's not the time to discuss this."

"Blood. Her blood." Croft's thought cut through the others speaking. He looked down at the wound on his side, the blood soaked into his shirt.

Seeing his movements, Wolf waved for Croft's attention. "No. It will do nothing. She's already connected. If you try, if you would even live, you'd be in a separate Realm space anyway. No Lovely occupy the same Realm space, even if they touch the same—" His words cut off as Croft grabbed his arm.

"Sielle." Croft pointed over Wolf's shoulder.

"Sielle," Wolf said as he realized the same thing.

"Yes," Sielle answered, stepping forward. "It's true. We occupied the same Realm space with the White stone. We never got to try any others, though."

"No, no," Cordelia said, choking on a small cry. "You can't do that. You might not ..."

"She's right," Prince Ren said, stepping to the opposite end of the half-sphere. "You'd be risking your life too. It's not a good idea."

"And it's my life to risk, yes?" Sielle said, determination behind her beautiful eyes.

No. Oh, no. I wanted to weep, to shout. Yet, I couldn't find my voice. Even more of my presence had thinned, turning into wispy ribbons, like the speckles of light inside the White stone Realm.

Sielle's shoulders arched back as she stood straighter. "If by some chance this doesn't work, please tell our father I am sorry, but I had to try. He will understand. And please also tell him about her, about Olean. Even in the short time I knew her, I felt her warmth and kindness. Her truth. But for everyone who knew her longer, please tell him about her. Share your stories of her youth, of her love. That will help him through."

Tears leaked from nearly everyone's eyes as they stood silently, listening.

Sielle wiped her own away, then extended her hand between Wolf and Croft.

Croft placed his hand in hers before leaning in and embracing her fully. She cried harder against him, the understanding and respect between them so natural and emotional my heart ached. The sensation slipped away quickly, disappearing into the expanse like everything else had.

I was fading. Thoughts had become languid as I tried to focus on the picture below me. Their voices and movements slowed, drawing farther away. I didn't fight, hoping that maybe Sielle's connection wouldn't come to pass. Maybe she wouldn't get to sacrifice herself for me.

Then the others were speaking, debating. Prince Ren lifted the knife outward, handing it over to Croft, while he kept talking. Explaining, I realized. Sielle replied, extending her arm.

"Her blood. Your blood. Connected."

Croft lifted the edge to her skin, then stopped.

"Connected," his thought repeated. Suddenly, his head shook, and he tossed the knife to the floor. The others reacted, voices asking why.

Croft motioned to Wolf and mouthed, *"It's wrong. We're wrong. They are the same. She will enter too and not exit. Their connection is needed here, not there. All the others were trapped there."*

"Because of their tether there," Wolf agreed. "A connection here will bring her back."

"Yes." Croft nodded, looking around.

"What is happening?" Sielle asked.

"We think the answer is your connection here. We need you to touch her, not join her," Wolf said.

Croft took hold of her arm again, this time walking her forward, taking care that neither of them touched the stone. He guided her hand above my face, then lowered it until her palm touched my forehead.

Within a moment, the bond fastened, like an unlatched lock clamping back into place. She released a cry that split through my ears, piercing and unrestrained. Her energy spread over me, recollecting the scatters of my presence and dragging everything back together. The pull was crushing and merciless. And as its intensity grew, I felt the force upon my physical body slacken, its relentless restraint loosening. Weight lifted as Sielle's presence took hold of me, securing us further. As her scream drifted, mine began, our energies mixing and twisting down, down, down.

The force disappeared, and my body jolted where I lay. A booming crack sounded inside the room. The stone split in half beneath me, dropping my legs and feet as it broke away onto the floor.

I opened my eyes to Prince Ren lifting me from the stone. In a daze, I looked around the room.

Croft's arms were wrapped around Sielle's middle, fully supporting her limp weight, preventing her from falling or touching the stone while she had held me.

"Move them outside," Wolf said, making way for everyone to pass through the doorway.

"Sielle!" I cried, reaching out for her as Croft laid her onto the floor. Prince Ren did the same for me, placing me at her side.

"Olean," was her weak reply as her head lifted, strands of her hair sweeping over her face. "You're here. You're all right."

I moved her hair, touching her face as her hand did the same, fingers skimming over my eyes, nose, and mouth. "We're all right. Thank you. Thank you."

"Olean!" Ivy's body fell against my back, her little arms wrapping around my middle.

There were no more words, only tears, as we lay holding one another, grateful to be alive.

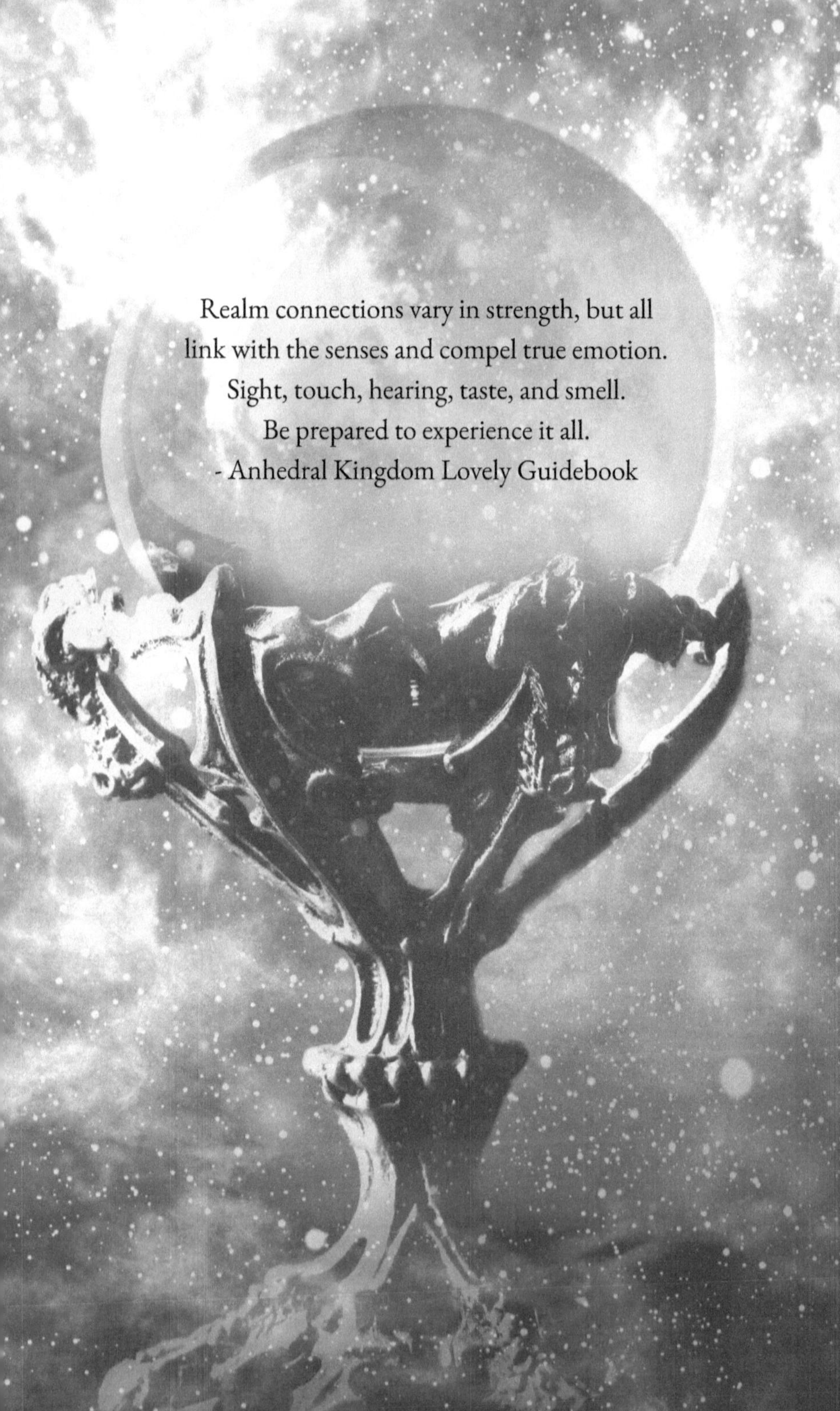

Realm connections vary in strength, but all
link with the senses and compel true emotion.
Sight, touch, hearing, taste, and smell.
Be prepared to experience it all.
- Anhedral Kingdom Lovely Guidebook

32

Two days passed with very little interaction between long stretches of sleep. Sielle was with me for the first day, also needing to recover from her time inside the Black stone. Its power was undeniable and almost fatal, having drained us to near death. They'd moved us both to my room, leaving us to rest in one another's arms, continuing our connection to help heal and prevent any fitful dreams.

The second night, Sielle returned to sleep and so did Ivy, who brought along her stuffed alpaca, Petal, and cuddled up beside us for her own comfort. I woke sometime in the darkness, unable to recapture sleep and in desperate need of a bath. While all the others were in their closed rooms, I was surprised to see Croft and Argo sleeping in the main sitting room. Like everyone else, he'd visited during the first span of time I was awake, watching closely as I ate the food they brought while everyone else recalled the events from the ball. His eyes stayed on me when I recounted my own version, explaining from how Hydra had used Ivy to trick me, on to all the rest I'd watched happen, unable to stop her in any way. But even though I'd heard a few of his concerned thoughts and met his eyes often, hoping he'd stay longer than the others so I could apologize to him properly, he didn't. That left me even more uncertain of how he felt, especially when he hadn't returned the next few times I'd woken. He'd been busy with Prince Ren, though, handling all the problems that came in the aftermath, to include assessing the injured as well as the damages to the castle.

On my way to the bathing room, I stepped quietly around the settee where he lay. Argo lifted his head but didn't bother moving otherwise. After some time, I emerged still feeling drained but also clean and relaxed. I readied myself for another silent walk, entering the dim main room. Croft still lay on his back, sprawled on the settee. Yet when I looked at his face, I found his eyes open and on me.

"Sorry to wake you," I whispered, wondering if he could see my lips at all. I hadn't wanted to disturb him. He had been through so much too and needed rest. But I was curious why he'd decided to sleep there.

Before I could choose whether to apologize again and go back to my room or tell him all the things I wanted to say, he motioned for me. I glanced around and discarded my used clothing onto the floor, while he sat upright and yawned with a stretch. A breath escaped him in a rush, and he grabbed his side.

The injury. He hadn't mentioned it once in the little time I'd seen him. I sat quickly at his side and touched his leg so he would look at me. "Are you all right? You were hurt."

"It's healing. Only sore."

"I'm sorry," I whispered again at the same time his next thought came.

"How are you feeling?" The question was all thought as his other answer had been, no motions or lip movements.

"Tired. My cut's sore too. But all right."

He nodded. *"So it is true. You hear my thoughts, understand me?"*

"Yes," I answered, pleased that he was willing to discuss it with me, that I'd finally have the opportunity to tell him everything.

"All the time?"

"No. Well, yes, here at the castle. I heard only a few words in Shadowstone when I first connected with you in the White stone. Your thoughts of sounds are different, but somehow, I can understand the stronger words you'd like to say. Not all your thoughts. And only when we're close."

His lips rolled, and he ran his hands back through his loose hair, taking a moment to process. *"How? Sielle and Ren explained it some, but I want to understand."*

So I began at the start, describing first contact with Sielle in the White stone and her reasons for giving me the information to link us. That while the purpose was to help with the other deaths, she also hoped I'd find her through Croft. I explained how I'd wanted to tell him but also knew he'd hate me after. And when he'd denied knowing Sielle, it made me more curious. Then as I learned more about his relation to the king, I'd found some solace in knowing he was meant to lead.

"It never went the other way. I was never able to hear you, see things, until the Black stone."

I twisted my fingers together but stopped myself from dropping my eyes into my lap, needing him to see my face fully in such low light. "I believe it's because you have no direct Realm connection yourself, so you wouldn't get anything back from me. But the Black stone opens the Realm with extraordinary power. That's why my thoughts projected to you through our direct link. It was the only thing I could do under Hydra's command because it was something she couldn't access."

When he didn't reply, tears welled in my eyes, and I admitted, "I never wanted to hurt you. But I understand that I did. I'm sorry that I used Argo. I shouldn't have done that either. I'm truly sorry. For everything."

"And you can fix it? Take away this ... connection?" His gaze stayed flat, expressionless. There were no emotions to be seen on his handsome face.

I nodded as tears spilled down my cheeks. It shouldn't have hurt, but it did. I couldn't expect him to be forgiving or understanding after all I'd done. And I certainly couldn't blame him for wanting me out of his mind as soon as possible.

Wiping the tears away in a rush, I replied, "Yes. Sielle told me how. You should only need to make your connection to the Realm. All you have to do is touch a stone you can connect with. It's best to do Clear first. But you probably already know that, and I ..." I was rambling in an attempt to cover my emotion. With a deep breath, I tried to regain my control, to not let my heart crack open and bleed all my sorrow in front of him. It was one more thing he didn't need from me. "I have the pendant from Cordelia. It was King Antin's. It has a small Clear stone inside. I was going to give it to you as soon as ... well, let me go get it for you."

I moved to stand, but he grabbed hold of my hand and stopped me, pulling me back down to sit.

"Not now. Tomorrow. Right now I ..." His hand moved to my face, his thumb wiping away more of my tears.

"No, no," I said, choking back a sob. "I understand. It's late. It's all right. I should go back to bed."

"Stay. It's my turn to apologize."

I shook my head. "There's nothing—"

"Olean." His hand dropped to the side of my neck, holding my face, staring between my eyes and lips. *"Yes. I do. I'm sorry you were in the prison. I'll never forgive myself for not considering what would happen when I walked away at your reading. And I'm sorry for not seeing you when I found out. I had to think about so much, had to prove myself worthy to the advisory council after learning about my father. There were meetings and discussions and ..."* He closed his eyes and shook his head before refocusing on me. *"I should have come to you. But I'm most sorry that during all of that, I didn't take the time to think about the missing information from Hemlock and Naomi. Ren told me about their readings. Something didn't seem right about the other deaths. I should have taken the time to really think it over. We might have known about Hydra before anything else happened. We could have stopped her before she got to you."*

"That's not your fault. I felt something was missing too. But none of us would have known. She was smart about her choices up until the end. I think she felt the pressure, knew that we'd figure out the truth soon enough. So she rushed, taking the chance while everyone was still distracted by the funeral and ball. It's no one's fault but hers."

"I thought I'd lost you. I thought ... I'm not sure what I would have done if I never saw you again, never got a chance to tell you ... I ..." His hand fell from my face and pointed a finger to himself. Clenching both fists, he crossed his arms and pressed them against his chest, then dropped them and pointed a single finger at me. *"Love you."*

A sob escaped me as his eyes welled up. I repeated his motions and said, "I love you too."

He gave a soft smile, then his eyebrows dipped lower and he clenched his jaw. *"I've been worried that it's not real. I know how I feel, and I decided that won't change. But how do we know that it's not mainly this connection?"*

"I've worried about that too, that maybe your feelings for me were only because of it, since I could understand you better than anyone else. But I don't think it's controlled or swayed our emotions in any other way. It let me understand you, let me discover so much about you, made me feel even more. I want to be with you. My feelings won't change either. And I won't ever lie or keep things from you again. Never again. But I also know you've decided on your role now, so I understand that it comes with a lot more responsibility and maybe you shouldn't—"

"I'll do whatever I want. No role will change that. And what I want is you." His hands lifted to my cheeks, spreading his fingers wide to the sides of my head. He leaned closer and pressed his lips to mine in a sweet kiss. I wrapped my arms around him, pulling his sleep shirt, needing him closer. Tears came again, streaking down my face, honest and raw. This time they weren't of regret, or shame, or guilt. This time they held all my love for him. And happiness. I was overflowing with happiness. Because he felt the same for me even after all I'd done. And because we were both here, alive. Together.

The kiss blossomed, his tongue meeting mine with long sweeping motions that sent shivers all through my body. We explored one another. The taste, the feeling. I couldn't get enough of him, and I could tell with each passing moment he felt the same.

"Olean. My Olean. My love."

His hands moved down my waist, then he leaned back and lifted me as he had the first time we'd kissed, drawing me up to sit on his lap. My knees settled at his sides, nightdress bunching around him, and I leaned in close, pushing my fingers deep into his hair once again, grasping firmly. His arms wound around my back, hands spreading wide, fingertips pressing into the thin material there, my skin still feeling every bit of his heat. The way he held me was marvelous. His grip was demanding and strong, yet every touch felt delicate and sensuous as if he were cherishing me, protecting me, and devouring me all at once.

I tipped my head back, gasping for breath. He pulled me even closer, his eyes gazing up at me as I tipped my chin down. "I think ... I don't think we can ... I mean, I want ..." Oh, I was messing it all up entirely.

He smiled, slow and wide, and I couldn't help but chuckle at myself. *"I know."* He shifted, kicking his legs up onto the settee and laying his body down fully. He gripped my thigh, gazing up at me. *"Stay with me."*

I hesitated for a moment, looking at my room, thinking of Ivy waking without me. But Sielle was in there with her. She would be fine.

So I readjusted myself, lying down. "Yes. All right." He helped settle me into position, my body half at his side and half on him, nestling my head onto his chest with a leg draped over his.

One of his arms bent upward, lying along my back, fingers tapping the rhythm of my heart. The other held the back of my hand pressed to his chest, where I felt the beat of his heart too.

"Sleep, my love. Tomorrow is our beginning."

The Realm tells all.
Whether the connection is for
entertainment, justice, or defense,
it never lies.
- Anhedral Kingdom Lovely Guidebook

33

We were awoken the next morning with Clem shouting, "Oh, nauseating!" at the sight of Croft and me lying together on the settee. That was effective in waking everyone else as well.

And even though I would have liked to have said it was the best sleep of my life—being against Croft's strong body and wrapped inside his arms—we agreed it definitely wasn't the best sleep as we stood from the cramped settee, stretching out our numb limbs and achy bones. He was just too big and broad to share such a small sleeping space with. So he gave me a wink, promising to share our own bed from that night on.

Breakfast had been brought up to us, most normal procedures already back into order during the days I'd been recovering. Immediately after, we'd been summoned for a meeting in the great hall since things had settled.

The gathering was for everyone who lived or worked in the castle, except for the limited amount who were on duty for patrols or posted at guard stations. They'd be filled in later. Croft and Prince Ren had obviously gone over the details because we arrived and there was no discussion ahead of time.

"This shouldn't be too long," Croft's thoughts assured as he kissed the back of my hand before letting it go. He'd held it the entire walk down to the great hall, drawing lots of eyes. Some attendants who weren't otherwise engaged in their duty, fell back into royal etiquette, giving Croft a small neck bow to show their acknowledgment of his new status.

He stepped onto the dais to stand beside Prince Ren. Queen Reina was also there, sitting in one of the high-backed chairs beside the thrones. Ivy waved to her, and she gave her a soft smile and waved in return. Wolf was also on the dais, though he stood at the edge, keeping watch of all who arrived. Tansy had decided to go join with Blodwyn and a group of the other Lovely, while Sielle and Cordelia stayed with me, Begonia, Clem, and Ivy. We were off to the side but still close to the front.

I nodded to some of the other Lovely, seeing Kalmia, Nettle, and Amaryllis. I'd heard two Clear stone Lovely and another from the Cloud stone division had died during Hydra's control. Unfortunately, they had been too close to weapons when she had given the final order. There was also a guard and three soldiers who didn't make it either. They had been casualties to the fights and also the initial quake that had caused stones to break and fall. Plenty more had been injured, most by the wolfdogs, which had also suffered some wounds, but thankfully all had lived.

"King Croft and I thank you for gathering with us today," Prince Ren called out, quieting everyone inside the hall. "We needed this time to tend to our dead, see to all those who were injured, and also assess all the damages. We are awaiting word from the Nurseries around the kingdom as well. Hopefully, the reach wasn't as extensive as that. As most of you are aware by now, Hydra was responsible for this attack and all its atrocities. She forced Olean's connection to the Black stone, controlling her within the Realm. While we plan to hold readings for anyone wanting more information or closure, there will be no trial. The only one responsible is now dead. That is also the case for Hemlock and Princess Naomi. While searching the castle, we discovered the lower cells of the prison experienced a total collapse during the quakes. Their retrieval is already in progress, but there will be no funeral."

He cleared his throat, and the dowager queen wiped at her eyes. Naomi's fate no longer being in their direct control had to be a great relief, but their grief would linger for a long time.

Prince Ren continued, "Your king promises to do his best in the coming days to help get things back to order here. But he also wishes you to know that there will be changes, most of which will be for the Lovely, those here at the castle and throughout our kingdom. Some Anhedral rules are antiquated. We all have agreed on this, especially after these recent events, the changes will be for the betterment of all our people. One notable change will be rescinding the Lovely indenture."

Gasps sounded all around. Excited murmurs were quick to follow.

Croft grinned wide as his gaze swept the hall. His eyes then locked with mine and held for a charged, heart-stopping moment before turning back to the prince.

Prince Ren smiled as well, slipping his hands into his pockets as he let everyone take in his words. "It's a lofty change, one that we will need help to achieve in order for it to be successful. We will have more discussions with Lovely in the coming days, but the goal is for voluntary placements with adequate pay, like we have for attendants, guards, and soldiers, to include food and housing for those wanting to keep their positions. And for those who choose to leave, we will wish you well in your future endeavors.

"For now, your king is asking for everyone's patience as he works with his council to sort through all the details. He is open to have discussions with anyone who wishes to see him as well. And the final announcement for today is that his official coronation will occur, but only after the rest has been taken care of first. Thank you all. Please come speak with us with any concerns," Prince Ren finished, turning to Croft and Wolf.

Applause rose from the crowd, and I turned to see all the smiles, including Sielle.

"He is something," she said, feeling my body shift at her side.

"Prince Ren? Yes. He's made quite a change. I'm sure he will do well in aiding Croft."

"Well, yes. But I meant Croft."

"Oh. He is something," I agreed, my entire being filled with admiration as I watched him.

"Yes," Cordelia said, joining in at Sielle's other side. The pride she felt lit her entire face.

"King Croft," Sielle said softly. "Never would have imagined hearing that as a child. But Pearla always did speak highly of him, even after he left school. I suppose it won't be long before I'm curtsying to my sister as well."

"What?" I released an amused breath.

The night before, I'd thought for a moment he would honestly reconsider us because of his decision to be king, knowing that I might not be suitable to be at his side. But I hadn't considered the reality of it when he silenced my concerns by professing his love, and I had done the same.

I supposed it did mean more, possibly …

"Come now, Olean. Even if we ignore how you both woke up this morning," Cordelia added, eyes still on Croft as well, "there is no denying how my son looks at you."

I kept my mouth shut, ignoring Sielle's soft giggles.

While Croft stayed with Prince Ren and Wolf, the crowd lining up, wanting to speak with them, we made our way back to the room to gather Sielle's things.

"You have to leave?" Ivy asked, clutching her alpaca as she moved to the table, not wanting to say goodbye yet.

"Yes, I do. I should get back to the house. Father will be home in the coming days, and I have to be there. But after he arrives, and I'm able to tell him all that's happened, I will call for you, Olean, so you can meet him."

"Send word and I'll be there. Anytime and anything for you. I'm beyond grateful that we have each other now, and I'm excited to know him too." I wrapped an arm around the side of her waist, not truly ready to let her go.

"Are you staying longer, Cordelia?" Sielle asked.

"I am." Cordelia looked at Begonia, Clem, and Ivy sitting at the table, eating the midday meal. "I hadn't been appointed any more children after they all left. So now, with these changes coming, I will ask what might be next for me."

Sielle nodded as she listened. "Will you stay here if you're given the chance?"

"Yes," Cordelia answered. "Everyone I love is here now. There's no other reason to return to Shadowstone. Unless they force me."

"That won't happen," I assured, understanding her unease for the dowager queen and the reason she'd been forced to leave the castle before. But things had changed, and her son was now king. "Croft won't allow it."

She gave me a little smile, that pride shining through again. During my days of sleep, they had finally interacted a couple of times. She admitted it had been awkward to start, especially after learning she'd stabbed him, but they were warming up to each other, even exchanging an embrace that morning before we all left for the great hall.

She placed a hand on top of Ivy's smooth head lovingly. "I'm looking forward to visiting the markets in the city again. It's been ages, and they have such lovely things. Maybe you all will join me. Clem, I bet they have wonderful books for sketching. Ivy, we will look for more puzzles. And, Begonia, they have so many beautiful hair clips and ribbons—"

"I'm no longer interested in hair clips," Begonia said, biting down on her lower lip. "But I would love to see the fabrics they have, maybe buy some to make my own gown."

I smiled as brightly as Cordelia at Begonia's response. She didn't seem so lost and conflicted anymore. She was finding herself.

"Good," Cordelia replied simply, deciding it best not to focus attention on her change.

A knock had us all turning, seeing Tansy and Blodwyn at the door.

"Are you ready, Sielle?" Tansy asked, moving inside.

"Yes," she answered. "I'll send word soon."

"I'll be waiting." I wrapped my arms around her fully, and she did the same. I owed her so much. Everything. With a sniffle, I lifted her bag of clothing that had been brought while we were recovering and handed it over to Tansy.

The others all said their goodbyes as well, moving with her to the door.

From out in the hallway, Blodwyn's voice came. "Croft—Uh, Your Majesty."

Through the bodies by the door, Croft's head tilted inside, searching for me. He lifted his eyebrows with a smile as soon as we locked eyes.

Everyone moved around him out into the hallway. As the others left, Cordelia spoke to Begonia, Clem, and Ivy. "I'm sure there are things we can help with. Let's go to the great hall to find out what needs to be done."

As Clem groaned in protest, Cordelia looked over her shoulder with a smile, then shut the door, leaving Argo, Croft, and me alone. Argo went to his mat at the fireplace, eager for a nap.

"Hi," I said as we met each other at the table.

"Hi," he thought and also mouthed. *"I don't have long. Need to get back for a council meeting."*

"All right." My smile was genuine. I knew I'd see him whenever possible, but I also knew he would be busy. He was no longer my personal attendant. And as much as I would miss being with him all the time, that didn't affect my happiness for him at all.

"I had to see you before then." He lifted a hand and trailed his fingertips along my jaw, over my ear. His eyes held so much, their look intense and loving. He leaned in, kissing my lips tenderly.

Hearing his thoughts and thinking about our conversation the night before, I pulled away. "Just a moment."

"What?" He watched me leave with a curious lift of a single eyebrow. Within seconds, I returned and extended a cloth containing what I'd promised.

He unwrapped the folds, seeing the chain and pendant. *"Oh."*

I flipped it over inside the cloth and waited for his eyes to lift to my face again. "The Clear stone is big enough to connect. As soon as you do, it should end our link."

With a nod, he took hold of the chain, lowered the pendant to the table, and took a seat.

I sat in the opposite chair, watching him examine the swirled background and his father's stacked initials.

"And then?" The question was a hesitant thought as his eyes lifted to me.

"And then ..." I smiled, understanding we shared the same emotion, anticipating how the detachment would feel. But we both knew there was no other choice. "Maybe you connect with the Cloud stone to see my thoughts."

"Oh, I do like that idea," he admitted with a glint in his amber eyes.

"And then ... we fight for what's important, make things better here for everyone."

"Yes. And?"

"And ..." I considered the motions I'd seen him use, hoping I wouldn't mess them up. I pointed to myself, then with one hand, I extended my fingers up in a straight line and touched the first to my chin. "I talk?"

His head fell backward, chin lifting, mouth open to the ceiling, and his body shook with silent laughter. After a few moments, he leveled his head again and looked at me with a radiant smile while I grimaced, embarrassed.

"I guess I need to *learn*, not talk."

"You're adorable, and your effort is the very best gift. I'll teach you anything you want to learn. Everything. And we will do it all together." He placed his hand over mine on the table, his warm fingertips trailing circles along my skin.

"I like that idea too," I agreed, heart overflowing with so much love.

We stared at each other for a silent moment, losing ourselves. Then I glanced down at the pendant. "You have a meeting ..."

"Yes." He lifted his hand and sat straighter in the seat. Using the cloth, he flipped the pendant to show the half-opened back and the exposed Clear stone.

I reached to his side, removing the attendant's dagger he still wore from its leather sheathing. Then, with a quick movement, I dug the tip into my finger and used the cloth to wipe the drop of blood over the stone's surface. "Having a focus is usually best."

"I'm glad it's you. It will always be you."

I leaned in and kissed him, wanting to show my feelings were the same. Though I'd miss his thoughts, I was excited for him to experience the Realm.

As soon as I leaned away, he pressed his finger to the stone.

And then ... our true connection began.

Acknowledgments

I must share my thanks to everyone reading this. You chose to pick up Dead & Lovely, and for that I am so grateful. I truly hope you enjoyed reading about Olean and Croft, and the Lovely world.

I purchased the pre-made cover a handful of years ago, in awe of its beauty and wanting so badly to create a perfectly suited story. The characters and plot formed slowly over these past years, utterly refusing any attempts to hurry things along, but I believe that was the very best for it.

As always, I need to thank my family, Will and Zoe, for a life filled with love and support.

Simone Nicole, thank you for your thoughts on the early chapters and for all the sprints and chats about anything and everything. To Amy Concepcion for coming out of a beta hiatus for this one. Your input is always and forever appreciated. Many hugs to Liz Parks for reading an early copy and offering your thoughts. If I could gift you a real trash panda, I would.

Ashley Slaughter, you're truly a gifted cover artist, and I'm so happy to have worked with you. Emily Lawrence, thanks for another round. You never fail to catch all the little (and some big) things with your stellar editing skills.

And to all the reviewers and content creators on socials who spread the bookish love, thank you, thank you, thank you! Reviews and shares mean the world and help tremendously. I wish you all the best bookish life. Happy reading!

About The Author

J.M. Miller lives on Florida's Emerald Coast with her husband and daughter.
When she isn't spending time with her family or being distracted by social media sites, she writes contemporary and fantasy romance novels.
More info at jmmillerbooks.com

Also by J. M. Miller
Senior Year Bucket List
Spied
Sever
Fallen Flame
Scattered Plume
Hidden Ember
Deep Breath
The Line That Binds
The Line That Breaks

9 781955 472104